SEARCHING FOR JULIA

LIZZY MUMFREY

To my beloved daughters, Philippa and Francesca, who mean the world to me.

TRIGGER WARNINGS

This book contains the following:

Racist language
Homophobic references
Inadvertent incest
Offensive language

FOREWORD

This story is written from my heart. I received a quintessentially white British upbringing but in more recent years my family has blossomed to embrace Vietnamese, Caribbean and Indian members. I thought that by this day and age racism, homophobia and class bigotry would have melted away, but I am increasingly made aware of how, sadly, this is not the case.

This novel has been read by a sensitivity reader because it contains references to extreme racist words and expressions as used reflexively by past generations, and examples of unconscious bias. I have included the sensitivity report as an addendum because it is important to understand the context within which this novel has been written and why it has been written in this way.

My story of the search for Julia is fiction but includes heart-rending true stories that I have taken from Lucy Bland's study *Britain's Brown Babies* with her kind permission.

THE BEGINNING

ONE

Emily Walker looked around at three generations of her very ordinary Yorkshire family, gathered for Great Granny's funeral at the Admiral Rodney pub in Sheffield.

They were just around the corner from where Great Granny Irene Bedlington nee Marshall, affectionately known as GG, had lived all her married life. They all agreed that she'd had a 'good innings' at ninety-four.

Only the close family remained since the other mourners had trickled away, and most picked lethargically at the debris of sandwiches and sausage rolls.

Granny Rosemary and maiden Great Aunt Cynthia, born 1950 and 1951 respectively and known throughout the family as The Boomers, were locked in earnest conversation, heads together, their indistinguishable white hair mingling as if they were one.

Emily murmured, "They're up to something."

The Boomers looked so alike that they were often mistaken for twins, with the same startling green eyes that they had inherited from Great Granny, but they couldn't be more different in personality. If they were dogs, Granny

Rosemary would be a lean Boxer and Aunt Cynthia a soppy, overweight Labrador. They had an irritating habit of speaking in tandem, talking over each other.

Emily moved nonchalantly to the table closest to them to listen in, drawing up a chair beside her three cousins with a casual nod and a perfunctory "Hi." She still couldn't catch what The Boomers were saying.

Emily leant down and, through a curtain of dark curls, heaved a bulky patchwork bag on to the table, a gift lovingly sewn by Aunt Cynthia from scraps of old fabric from countless family garments over the years. She started rummaging in it to make it look like she wasn't trying to eavesdrop. Emily had no idea that everything she thought she believed in was about to be shattered.

Emily watched The Boomers look furtively around the bar of the Admiral Rodney before scuttling out of the room together, looking shifty.

What are they up to?

Emily was frustrated that she hadn't been able make out what they were whispering about. You never knew with Granny and her murky past.

Granny's claim to fame, designed to shock, was that she was a pot-smoking hippy in her heyday. She went on about it at every opportunity. Granny's husband died twenty-one years ago, and she had been parading an endless train of unsuitable lovers ever since. On the other hand, Aunt Cynthia, always known as Cyn, had never married because of an unrequited love. Granny said it was because she let herself go and was fat.

Emily turned to look at her parent's generation to see if they had noticed Granny and Aunt Cynthia's surreptitious behaviour and disappearance.

Granny's two regularly embarrassed daughters, Emily's mum Lisa and Aunt Jennifer, were born in 1969 and 1971,

Generation X. They could have come from two different fathers, or indeed mothers, they looked so unrelated: Jennifer tall and willowy with The Boomers' green eyes and blond hair that would go silver in old age. Mum, who Granny always said was too lazy to grow upwards, was mousy haired and plump, with mud-coloured eyes.

Aunt Jennifer and Emily's mum were leaning back in their chairs tutting, looking towards the bar in the hope of hurrying along Emily's henpecked dad, Mike, with their latest wine order. Emily thought that Mum looked as if she'd had quite enough to drink already. She was waving her arms around and getting very loud. "Hey Mike, where are those drinks? We're dying of thirst here."

Mum, please, so embarrassing. He's being as quick as he can.

Uncle James, Aunt Jennifer's husband, came lumbering in through the French doors and squeezed his not inconsiderable bulk behind Emily's chair. She received a strong gust of sweat mixed with pungent aftershave and revolting cigarette smoke, definitely tobacco, although Emily suspected that he preferred ganja when at home in Kingston, Jamaica.

I bet he supplies Granny on the quiet on his infrequent visits. She always seems to be inordinately pleased to see him, despite him being such a pain in the arse.

Emily watched as James sat by his wife and threw a casual arm over her shoulders, his garish gold watch flashing. Aunt Jennifer patted his back and obviously found it dry. "It hasn't rained then, James?"

"Yeah. A bit of a surprise for a Sheffield summer. It's warm but nothing like what we're used to." He reached across the table and snatched a lonely sausage roll from a plain white plate, took a dramatic bite, chewed vigorously, grimaced and spat it out into a serviette.

"Where's Mike with those bloody drinks?" He swivelled around, sniffed for no reason, an annoying habit, and then rumbled, "Hey, Jennifer, have you told Lisa about the new villa yet?" Jennifer frowned and shook her head at him. James pressed on regardless with a sly look at Lisa. "Yeah, we wanted somewhere to go and chill outside of the city, so we've bought a place, right on the beach at Montego Bay. Lisa, you'll have to come out and visit us, won't she Jennifer? You'll love it. Five bedrooms, so plenty of room for everyone and an infinity pool."

Lisa jutted her jaw towards James, swivelled in her chair to glare at him, almost falling off her chair. "Oh, shut up, James. We know all about the money coming out of your ears, you never stop going on about it. Despite slogging our guts out all our lives, some of us can barely afford the rent and can't even find the bus fare into the city, let alone fly all the bloody way to Jamaica."

Jennifer laid a comforting hand on Lisa's knee with a condescending smile. "Perhaps when you inherit a bit from GG you might be able to."

Lisa pushed Jennifer's hand off. "Well, I hope we bloody well do get something." She glared, somewhat unfocussed, at Jennifer who sat back looking surprised at such vehemence. "Well, you don't bloody well need it do you? We do. The car's about to pack up, it's on its last legs..."

The fiery exchange was damped down by an interruption from Emily's little sister Ashley, who sidled up to her mum and whispered in her ear. Emily knew that this time it wasn't tantalising secrets passing between family members, just Ashley being soppy and nauseating.

Ashley had been a surprise late arrival to their family after her mum's thirtieth birthday celebration. At only nine years old there was an enormous age gap between her and Emily's twenty years. Emily couldn't relate to Ashley as a sister; she was more like a niece, a particularly infuriating one.

Mum pulled Ashley into her and gave her a sloppy kiss on the cheek. "Come here my little darling. What you been up to, eh?" Ashley whispered back. "On the climbing frame? I hope you were ever so careful. You should have asked Emily to help you."

Emily grimaced.

Why is she made out to be my responsibility? I'm not her babysitter.

Mum gently brushed Ashley's blond hair off her face. "Have you got sun cream on?"

Mum was devoted to Ashley and ever since her arrival had lavished her with affection, with seemingly none to spare for Emily. It made Emily sad. It was even more annoying that Ashley had inherited the family's green eyes and blond flowing locks and Emily hadn't. Emily conceded that her own eyes were more sludge coloured, her height on the minimum side and her build chunkier like her mum – and her hair couldn't be darker if it tried.

Emily realised that she was staring at Ashley and that Ashley was glaring back over their mum's shoulder. Ashley put a possessive arm around Mum's neck and nestled in, a smirk of triumph on her face. Emily sighed.

At least I have a brain, the only thing in my favour.

Emily was the first of her family to have got into university. Her pride at getting a place to read Chemistry at Edinburgh had been somewhat dented by the reaction from her parents, particularly her miserly dad. "Why can't you go and get a job like a normal person? We all got on with it and didn't fanny around with higher education, leeching off our parents."

Emily spluttered, "I thought you'd be pleased for me. I'm not taking a penny off you. I've got a student loan."

"But what do you contribute to the household when you are home in those ridiculously long holidays? You eat like a horse, and I've never known a person have so many showers using up all the electricity. So much for your mantra of saving the planet's resources."

Emily had bitten her tongue, literally and metaphorically, so she didn't answer back.

Emily's tight-fisted dad returned from the bar with a tray burgeoning with drinks. He wasn't paying – the Boomers were running a tab – and carefully placed one in front of each family member in generation order like an obsequious waiter. Emily found it odd that both her mum and dad behaved so differently when they were with The Boomers, the one drunk as a skunk and the other overly subservient.

Emily caught sight of The Boomers bustling in from their secret mission. Aunt Cynthia was mysteriously clutching a plastic orange Sainsbury's carrier bag as if it contained something she had just stolen. Emily couldn't help but frown at The Boomers profligate use of non-sustainable plastic.

By the time the Millennials had been served assiduously by Dad, Granny was standing in front of her descendants, Aunt Cynthia dutifully located just behind her shoulder, tapping a glass with a knife. As one, the family fell silent and looked at Granny, now the newly crowned matriarch of their clan.

"I want you all to listen carefully. Cyn and I have something to share with you." Everyone looked at each other, a bit worried. Granny was being so solemn that it could hardly be good news. Aunt Cynthia picked up the Sainsbury's carrier bag and put it on the table in front of her, delved into it, pulled out a pile of large envelopes like a conjuror's assistant, and presented them to Granny.

"Now, Mike, if you could kindly hand out one of these to everyone..." Emily's dad obliged with a deferential bow. He had become resigned to be being bossed about by Granny years ago. Each family member took one and started picking at it. "Don't open them until I give you the word." More exchanged glances.

"Is this GG's will by any chance?" asked Lisa.

"No," Granny spat out before muttering something under her breath. Emily thought she'd said, "Mum's only been dead five minutes." Granny had a venomous look in her eye, she wasn't one for hiding her feelings. "Just wait a minute. Have you all got one?" Murmurs of assent. "I want you to open your envelope, read the letter inside and put up your hand when you have reached the end of it. No-one is to say anything until everyone has had a chance to read. Agreed?" Emily giggled to herself; Granny sounded just like an exam invigilator. There was a murmur that was taken as agreement. "You can open them now."

Emily tore the top off the envelope amidst a cacophony of ripping sounds. The letters all rustled like test papers simultaneously being turned over as they were drawn out of the envelopes.

At least the paper and envelopes are recyclable.

Emily started to read.

My Dear Cynthia and Rosemary,

It does seem so very odd to be writing to you in this way. I am alive as I write but you will be reading this when I am dead. Please know that I had a wonderful life and I loved you all so much. I hope that you will remember all the happy times that we had together.

I have left this letter for you to open on my

death because I have news that is going to come as a shock to you. I can't think of any way of softening the blow. I had a daughter in the war, before I married my darling Bill and went on to have you, my beloved girls.

When I was eighteen I worked in a hospital, very much as a skivvy, in Henley-on-Thames, doing my bit for the war effort and to get away from the incessant bombing at home in Sheffield.

I fell in love with a GI and, with the fear of death always on the near horizon, we had a whirlwind romance. I loved him, truly and deeply, and he asked me to marry him. It meant going to live in the United States of America after the war, but I loved him so much that I was very happy to follow him to all ends of the earth.

Apparently, because he was American, I would need permission from his Commanding Officer for us to get married and since they were all going away fighting that wasn't going to happen very soon, so we decided to wait until he came back. Our engagement was therefore secret and we were determined to marry on his return from his forthcoming, very hush hush, posting.

He left Henley in May and went somewhere, I didn't know where, I didn't know why, and of course I didn't ask. There were so many secrets then and we were all good at keeping them. He and many others like him were about to take part in the most courageous and ingenious event ever. The big secret was D Day, June 6th 1944. Nobody knew.

When we found out, everyone was amazed and so excited. We read the news reports and watched the Movietone News to glean every bit of information that we could. Those of us with men who had suddenly upped and left all assumed that that must be where they had all gone. We talked about it endlessly.

It was not long before I found out that I was expecting. I was thrilled, but also apprehensive, and wrote to tell him about it. I didn't receive a reply. I knew they were in the thick of it so assumed that was why. I didn't tell a soul that I was pregnant but we all talked about our chaps and what they might be up to. Others thought that they had been abandoned but I knew in my heart that Lloyd and I loved each other so much that that would never be our case. I was unwavering in my determination to wait for him and was desperate to hear from him.

I didn't tell my parents about the baby and carried on working in ever baggier clothes and kept writing to him.

It was soon obvious that I was pregnant. Everyone was incredibly shocked and insisted that I return home to my parents. I couldn't possibly carry on working at the hospital in my condition and indeed I had proved myself to be a complete slut, apparently, and therefore not suitable to show my face. They told me I was an absurd, deceived fool and deserved to be abandoned for being such a degenerate hussy.

I was sent home in disgrace.

My parents were of course horrified and ashamed and tried to hide me away. When the baby was born, I named her Julia. I don't know why. I just liked the name, and it suited her. Of course, I wrote to Lloyd immediately and asked him to write to at least let me know that he was happy with my choice of name for our daughter and asking him for his mother's name so we could use it as her second. I heard nothing in return.

I insisted that her father was named on her birth certificate. After all, he is her much-loved father and I thought he would come back for us. I had still not heard from him and everyone was convinced that he had never meant to marry me at all and that it was all poppycock.

I was held prisoner in my own home and was strongly discouraged from taking my daughter out where we might be seen by the neighbours. But where else could I go? It was such a heinous crime to have a baby out of wedlock.

Julia's father never returned. I didn't hear from my beloved Lloyd again.

After five months of motherhood bliss, they found a Dr Barnardo's home that would take her. They told me it wasn't easy to find her a place and had called in a favour from the curate who had just taken up a new post down south. He lobbied on my parents' behalf, and I was meant to be grateful.

When they took her away from me, I was heartbroken. I cannot find the words to describe it. A last kiss.

I didn't know that Julia's father was killed on Omaha Beach some months after D Day. I found this out much later when the war had ended. He was one of the first of his battalion, the 320th Barrage Balloon Battalion, to land on the beach. I have never been able to find a clear explanation of how he died. I don't know whether he received my letters.

There was no reason that I would have been informed of his death because as far as the American Army was concerned our relationship didn't exist. I don't even know whether he knew that we had a child. I was distraught when I found out that he was dead and of course I wanted to go and get Julia back, but no one would allow it, however much I pleaded. I had to accept that I had lost them both.

I told your dad all about Julia before we got married. We had no secrets and I promised him that I would not look for her in my lifetime. We decided that it would be too difficult for all of us.

As you know from your birthdays, I had you two as soon as I could and I have loved you, treasured you so much and never let you go. But at the same time I have never forgotten Julia.

Because you are reading this letter it means that I am dead now so please find her. Please. Find her and tell her that I loved her so much just as I have loved you. Give her the note that I have enclosed and tell her I'm so sorry.

Go and find her, my darlings. Your half-sister, your flesh and blood.

My love forever,

Mum xxx

Everyone was relatively silent as they read their copy of Great Granny's missive, just the odd loud exhalation now and again. The flutter as a page was turned was like the rustle of trees in the wind.

Upon reaching the end, Emily's mind was in turmoil.

Who'd have thought it? Great Granny Irene. Cuddly, kind, cosy GG. I'd always thought that Granny was the rebel. Well, Granny, you have been well and truly usurped! This is amazing. How extraordinary. And her name is Julia. Our family name. Granny is Rosemary Julia. Mum is Lisa Julia and I am Emily Julia. Well, well, well.

She started again at the beginning to try and take it all in but became aware of arms going up around the room. It made Emily want to giggle.

Are we back at school?

She looked around and grinned at her cousins and her sister, but they were all looking very solemn. Ashley just looked baffled.

Why aren't they all incredibly excited? This is fantastic. We need to go and find her. We need to go and find Julia.

Emily put her hand up to show that she had finished reading it.

Granny spoke, an explosion in the silence. It made

Emily jump. "You've all read it?" Mumbles of assent. "So, what are we going to do?"

Everyone looked at each other.

Uncle James started, always keen to be the first to give his opinion on everything. "Did you know about this Rose? Cyn?"

"No, definitely not. Not even a whisper," Granny replied crisply. The Boomers were shaking their heads vigorously. "We found this letter along with all her other papers and stuff when we made a start on clearing Mum's house."

Uncle James turned to Generation X. "You, Lisa? Jennifer?"

Mum looked at Aunt Jennifer who raised her hands in a questioning gesture and turned back to Uncle James. "No. Why would we?" Lisa responded as if insulted; her voice was very slurred.

Why do drunk people always sound so exaggeratedly indignant?

Ashley piped up, "I don't get it. How come there is another sister?" But nobody answered because the room was quickly becoming like the Tower of Babel. No-one was listening to anyone else and so the points of view just became louder and louder.

Granny resorted to the knife on glass again but at a frantic pace. She yelled out, "Will you shut up you lot?" Seniority counted in this family, so everyone did indeed quieten down and looked at her. "Right. Now I can hear myself think let's talk about this one at a time. Has anyone anything they wish to say?" Everyone just looked at each other like a bunch of mad startled hens.

"Mum?"

"Yes, Lisa?"

"This isn't really anything to do with us, is it?" She was

swaying as she said it. "I can see that you and Aunt Cyn are shocked to find that you have a sister, actually a half-sister, even a quarter or a third sister, who knows, but we are a generation away and I'm not sure that I feel it in quite the same way." Emily was a bit surprised by her mum's reaction, as well as baffled by her drunken rambling.

Why wouldn't you want to find a long-lost relative, your half aunt? Granny and Aunt Cyn's secret sister? Aren't you fascinated? I am.

Granny bristled. "You have an aunt that you knew nothing about. Doesn't that at least... arouse your curiosity?" Emily nodded firmly and stared at her mum.

Totally agree, Granny.

"No, not really. I'm sure it happened an awful lot during the war. Live and let live is how I feel. What if she doesn't even know that she was adopted? The poor love is probably completely ignorant of her background and would be horrified to have it shoved in her face. Horrible for her. Don't you think, Jen?"

Jennifer nodded. "It would be a bit different, Mum, if you had a daughter that you hadn't told us about. She would be young enough to go looking for and things are just so different these days, aren't they? I mean, we all know that Lisa did the decent thing and decided, in the end, to keep her illegitimate daughter rather than giving her away like GG did."

Emily gasped and turned round to stare at Aunt Jennifer.

What the hell was she implying by that?

Emily stared at her mum and tried to catch her eye. Her mum slapped at Aunt Jennifer's thigh, put the finger of her other hand exaggeratedly to her lips and sort of shushed. It came out as a rather dribbly whoosh. She harrumphed, folded her arms and stared fixedly at Granny.

What the chuffing heck is going on here?

Aunt Jennifer continued as if she hadn't just detonated a bomb. "And anyway, I feel that if she had wanted to find her, she should have done it herself. What's the point?"

Should I say anything? Should I ask what the hell they are talking about? Shall I wait 'til after?

Emily missed her moment to speak out as a furious Granny replied, her green eyes becoming slits. "Believe me, I do not have any bastard children or any secrets. What you see is what you get, you know that. Just what sort of mother do you think I am? And please, use your nous. It would have been a completely different situation back in 1945." Her offspring looked as if they were going to speak, obviously thought better of it, and instead just looked at each other, raised their eyebrows and shrugged.

Despite Aunt Jennifer's revelation completely rocking Emily, she realised that this was not the right time to pursue it. Her head was buzzing with this whole maelstrom of surprises, but she still felt that she wanted to have her say about Julia. She just couldn't understand how no-one else seemed eager to find her. "But Mum, she – Julia – is our flesh and blood. She's family. We have her name as our middle name – well, Granny, you and I do. Perhaps she has been looking for us all this time? Maybe she thinks we don't care. We can put that right."

Lisa flapped her arms vaguely as if shooing Emily away. Aunt Jennifer, marginally more sober, frowned at Emily and added her penny's worth. "Maybe Emily, but I'm inclined to go with your mum. If she doesn't know that she was adopted, we could put an enormous cat amongst the pigeons. I can't imagine how awful that would be. I'm sure that she would have made some effort to find us, if she was indeed looking for us at all. There are so many programmes on telly about reuniting long-lost families that she would have been sure to get in touch with the right authorities. It's so easy nowadays. Don't you think, James?"

Uncle James took a swig of a brightly coloured drink with a silly little umbrella poking out of it.

Why an umbrella? It's always an umbrella. Why not a flower or a walking stick? And I hope it isn't plastic.

Uncle James ponderously replaced his glass on the table and stated condescendingly, "I rather think it is up to you ladies to decide." Despite his overinflated ego Uncle James knew when to stay out of things.

"Kids?" All three of Aunt Jennifer and Uncle James' children shrugged in unison.

Aunt Jennifer turned her head and asked, "Mike?"

"I'm with James. Up to you." Emily knew that her dad would take the line of least resistance. "She must have been a teenager when she had that baby, even younger than Lisa when she had Emily."

Silence. Emily felt uncomfortable. More uncomfortable than she normally did when her parents brought up the whole unplanned pregnancy thing. She had always known that her parents had got married because of her. It was a hard fact to hide when her birth date preceded their wedding anniversary.

Granny looked at Aunt Cynthia. "What do we do?"

Emily couldn't believe the lack of curiosity. How could anyone refuse Great Granny's heartfelt plea? She stood up and spoke out. "Well, I for one want to find Aunt Julia. At the very least we need to make enquiries to see if she had been trying to get in touch with her birth mother."

It seems odd to be referring to GG as a birth mother. It doesn't fit our lovely, homely, cuddly old GG.

Murmurs of "I suppose so."

"Look, I am more than willing to help. I don't go back to

university until October, although I might do some stuff with Dylan. My boyfriend," Emily added as puzzled looks were exchanged. "So, I'm as free as a bird." She glared at her woeful, unhelpful family. "I can start doing the research and then we can go in search of Julia and potentially a whole new branch of our relatives. Who else is going to help?"

"We've got to go home in any case..."

"Emily's got a boyfriend. That's a turn up for the books."

"Let sleeping dogs lie, Emily..."

"We've got to get back to work..."

Emily was indignant. "Well Granny, Aunt Cyn, it looks like we're it. We need to make plans."

The Boomers exchanged glances. Granny scowled at the rest of the family before saying to Emily, "Come round to ours in the morning and we'll go round to Mum's house and make a start. We can show you all the papers that we've found. I'm too tired to do anything right now." She turned towards Cynthia, her lips pursed and shook her head, looking disappointed by the lack of interest shown in Julia. Cynthia patted her arm and gave a little squeeze. That seemed to bring the proceedings to a close.

Poor Granny, she looks defeated, and she never *looks like that.*

Emily picked up her copy of Great Granny's incredible disclosure, folded it carefully, and put it in her pocket. Then she scooped up the extra ones that had been abandoned unwanted on the chairs, shoving them into her capacious patchwork bag for later recycling.

Emily said cursory goodbyes to her aunt, uncle and cousins before giving The Boomers a giant hug and a kiss before climbing into the car so her dad could drive the four of them to the Premier Inn. Mum was completely pickled.

Dad had to pour her into the front seat of the car, and she kept laughing for no reason at all. Emily cringed.

Dad started up the car and they cruised out of the car park. Emily's head was spinning and she was thinking of all the things that she could be looking up on her laptop to start her search for Julia. She'd begin as soon as they got to the hotel.

Mum was fiddling with the radio and turned it on super loud. Ashley put her hands over her ears. Dad leant across to turn it off and nearly collided with a white van. "Leave it be, Lisa." Mum cackled. Ashley exaggeratedly brought her arms back down and 'accidentally on purpose' flicked Emily's head.

"For god's sake, Ashley." Emily slapped Ashley's arm out of the way.

"Mum, Emily hit me..."

"Pack it in, Emily." Mum shouted in a silly sing-song voice. Emily rolled her eyes and looked out of the window. Mum belched. "Pardon me." An uncomfortable silence ensued for a few minutes until Mum abruptly barked over her shoulder.

"And what do you want to go on a wild goose chase after this complete stranger for, Emily?" Emily's silence did not put her off as she added, "Eh? Emily?"

"Do you mean Julia? I think it's very important to Granny and Aunt Cyn."

Dad added his predictable penny's worth, "Aye, but who's going to pay for you to gallivant around the place? Are they paying?" Emily wasn't up for a fight. "Eh, Emily?"

"Don't worry, Dad, it won't cost you a penny. I'll make sure of that."

Emily was itching to get going with her research.

I WILL find Julia.

TWO

Emily was a bit annoyed that she had to share a room with Ashley. But it was the lesser of two evils because it was either that or she had to pay for her own room herself. She cringed as she heard a hideously loud shout from Mum much further down the corridor. "See you downstairs for tea in fifty minutes."

Emily swiped the key, pushed open the door and, holding Ashley back with one practised arm, went into the room first. Ashley squeezed past her to the first bed and dived on to it. "Shotgun this bed."

Emily felt a little smug because she didn't care which bed she got. They looked equally enticing, plump and white like Pavlovas, but she was after the one comfy chair. She sat down in it with purpose and plonked her laptop on top of the table. "You can have any bed you want, dear sweet little sister." Emily gave Ashley a saccharine smile. Ashley looked suspicious.

Emily was keen to get going with her research, but the parents had insisted that they all go out for a meal, even though Emily was full after all those sandwiches that had seemed to appear like a never-ending flood. She didn't want to eat, she wanted to get googling straight away. She checked the time on her laptop.

A good three-quarters of an hour until we meet up in the foyer.

She was energised by this amazing new project to find Aunt Julia. It was a great distraction from the looming long uni holiday. It was funny how at uni you got used to being buried in research and reading and learning all day and then suddenly it stopped dead for months on end. Emily always found it hard to switch off.

She'd made some vague plans with Dylan to go somewhere and do something, but she didn't approve of flying anywhere, adding to the planet's disastrous climate problems. Neither of them seemed to have been able to come up with a plan that suited them both. He'd left it up in the air as he said his goodbyes at the station, perfunctorily giving Emily's shoulders a squeeze and dropping a brief kiss on the top of her head. "I'll message you. Bye, babe. See you later." Emily hadn't found it a very satisfactory farewell – and she hated being called 'babe'.

With these thoughts of Dylan, Emily went to retrieve her phone, "There might be a message from him now."

"Who?"

"Dylan."

"Oh. Boring." Ashley trundled into the bathroom to use the toilet.

She checked her phone, but it was dead.

You idiot, Emily. You forgot to turn it on at the wall.

She checked that she had plugged it in firmly, flicked the switch and went back to her laptop with relish.

"Now we begin." She thought for a moment, tapped her neatly trimmed nails on the table, and then leant forward and googled 'finding people who have been adopted.' Up came a list: ancestry.co.uk, adopted.com, genes-reunited.com, www.gov.uk Adoption Records: The Adoption Contact Register...

This is gold.

"What are you doing, Emily?" A whine came in her ear.

"I'm busy doing what everyone else in this family should be doing and searching for GG's Julia."

"I'm bored."

"No such thing as bored, just boring."

"I hate you, Emily."

"I know you do, Ashley, but I can't be bothered to have a puerile conversation about it with you."

"What's puerile mean?"

"For heaven's sake, Ashley just..." Emily nearly said bugger off but knew that this would be reported to Mum and Dad, "...go away. Go to Mum and Dad's room and I'll meet you later."

"But I can't go all on my own."

"Ashley, you are nine years old and they are literally ten rooms away on this floor." Ashley distorted her face into a ridiculous grimace as if she was about to cry. Emily knew that it was all just amateur dramatics. "Oh for..." Emily kept that expression to herself as well. "I will watch you down the corridor."

Ashley immediately rearranged her appearance into a look of triumph, put her head on one side coquettishly and stretched out a limp hand. "Take me Emily, please." Emily clenched her fists and counted to ten, under her breath but loud enough that Ashley would hear.

They walked to Pieminister to eat. Mum, still decidedly unsteady, was hand in hand with Ashley, both of them giggling because they thought they would catch Emily out and somehow make her eat a meat pie. They always seemed to find it a huge joke that Emily had chosen to become vegetarian for the good of the planet and her health. It was supremely irritating.

They did it whenever she was at home; as giant roast chickens were paraded on the table with pigs in blankets they would say, "Do have some gravy with your vegetables." From the smirking, it was obvious that it was made with meat stock. The one that really pissed Emily off was, "Would you like a boiled chicken embryo for breakfast? You seem to find that palatable." In a way though, they could be right. Perhaps she should go vegan.

Emily ambled along behind with her dad, who never felt it was necessary to say anything just for the sake of it. In a world of his own, he seemed to be watching his sloshed wife who meandered unsteadily along the pavement.

Mum and Ashley managed to keep the irritating conversation going all the way to the restaurant and while they were seated, finally shutting up when they were handed their menus. Of course, Pieminister had vegetarian, and even vegan, options and Emily was amused that her pie of choice was called Kevin.

Who on earth names a pie Kevin, and a vegan one at that? Love it.

Once the menu choices were given to the waiter, Mum twittered, "Well that went well, I thought."

Emily immediately thought they were going to discuss Great Granny's revelation. "What, finding out about your Aunt Julia?"

Mum flapped a hand inanely. "No, the funeral and everything. Nice church, nice burial. She'll have a lovely view from that Wisewood cemetery down the valley, nice wake afterwards. The Admiral put on a good spread. A good turnout. A funeral is such a good way to put a full stop on someone's life. Don't you think, Mike?"

Emily's dad gave an undistinguishable murmur. A man of few words, except when it came to the cost of anything and everything. Mum mumbled on, reliving the conversations that she'd had reminiscing about Great Granny Irene and what a kind and caring Nan she had been to her and Jennifer, and how she had been the only one on her side when she unexpectedly had 'the baby'. Emily was stone cold sober and found this tittering, silly version of her mother irritating.

Why is she being like this?

She gritted her teeth when the conversation turned to 'the baby'.

That's me, Mum. I'm here. I have a name. I have feelings.

The waiter delivered their pies. They looked crusty and golden and Emily suddenly found that she was hungrier than she had thought. The moment he departed, Mum immediately started on a new tack but an old topic, "That James, he makes me hopping mad. He was quite deliberately lording it over all of us going on about their new villa. 'Why don't you come and use it, Lisa?' Blah, blah, blah." Mum mimed a duck quacking with one hand while waving a forkful of pie around in the other. A drip of dark gravy plopped on to the table. "Chance would be a fine thing." Emily silently agreed that Mum really could do with Great Granny's money far more than Jennifer, who had been blessed with the looks as well as a wealthy husband. "How Jennifer can put up with him I don't know, with all his airs and graces. Who does he think he is?" She paused, took the mouthful off the end of her fork before pointing it in Emily's direction. Her mind had changed tack again. "Emily, why do you think it's such a good idea to start digging up lost relatives? Poor thing, whatever her name is..."

"Julia. Like your middle name. Hasn't that occurred to you?"

"I always assumed it was because it's Mum's middle name too."

Emily could imagine Julia. The third pea in the pod next to Granny and Aunt Cynthia. She had a romantic notion of their reunion, tears and joy all round, finding your long-lost sisters. Being able to tell Aunt Julia that she was loved, not unwanted. She couldn't understand why no-one else felt the same way.

Mum shook her head, "That's as maybe, but she's probably spent a very happy life not knowing anything about us lot, so why should she suddenly want to be introduced to us all? I wouldn't if I were her. Let it go."

Emily was indignant and put her knife and fork down with a clatter. "It's what GG wanted."

Mum, Dad and Ashley jumped at Emily's fervour. Mum waggled her finger at Emily. "But GG is dead so she won't know one way or the other."

Emily spluttered at such bluntness. "But Granny is alive, and she and Aunt Cyn are obviously keen to do what GG asked."

Mum went to rest her chin on one hand but it slipped off clumsily. "I think they're mad. Heavens knows how it will turn out. I think it's a really bad idea. You might find that the half-sister –"

"Julia."

"– is a drug addict or a prostitute or worse..."

"Mum, what could possibly be worse than a drug addict or a prostitute?"

Mum sat back looking rather pleased with herself, nodded her head firmly and attacked her pie. Speaking with a large chunk on her fork she sputtered, "What's funny is that it could be you, Emily."

"What do you mean?" Emily froze, on full alert. Mum shovelled the dripping forkful of pie into her mouth. Emily stared, waiting for her to go on.

After chewing for ages and then swallowing with a noisy gulp, she continued, "Well, we thought of having you adopted."

Emily was horrified.

So, Aunt Jennifer's hint was true. Mum is admitting it.

She had heard for as long as she could remember about being the unwanted baby, in contrast to Ashley who it appeared was the 'happy surprise'. But her mum had never been so direct before. Emily leant forward, stared directly at her mother and hissed, "You wanted to give me away?"

"Well, you weren't planned, and we hadn't even talked about getting married so we thought you might have a better life with someone who wanted you."

Emily was stunned.

Wanted you? Ouch. She gave birth to me and instead of being thrilled to meet her own daughter, she wanted to get rid of me.

A tight band of pressure threatened to crush her skull. "So, you admit it, you didn't want me?"

They were prepared to give me away to a complete stranger. I can't believe it.

Her mum shook her head, "Not at the time, no."

Mike grabbed ineffectually at Lisa's arm and wheedled, "Shut up, Lisa. You're pissed. You don't know what you're saying." He looked embarrassed.

Emily was fuming. "I think she does." It came out sounding like an insult.

"Indeed I do. Did that come out right?" Lisa put her head back and her mouth dropped open. "Not sure." She brought her chin down and looked vaguely at Emily, "Anyways, we did get married, and we did keep you. And Mike is your dad although I'm still not entirely sure about that because you certainly didn't get your brains and work ethic from him." She laughed, a horrible cackle.

Emily didn't think she could feel any worse but that was like a stab in her solar plexus.

"What are you saying, Mum?" It came out as a shout. Her mum shrugged, looking ridiculous with a smear of green mushy peas dribbling from the corner of her flaccid mouth.

Emily turned furiously to her dad. He was stoically sawing at his pie crust as if he hadn't heard a word of what Mum had been saying. Emily sat back, gobsmacked by her mum's revelation, and feeling icy cold. She abandoned her pie and sat rigidly while the others continued to peck at theirs in silence. The frigid atmosphere was weird. Neither her mum nor her dad would make eye contact with her and simply said nothing. Even Ashley had the good sense to keep quiet. Emily couldn't stand it.

"Look, Mum, Dad," *if you are my dad*, "you can't just say something like that and then –"

Dad said quietly, "That's enough. Everybody eat your bloody pies and let's get you out of here, Lisa."

It was hard to put one foot in front of the other, to walk along the pavement in such proximity to her parents and yet a zillion miles apart, to go into the hotel, to cram into the lift trying to press back into the corners to stay as far apart as possible, with no-one saying anything at all like complete strangers.

The lift intoning 'doors opening', in an irritating received pronunciation accent, broke the silence. Emily stepped out, turned to her parents and said, "Goodnight", although there was nothing good about it at all.

The thoughts cycled frantically through Emily's head as she fled along the corridor towards the room. Ashley followed bleating, "Wait for me."

'Someone who wanted you.' Is Dad my dad? How can you just come up with something like that and then just clam up and not say anything more? Jesus. This definitely needs talking about when Mum has sobered up. Breakfast time.

They aren't getting away with this.

THREE

Emily turned from the door of the hotel bedroom and watched as her parents drifted off nonchalantly towards their own room. Ashley rushed along the corridor towards Emily like an innocent spring lamb suddenly finding its mother.

"Shotgun the bathroom first." Ashley ducked under Emily's arm and headed for the bathroom to clean her teeth and get ready for bed.

Emily sighed and went to get her phone, feeling numb.

A message. I bet it's from Dylan. Thank God for that. She wriggled into the comfy chair and tucked up her legs ready to see what her boyfriend had to say.

> Hi hope funeral went OK. Been thinking lots today.

That's thoughtful. I need that right now.

Congrats on your results. I'm not looking forward to resits. Seems we're very different. I like steak, drinking and travelling the world. I want to have fun. You don't.

Emily frowned as she read that bit. *That's a bit antagonistic.*

I guess that we aren't meant to be together.

Emily stared at the phone, shocked. *Oh my god, he's breaking up with me. By bloody text.*

Sorry. Tried to call but your phone not on.

"You utter bastard."

I need a bit of space. Will contact you when I can.

Emily's heart lurched. An enormous mass lodged in her throat, making it hard for her to breathe. "Miserable cowardly twat."

Ashley walked into the room. "Don't talk to me like that. I'll tell Mum and Dad."

"For God's sake, Ashley, not everything is about you."

"Well, anyway, I want to go to bed now, and I want it dark, so you'll have to turn the lights off."

Selfish little twerp.

Emily ignored her and reread the message from Dylan twice. *I will not cry. I will not bloody cry.* She hit the Facetime icon and swiped Dylan. She didn't care that Ashley would be earwigging. It rang. It kept ringing.

"Answer you bag of shite." It kept ringing. She wondered if she had somehow done it incorrectly, got the wrong number perhaps. She swiped right and tried again. It rang.

She tried calling him on the phone. It rang once and went to voicemail. She was so incensed that she didn't know what to say, so she hung up. She thought about it, planned a message, and rang back. "Please ring me. That is all." He would see two missed calls.

She texted him a curt message.

Ring me. We need to talk.

She felt helpless and adrift. She wanted to howl but instead just chanted under her breath, "Bastard, bastard, bastard."

"Shut up, Emily," wailed a voice from the bed. "I want to go to sleep. Turn the lights off."

"Oh, for God's sake don't whine, Ashley."

She didn't know what to do next. She read the message again. There was no way she would be able to sleep after that second bombshell. She tried Facetime and wondered how long it would ring before it cut out. It must be driving him mad. Surely he would pick up. She tapped her fingers on the screen and jiggled her leg up and down.

"Dumped? And on the same day I am reliably informed by my own mother that I am an unwanted bastard and she isn't certain who my father is. Can it get any worse?"

"Shut up, Emily, you're being so annoying. I'm going to go and get Mum and Dad."

Emily sighed. "Don't bother, Ashley, I'll turn the lights off."

She sat huddled in the dark. She caught sight of her reflection in the room's mirror; her face looked haunted in the glow from her phone screen.

She let the tears creep silently down her cheeks as she reached for her laptop.

FOUR

At breakfast, her parents point blank refused to talk about the whole adoption thing. Emily was seething.

"For heaven's sake, Emily," Dad said wearily, rubbing the bridge of his nose, "your mum was just talking a whole load of drunken nonsense. It was all total rubbish. She didn't mean any of it. So just forget it."

Mum piped up, "God I feel awful. Your dad's right, Emily. Just ignore me. The rest of you, I have a cracking hangover so be nice to me. Just pour me some more coffee, Mike. Heaven knows what I was drivelling on about."

"But...did you consider having me adopted? Did you? Aunt Jennifer implied it and then you stated it quite clearly –" Emily persisted, staring hard at her mum.

Dad put both hands up in a stopping gesture. "Leave it out, Emily, for God's sake."

Emily whipped round to look at her dad. "And what about my parentage. Are you my dad?"

"Of course I am, so stop going on about it." He didn't look at her, picked up a knife, reached across to swipe a blob of butter, and started spreading it on his toast.

Emily gritted her teeth. It was quite clear that she wasn't going to get any more from him, so she turned back to her mum. "Mum? Is he? You said..."

"Please stop, Emily, with all these silly questions. I just can't take it." Mum flapped her hand in Emily's direction like a limp flag, buried her head in her hands, groaned and rubbed at her temples. Emily fumed but knew there was no point in pursuing the matter further. Her 'parents' could be very stubborn.

They were being so obstinate and uncaring that she wasn't even going to tell them about Dylan. She fiddled with a teaspoon, stirring her fruit smoothie, took a sip, stared around the room and, after some pondering about the fact that she wasn't getting anywhere, she decided to change the subject completely.

"I need to pop over to Granny and Aunt Cyn's so I was wondering if you could drop me off there, Dad."

Mum answered on his behalf. "Not this daft notion about finding the lost aunt again, Emily. Your dad and I were thinking we could all go to the tropical butterfly place before heading off home."

"Not really my thing. I can't think of anything worse than all those poor creatures held in captivity so that humans can go and gawp at them."

Mum sighed with an exaggerated droop of her head. "For heaven's sake, Emily, get over yourself."

It was Dad who came to her aid, although not in the supportive way she would have hoped. He always sat on the fence. "Perhaps it would be best that you go over to The Boomers. You can take the tram or a bus, Emily. We can pick you up later and then all drive home from there."

Emily got the bus to The Boomers. It gave her time to go over – and over – everything that had happened in the last twelve hours. Waves of misery and confusion kept catching her unawares, but she managed to hold herself together and tried to think positively about the whole finding Julia opportunity. She could hear Granny inside her head. "Stiff upper lip, lass."

She alighted at the familiar bus stop and lumbered up the hill to Granny's house, her heavy bag slung over her shoulder making her feel weighed down, literally and metaphorically.

She didn't need to ring the bell because the door was flung open and she was greeted on the steps by Granny with a quickly administered, deafening kiss in her right ear. Aunt Cynthia then enveloped her in a cosy cloud of Johnson's baby powder. Emily breathed it in and felt some of the tension dissipate with the familiar fragrance. Granny and Aunt Cynthia always made her feel loved and wanted. Despite Granny's attempts at being seen as strong, powerful and somewhat frosty within the family unit, Emily knew that underneath the bluster she was as soft as a comfortable pillow.

"What on earth are you wearing? You look like you're wearing pyjamas," came from Granny and "You're looking lovely today, very snazzy," from Aunt Cynthia.

"These are my harem pants from India. I got them from a charity supporting widowed mothers. They're ever so comfortable, and ethically sourced."

"And I suppose going all native is why you've got that silly stud in your nose these days as well as all those earrings. I spotted that yesterday." Granny turned to go inside. "Don't forget to wipe your feet."

Aunt Cynthia gently tapped Emily's nose, gave a wink and ushered her inside. "Someone had their beauty sleep,

I see," Aunt Cynthia said. Emily knew that she didn't really mean it, particularly after the night she had just had. A quick glance at her reflection in the hall mirror told her that she had black bags under her muddy eyes, but she was grateful that The Boomers always set out to make her feel more acceptable and give her confidence in herself.

She took her customary seat at the kitchen table, wrestling to control the bulk of the patchwork bag which always seemed to have a mind of its own.

Aunt Cynthia smiled benevolently. "Still using that bag, Emily?"

"I don't let it out of my sight. It holds everything that I need. It is my special sustainable, upcycled, bag for life – and it makes me think of you and all the clothes that you lovingly sewed for me as a kid." Emily smiled back but it came out as a bit weak and wobbly.

"Aww, dear. My pleasure." Aunt Cynthia patted Emily's shoulder.

Emily couldn't think where to start with her tales of woe so blurted out, "I got dumped by Dylan." It came out as a whine, as pathetic as one of Ashley's.

Granny plonked herself down at the table. "Who is this Dylan anyway? Have we met him?" and from Aunt Cynthia, "What do you mean dumped, dear?"

With The Boomers she never quite knew who to answer first when they talked in stereo.

"My boyfriend. Well, now my ex-boyfriend. We were so-called 'together' at uni. And the bastard gave me the elbow by text and I'm quite certain that he's blocked me because I can't get through on the phone or through Facetime, and he hasn't answered my texts."

Granny huffed. "Sometimes, Emily, you speak a completely different language than other human beings," and Aunt Cynthia declared, "Oh dear, that doesn't sound very nice whatever you mean."

"Sorry, I'm just very sad. And I've no idea what I'm going to do all summer but at least now I can go on my mission to find Aunt Julia without any encumbrances."

"You're far too young to be getting serious," Granny declared, and Aunt Cynthia added, "Better off without him by the sounds of it, you're far too good for him." Emily shrugged. She had hoped for a bit more conventional sympathy, but knew that The Boomers always had her welfare at heart.

"Pop the kettle on, Cyn."

"Of course, Rose. There's nothing like a brew to set things right." Aunt Cynthia gave Emily's shoulder a pat as she headed for the kettle. The kindness punctured Emily's steely self-control. She burst into tears and all the rest of her troubles started tumbling out.

"Mum and Dad – if he even is my dad – don't want me! They wanted to give me up for adoption, they said so, and I'm sure they meant it even though Mum said it was only because she was pissed." The Boomers exchanged shocked looks.

Granny said briskly, "But they did keep you, didn't they?" and Aunt Cynthia, "Oh dear, love. How horrid for you to find that out."

The Boomers looked at each other as if not being in total agreement was a shock. Granny leant across and took hold of Emily's hands. "Look, love. That was all a long time ago."

"Mum casually dropped it into the conversation that I was almost given away and then, to make it worse, implied that Dad might not even be my actual dad. They won't discuss it with me. Just keep fending me off."

The Boomers looked at each other again across the

kitchen. Aunt Cynthia nodded. Granny replied on their behalf, "I expect your mum was shaken up by the whole lost, secret aunt situation. That's the only way I can explain why she was behaving so badly and drinking too much. With it all coming out so suddenly it must have triggered how she felt when she fell pregnant with you. She would have gone through a lot of the thought processes that GG did, even though it was in less judgemental times." Emily sniffed.

But Mum was well away before the announcement so that isn't an excuse.

Aunt Cynthia gently placed a couple of tissues in Emily's hand and a mug of tea in front of her. She didn't like to say that she didn't drink tea any more. It seemed inappropriate. Granny released her hand, and she had a good blow. Aunt Cynthia retrieved the soggy pile, patted Emily's shoulder, and popped the mess into the bin.

"But what did happen? You must know."

"I'm not sure that it's our place to say..." Granny looked at Aunt Cynthia for support, Aunt Cynthia shrugged, nodded. Granny turned back to Emily. "As far as I remember it, yes, your mum was horrified when she found out she was pregnant. It wasn't at all what she had planned. She was doing well at work, she was going to night school to better herself and I was so proud. Then everything came crashing down. She kept hoping that it wasn't true and hid her head in the sand."

Aunt Cynthia gently placed her hands on Emily's shoulders. Emily felt comforted by the unspoken gesture of love. "Even then it wasn't the done thing dear, to have a baby when you weren't married. Frowned on. It was all still a bit old-fashioned around here."

Granny continued, "And by the time she told me, it was too late to do anything about it. Be thankful for that."

Emily gasped. "You mean she was thinking of getting rid of me...?"

Bloody hell, this just gets worse and worse.

Granny rushed on, "Yes, love, but you weren't. So, along you came anyway, and we were all thrilled, especially your GG... and me."

"And me," chipped in Aunt Cynthia, earning a frown from Granny. "You were adored from the start."

"Your mum obviously wasn't thinking straight, and she really did believe you would be better off if you were adopted, but your GG was having none of it. We all know why now, don't we? So, the arrangement was for your mum to carry on much as before your arrival, staying in her regular room at the back," Granny flicked her head towards the stairs, "with you in the cot that your mum and Aunt Jennifer had grown up in, and your GG came in during the day to look after you while we were all going to work and such. We always did things like that in those days, rallied round, it was how families worked."

Aunt Cynthia chipped in, "Still do, love." She gave Emily's shoulders another squeeze.

Emily took a quavering breath that ended in a hiccup. Granny continued. "So, Mike stepped up to the plate, even though your mum could've done much better, he's not much of a catch." Emily was taken aback at her bluntness, although Granny had never hidden her feelings on that matter, "Your mum seemed pretty adamant that you were his. They did get married and they did keep you. Thank God. I'd have hated for you not to be such a big part of our lives while you were growing up."

"But how do I know whether Dad is my dad?"

Granny was forthright. "He's always been your dad. Do you need another one? I know he's sometimes tough on you, but his heart is in the right place. I think he just finds you a bit flummoxing with your intelligence. Your brains definitely came from your mum, that's for sure." Emily wasn't satisfied. It didn't seem quite right.

Aunt Cynthia was more gentle. "In all probability it's most likely that he really is your dad anyway, dear. Why don't you just hang on to that, eh?" Emily wasn't convinced but didn't think The Boomers had any more idea than she did. She sighed heavily.

Granny smacked her hands on the table and gave a robust nod to Aunt Cynthia. "That's all history, Emily. There's nothing that you can change about the past. You're here, you've got a family that loves you. Now, let's change the subject. And as for that chap with the ridiculous name there's plenty more fish in the sea, but don't turn that into a lecture in sustainable fishing, please, Emily." Emily had to grin. Somehow, The Boomers could make her feel better just by being totally rude.

Aunt Cynthia added, "Right, cheer up chicken, and let's tell you some good news." Aunt Cynthia lifted her hands from Emily's shoulders, clapped like a seal and scuttled around the table to take her appointed place.

"Okay?" Emily looked warily at a beaming Aunt Cynthia and a smug looking Granny. "Is this about Julia?" What other bombshells were going to come her way? She was exhausted from all the emotion. At least this was being hyped as good news.

Granny continued to keep up the suspense. "We weren't going to tell you until we went over there but we might as well do it now."

"This really will raise your spirits, dear." Aunt Cynthia giggled.

"Tell me what? Come on, stop teasing, please."

The Boomers grinned at each other conspiratorially and Granny burst out, "She only went and left you the house!"

and Aunt Cynthia, beside herself with excitement, "Mum's house, it's yours!"

"What do you mean?" Emily shook her head. She couldn't take it in. Were they saying that Great Granny's house would be hers, or was she turning two and two into five? She knew she was gawping.

Granny leant back in her chair and raised her eyes to the ceiling. "Don't be so thick, Emily."

Aunt Cynthia did her idiosyncratic clap like a crazy seal. "Your GG. In her will, she left her house to you."

Emily looked puzzled. It was so randomly unexpected that it wasn't sinking in.

Granny growled, "For God's sake, Emily, you twit, look happy about it." Aunt Cynthia simpered, "Say something dear."

"Um. I'm not sure what to say. Are you sure?"

"Of course, you silly fool," and "Yes, yes, it really is true."

Who knew there were so many ways to call someone an idiot?

Emily was frankly amazed. It had never even crossed her mind that Great Granny might do that. She had always assumed, probably like everyone else, that it would be divided between her daughters. She shook her head.

That is incredible. It's amazing. The house. How much must that be valued at? It must be worth a bomb.

Emily was letting the excitement grow but then she had a sudden thought which brought her back down to earth. "But what about you two? That isn't fair."

Granny rolled her eyes and scowled. Aunt Cynthia tutted and said, "What a silly chump."

Granny added, "Look, love, it couldn't be better. Me and your Aunt Cyn are delighted for you. Mum specifically left us her rings, Mum and Dad's wedding carriage clock..."

Aunt Cynthia chipped in, "And the silver tea service, though gawd knows when we'll use that."

Granny continued as if Aunt Cynthia hadn't said anything, "I own this house outright, your Grandad did me well, we've got our pensions and to be honest, I'm not sure that we would really want to take on another house," and Aunt Cynthia, "And go through the palaver of having to sell it."

So, it was okay with Granny and Aunt Cynthia but a wave of uneasiness rose making Emily feel a bit anxious. Out came a whisper. "But what about Mum?" A pause.

After a deep breath, Granny answered, "She's stipulated the princely sum of three grand for your mum but nothing for Aunt Jennifer and that reprobate of a husband, she never did like him, arrogant sod." Aunt Cynthia added, "I'm sure your Mum and Dad will be glad to see you independent." Emily wasn't quite so convinced by that but didn't know what else to say. She shook her head and raised her hands in surrender.

The niggle about Mum's reaction remained. Would Mum be satisfied with three grand? It was an enormous sum in anyone's mind, but not so much when compared to Emily getting the house. "Well, I just don't know what to say."

"Well, well indeed," Granny said. "We need to get going sorting Mum's things out, so put that miserable face in your ridiculous great monster of a scrap bag and get a wiggle on," and a faint protest from Aunt Cynthia, "Hey, Rose, I made that bag."

"Let's go and visit *your* house." Granny chuckled in delight. Aunt Cynthia giggled and chucked Emily under the chin, as if she was six years old.

FIVE

Emily was in a complete daze as they walked down the hill and along Loxley Road. If she was going to inherit Great Granny's house a whole world of possibilities suddenly opened up. What was she going to do? Should she keep it to live in, or should she sell it? Selling it didn't seem quite the right thing to do but did she really want to move back to Loxley permanently? Would this be her final destination after uni?

It was a walk that Emily had taken so many times in her life when she had stayed with The Boomers, just around the corner from Great Granny. She'd been with The Boomers every school holiday that she could remember while her mum was working, as well as when the unexpected baby – that was Ashley, the happy surprise – arrived, in order to keep her out of the way. Loxley felt familiar and comforting and more like home than anywhere would ever be.

They had always spent a great deal of time with Great Granny, at her insistence. Many happy hours had been spent having tea around the table with the big brown teapot and scratchy Denby pottery plates, picnics in her garden, going up to the playground, popping to the post office with pocket money to buy sweets. Emily smiled to herself. Happy memories. Emily couldn't help but share them. "Do you remember when we went to the park and GG got wedged into the slide?"

Granny burst into hoots of laughter. "Indeed, I do. Silly old Mum. Her bum was far too big for that slide."

Aunt Cynthia giggled, "Oh yes, I so remember that. We laughed 'til we cried, and you wet your knickers, Emily."

"I never did." Emily was laughing out loud.

Ever practical Granny added, "Ah, but I always carried spare kecks just in case."

"You did, Rose. On that occasion we all needed them." They all sniggered like they were young kids.

Granny stopped to catch her breath and inhaled heavily. Emily was taken aback. "What's up Granny?"

"Dicky heart. No point complaining but I'll be needing a few running repairs if this goes on."

Emily was horrified. There she had been wallowing in her own troubles and distracted by her unexpected good fortune, and there was Granny with real, life-threatening problems of her own. Emily caught a worried look on Aunt Cynthia's face before it was quickly transformed into a reassuring smile when she realised that Emily was looking at her.

Giving Granny a moment to recover, Aunt Cynthia turned and looked out over the Loxley Valley. "I never tire of this view." Emily took the hint and admired the incredible panorama.

The view hadn't changed since Emily was a child: the hills and diving vales marked out with their stolid stone walls, a procession of trees following the route of the River Loxley. She was amazed at how, despite being in a suburb of the city along a major, busy road, it was possible to reach out and touch the wildness of the Peak District from here.

"Well, don't stop and stare all day, you two, or we'll never get to Mum's at this rate." Granny's peremptory command jolted Emily out of her reverie, and they set off again, Emily trying very hard not to be too obvious as she kept an eye on Granny's progress. They turned right at the Admiral Rodney pub, where the great revelation about the forsaken Aunt Julia had been pronounced. Then slowly, matching Granny's now much more measured pace, they proceeded steadily up the hill to Leaton Close, arriving at Great Granny's house at the end of the cul-de-sac.

Granny had a key, although Great Granny's house had never been locked before in living memory. It was strange to be going into her house, to pass the tweed coats amassed as usual on the hall stand topped with an array of felt and knitted hats, and not to be greeted by a quavering 'woo-hoo, I'm in the lounge'.

And this – this house – is now mine.

Emily stood in the hall taking it in. She looked up the stairs imagining Great Granny inching down, clutching the banister as if her life depended on it, which it probably had since they were so steep. Aunt Cynthia put an arm around Emily's shoulders and gently moved her aside. "Emily, don't stand in the way, you silly goose, we have lots to do."

Granny had her industrious expression firmly pinned to her face and clapped her hands together. "Indeed, we do."

Is it a family trait, all this hand clapping? Perhaps I will start doing it too.

Emily felt a bit reluctant to go through to the empty living room but dutifully followed The Boomers.

It still smelt of Great Granny; her favourite scent, Blue Grass, was infused into the swirly patterned carpets, flowery curtains and decorative wallpaper. It had been the family's go-to Christmas present for years and Emily suspected that upstairs there was a bedroom with a secret cupboard stacked with the stuff. Whenever she had unwrapped their gifts, she would always appear surprised, open her vivid green eyes wide and coo, "Oh my love, Blue Grass, my favourite, thank you so much."

Such a sweetie, and she definitely wanted Mum to keep me and loved me unconditionally. And now we know about her past it isn't surprising she felt so strongly.

"Now, Cyn and I made a first stab at sorting out all the paperwork the day before yesterday. We found the will. That's how we know that your GG wants you to have the house. It'll need a lot of sorting out with the solicitors and all. They're the executors of the will so they will need to apply for probate before anything can be divvied out."

"Probate?"

Aunt Cynthia answered, "Yes, dear, there are laws of the land that we have to follow."

Granny frowned at her and looked back at Emily. "You don't need to know all the details but basically, they have to get everything valued down to the last trinket, send all the figures to the government who take their slice and then grant probate to the executors. It's only then that they can fulfil Mum's wishes as per her will. At that point, and only then, are they obliged to contact the beneficiaries."

"Sounds complicated."

"It is, and long winded. Those solicitors will drag it out so they can get their fees, no doubt. Anyway, it means that nothing is official yet so we'd better keep it under our hats, but we wanted you to know"

Emily couldn't help but imagine a wax sealed parchment poking out under one of Great Granny's favourite felt hats from the hall stand.

Aunt Cynthia was hovering, waiting to get her penny's worth in. "And, Emily dear, this is ever so exciting, we found Mum's letter and some other bits and pieces all bundled together. And, this is sensational, Julia's actual birth certificate!"

It was beginning to sink in that the house and everything were now hers but the prospect of finding Julia trumped all the other revelations that had poured out since Great Granny's letter. At the sound of a real life birth certificate for Julia, Emily's curiosity was piqued and her excitement at the prospect of finding Julia was rekindled.

Now, that is what I am going to be doing this summer break. I am going to find Julia and deliver GG's note.

"Can I see it?" Emily asked in anticipation.

"All in good time, but first of all why don't you take a look around with new eyes at your very own house? We need to sit down and write a list of everything that we need to do."

Emily was itching to see that birth certificate.

"Did you find the note that GG wants us to give to Julia?"

Granny retorted, "Yes, but it is sealed and marked 'For Julia's eyes only' so we must respect that. Not much else otherwise." Aunt Cynthia added, "It was with a notebook and bundle of papers fixed with a rubber band."

"Last night I did loads of googling and I've bookmarked some useful sites. So many people have done this before, tracing relatives, so there's a mountain of useful information..."

The Boomers were looking at her as if she was speaking Greek, then Granny flapped a hand dismissively. "Yes, yes, but let's not worry about that now," and Aunt Cynthia, "We need to go through all this again and check that we haven't missed anything. That has to be the first thing on our list."

The dining room table was loaded with paperwork. It appeared that Great Granny had kept every single piece of paper that she had ever received. Emily was very impressed by her 'waste not, want not' attitude. It matched her own ecological ethos, although she wasn't quite sure what Great Granny had intended to do with all the rubber bands, odd pieces of string and carefully folded wrapping paper from ninety-four years' worth of birthdays and Christmases.

Emily picked up a Barclays Bank statement going back to just after the war and studied how it had all been carefully typed on a pre-printed sheet with columns for Date, Particulars, DR, CR and Balance. A whiff of dry leaves wafted up. The paper was brittle and yellowing with age. It took Emily a moment to decipher the numbers which were written like a bank sort code with three items.

Twit. It's the ancient currency of pounds, shillings and pence.

It must have taken ages and an army of typists to do those. Obviously, some of them weren't very good at their jobs because the columns were all over the place.

This belongs in a museum.

Granny crept up behind her and whisked it out of her hand. "Emily, if you read every piece of paper on this table, I will have passed away myself before you've finished." Emily jumped a mile and the whole lot cascaded on to the floor.

"Oh, Emily." And as an echo from Aunt Cynthia, "For gawd's sake!"

Emily wasn't ready to take possession of Great Granny's home while it stood exactly how it had always been: the G Plan chairs, the carriage clock on the mantlepiece above the gas fire, the photographs of them all alongside. It was still her great-grandmother's home; the place felt as if she'd just popped down to the post office and would be back in a moment. So Emily decided to get on with her research despite The Boomers' lack of interest.

Once the papers were restacked on the table, she sidled

around and found a partly used lined notebook with a few shopping lists in Great Granny's loopy writing. She sniffed it to obtain a whiff of Great Granny but was disappointed that it smelt of curry powder. It had a sticker with a weird symbol on the front, '1/-'. She wondered what that meant.

One of many?

"Can I use this?"

"Mum won't have much use for that now, will she?" Granny said, overlaid by Aunt Cynthia saying, "Yes of course, dear."

Emily discreetly pinched the pile of old papers that looked distinctly like the bundle with the birth certificate. Then she scuttled to the other end of the room where she hopped into a chair with her back to The Boomers and had a good look at her stolen treasure.

For a moment, out of all the thoughts that were running crazily through her mind, it struck her that she ought to try contacting Dylan again. She needed to have it out with him. How dare he dump her by text, so rude. She had realised that he must have blocked her. It was the only explanation for him not picking up her Facetime calls.

I wish there was some way of knowing whether someone had read your texts. On WhatsApp, the little blue tick gives people away.

"Bastard. Sod him."

"Emily!" and "Language!" were thrown in her direction.

"Sorry, so sorry."

I will forget all about that scrawny little carbon guzzling, dead animal eating, alcoholic... damn, run out of words.

She shuffled through her booty and instantly spotted the letter for Julia. She couldn't help but clasp it to her chest and hunch her shoulders. It smelt clean and fresh and faintly of lavender. "I will get this letter to you, Julia, I promise," she whispered.

She replaced the poignant missive on the pile, unopened. Emily picked up and avidly read the birth certificate, beautifully written in meticulous handwriting, and wrote all the details down in the 1/- notebook.

When and Where Born: 23rd March 1945
Hallamshire Maternity Home, Sheffield
Name if Any: Julia
Sex: Female
Name and Surname of Father: Lloyd Franklin King

Julia's father. GG's lover. A very American name. Much better name than Dylan, manly and strong.

Name, surname, maiden name and address of
mother: Irene Ada Marshall, 8, Laird Avenue,
Sheffield.

Yup, that's GG and presumably where she lived with her parents.

Emily looked on Google Maps and found Laird Avenue just a few blocks down the road. This family had not wandered far in their lifetimes. She wondered how different it would have been then, before Loxley was enfolded by Sheffield in the 1970s and became 'no longer a village but a city suburb', as Great Granny was always telling her.

Sheffield would have been very different then with its thriving steel industry. Great Granny always went on about the local firms who diligently manufactured the furnace bricks that made the industry possible. She recited all their names like poetry: 'Bramalls Siddons Bros; Thomas Wragg & Sons; Thomas Marshall and Co, no relation to my branch of the family; and Hepworths.' Great Grandad had been very proud to work for Hepworths, and Emily's mum had been equally proud to work for Bramalls until she had married Emily's dad in 1992. Emily had been born in 1991.

I wonder if Mum would have married Dad if she hadn't been forced to? And would Dad, if he is my dad, have married Mum if he hadn't had to? Or perhaps I'm just not very likeable which is why Dylan has dumped me and Mum and Dad didn't want to keep me either. Perhaps my parents really would have preferred to have me adopted like Aunt Julia was.

Stop whining, Emily. You're getting as bad as bloody Ashley! Now just get on with finding Aunt Julia.

Occupation of father: Master Sergeant

Definitely a soldier as stated and a strange American rank.

Signature, description and residence of informant:
Squiggle, mother, 8, Laird Avenue, Sheffield.

"This is incredible, so much information in just one formal document telling a family history. Wow"

Granny grumbled, "Emily what are you doing now?" and Aunt Cynthia echoed, "What, dear?"

"Sorry Boomers, I caught my shin on the coffee table and was saying ow...?"

"You are always so clumsy, something else where you take after your mother," harrumphed Granny overlaid with, "Well don't make such a fuss, dear, we're up to our eyes in paper here," from Aunt Cynthia.

The next of her secreted documents was a brown envelope marked 'Favourite Recipes'. Not likely to be very interesting except from a historical perspective, but Emily opened it anyway and drew out a book with a flowery cover stating, very boldly in unnecessarily large writing: 'Recipes'. It emanated a slight whiff of mothballs as if it had emerged from GG's blanket box. Emily flicked through it and recognised Great Granny's writing. Exactly the same as her poignant letter from the grave.

It's funny how everyone's writing is so unique. Like our DNA. The DNA that I share with GG and Julia... and Mum... maybe with Dad.

Some good vintage recipes though, and many of them vegetarian: Vegetable Cottage Pie, Bubble and Squeak, Eggless Chocolate Cake.

They were into their vegetarian food then too, although perhaps not Spam Hash. That sounds unattractive, but what on earth is Spam? Is it a vegetable?

Emily carefully turned the pages. They were brittle. She was scared that she might tear them.

They certainly knew how to make do and mend in those days. No food wastage, paper bags, no everlasting plastic, fabric nappies, all the washing dried on a line. I assume that they still had rationing and ate very limited amounts of meat. I wonder if they knew they were saving the planet only for us to come along and ruin it?

As she sat back in the chair and lifted the book to read, a plain envelope slipped out. More recipes? She looked inside and found a bundle of letters tied with a thin, pale pink ribbon. The little hairs on the back of her neck bristled. She glanced guiltily at The Boomers but they were in their own little world chattering like rooks. Emily wiped her fingers on her harem pants, just in case, and carefully undid the neat bow and started reading.

23rd March 1946

Dear Miss Marshall,

Great Granny Irene as an unmarried lass... wow.

I know that you have been immensely distressed regarding Julia who was placed with St Christopher's Home within my parish on my recommendation. I am able to visit frequently. It is a happy place and the children are comfortable and well cared for. Julia has been content since she arrived. It is indeed fortunate that she has found such an ideal placement and you can rest assured that she is in good hands.

It is not permitted to provide you with further information regarding Julia in the future, which I trust you understand.

Yours sincerely,
Reverend John Partington

Emily sat up straight, rigid, the hairs standing up on the back of her neck. She gasped, then looked round at The Boomers, but they seemed to be playing a mad giant card game with mounds of papers.

This is gold! Reverend Partington? He must be the one that was mentioned in GG's letter. The curate. Emily dug out her copy from her pocket, horribly creased from the number of times that she had read and reread it. *It makes sense.*

Saint Christopher's Children's Home – an enormous clue to finding Julia. She grabbed her laptop and typed into Google, 'Saint Christopher's Children's Home' She scrolled through the results. One turned out to be an old people's home not for children at all. *I'm just not doing this right.* Her research at uni had taught her that the world wide web was like that. You had to know what you were looking for in order to find it, which was extremely annoying and contradictory.

Sighing with frustration, Emily looked at the next missive, plucking it delicately from the pile as if she was extracting a piece of fragile tissue paper.

Perhaps there will be more clues.

Dear Miss Marshall,

Thank you for your letter and the enclosed gift.

I understand from my parents that congratulations are in order and that you have impending nuptials. I am delighted for you although somewhat envious of your prospective spouse. You must know that I always held a candle for you.

Gosh, GG – heart breaker!

When we last wrote, I informed you that I could not provide further information regarding Julia and I am afraid that this must stand.

That's really mean.

I will however give her the golliwog anonymously. I am sure that she will be most grateful. Please do not send further gifts as it places me in an awkward situation with the staff *and the other children and I do not wish to jeopardise the trust that they have in me.*

Yours sincerely,

Reverend John Partington

How unkind! Poor GG. And a g— urgh, I don't even want to think that word. But a black doll like that was considered an acceptable gift? It doesn't seem possible that there was a time when such toys were given to children. I wonder when they were finally labelled racist. Jesus, GG was living in such a very different world.

Emily shuddered. She carefully put the offensive letter to the back of the bundle, wiped her fingers thoroughly on her shirt, and read the next plain postcard addressed to 'Mrs W. Bedlington, 8, Leaton Close, Loxley, Sheffield, West Riding of Yorkshire'

23rd March 1948

Dear Mrs Bedlington,

Please be advised that Julia continues to live a content and happy life at St Christopher's. Her third birthday was celebrated with a small party with her friends.

JP

A bit abrupt. Maybe even callous? Emily rubbed tenderly at the smudges on the ink. *Tear stains? They could be. I would have been in floods if I'd been GG.*

Another plain postcard followed.

'23rd March 1949

Dear Mrs Bedlington,

Please be advised that Julia continues to live a content

and happy life at St Christopher's. Her fourth birthday was celebrated with a party which all the children very much enjoyed.

JP'

At least he was keeping Great Granny in touch with the progress of her daughter, albeit in a rather miserly manner. Then another letter rather than a plain postcard.

23rd March 1950

Dear Mrs Bedlington,

I am writing to advise you on Julia's fifth birthday that this will be my last letter to you as Julia is no longer at St Christopher's. A respectable Christian family, the Levetts who farm nearby, have now formally adopted Julia. They have a son called Charles but sadly lost a much beloved daughter when she was a baby.

I have not seen her since she left St Christopher's, understandably, but am reliably informed that she is very happy. Apparently they tried to call her Molly but she refused to answer to it which amused the staff greatly. She is quite the character.

I understand from my parents that you have a thriving daughter. I wish you well for your future happiness as a legitimate family and must now conclude my correspondence with you.

JP

"A legitimate family. How bloody rude!" It came out rather louder than Emily had expected.

Aunt Cynthia asked kindly, "Who's rude, dear?" with a

synchronised, less kind, "What are you going on about?" from Granny.

Aunt Cynthia added gently, "Honestly, Emily dear, you are always talking, muttering and laughing to yourself."

Granny's opinion was, "People will think you are potty, which you are, so it isn't surprising."

"Sorry, Boomers. I was just trying to tie up some dates. Can you remind me of your actual birth dates, please?"

"My *actual* birth date is twenty-second of May 1950 and Cyn's is tenth of September 1951. Why do you need to know that?"

"I'm just trying to get a timeline straight in my head, you know, when GG got married and had each of you two."

Aunt Cynthia chipped in, "Mum and Dad got married on twenty-third of July 1949. Their wedding picture is over there on the dresser. Not a very fancy occasion by all accounts but Sheffield was a mess from the ruinous bombing and there was still rationing. Mum would've had to beg for clothing coupons to get enough fabric for a dress."

So, GG must have married Great Grandad soon after she found out about Julia's dad being killed. Nothing wrong in that. And she most definitely cracked on to have Granny and then Aunt Cyn.

Emily counted the months out on her fingers.

Blimey, ten months from when they got married and then only sixteen months between the two of them.

Emily read every single letter and postcard again, took pictures of each of them, compared dates, and carefully wrote the facts that she had discovered in the 1/- notebook. She couldn't bring herself to record the 'G' word.

What must GG have thought when she received each of those postcards and letters? Was she sitting here in the lounge, or in the kitchen? When she got that last one about Julia being adopted, Granny would have been toddling, on this very carpet probably, and Aunt Cyn would have been on the way. Hard to imagine Granny as a toddler, I bet she was naughty.

Emily jumped as Granny suddenly barked, "Emily, instead of fiddling with your computer could you make yourself useful and make us a brew?"

Aunt Cynthia pleaded, "Oh yes, dear, I'm gasping."

"Of course." Emily smiled to herself, hiding her incredible discoveries for the moment – she had far more work to do with this goldmine of information – then leapt up and went into the kitchen. She boiled the kettle on the gas hob, pulled the giant-sized brown teapot that she had known all her life out of the cupboard, warmed the pot (she had been well trained) and spooned in Yorkshire Tea – leaves, not bags of course. She didn't like tea herself, an aberration considering her upbringing where a brew was the answer to everything. She poured in the boiling water and left the tea to 'brew 'til you can stand a spoon up in it'. That's what Great Granny had always said.

Emily ambled into the garden, turning her face up to the warm sun that always flooded the bountiful south-facing garden, when it wasn't bucketing with rain as it was wont to do in Sheffield. The plot was already becoming overgrown without the loving ministrations of Great Granny who could often be found turned upside down like a duck to dig out a weed and pinch off spent flowers while quacking about the slugs.

Emily picked herself a handful of mint. As she came back into the kitchen sniffing the fragrant sprigs with pleasure, Granny was calling, "What are you doing, Emily, picking the tea?"

Emily grinned and shouted back. "Yes, indeed I am."

"Don't be daft, Emily."

Aunt Cynthia giggled, "You are so funny, Emily."

With The Boomers served their tea, in exchange for a heart-warming hug and a noisy kiss, and a steaming mug of mint tea next to her, she wondered what to tackle next.

Okay, I must start digging deeper and more intelligently. Think, Emily, think.

She went back to her first clue: Saint Christopher's. It had to start there. She looked again at Great Granny's letter. Dr Barnardo's home. She tried googling that instead.

Ah, this is more like it. A list of children's homes.

She clicked on the link and there was a list of all Dr Barnardo's homes by county. She worked her way steadily down the list; there seemed to be so many and for some reason a preponderance in Essex. Her finger was leaving a bit of a snail trail down her laptop screen where she had poked at the mint in her tea.

And suddenly there it was. Directly under 'Tunbridge Wells Home for Incurables', 'St Christopher's, Pembury Road, Tunbridge Wells, Kent'. Emily's mind raced and her heart pounded.

OMG. Kent. Why Kent? So far from Sheffield. Weird. And Tunbridge Wells sounds very posh. Better check that there aren't any more Saint Christopher's. Hooray for Control F.

Emily was overcome with a burst of excitement. She wanted to jump up, shout and sing and dance but instead she managed to control her enthusiasm, sat back and took a slug of mint tea, grinning to herself.

Tunbridge Wells! I'm amazing at this research malarkey. At least I'm good for something in this world.

But how could she use this amazing information breakthrough?

Back to basics, Emily.

She returned to the 1/- notebook and the curate's letters to assess the next potentially significant clue.

A respectable Christian family, the Levetts who farm nearby, have now formally adopted Julia.

Okay, farmers... and an unusual surname. I would expect it to be Leveret like the baby hare but it isn't, unless he spelled it incorrectly. Could he?

She tentatively searched Yellow Pages for the Tunbridge Wells area to see if there was still a Levett, or Leveret, farming in the area. Up popped:

William C. Levett, The Oast, Oak Tree Farm,
Lamberhurst, Kent. 01892 785419.

What does Oast mean? A bit confusing. She scratched her head with both hands, massaging her scalp; it was calming and kept her usual vocal outbursts suppressed. *How can I check it out further? Even if they're just relations they might know of the whereabouts of Julia, or the brother named as Charles in the Curate's letter.* Her rookie research at the Premier Inn last night into 'how to find lost relatives' came in handy and she decided to try the electoral roll for Lamberhurst.

She tapped in the website address, typed in Levett and found: William C Levett, Elizabeth A Levett, Charles P Levett, Catherine J Levett.

"There is a Charles," whispered Emily with great restraint, glancing at The Boomers to make sure they hadn't heard.

Elizabeth and Catherine could be wives or other daughters, but no Julia or Molly. Being female, it was likely that Aunt Julia had moved away from the family home after she was married, as her own mother had done, and would by now have a completely different surname. That made things much trickier.

Why do women have to change their names to their husband's? I most certainly will not, if I ever do get married. I'm not a bloody chattel.

A quick search for Levett on BT.com came up with the same William C. Levett at the strange Oast address. The second entry was for 'Charles P. Levett, Oak Tree Farm, Lamberhurst, Kent. 01892 785207'. A weird sensation snaked up her back. Was this Julia's brother? It surely must be. Emily did a wiggly dance move with her arms and the papers cascaded onto the floor. The Boomers glared at her. "Sorry, sorry." She wondered whether to say anything to them yet, but she wanted to be absolutely certain.

Perhaps I could phone that number?

She was tempted but realised that it would be wrong to just pick up the phone to a complete stranger and blurt out what Great Granny had revealed before she had amassed – and confirmed – more information. She made notes of her discovery and decided to continue.

She needed to find out Julia's married name. She went back to ancestry.co.uk, that she had discovered only yesterday but was an absolute mine of information. They told her that there were 117 records for Julia Levett and just in case, 9 for Molly Levett. It was frustrating that to get at them you had to sign up for a free trial.

Worth the risk? Go for it, Emily.

It seemed to take forever to sign up and they insisted on having her debit card details despite it being 'free'. Her card wasn't in her purse. It seemed to be hiding somewhere else in her enormous bag. She rummaged amongst her Hydro water bottle, all the spare copies of Great Granny's letters, her 'cagoule in a bag', hairbrush, wet wipes, wash bag, tissues and other very useful items. She hunted it down between the covers of Great Granny's service sheet.

I need to sort this bag out. God knows what else is lurking in there.

Logging into ancestry.co.uk revealed a treasure trove of information and a very long list of Julia Levetts. Emily sighed with frustration.

C'mon now, patience Emily, this is going to take time.

She realised very quickly that she could pass on most of them because the dates were 1885 and suchlike, but irritatingly the list wasn't in date order, so she had to be careful. She was getting bug eyed so decided to take a break, went to the toilet and, while she was upstairs, poked her head into the bedrooms – *her* bedrooms now.

First door was the spare room. She looked at it with new eyes. It was such a very old-fashioned room with tall, wooden twin beds, and rather garish sixties wallpaper. Great Granny must have had a funny five minutes as it was not her usual style, or perhaps it was Granny and Aunt Cynthia's choice when they were groovy teenagers sharing this room. The frilly curtains were in stark contrast.

My house now. Weird. Very kind of GG. It will set me up for life, pay off all my tuition debts. Amazing. I can get out and have some real fun at uni next year without scrimping and constantly worrying about how I'm going to pay it all back. It's going to change my life.

She sat on the bed nearest the door and with a creak of the rusty bedsprings, was consumed into the deep, enveloping hollow of the squishy mattress, her arms and legs thrown gawkily in all directions. She stayed for a moment in contemplation as her mood swung suddenly from amusement to misgiving.

Mum will be livid though. And Dad. I wonder how they'll react when they find out?

Emily found herself torn between feeling guilty for her mum but at the same time thinking that it served her right for even considering getting rid of her, even before she was born, as well as afterwards. If it hadn't been for Great Granny, Granny and Aunt Cynthia she wouldn't even be here now, in this house at all. She could be living a life with a completely different family, and she wouldn't know anything about her real kin at all. Like Aunt Julia. Lost. Abandoned.

Sod you Mum. Best not tell her yet.

She scrambled to her feet, ventured down the short landing and softly opened the door into Great Granny's darkened bedroom. The room still smelt intensely of Great Granny, and Emily inhaled deeply.

Perhaps I might find GG's stash of Blue Grass as I uncover all her other secrets.

She crossed the room, drew back the curtains, perched on the bedroom chair next to the kidney shaped dressing table with its flouncy skirt, and looked at the view out to the hills beyond. "Thank you so much, GG. Not just for this house but everything, all the love and cuddles. And for stopping me from being adopted."

She spotted a tortoiseshell hairbrush on the dressing table, silver hairs sparkling in the sunlight from the window.

Now that I am a super sleuth, perhaps I should keep that for DNA purposes.

Emily smiled to herself. She couldn't believe how far she had come in just a few hours of 'fiddling with my computer'. She was so excited. "GG, we will find Julia," she promised the scent laden room firmly. "I have already found out where she went and who her family are. It's just so exciting, GG. Never mind that they wanted to get rid of me, thank you for saving me and I hope I can return the favour by finding Julia for you. Now, I'm going back to work. And sod Dylan, he can just go and... stuff his face with dead animals." Emily got to her feet and walked with intent back across the room, patting the flowery eiderdown as she went past the bed. Great Granny had always refused to use a new-fangled duvet. She closed the door firmly to lock in the special aroma.

In the kitchen, Emily topped up her mug with hot water, refreshing the limp mint leaves. Then she sidled back into the lounge to take her place in the armchair and toil on with her research where she had left off. She kept plodding on and on through the long list of Julia and Molly Levetts.

She became very tingly when one particular post eventually popped up.

'23rd November 1965. Julia Levett to David Merripen, St Mary's Church, Lamberhurst, Kent.'

A little 'eek' squeaked out before she could stop it.

"What?" The Boomers spoke in unison and turned to frown at her in perfect synchronisation.

"Julia got married!"

A sigh from Granny, "What are you talking about?" overlaid with Aunt Cynthia's, "Who married who, dear?"

"It's here... look..." Emily leapt up from the chair, picked up her laptop and thrust it towards The Boomers, sending her mug of mint tea flying.

"Emily!" was bellowed out in stereo.

To be fair, you can't see anything on the swirly patterned carpet, and it is now my carpet.

"Sorry, I'll clear it up while you look at this. Just look at it. Please."

They both stretched their necks, wrinkled their brows in unison, and squinted at it. They looked identical.

"I can't see what it says," and, "What is it?"

Emily took her laptop and put it on top of a stack of fading magazines from the eighties. "Sorry, but I just can't keep this from you both any longer. It's details of Julia's marriage to a man called David Merripen. I've found her. Your sister. And it's Lamberhurst Church – that ties in with the farm address and her brother Charles." Emily couldn't understand The Boomers' lack of response.

Granny frowned. "Emily, what are you gabbling about?" matched with "You've found someone who married someone else? But who?" from Aunt Cynthia.

Emily was beaming. "I'm ninety-nine percent sure I've found Julia. It's a pretty good match I would say. GG has made this so easy for us." Emily was grinning proudly and stood with her arms out waiting for an accolade. "Ta da."

Granny frowned at her, looked closely at the screen then back to Emily. "You've found Julia? Are you sure?" Aunt Cynthia craned her head forward towards Granny as if hard of hearing, then peered at Emily. "Have you?"

"I have." Emily nodded and folded her arms in triumph.

"Are you certain, Emily? You could be barking up completely the wrong tree. You've only been at this for a few hours, and you can be very impetuous."

Typical of Granny to question it. Emily gritted her teeth. Aunt Cynthia nodded in agreement but looked a bit bemused.

Emily was getting miffed that The Boomers didn't seem to be taking her seriously. Her face fell. Granny spotted it and frowned. "Don't sulk please, Emily. You can't just gabble away with all this nonsense and expect us to understand."

Aunt Cynthia snaked a comforting arm around her shoulders, "Now dear, I'm quite sure that you have done a fantastic job. We can't thank you enough, but please talk us through your findings calmly and in some semblance of order."

Emily realised that she had gone completely overboard

with her eagerness and switched to 'objective researcher explaining a thesis', but the overwhelming feeling of excitement was bubbling up again. As she tried to be calm, her voice got steadily squeakier as she took The Boomers through her notes, the birth certificate, and the correspondence discovered at the back of the mothball smelling recipe book. "It's all there, in the letters from the curate bloke. Bless him – he kept GG updated about Aunt Julia when she ended up at Saint Christopher's Children's Home. Isn't that amazing?"

The Boomers stared at her in bafflement. "Letters from the curate?" Granny asked. Emily dashed to the sofa, picked them up and waved them in front of The Boomers. Granny took them from her as if they might bite her and glanced at Aunt Cynthia who shook her head and raised her eyebrows.

Emily took a quick breath and continued in a rush, "And that meant that I could locate Saint Christopher's in Tunbridge Wells, which meant I easily unearthed the Levett family and then I knew what her name was so I could obtain Aunt Julia's marriage details. So we know who she is and where we can find her." Emily looked between The Boomers, her face glowing with exhilaration.

Why aren't they jumping up and down?

Granny looked at Emily with a completely unexpected blank face. "Now calm down, lass. This needs to be looked over. We need to take it steady. If you're right this is indeed astounding." Emily instantly felt deflated.

I am right. Granny can be so annoying when she doesn't take me seriously.

Aunt Cynthia nodded, and gave an "Mm," clearly letting Granny take charge.

"So, steady on Emily. You're going back home to Newcastle this afternoon, we presume – unless you want to stay of course? Nothing more is going to happen in the meantime, is it? So, for now, just hold your fire. We'll have a read of these letters..." Granny flapped them like a fan. "Look at your notes and go from there."

Emily was so frustrated. "But..."

"I don't think we will find anything more in the way of revelations in Mum's papers, but they still need sorting," Granny continued. "The whole house needs sorting. Let's get everything straight. The house might be yours, love, but we can't leave it all to you and it's proving quite cathartic. Now, we've waited all this time to even find out about Julia, we can wait just a bit longer. Yes?"

Emily mumbled, "Okay." She was disappointed. 'Merripen' was echoing in her head. Her fingers were itching to get going again. She folded her hands tightly as if in prayer. It was very tempting to stay. In all truth, since her parents' hideous revelation, she would much prefer to be with The Boomers than them. Unfortunately, she hadn't packed for that eventuality.

Perhaps I can come back, do my research here where they're as interested and excited as I am. And I'm embraced here, literally and metaphorically.

Granny placed the letters on the table and continued steadily, "I'll get Lisa and Mike to come over and help this afternoon. I presume they're picking you up to go home to Newcastle." Emily nodded. "Jennifer's lot are as much use as a chocolate teapot – too used to their cohort of servants. But they might all want to choose a keepsake to remind them of GG. In fact, Emily, you'd better have a rummage through the lounge cupboards and Mum's jewellery in her bedroom before they get here. Make sure they don't choose anything that you want to keep. There's no need to tell them the good news about your legacy yet. We'll get back to this once we're all sorted, there's no rush."

"Okay, Granny," Emily said, although secretly she was

thinking about all the research rabbit holes she was going to explore when she could get back onto her laptop. "What I'd really love is old photos of everyone."

So I have a collection to show to my new relatives when I find them. And GG's hairbrush, just in case. For DNA purposes. Actually, that is a way I could find out whether Dad is my dad. But he doesn't have any hair so perhaps a toothbrush might do.

Granny nodded, "You can have as many of those as you like. There will be plenty, Mum kept every single blooming picture that was ever taken. There are shed loads of them. Where will they be then, Cyn?"

Aunt Cynthia thought for a moment, "There should be stacks of old albums somewhere. I think they might be in the attic."

Emily wasn't going to give up on her quest to search for Julia, even though The Boomers seemed content to procrastinate. "And can I take all the Julia papers home with me? If you read them while I'm rummaging, then I can organise them for you and keep going on my research..." Emily looked at Granny pleadingly.

Granny smiled, "Go on then, love. You're obviously keen to get on to it and you seem to have done a good job so far." Aunt Cynthia gave Emily one of her comforting pats, "I don't think we'd be able to stop you."

Emily grinned and placed the pile of appropriated documents, and the letters that she was desperate for The Boomers to read, on the table.

She gave them a tap. "There we go, have a read, it's incredible." Emily beamed and gave each of The Boomers the most generous hug that she could muster. She inhaled Granny's glorious smell of Fairy Snow washing powder – "Give over, Emily," – and Aunt Cynthia's baby powder – "That's lovely, love," – and headed upstairs.

SIX

Emily was sweating like a pig after rummaging in the attic. It was very hot in this unexpected spell of warm weather, and it had taken a lot of effort getting stuff down the ladder and into the hall where she was creating a stash of photo albums to take. Granny was right, there were shed loads of them indeed – a warehouse load even.

Carrying an armful of the heavy books, Emily negotiated the stairs very carefully. They were steep, and the carpet was worn from generations of her family going up and down over the years. Ashley flung the front door open and wandered in as if she owned the place.

But I do, Ashley, not you.

Mum and Dad followed, ignoring Emily perched at the top of the stairs, and wandered into the lounge.

"Hi, Mum, Aunt Cyn."

"Hey up, Rose, Cyn. How's it going?"

Granny answered, "We're getting stuck in, that's for sure," and from Aunt Cynthia, "We're doing very well thank you, Mike." More murmurings.

Emily listened in for a while, wondering whether her

parents were going to start asking questions, and then continued down the stairs to follow them into the lounge. Her family stood in a row staring at Granny and Aunt Cynthia. The conversation was obviously finished, so she made her presence known. "Hi," she deliberately sounded cheerful, "how was the butterfly place?"

Mum turned and looked at her with an impassive expression on her face. "It were grand. We had a lovely time and there were so many interesting species. They explained everything they're doing for nature conservation." That came out as a bit hostile. "You'd have enjoyed it if y'd come."

Emily couldn't even start to think how to unpack that statement, where so much was being said behind the actual words, so she pressed on. "I've had an incredible morning." Granny flashed Emily a warning glance.

*Don't worry Granny, I'm not letting **that** cat out of the bag.*

"I've found Julia." No reaction. Perhaps her parents were as cynical as Granny and Aunt Cynthia about finding her so quickly. "I am ninety-nine per cent certain I have found her. In Kent. That's where she was sent. She was then adopted by farmers, the Levetts, when she was five years old, and she got married..."

Her mum waved a hand at her, a slow down gesture. "Okay, love. That's all very well but it's only three seconds since we found out so just rein it back a bit, will you? We've plenty to sort out before we get on to that." Emily was deflated. Mum turned to Granny. "So what else have you turned up?" She was after the will. Emily knew it.

Granny stared back, a blank canvas, "No end of rubbish. That's what we've found. Mum was a hoarder and it's going to take forever to get to the bottom of it all."

Mum looked frustrated and burst out, "But what about the will?"

Granny kept her face straight. "That'll be with the solicitor, I'm guessing. Mum said that they were her executors. We'll get on to them and find out. They'll be needing access to this house and all Mum's things as a start before they apply for probate." Granny changed the subject pointedly. "So, are you here to lend us a hand?"

Mum said, "I think we'll leave that to you. We've got to get back."

Granny let a small frown cloud her face. "But you'll be needing a bite to eat or a brew before you get off, won't you?"

Aunt Cynthia smiled, with a friendly tilt of her head towards them. "I can put the kettle on." Emily could see her eyes sparkling mischievously. Her mum and dad looked at each other and frowned. They obviously knew that something was up. Emily kept very still and silent. She didn't want anything to slip out.

After a pause, Mum said, "Thanks, but no thanks. We ate at the butterfly place. Best get going I think." Her dad nodded.

Aunt Cynthia wheedled, "But don't you want to take a few mementos of your Nan?"

Mum shrugged and looked around the room. "The carriage clock maybe. That would look nice..."

Granny butted in, "She left that to me."

Aunt Cynthia soothed, "A bit of her jewellery or something as a keepsake? Not her rings, she wanted Rose to have those too, but she has quite a collection of costume jewellery."

Mum sighed, "A few bits of bling won't pay the bills but thanks anyway." She turned to Ashley. "Now go and use the toilet and we'll be off."

Ashley wiggled, took Mum's hand and simpered,

"Come with me, Mum. I'm scared to go past where GG passed away on my own."

"Okay, my love." They climbed the stairs hand in hand. Emily grimaced and realised that both Aunt Cynthia and Granny had the exact same look on their faces.

The whole bequests and will conversation was making Emily's heart hammer, so when she spoke it came out as a squeak. "Dad, I've got a whole lot of stuff that I need to put in the car for my research. It's in the hall." She waved an arm vaguely in the direction of her heap.

"You mean that lot at the bottom of the stairs? You must be joking, lass. We're not taking all Irene's rubbish home with us."

"But–"

"If you want to look at all her old junk then you can come back here. Your Gran and Aunt Cyn will have you back any time, won't they? After all they've always thought that you never left Loxley." Granny and Aunt Cynthia raised their eyebrows at exactly the same moment.

Granny puffed. Aunt Cynthia chirruped, "Of course, Mike. You know she's always welcome with us." Aunt Cynthia stepped forward and put a possessive arm around Emily.

"Yeah, I know that." Dad sighed and sounded sullen.

Mum reappeared with Ashley. "Right, let's get going, we don't want to get caught in the rush hour traffic." She clapped her hands.

This is definitely an inherited family thing. I'll find myself doing it next.

"Bye Mum, bye Aunt Cyn." Mum stepped forward and pecked them each on a proffered cheek awkwardly, avoiding eye contact. "Ashley? Say goodbye to Granny." Ashley stepped up and flung her arms round Granny and

Aunt Cynthia's waists with a quick squeeze as if to get it over and done with as quickly as possible.

Emily's dad wasn't one for kissing so just said his farewells. "Bye then, Rose, Cyn. See you later."

Emily was flustered by this rushed departure and frantically turned to The Boomers. "Did you read them? While I was in the attic? Did you?"

Granny nodded. "We did, and you're right. It is a miracle and an amazing one at that. Best you take them all with you. We can catch up on the phone, or even better you must come back and see us."

Aunt Cynthia turned to the table to scoop the pile up. "Isn't it wonderful, dear. It really is incredible. You've done so well to get so far so fast. Give us a ring and keep us posted."

Emily tucked away the treasures into her bag.

"Got everything?"

"Yup, Aunt Cyn, I have." She patted her faithful bag before launching herself for an enormous hug, whispering in Aunt Cynthia's ear. "Thank you. Thank you so much." Aunt Cynthia grinned.

Emily then flung her arms around Granny. "I can't thank you enough. For everything." Emily gave her a meaningful look hoping that Granny understood her clandestine meaning.

Granny shook her head. "Get away with you, lass. Now off you go, get your research done properly, come back when you've sorted it all out and tell us everything that you've decided. Okay?" Emily grinned and nodded. She couldn't resist going in for a boisterous kiss of Granny's proportions. Granny laughed out loud, not a very frequent occurrence.

Granny and Aunt Cynthia followed them to the steps and waved them off. Emily was still grinning as her dad drove down Leaton Close, turned left and past the Admiral Rodney. Emily looked at her phone and couldn't believe that it was only twenty-four hours since the discovery of Aunt Julia, finding that she herself might not have existed at all or could have been parcelled off to a completely different family, and that she was soon to be a homeowner. As an afterthought, she realised that being dumped by text by the hideous carnivore Dylan paled into insignificance.

Mum started fiddling with the radio.

"Turn it to Five Live, Lisa."

"Me and Ashley don't like sport," Mum said distractedly. Emily wondered where her own preferences came into it.

Dad sighed. "What do you want then?"

Mum shouted over her shoulder. "What do you want Ashley?" Ashley shrugged. She had already started playing some game on her iPad, her thumbs manically twirling, pressing random spots which seemed to be creating tinny, high-pitched beeps. Very irritating. "Let's go for two then."

"Before you do that, Lisa, I have a question for Emily." Emily's thumb froze over her phone screen. "Emily?"

"Yes Dad, I'm listening."

"When you left us this morning you had a right face on." Pause.

"Yeah." *Or should that be, no? An impossible statement to answer.*

"When we came and picked you up you were looking as chuffed as monkeys."

"Yeah." *Or no?*

"So, what's that all about then?"

Emily felt a wave of anxiety whoosh through her body ending up as a blush.

Do they know about the will? They can't. How would they know? "Umm." Mum had twisted around in her seat to look at her. Emily hoped that the guilty flush had subsided. Her reply came out in a rush. "I told you. It is dead exciting that GG had kept letters from the curate and it enabled me to find where Julia had been sent and who adopted her. And then I found out that her brother is still alive and who she married so I can track them all down..."

Mum swivelled back. "Oh, that old nonsense." Mum turned the radio up. Emily let out a huge breath and relaxed into her seat. She rummaged in her bag and found the 1/- notebook and reread her notes. She then spent the next ten minutes finding her pen and pencil; they turned out to be hidden behind some Bonio dog biscuits that she couldn't remember ever putting in there.

Emily sat back and pondered her next research angles.

SEVEN

A whole week had passed since Great Granny's revelations. Avoiding anything controversial, and definitely not mentioning anything whatsoever about Great Granny's house, had allowed the dust to settle at home and Emily had been getting on well with her mum and dad except for the occasional spat.

Emily offered to cook to give her mum a few nights off, which her mum really seemed to appreciate. A respectable offering of macaroni cheese topped with juicy slices of tomato and bubbling cheese went down well. What didn't go down so well was Emily's next offering; sausages, mash and beans. Ashley took one bite and exclaimed, "Yuck. This sausage is disgusting."

Dad was looking worriedly at his plate as if something might bite him. Mum was more blunt, "Where did you get these sausages from, Emily? They're rubbery and tasteless."

Emily giggled, "Damn it, I thought I would get away with giving you vegan ones, but obviously not. I think they taste great and much better for the planet as they're plant based."

Mum and Dad looked at each other and sighed before

turning to Ashley. "Ashley, just chuck them in the bin and I'll fry you some bacon and eggs instead."

Emily protested, "I'll eat them. They're delicious."

Her mum raised her eyebrows and looked at her witheringly. Emily smiled weakly, hoping her mum would do the same.

That didn't go down well. You win some.

The other spat was with her dad. Emily had originally planned to get a holiday job so that she could get some cash and 'contribute to the household' but her need to find Aunt Julia was like an addiction. It had become her sole focus when the rest of her life seemed to have crumbled, but her dad had not been at all impressed.

"Why aren't you out there looking for a job?" he challenged her when she joined the family at breakfast.

"Why aren't you telling me the truth about my parentage?" she snapped back.

"For God's sake, Emily, cut it out. I'm off to work now. You know what that is? It's where they pay you good money for a day's toil so that you can pay your way." He pushed back his chair, levered himself up and walked out. The atmosphere was distinctly frosty. Emily tried to look nonchalant as she sipped her juice and bit into an apple.

How can I find out if he really is my dad? Perhaps I can tie it in with this whole family research thing. I must follow up on the DNA testing possibilities.

And I haven't thought of Dylan for days. The bastard still hasn't contacted me. Stonewalled by Dylan, stonewalled by Dad. I wonder where that expression came from. Not a Peak District dry stone wall, you'd just be able to shout over it so that wouldn't be any good.

~

Mum had taken time off from work and seemed to be enjoying going on outings with Ashley. They seemed to be places only suitable for children otherwise Emily might have considered joining them when invited. She used the excuse of her research so as not to offend each time she declined. Meanwhile, Emily was exceedingly happy to spend her time finding out what she could about Julia.

She had set herself up in her paltry bedroom where she had found the perfect position on the bed for her research. With a pile of pillows behind her back, she could balance her laptop on her knees and access her papers from her bottomless bag by propping it up against the bedside table.

Her room was the smallest in the house. Somewhere in history someone in a grey suit had set the standard British model for bedrooms in homes: two doubles and a single, where the single was usually more of a box room.

It annoyed Emily that she was squeezed into the tiny bedroom while Ashley had always had the large one. To be fair, the room was probably the size of Emily's old bedroom in halls at uni, and it was only right that Ashley should have more space at home now that she wasn't there. It still rankled a bit when Emily squeezed into the single bed next to an array of drying washing and Mum's unused exercise bike that had taken up residence the moment she went to Edinburgh. There was a faint smell of sweat hanging in the air overlaid with the chemical smell of environmentally damaging biological washing powder.

Emily felt like a real detective. She could not believe what you could find on the internet with a little determination. Each birth, death and marriage was easy to find once you knew how and with the help of her free trial. Her 1/- notebook was getting filled up with the most amazing snippets of information, and she had put together a comprehensive family tree for the Levetts.

John Levett (born 1920 died 1981)
married Margaret Buss (born 1925 died 1984)
Charles P Levett (born 1943)
married Lorna Burgess (born 1944 died 1979)
Julia Levett (born 1945 adopted 1951)
married David Merripen (born 1943)
Genevieve Merripen (born 25th August 1966)
married Nicholas Pennington
Daniel Pennington (born 29th October 1991)
no further information found
Matthew Merripen (born 17th May 1968)
no further information found

She was thoroughly enjoying herself sifting through births, deaths and marriages when suddenly, there it was: Julia Merripen nee Levett had died on the 24th of April 1992.

No, no, no. It can't be.

Emily did a quick sum in her head.

She was only forty-seven years old. What happened? It must have been an accident or some dreadful illness.

Emily scrabbled around and googled, trying to find anything that came up when she linked Julia Merripen with different causes of death, but she couldn't find anything at all. She knew she was being sloppy and taking too much of a scattergun approach.

I need to delve deeper. But where?

Emily needed a break to ponder on this and decided to go for a walk to keep up her ten thousand steps a day. She walked the long way round to Walbottle Community Orchard, looped back the other way via Hospital Lane, all the time googling new ideas. It wasn't long before she had uncovered a whole new line of enquiry: newspapers. Full of eagerness, she jogged back to her laptop, where the bigger screen made it so much easier to find everything. After an hour perched back on her bed, she was ready.

Right, I need to tell The Boomers.

Emily snatched up her phone. Granny answered with her usual "Hello, Loxley 4196."

"Granny, it's Emily."

"Hello love, how are you?"

"I'm fine but feeling a bit devastated."

"Devastated?"

"I've just found out that Julia is dead. She died years ago, and we didn't even know."

"Oh gosh, that is terrible, lass. When did she die? How did you find out? Are you sure?" Granny doubting as ever.

Emily could hear Aunt Cynthia in the background. "Who's died? Rose, who has passed away?" Emily could imagine Granny frowning and flapping a hand at Aunt Cynthia to stop interrupting.

"I found it on the register of deaths. It has to be Julia. Surely nobody else would be called Julia Levett and married a Merripen"

"Is that right? How did she die? Be quiet, Cyn."

"I can tell you that it was the 24th of April 1992, but I can't tell you anything else yet. She was so young. She could have died for any reason. Perhaps she was ill or in an accident or something."

"Ah well," Granny sighed. Her voice became muffled, obviously talking to Aunt Cynthia with her hand over the mouthpiece, something she'd done since time immemorial. "It's Julia, Cyn. She passed away." A pause. "1992. We'll never meet her now." Another pause. "I know, it's more than sad, it's bloody tragic. That brings an end to it surely?" She paused again. Emily thought she might have caught a sniff and could hear distressed squeaks from Aunt Cynthia.

Granny's voice suddenly came back booming, "Thank

you for all your digging. It's grand that you found her and so much about her. We'll hang on to that. It is much appreciated and at least we know now. If you can write it all down for us..."

"But Granny, there are still hundreds of people who can tell us so much more about her. Her brother Charles, her husband David. And she had children, two of them: Genevieve and Matthew, and she has a grandchild, Daniel."

"Good heavens! Well, you have been busy. I must say it's very strange finding out about all these people we had no idea existed and are part of our family. I'll tell you in a minute, Cyn. Let me see now, a cousin, a brother-in-law, a niece..."

"And a nephew and a great nephew."

"So, Emily, what do you want to do now?"

"I feel that I've only just started. I want to find out how Aunt Julia died. I want to find her children, her husband – if he's still alive, I haven't followed that one through yet. I want to meet them and find out what her life was like. I think most of all I want to make sure that she was happy and had a fulfilling life even though it was cut short."

"Well, you have got a bee in your bonnet. I hope this isn't costing you too much."

"So far it isn't, but I will I have to start paying soon for any more electoral register enquiries and some of the newspaper archive sites and the British Library charge for printouts of articles. And those buggers at the ancestry site have only gone and charged me for an annual subscription after I took them up on their free trial offer."

"Why on earth do you need all those?"

"I can find out the names and addresses of people wherever they live through the electoral register and generally just find out more information. I'm particularly keen to find out more about how Aunt Julia died. I need to go to the newspaper archive and have a dig around. They've started getting stuff online but not all of it, so I can look on microfilm, or as a last resort, I can look at the original papers."

"Emily, you make my brain spin with all your babble. And where do they have this archive?"

"The British Library. They have a branch in Boston Spa, between York and Leeds, just off the A1. It's the home of the UK national newspaper collection. Did you know that they have more than three centuries of local, regional and national newspapers? Three hundred years."

Granny grumbled, "I do know what three centuries is, Emily."

Emily smiled to herself, typical Granny, and continued, "Isn't that amazing? And there's free access to more than twenty million digitised pages of historic newspapers, and you can order newspapers on microfilm from London. Who knew that such an awesome research resource even existed?"

"Okay now, so what's all this to you then, lass? You really do need to learn to try and make sense."

Emily laughed. "I've found out that the local rag covering the Lamberhurst area is the Kent and Sussex Courier, so I can go through it and find out all about Julia and anyone else that I have found connected to her. I'm hoping that there might be some clues to how she died, particularly if it was a car accident or something like that."

"Right, now you *are* making a bit more sense. So how do you propose to get there to read all of this?"

"Well, I can get a train to Leeds and then a taxi but if I had a car I could go straight down the A1 from home or the M1 then A1." Granny went quiet at the other end of the line and then there were muffled sounds again as Granny consulted Aunt Cynthia. "Hello? Are you still there?"

"Yes, we were just discussing an idea."

"An idea. About what?"

"Your passion is infectious, Emily. I'd like to say that we would come with you, but it's all a bit much at our age gallivanting around the country on what could be a wild goose chase, especially with my heart. And too much time spent with you blathering on makes my head spin. I'll have another word with Cyn and see how we can help you. I'm already thinking that you could borrow our car to save on train fares and such, and we can give you a cheque to cover your expenses." Emily was delighted that they were able to help. It would get her dad off her back. "If you come down here on the train, you can pick up the car and fill us in on everything that you've found."

Emily was thrilled by The Boomers' equal enthusiasm. She'd be able to get going on her research and find out so much more about Aunt Julia, but she knew that there was much more still to be found. "I'd love that. I am most definitely coming as soon as I can."

"Anyway, what I think I am saying is thank you, Emily – fantastic work, and please carry on. Keep us posted as to when you expect to get here."

Grinning with pleasure, Emily said, "Thank you Granny, I will."

"And have you had any thoughts about the house at all? You need to be getting organised for when you sell it."

Emily frowned. She wasn't ready to think about that yet. She was so worried about Mum's reaction, she knew it wouldn't be good, and she'd deliberately shoved it in the 'later rather than sooner' pile. "No. Do I need to decide now?"

"Have you told your mum and dad?"

Emily's excitement was washed away by guilt. She whispered, even though her parents weren't even in the house, "No." Emily shifted in discomfort. "Granny, can't you tell them? It would be better coming from you." A pause. "Please, Granny."

Oh God, I sound like Ashley.

Granny went silent but Emily could hear her breathing. "Tell you what, the solicitors still haven't sorted out probate. I can't think what's taking them so long, but we'll wait for the solicitors to send an official copy of the whole shebang to your mum and you as beneficiaries, and we can say that we all got our copy at the same time. But God help you if you ever – and I mean, *ever* – let on."

"Oh, Granny, you are a miracle worker." Emily's spirits had returned to their previous level of excitement. "I promise I can keep it a secret, I swear on GG's grave. And if I come down to you and collect your car and then stay with you for a bit, I can cope with the fall out at a distance."

EIGHT

Emily's dad had left to go to work, he had an early shift on a Saturday. Her mum was boiling an egg for Ashley to go with her soldiers. She was humming, a happy sound, stopped and said brightly, "How about a visit to Alnwick Castle today? We could take a picnic. What do you think, Ashley?"

Ashley shrugged and pushed her long blond hair back from her face, shaking it out like she was in a shampoo ad. "I don't mind."

Emily wondered if the throwaway line had included her in this plan so said encouragingly, "That would be great. A family day out. You love Harry Potter, Ashley." It really would be nice to do something together, something fun that they could all enjoy before she went off on her research expedition.

Ashley ignored Emily. "Is my egg ready yet, Mum?"

"Just one minute."

Emily googled Alnwick, "Hey, Ashley you can learn to play quidditch and have a go at archery." Emily took a hearty bite of toasted white sliced bread, nothing like Aunt

Cynthia's delicious home-made loaves, and a slurp of orange juice.

Looking over her shoulder, Mum asked Emily crisply, "So you're going to come? That would be nice for a change."

Emily responded carefully. "Yeah, Mum. I've done all I can with online research so it would be a great finale before I go back to Loxley."

Turning from the stove, Mum's voice had suddenly changed to wariness. "When are you planning on going to Loxley, then?"

"I thought I'd go tomorrow, then I can get going on my research at the British Library on Monday..."

Mum whirled round, hands on hips, and looked in shock at Emily. "Who's going to look after Ashley, then?"

Emily was taken aback. "I didn't know that you were expecting me to look after Ashley. You haven't asked. I thought..." Emily was baffled. Why on earth would they have assumed that she would be babysitting Ashley?

Mum rolled her eyes. "You don't think, do you? I shouldn't need to ask. She's your sister, and I've got to go back to work on Monday. Dad's got his shifts and we can't leave her on her own all day, can we?" Mum's voice raised into a sarcastic tone, "School holidays, Emily." Mum shook her head and pursed her lips. "Honestly, Emily. I really do not get you at all."

That's pretty obvious.

Emily didn't know what to say. She tried to be reasonable. "If you'd discussed it with me, Mum..."

Mum turned her back on Emily, muttering. The egg timer went off and made Emily jump. Mum scooped the egg fiercely from the saucepan and said over her shoulder, "Well Ashley, since your own sister won't look after you, we'd better be finding a nice summer camp or something. Heaven knows if we can get you in anywhere at this late notice and it'll cost a fortune. Either that or I guess that I'll have to persuade Dad to take more time off..."

Emily slowly got to her feet, lifting her chair so that it didn't scrape, and tiptoed out of the kitchen, but her mum had ears like a bat. "I've just tried to make today a nice family day out for us all. Why do you have to spoil things, Emily? Running back to Loxley at the first chance you get." Emily scrambled up the stairs, trying to hold back bleak tears. She could still hear Mum muttering on about finding childcare as she dashed into the sanctuary of her bedroom. She resisted slamming the door.

She hadn't planned to leave until tomorrow but this abrupt shift in mood was just too much to bear. It had been going so well. "Why can't I ever do anything right?" Emily sniffed as she bundled clothes into her rucksack. "And is that all I'm good for in this family – child minding?"

She carefully gathered up all her research papers and her laptop, and shoved them into her reassuring bag. It was bulging and Emily could see a seam stretching precariously, a few stitches sprung loose. *Aunt Cyn can patch it up for me. Her forte, and she'd love to be asked.* Emily felt less fretful at the thought of The Boomers.

"Right, that's it." Emily looked around the room, lifted her rucksack on to her back and her treasured bag on to her shoulder and negotiated the stairs. It was a bit dangerous when quite so laden, but Emily took her time, also trying to put off the moment when she reached the bottom and had to face her mother. Her stomach clenched as she approached the kitchen door. Mum was now sitting at the table clutching a mug of tea, looking depressed. "Well, Mum. I'll be off then."

"Thought you weren't going until tomorrow."

Emily sighed and looked at the floor. "Sorry, but I think it's for the best if I go now, Mum."

Her mum sighed, "Well, off you go then. Bye."

Why did she have to be like this? Thank God she hadn't heard about the house yet. "Bye, Mum. I'll let you know how I'm getting on with my search for Julia." Silence. It was impossible to manoeuvre into the kitchen with everything hanging off her. Emily peeled off her bag, wriggled out of her rucksack and crossed the few steps to her mother. Mountains and Mohammed came to mind.

Emily leaned in. Mum looked down at her hands. *Are those tears in her eyes? Is she that angry?* Emily sighed with frustration and softly kissed the top of Mum's head. "Sorry. Bye, Mum."

Mum mumbled, "Bye then."

Emily said, "Bye Ashley, have a fun summer hols." Ashley didn't answer, just continued poking her soldiers into her egg.

Emily turned, feeling bereft. She dragged her luggage to the door, opened it, stood on the steps to pile everything on again, turned towards the kitchen. "See you later."

She closed the door quietly.

Two and a quarter hours on the train gave Emily too much thinking time. Her simple, boring, uneventful life had suddenly turned into a swirling maelstrom since Great Granny's funeral. She replayed every event and every conversation that she'd had with each family member since that day. Her emotions seesawed erratically between mortified, grief-stricken, a bit of pride, hints of pleasure and guilt.

How much should she say to Granny and Aunt Cynthia, who would be sure to ask why they were seeing her a day earlier than expected? She had called them to let them know she was on her way, saying, "I couldn't wait to come and see you both." Emily knew that it sounded a bit lame, but she might get away with it.

In her rush to leave 'home' she had forgotten to fill her water bottle and refused point blank to buy a plastic bottle from the buffet, so thirst only added to her misery. She distracted herself by firing up her laptop and doing a few searches related to Merripen, and when they came to nothing, decided to explore property prices on Rightmove. The guilty feeling crept back, and she found herself looking furtively around before she typed Loxley into the search field.

Two properties came up. One a cute cottage built in the local grey stone with a dark slate roof right by the river, which was nothing like GG's house, and an astronomic price of £750,000. The second was very similar in layout to GG's and marked £275,000.

"Wow. £275,000." Emily sat back and thought about it for a moment. It would pay off her student loan and give her spare change. She paused, trying to think what she wanted to spend her 'spare change' on. Never having had that as an option and having had a frugal upbringing – where she had been reminded every minute of every day that there was not enough money to do anything but basic living – it was difficult to imagine. That made her feel sad for her mum and dad's life. Had they wasted it always wanting more and not appreciating what they had? Emily shook her head sadly.

Or she could live in Great Granny's house and let out the spare room, with its jazzy wallpaper. Or she could go and volunteer on a project in Africa or India, perhaps the widow's cooperative, although she couldn't help them make their trousers as she was hopeless at sewing, that was Aunt Cynthia's domain.

"The next station stop is Sheffield. Please make sure you take all your belongings with you when you leave the train..." Emily packed up her laptop and put it in her bag, grabbed her rucksack from the rack above and headed for the door. She scrolled through the Refill app as she waited to arrive at the platform.

"The moment I step off this train, I am going to find a refill station."

A woman with a hangdog expression, waiting by the door, looked at her curiously then looked away.

Okay, I'm talking out loud again...

NINE

As she staggered up the hill to Granny's house Emily felt a sense of relief. The tension was beginning to dissipate as she got closer to her safe haven. As ever, The Boomers pounced on Emily the moment she set foot on the first step up to the front door, wresting her rucksack and bag off her. *They must lie in wait for me.* It made Emily feel valued.

She was barely in through the door before the questions started about her research.

"How's it going? What else have you discovered?" from Granny.

"Do you know anything more about how she died?" from Aunt Cynthia.

And they are so interested in my Aunt Julia mission.

"I'm not going to find out anything more until I get to the British Library so you'll just have to be patient." *I sound just like Granny.* It made Emily grin.

~

The British Library was a treasure trove of all the newspapers that had ever been published, even though it looked like a prison from the outside.

The reading room was like a portal into its vast riches. Emily was flabbergasted by the amount of information that was buried here. She was even more excited when she discovered on checking in that the British Newspaper Archive held a database of newspaper articles searchable by keyword and that the Kent and Sussex Courier was one of them.

She took a seat at one of the computers, rummaged in her bag for her 1/- notebook and a pencil. It took some time to hunt them down.

Really must sort this bag out.

Every Kent and Sussex Courier newspaper for the period from 1965 to 1978 had been catalogued and could be searched by keyword. She simply had to type in the surnames that she was interested in and up popped any articles that referenced them, with the name highlighted.

How incredible is that?

"Wow."

There was a polite little cough came from the large woman at the computer next door whose substantial frame dripped over the sides of the plastic chair.

"Sorry about that. It's just so exciting to find this resource. I'm looking for my Aunt Julia, she was adopted as a baby and..." The substantial woman wobbled her head, making her chins oscillate, and looked worriedly down at her keyboard. Emily smiled at her politely, shrugged and turned back to her own screen.

Here it all was, a lifetime shown in newspapers. She was severely tempted to search for The Boomers in Sheffield papers but was rather afraid of what she might find in Granny's case.

Thinking of The Boomers made her realise how great it had been to see them and sit around the table with a brew, chatting through everything that Emily had found out about Aunt Julia. They were always so interested in everything that she did, unlike her parents who tended to look at her blankly and say nothing at all.

The Boomers had been so excited, in their own inimitable way, when she had become the first of their family to make it to university. 'You clever old thing,' and 'Who ever knew you'd turn out to be such a brainbox?' They had sent her a card with a £10 note enclosed when she set off on her big adventure for the first time. A fortune to them. A much more gratifying response than 'Don't let it go to your head, love, you're still our Emily from the back streets of Newcastle,' from her mum.

She realised that she felt closer to The Boomers than she did her own mother.

Was that wrong?

The revelation about her mother not wanting to keep her made sense. Perhaps she had always known that on some level.

Anyway, to the job at hand...

She clapped her hands together and rubbed them vigorously. "Let's be having you Aunt Julia."

Damn, I've definitely inherited the clapping hands thing, and I said that out loud again.

Glancing out of the corner of her eye, she saw that the substantial woman was doing the same. She quickly swivelled her eyes back and determinedly typed in 'Levett'. It was faintly irritating to her rather OCD brain that the name wasn't Leveret, but at least it would surely narrow things down. A whole list of phrases came up; it was like magic. She scanned each entry, eagerly seeking references to Aunt Julia.

'John Levett.' Emily checked back in her 1/- notebook. Aunt Julia's father. 'Champion Romney Ram at the Paddock Wood Fat Stock Show in 1935,' and then again in 1937. And again in 1938.

So, they were genuine multi-generational farmers. I wonder what happened in 1936. Perhaps the rams weren't fat enough.

'1941 Performance in aid of the Kent Spitfire Fund by Mrs Margaret Levett accompanied by Mrs Maude Manwaring on the piano.'

Wow. Mrs Levett a singer.

Emily found it amazing how these people were coming to life. Looking at births, deaths and marriages was so anodyne, but suddenly they were becoming real people with jobs, hobbies and talents.

'1941 Mr Levett reporting the Penny-A-Week Red Cross Scheme stated that in the first seven months of the year £100 8s 9d had been collected.'

Doing his bit for the war effort, a good man. Presumably as a farmer he didn't go to war and was busy digging for victory.

'1943 Wanted by Mr John Levett, Oak Tree Farm, farm labourer able to dress, string and twiddle hops.'

Emily couldn't make any sense of that at all. She knew that hops were used to make beer but why did they need to be dressed? And in what? And what was stringing about? Hop puppets? She giggled, glanced nervously at the fat woman and turned it into a cough.

She carried on reading through every entry related to the Levetts; it was such fun and fascinating, but she realised that she could be at it all year if she kept going at this rate. She selected a later set of years and continued her pursuit of the truth about Aunt Julia. Suddenly a bold headline popped up:

TRILOGY OF SUCCESS AT KENT FESTIVAL

At the Kent Festival, held this year in Folkestone, Miss Julia Levett won the Alfred Deller Memorial Cup for best vocal performance under 16 for the third year in succession. Her rendition of 'Early One Morning' was highly acclaimed by the adjudicator, Miss Rowe, Head of Music at Ashford School. Mark Deller, presenting the trophy, regretted that Miss Levett would not be winning the award again as this was the last year she could compete, next year being ineligible through age.

Ooh. Aunt Julia was a very talented singer. Obviously got that from her father, not our branch of the family. Granny says that although I didn't get the blond hair, green eyes and slender figure I have inherited the ability to sing like a strangled cat.

Emily tried out a few notes of 'Early One Morning'. They were very bad. The substantial woman scowled, gathered her bits and pieces and marched away, her body rolling and lurching. Emily snorted. She peered at the monitor, her face nearly touching the screen, trying to make out the black and white hazy photograph that seemed to be part of the article.

Was this Aunt Julia?

Sadly, it was only a back view as the photographer seemed more interested in the worthy gentleman who was handing Aunt Julia an enormous trophy. Aunt Julia was wearing a white shirt that glowed, a military looking A-line skirt and dark tights. School uniform? She was nearly as tall as the man and had very long legs. Her hair looked dark and curly like Emily's and was pulled into an overstuffed bun. So, not blond like The Boomers. It was so frustrating to see her but not be able to distinguish what she looked like. Emily lingered on the image and touched it, leaving a smudge on the screen.

At least she could find this again if she wanted to. She wrote out the reference to the page so that she could request a hard copy.

"Now, get on Emily, otherwise you'll be here forever."

She came across a whole set of references to Charles Levett. He was obviously a pillar of the community and was elected to the parish council. There were several references to his election, and his ongoing contribution including a hilarious article that made Emily laugh out loud. 'Charles Levett, commenting on getting rid of moles on The Downs, said that they'd only come back.'

Seriously? Newsworthy? Country life. So profound. Now, this next one looks more interesting.

May 1965

INCIDENT AT ELIZABETHAN BARN

Police were called to deal with a fracas at the Elizabethan Barn. Fighting broke out between local men David Merripen and Charles Levett. Both men were taken to Tunbridge Wells police station. Neither protagonist wished to press charges and they were therefore released with a caution.

Oh, I wonder what that was all about. David Merripen is Aunt Julia's husband and there he was fighting with Aunt Julia's brother, Charles. The upright parish councillor involved in a set to. Perhaps he was a scrapper?

Emily wondered if Charles Levett would show any more bad behaviour, but all that she could find were endless references to the Lamberhurst Cricket Club, with some rather low numbers of runs, and the odd mention associated with the parish council. Obviously, his misdemeanour was a one-off and had not caused him to be excommunicated from such a hallowed institution.

She slogged through more yawn-inducing cricket mentions with single figure scores. *Not as good an innings as GG.* An enthusiastic cricketer but obviously not that good by the look of things. She was beginning to lose concentration when suddenly there it was: a mention of Aunt Julia, at last.

> The marriage of Miss Julia Levett to David Merripen took place at Lamberhurst Church on 14th November 1965. The bride was given away by her father John Levett of Oak Tree Farm. The best man was Charles Levett, the bride's brother. A reception was held at Oak Tree Farm and the honeymoon is to take place in the Norfolk Broads.

Hang on a minute. So, despite the fight at the Elizabethan Barn, Charles Levett – Aunt Julia's brother – was the best man. What on earth? They obviously made up. But what did they fight about in the first place?

So many questions, but Emily was really excited to see an accompanying black and white photograph that showed the bride with, presumably, her father. A very bouffant veil covered her face and she was carrying an enormous bouquet of flowers. With the addition of the veil she was so much taller than her father. *Must be those long legs.* Emily tried to zoom in to see what she looked like but couldn't see any details; it was all too fuzzy. It could have been anybody, but at least she had now 'met' Aunt Julia face to face.

"Hello Aunt Julia. It is so brilliant to meet you." She sat for a moment and just stared with a happy smile, feeling satisfied and thinking that The Boomers were going to be thrilled.

So, now Julia was Mrs Merripen. Emily decided to continue her search using the new surname. With such an unusual surname, the references were far fewer except that it seemed that David Merripen was also a keen cricketer and his batting scores kept coming up. It appeared that he was far more talented than Charles Levett, most of his scores were in the double figures.

At least they weren't fighting each other.

Then there was a really shocking one that caused Emily to yelp, "Holy Mother of God." After looking around anxiously to make sure she hadn't inadvertently disturbed anyone again, she bent forward to read the article.

LAMBERHURST BLAZE INJURES CHILD

David and Julia Merripen were extremely fortunate to escape a blaze at their home, Wayside Cottage, Furnace Lane, Lamberhurst unscathed. Julia Merripen was able to carry daughter Genevieve, aged five years old, to safety but David Merripen, despite his valiant rescue attempt in the face of fierce flames, was unable to prevent their son, Matthew, aged three years old, from receiving severe burns.

Emily gave a huge gasp but managed to keep her thoughts inside her head for a change.

Poor little boy, how appalling.

> The fire was discovered by David Merripen at 10:30pm on his return from a Lamberhurst Cricket Club dinner at the Elephant's Head, Bells Yew Green. Neighbours immediately alerted the fire brigade and tenders from Wadhurst attended the scene.
>
> David Merripen bravely faced the fire and entered the house to evacuate his family. His wife, Julia Merripen and daughter Genevieve were able to escape unscathed but son, Matthew was seriously burnt.
>
> Neighbours Mr and Mrs Beech, who had called the Fire Brigade, told our reporter that they were extremely shocked by the injuries received by Matthew Merripen. Matthew remains in hospital and is in a stable condition.

The black and white photograph showed a rather ugly, small, square house surrounded by fire engines and firefighters with hoses jetting water on to it. Emily's heart was pounding. Sadly, no picture of Aunt Julia herself.

Poor Aunt Julia. What a horrible thing to have happened. Poor Matthew, I wonder how badly he was hurt. At least the rest of them were okay.

After that, there was very little more except for some more great batting by David and some mediocre scores from Charles Levett. Emily was getting a bit bored by the endless 'man of the match' and 'great innings' when something more interesting popped up.

August 1976

BABES IN THE WOOD

Search parties frantically sought two children, Genevieve Merripen, aged 10, and Nicholas Pennington, aged 12, when parents reported them missing at seven pm after they failed to return home. Both children live in Hoghole Lane, Lamberhurst and often play together, but mother Julia Merripen told police that this behaviour was completely out of character.

Hoghole Lane – hilarious name, sounds rude. A good name for bloody Dylan. 'Hey Dylan, you're a hog hole.' I wonder if that is a spelling mistake?

The children were discovered by Genevieve's father, David Merripen, at nine pm in woodland off Sweetings Lane, when smoke alerted him to their campfire and encampment deep in the woods.

According to Sarah Pennington, mother of Nicholas, "I am extremely relieved to have Nicholas home safe and sound. He is fine. They had made a watertight shelter and had food and drink from home. But I am very angry that it was Genevieve who suggested camping out without telling us parents."

Oops, naughty Genevieve. I bet her mum was livid to find that there was fire with smoke involved after the previous story. But hang on a minute... Nicholas Pennington?

Emily frantically turned the pages back in the 1/- notebook to look at the family tree that she had been growing.

Duh. Nicholas Pennington, you nitwit. Married Aunt Julia's daughter, Genevieve Merripen. The babes in the wood got married!

She made a note of Sarah Pennington, mother of Nicholas.

There was disappointingly little after that. There were a few more great cricket matches which, now that she had clocked and noted the name Pennington, seemed to include a Jolyon Pennington.

Very posh name.

Most of them also included Charles Levett and David Merripen. After that, the newspaper archive came to an end.

"Right, one more trawl through with this Pennington lot and then I'll be done."

Emily knew that then she would have to move on to the microfilm records.

She feared it wouldn't be quite so easy but was thrilled that she had found out such amazing events in the lives of Aunt Julia, her husband David Merripen and her brother Charles Levett.

Before embarking on her last sweep, Emily needed a break, so she wandered through to the café and plonked her burgeoning bag for life on the chair next to her, where it drooped over the edges like the fat woman in the reading room. She rang The Boomers.

"Emily, love, how are you getting on? I've got you on speaker so that Cyn can listen in."

"It's brilliant here. I can't believe it. I've got to know so much about our relatives."

"What have you found out?" and "Do tell us what you've found, dear." Emily was delighted that The Boomers sounded as excited as she was.

"The Levetts are farmers, and from what I can gather they're still living on the same family farm even now. Aunt Julia's dad seems to have won loads of prizes for his rams at fat stock shows. I'm not entirely why the stock has to be fat but –"

"Get on with it, Emily," said Granny, while Aunt Cynthia's protests were somewhat muffled.

"I skipped a whole lot of farming stuff and there are loads of references to cricket but I skated over those." Emily flicked through her notes. "Then I found Aunt Julia's wedding at Lamberhurst Church, which matches up with the certificate that I found. There is a tiny photo and it is hard to see her but it is there. I have met Aunt Julia. I've requested printed copies for you."

Huffs of pleasure were coming through Emily's phone.

"Then there was a terrible fire at Aunt Julia's home. That isn't when she died. They all got out alive, Aunt Julia and her husband David, the two children Genevieve and Matthew but apparently Matthew got badly burned. Isn't that sad?"

Granny sounded more animated than she ever did normally, "Well, I never." And from Aunt Cynthia, "What a terrible thing to happen."

"I've asked for a print of that article too."

Granny said, "It really does bring them to life, doesn't it? Thank you ever so much for carrying on with this. Is there anything more that you can find out there?"

"The most important thing to find out was how Aunt Julia died but that was in 1992 so it won't be in the newspaper archive because that only goes up to 1987." Emily checked the 1/- notebook again, "Oh wait, but I have found one more story. Aunt Julia's daughter went missing when she was ten years old and they called the police." Gasps from the Boomers. "Yes, Genevieve went off with a local friend, a boy just a bit older than her, and went camping in the woods. All found safe and sound. And then, can you believe it, Genevieve ended up marrying the boy, Nicholas! Isn't that adorable? And this family, the Penningtons, the ones that Genevieve married into, keep popping up so I will do one more trawl through the archives to find out anything I can about them. That's it for now, except for endless cricket scores. I've nearly got to the end of the searchable newspaper archive. It's on to the microfilm next which isn't indexed so it won't be as easy."

Granny continued, "It's all good stuff, except for the fire of course, but it really is bringing her to life, isn't it? Our sister," and Aunt Cynthia added, "I wonder if you can find a good photo of our Julia, now that really would be marvellous."

"I'll keep trying to find one where we can see her and will make sure you get a copy as soon as I do. Bye for now and thank you for the use of the car. It's made my life so much easier."

"Bye love, well done" and in stereo, "Bye Emily, fascinating."

As Emily ended the call, she suddenly remembered that she hadn't mentioned the singing prize. That would have made Granny and Aunt Cynthia chuckle.

On returning to the library, Emily headed to the same computer as before. There was only one other person in the reading room – a scruffy man with greasy looking hair and a bottom lip that drooped when in repose making him look gormless – but he was far enough away not to bother Emily, and not to be bothered by Emily.

"Now for the Penningtons." She linked her hands and cracked her knuckles, overdid it and it proved painful. "Ow."

The marriage took place on 22nd May 1965 between Miss Sarah Digby-Watson and Jolyon Pennington at St Paul's Church, Langton Road, Rusthall. The bride was given away by her father Colonel Digby-Watson and attended by her sister Annabelle Digby-Watson, her younger sister Fenella Digby-Watson, and two nieces. The best man was Robert Harrington-Smythe. The reception was held at The Spa Hotel and the honeymoon is to be spent abroad.

Is this the same Pennington branch? It makes sense as the bride is Sarah. Better check out Nicholas Pennington's birth certificate to see if this Sarah is his mother.

She scribbled a note in the 1/- notebook. The accompanying photo showed a bride, with jet black hair, dressed in a voluminous meringue and the groom in a grey morning suit with a hilariously shaggy, unkempt hairstyle. She looked deliriously happy whereas he appeared distinctly sheepish.

Now that has got to be a very posh wedding. Enough double barrels to shoot a man dead. And why did brides in those days think they were so stunningly beautiful in their flummery when they looked outrageous?

Emily pressed on. The Penningtons weren't very

noteworthy it seemed. After reading endless cricket match scores, Emily judged Jolyon Pennington to be better than Charles Levett but not as great as David Merripen.

What am I doing? Putting these people into a fantasy cricket league!

Up came the same report that she had picked up on before about the babes in the wood, where Sarah Pennington had a go at Genevieve suggesting they go camping.

Okay. Nothing more to see here. It's on to the microfilm. I'll grab a bite to eat and then crack on.

TEN

Microfilm proved to be horrendous. There were no keyword searches that took you straight to what you were looking for and no conveniently highlighted search words on the screen. Instead, Emily was having to read every single line and every single page of every single newspaper. There was so much of it.

Talk about needles in haystacks.

She was carefully logging each and every edition that she checked and hoped to make a note of what, if anything, she had found. She used a pencil since ink wasn't permitted in the reading room.

Probably a good thing, knowing my clumsiness.

Charles Levett was still making cameo appearances as a parish councillor. His main topic seemed to be about a proposal for a Lamberhurst bypass. Apparently, the village became gridlocked on sunny days from all the traffic heading for the seaside. The pages of her 1/- notebook were getting very smudged and the table a bit messy with the debris from her pencil sharpening.

The whole thing was proving very tedious. She didn't

even bother to look at the sports pages; there are only so many cricket matches that a girl can take. Perhaps she needed to be more discriminatory. Emily went for a coffee in the café to wake herself up from her stupor and to take stock of the situation.

With Julia's exact date of death, it must be possible to track down the right story on the microfilm records more efficiently. I must narrow down the stuff that I look at before I go insane.

She swigged back her coffee and returned to her workstation refreshed.

She put aside a whole pile of the microfilms that the library had kindly provided, sent up from London especially for her, and picked out the first edition published after the actual date that Julia had died. Thank God the paper had only been issued weekly rather than daily. The edition she had was dated Thursday 30th April 1992. She carefully slotted it into the reader and scanned the records on the screen, very carefully, not wanting to miss a thing.

Another picture of a burning building, in black and white, flames leaping from it with firefighters and their appliance silhouetted in front. The headline was: POLICE INVESTIGATE FARM BLAZE. It caught Emily's full attention.

An article below said 'Fire engines were called to reports of a fire in an agricultural building at Oak Tree Farm, Lamberhurst late on Monday night.'

"That's the Levett's farm where she was brought up." Her heart was hammering.

Crews from Wadhurst, Southborough and Tunbridge Wells attended and crews wearing breathing apparatus used hose reel jets to extinguish the flames and bring the conflagration under control. One casualty, a woman named locally as Mrs Julia Merripen, is believed to have died in the fire. Enquiries and further investigations are ongoing to establish the cause.

Emily squeaked in horror and put her hands over her mouth. She sat back in her chair, shaking her head and trying to take it all in.

A fire? How awful. Poor Aunt Julia. What a hideously awful way to die. What started the fire? How did it happen? I wonder why she was in a barn. Why another fire? Fire seems to be figuring highly in Aunt Julia's life. Was it a coincidence?

She read it again and made a note to request a hard copy of the article. She then sat and pondered, letting the horror of Aunt Julia's death sink in.

How am I going to tell The Boomers? They'll be appalled. With a story like this, there surely must be more in the next week's papers. They'll have to follow it up.

Emily trawled through each of the consecutive weekly papers, scanning each page carefully. She read from left to right and top to bottom, following her finger as a guide so that she didn't miss anything vital. It made a nasty smear on the glass, which she rubbed off with a tissue.

It was mesmerising looking over each page, and the movement as it swung across the screen was making Emily a bit seasick. She had to look away to allow the nausea to settle and found that studying the bearded man was the perfect way to relieve it.

I wonder what he is researching so avidly. Is he looking for a lost relative too?

She realised that he had looked up and met her stare and he didn't look very friendly. Smiling to show no ill harm was meant, Emily blushed and turned back to her screen.

Getting to the end of a page, she realised that she had just let her eyes float over the reams of words and pictures without taking it in and that her mind was wandering.

This bloody microfilm is a nightmare. Concentrate Emily, concentrate.

Striking her thigh to wake herself up, she forgot about the sharp pencil in her hand. She stifled a squeak as she stabbed her leg. It hurt.

Emily was suddenly on high alert. The name Merripen jumped out at her.

MERRIPEN INQUEST OPEN VERDICT

The inquest into the death of Julia Merripen took place this week at Tunbridge Wells Coroner's Court. Eight witnesses gave evidence to Coroner Susan Evans over four days including concluding proceedings. Susan Evans, coroner, said: "To come to a conclusion of unlawful killing or suicide I am required to provide a judgement beyond reasonable doubt. On this occasion it has been ascertained that the cause of Julia Merripen's death was not the ligature around her neck but inhalation of smoke and injuries caused by fire.

Emily put a hand over her mouth to stifle the squeal that was trying to escape.

Bloody hell! Ligature?

> The fire was started by a Tilley lamp combusting with piles of straw and hay on the floor but it cannot be ascertained whether the fire was started accidentally or deliberately. I am therefore required to record an open verdict.

What the hell is a Tilley lamp? Accidental or deliberate? What on earth does that all mean? Jesus, it sounds awful.

> A spokesman for the family, Sarah Pennington, expressed her regret that the inquest had been inconclusive but hoped that Mrs Merripen could now rest in peace. The matter was closed and her relatives would be able to get on with their lives without further speculation.

Why on earth is Sarah Pennington, mother of the other babe in the wood, representing the family? She seems to like having her say in the newspapers. Speculation? Is this significant? Aunt Julia's best friend as well as mother-in-law, but not mother-in-law as such, oh for God's sake.

Emily scrabbled back through her notes to her family tree.

I need to dig around there a bit more.

Emily read the article three times, took a photo with her phone and wrote out the words in her 1/- notebook with an action to follow up on the significance of Sarah Pennington. Tapping her pencil on her nose, the thought struck her that she needed to investigate these Penningtons. The web was spreading.

She headed pages in her 1/- notebook with the names that she was researching and made a note of what she knew about each.

Sarah Pennington – Friend of Aunt Julia, related by marriage of son to Aunt Julia's daughter. Referenced in babes in the wood and inquest.

Sarah Pennington was easy to find through the electoral register. She was registered at an address in Tunbridge Wells. Emily wrote it down. She lived on her own. There was no Jolyon. Had he died? Another thing to check. Sarah obviously knew Aunt Julia very well and then became her in-law so she should have plenty of information to reveal.

Jolyon Pennington – Sarah's husband. Father of Nicholas. In-law to Julia. Cricketer but nothing else significant found. Not in the electoral register and a Google search didn't find anything.

Nicholas Pennington – Son of Jolyon and Sarah. Babe in the wood. Married Genevieve, Aunt Julia's daughter. Emily could find no sign of a Nicholas Pennington in this world for love nor money. He was still alive as there was no record of his death, but he had vanished from the web. No Facebook, no LinkedIn.

Genevieve Merripen/Pennington – Aunt Julia's daughter. Genevieve Pennington didn't seem to figure either. No Facebook, no LinkedIn. It wasn't exactly common, but Emily found sixteen people on Facebook that had the same name. None of them were the right age group or location, though. Many were in the States. Could she and Nicholas have moved to the States? It needed more hunting.

David Merripen – Aunt Julia's husband. Likewise, no mention anywhere beyond the early newspaper references. Nothing on social media but that could be just because he was old.

Matthew Merripen – Aunt Julia's son, Genevieve's brother. Burnt in fire when aged three. Nothing.

Daniel Merripen – Emily found one Daniel Merripen on Facebook but couldn't work out if he was the right one. The right sort of age but by his posts he seemed to be living somewhere in Wiltshire, miles away from Kent so probably not. Most of his posts were about animals.

All seemingly alive unless I have missed their death certificates. Where are they all hiding?

I think it's time I tracked down and spoke to some real people.

ELEVEN

Back with The Boomers, Emily managed to survive a thorough interrogation and disclosed everything that she had found. Inevitably, The Boomers laughed heartily over Julia's singing prize and Emily's complete lack of talent in that department.

Not so amusing was their cross-examination regarding what she had, or had not, told her mother about GG's house. Emily's guilt weighed as heavily as her overstuffed patchwork bag. Granny prodded her, literally and metaphorically, "We need to get on and work out how to sell the house. I've got some paint colour cards but I do think it's best to stick to something simple like magnolia." Emily escaped to the toilet to avoid the inquisition.

Having decided that it was time to speak to real people, her newly discovered relatives, Emily decided that the best approach would be to write a letter to them.

She thought that the old-fashioned form of communication was perhaps a little less threatening than an out of the blue phone call, and it left more options open should the letter be ignored. She wrote a draft letter and read it out to The Boomers at breakfast to see what they thought.

> *Dear Mr Levett,*
>
> *My name is Emily Walker. I am the great granddaughter of Irene Bedlington (nee Marshall) who sadly passed away recently. She left a letter for us, her family, to be read on her death which included the revelation that she had given birth to a daughter in 1944 out of wedlock. She deeply loved the father of the baby and had hoped to marry him but this did not happen because he was lost in the war. I enclose a photocopy of her letter so you can read it for yourself.*

Aunt Cynthia didn't look impressed. "Hmmm, dear. It is very good but I'm not sure this is quite the thing," and in echo Granny got straight to the point, "Blah, blah. You do go on rather. What's with all the 'I, I, I' and why say all of that when it is said much better in Mum's letter? You've said that you're enclosing it."

Thanks Granny, blunt as ever.

Emily crossed most of her crafted words out and continued.

> *My research shows that the baby was indeed put up for adoption by Saint Christopher's in Tunbridge Wells and was subsequently adopted by your parents, John and Margaret Levett. I believe*

that you are the adoptive brother of that child, Julia. Research also shows that Julia sadly died in a fire at your current address.

Granny blustered, "He knows all that," in stereo with Aunt Cynthia's "Why are you telling him things he already knows?"

Emily protested, "Supposing I've got the wrong person? I'm just checking."

Granny bridled. "Don't be daft. You've either got the right person or not. You keep telling us you've found Julia."

Aunt Cynthia patted Emily. "I'm sure they'll soon tell you, love."

Emily sighed and rather wished that she hadn't shared her ideas. She crossed out more words.

Our family are very keen to meet people who knew Julia and find out more about her life. We have a letter that Great Granny Irene wrote for Julia and it would please us all if this letter could be shared with her children.

Granny nodded firmly, "That's more like it. Cut to the chase, get rid of all the faff," and a gentle, "Wouldn't it be better if you just asked to come and see him, dear?" from Aunt Cynthia.

The Boomers can be irritatingly direct. I don't think I will bother to share my drafts in the future.

I understand that Aunt Julia married a David

Merripen and that there were two issue, Genevieve and Matthew...

The Boomers burst out laughing simultaneously, "Issue! What do you mean issue?" Aunt Cynthia was rocking with laughter and added "Oh, Emily. What are you like?"

"That's what they are called on all the websites." Emily was getting annoyed but pressed on.

I have tried to discover their whereabouts but have been unable to locate them and would be most grateful if you were to be able to do so for me. Also I have identified a Sarah Pennington who I believe may be a close friend. I look forward to hearing from you and would be delighted if we were able to meet.

The Boomers were still guffawing and chuckling. Emily held her hands up and shook her head in irritation. "Okay, okay. I will have another go at it."

And I won't be showing you two the final copy.

An hour later Emily crept down to the post office on the pretext of getting in her ten thousand steps a day. "Just going for a walk along the river."

Reaching the front of the queue, the post office owner, Mrs Harrington, who had known Emily all her life, expressed delight at seeing her. She exclaimed in her squeaky voice, which didn't match the extreme bulkiness of her body, "How are you love? You're looking well. Sorry to hear about your Great Granny. She will be missed, such a lovely lady. How's that fancy university of yours? Are you staying in Loxley long?"

Not being entirely certain which question to answer first, Emily muttered "Very well thank you, uni's great and I'm just staying with Granny for a while." It seemed to satisfy Mrs Harrington who beamed at her with her moon face over her ample bosom. Emily bought stamps, stuck them on the envelope and posted it in the old-fashioned, bright red post box that stood like a sentry in the middle of the pavement outside the post office. The whole process felt strange and old-fashioned, almost biblical. The feeling of that solid metal mouth around her fingers as her letter dropped with a rustle into the void, made her a bit nervous. She whipped her hand out quickly. But when the deed was done, she felt a strange lightness and satisfaction.

I wonder how soon I'll hear back.

TWELVE

Strolling along the well-worn path beside the Loxley River, Emily was enjoying the friendliness of strangers she passed: "Nice day again, isn't it?" and "Looks like there's some weather coming down the valley".

She had posted the letter to Julia's brother, Charles Levett three days ago in the hope of eliciting a positive response and a potential meeting. That done, she was now at a bit of a loose end and feeling very frustrated. If she had received such a bombshell of a letter she would have replied straight away or rung or something. To ease her impatience, she tried to enjoy the coolness of the shade from the trees, respite from another unusually hot and sunny day. She patted a rather fine oak.

I wonder how old these trees are? Must be at least a hundred. Older than GG. Perhaps GG wheeled Julia along here in her pram before she had to give her up for adoption, if she was allowed out at all. And GG would have wheeled The Boomers along here too. And Granny would have done the same for Mum and Aunt Jennifer – and me too. Just think what these trees must have witnessed. So many life stories absorbed into their rings.

~

Emily drifted up the steep hill back to Granny's, reflecting on the last few days of frustrating anticipation. With no contact from Julia's family, she had spent her time at Great Granny's house helping Granny and Aunt Cynthia get to the bottom of Great Granny's piles of stuff. Anything valuable – in terms of memories rather than monetary worth – had been carried off to Granny's house for safekeeping. Emily had bagged Great Granny's blanket chest; she loved the smell of old-fashioned moth balls when she lifted the lid.

The house clearance people had been in and valued all Great Granny's remaining furniture and treasures at a paltry couple of hundred quid. They removed it all in a trice with no show of respect.

Once they'd gone, Emily had shuffled inside Great Granny's house for a long despondent look. "It doesn't look like GG's home any more." Emily hadn't realised that it would be like this. Great Granny had gone. Her scent was fading, had all but disappeared, and it just didn't feel right without the furniture, the ranks of family photographs and the knick-knacks. Stripped of its homely trappings, the house looked naked.

She wandered into the hall and stared up the stairs. "Where have you gone, GG?" She crept sadly out through the front door into a sudden burst of sunshine.

A thought struck Emily. *Is this a sign that it isn't GG's house any more? It is mine.* She looked up at the blue sky. "Thank you GG, thank you so much wherever you are."

She arrived back at Granny's in time for dinner, feeling a bit down and wanting to talk, but Granny and Aunt Cynthia pounced on her the moment she stepped through the front door. "Emily, we've had a phone call," and "She's received it in the post and she's rung."

A frisson of excitement shivered through Emily. "Julia's brother?"

But they said she?

Granny pressed her lips together, a sympathetic look, "No, love, your mum," and Aunt Cynthia patted her, "Your mum, dear."

"Oh." Emily's face drained of colour. "Okay, so what has she said?" Emily checked her phone. "She hasn't rung me."

Aunt Cynthia gestured at Granny to take the lead. "She's not happy. Come and have a brew and I'll tell you all about it."

Emily sighed and shivered with discomfort, followed Granny into the kitchen and sat at her place, cuddling her patchwork bag for comfort. Aunt Cynthia fiddled around with the kettle, opened and closed cupboards loudly and clashed mugs together. Finally she placed a steaming mug in Emily's hand before taking her place.

"Ta, Aunt Cyn."

It doesn't matter how many times I say that I don't drink tea, they keep giving it to me.

Granny bustled in her seat like a hen settling on her nest and slapped the table. "Right." Emily jumped, sending a wave of tea across the table. She was feeling very tense. Aunt Cynthia then wasted what felt like another age mopping up the mess before Granny cut to the chase. "This is what she said, a précised version otherwise we would be here for a while." Emily shivered. "As I said, she's not happy. Obviously, she is pleased to get some cash but thinks that GG had stashed away far more than that – which, to be fair, she did – so your mum thinks GG has been deliberately miserly, and that's annoyed the hell out of her.

But the main thing is that she just can't see why you've been given the house. Why hasn't it gone to her and Jennifer? Why you specifically? Why not you and Ashley? She sounded very tight lipped." Aunt Cynthia nodded and Granny continued, "I've told her that when me and Aunt Cyn pop our clogs that we will make sure she gets this house, but I don't think she were listening." Emily breathed out heavily. She hadn't realised that she'd been holding her breath.

Emily felt a bit tearful, "That's it?"

"In a nutshell, yes." Granny folded her arms, lifted her chin and sniffed.

"So, what should I do?"

Granny shook her head. "Nothing," and Aunt Cynthia reached out to pat Emily's hand. "What can you do, dear? It wasn't your decision."

Emily checked her phone again nervously. Mum definitely hadn't rung her. Emily thought that she would have done now that the whole thing had been exposed. "Don't you think I should ring her, though? I've got to speak to her about it sometime."

Granny seemed adamant, "I'd wait until she contacts you. Let her stew for a bit then she might be more reasonable about it and actually be pleased for you instead of mardy. Now let's have a bite to eat. I've got a few slices of haslet for me and Aunt Cyn's dinner and loads of rabbit food for you, Emily."

Oh my God, Mum knows. She's not happy. To be fair, I'd probably be furious if I'd been passed over like that, but I think we can all see why, the way Mum had behaved, it's no wonder. And at least I'm tucked away safely here and not at home having to face her resentment.

Despite that, Emily's stomach lurched.

I don't think I could possibly eat a thing.

THIRTEEN

Emily woke the next morning with a feeling of dread.

Mum knows. When's she going to call? She'll be furious. What am I going to say?

She could hear the neighbour's yappy dog. It was so loud that Emily could hear it through the bedroom wall. Although it was irritating it did mean that it announced the postie was on their way. Emily listened and heard the letter box snap, signalling post. Scooting out of bed, she shimmied down the stairs as she had ever since she'd mailed her missive, just in case she had received a reply.

There was one white envelope with exuberant writing on it, and it was addressed to Emily. The postmark was Tunbridge Wells.

Hooray, at last!

She shouted, "Granny, Aunt Cyn! I've got a letter! It must be from Charles, Julia's brother."

Granny called back, "No need to yell, Emily, we're only in the kitchen," and from Aunt Cynthia, "A letter, dear. How exciting."

Emily skipped into the kitchen.

Granny grumbled, "But you're not dressed, Emily."

"I just couldn't wait to show you..."

"Well, just this once. This is a civilised household. We don't breakfast in our pyjamas and well you know it."

Emily grinned at Granny's exacting standards, "Sorry Granny. But this is so exciting..."

Granny grunted, "Open it then, what are you waiting for?" and from Aunt Cynthia, "I wonder who it's from? I'll put the kettle on."

Emily went to pick it open clumsily, all fingers and thumbs. Granny raised an eyebrow and handed her a knife. Emily slit open the envelope, pulled out the contents, and started to read.

Dear Emily,

What a wonderful surprise for us to receive your letter out of the blue about Aunt Julia. I am Charles Levett's daughter, and I am replying on his behalf as my father is very frail.

"It isn't Charles, it's his daughter."

Granny said with exasperation and more loudly than necessary, "Read it out loud, Emily."

"Okay, okay." She grinned at Granny and started again from the beginning before continuing.

You are correct that Aunt Julia sadly died on 24th April 1992. It is a shame that she never received the letter from her mother and was made aware of her history and that she was so loved. Something that we all need, I believe. What a lovely idea to pass it instead to her daughter and son.

Hooray for such a positive response.

I do have an address for the Merripens. They moved to Wiltshire soon after Aunt Julia died, and I haven't seen them since although I do correspond regularly on anything of note within the family. I assume that they receive my letters and invitations, but I can't be certain that they have not moved from that address: 2, Harepath Cottages, Bourton, Wiltshire SN10 7QQ. I did have a landline telephone number but that hasn't worked for years and I have no others to offer.

Excellent! I can follow that up now easily. Electoral register here I come.

With regard to Sarah Pennington, she was indeed very much involved in Aunt Julia's life particularly in respect of the marriage of her son to Aunt Julia's daughter.

Now that is interesting... reading between the lines there seems to be more there than meets the eye. A bit stilted?

It would be wonderful to meet you, the great grandniece of Aunt Julia, and I know that my father, your Great Uncle Charlie, would love to talk to you about the happy childhood that he shared with her. Please come and see us. Give me a ring, number at the top, or send me an email, address likewise at the top, and we can make a date.

Yours, Cathy Levett

PS Can't believe that this has happened. So excited to meet you.

Granny's eyes were lit up with excitement. "So, what next, Emily?" Aunt Cynthia, doing her seal clap, added, "What a lovely letter, dear."

"I definitely want to go and see Cathy. She sounds lovely. And now I have somewhere to start with the Merripens I must follow that lead. And I can send a letter to this Sarah Pennington. Then I can go down south and see them all."

Emily was so happy she managed to forget her feelings of dread about the house and her mum.

Within twenty-four hours, Emily had made great progress. A quick check on the electoral register showed both David Merripen and Genevieve Merripen at the address given by Cathy Levett, so Emily wrote them a letter. She didn't show The Boomers her draft this time in case they got picky again.

She already knew where Sarah Pennington lived, so she wrote to her as well. The Boomers had shown her how to write the address correctly with little indents all the way down to make a nice, neat diagonal and given her a hugely long lecture about ending the letter 'Yours sincerely' or 'Yours faithfully' which Emily had chosen to ignore.

Crazy way of carrying on and so many rules that no-one knows about. Long live emails and texts. Except when your boyfriend blocks them. Ex-boyfriend, I mean.

It suddenly occurred to Emily that she hadn't thought

about Dylan for days. And she hadn't once thought about whether her father was really her father. Since the letter had arrived yesterday, she had stopped dreading that her phone might ring in case it was her mum. Mum hadn't made contact, was that a good or a bad sign?

No wonder I'm feeling so good. This whole searching for Julia is a huge distraction.

She wandered to the post office. Mrs Harrington beamed at her, her eyes disappearing into the plump folds of her face, "You again, love. You're a busy little correspondent. How are Rose and Cyn, your Gran and Auntie? They bearing up?" Emily nodded politely; it was all that was required.

Sticking on the stamps and posting the letters, it was as if she'd been doing it all her life. As she sauntered back to Granny's she thought that it was all very well using the snail mail for this venture, but it took forever to get a reply, so exasperating. Just as well then, that she had taken Cathy's lead and put her email address on each of the letters in the hope of speeding up a reply.

FOURTEEN

Emily had spent the last two days since posting the letters as a slave in Granny's sumptuous vegetable patch. There was always something to be done, pinching off tomato shoots, feeding, watering, and weeding. Granny was determined to keep Emily busy as a distraction from her frustrating wait.

As a reward for her horticultural endeavours, Emily was sat at the kitchen table with Granny and Aunt Cynthia stuffing a fat cucumber sandwich into her mouth.

Aunt Cynthia was a master baker, as well as a seamstress, and had baked the bread. The whole kitchen smelt of it. It was heavenly. The home-grown cucumber tasted nothing like the watery ones that came from the supermarket. The butter, cutely named 'Our Cow Molly', came from a farm literally just down the road. Emily savoured the delicious combination, and all with the smallest possible carbon footprint. She was in heaven.

An email pinged in on Emily's phone and she reached into her trouser pocket for it. "Not at the dinner table, Emily." Granny barked. As she withdrew her hand, Emily wondered with a shiver of apprehension whether it was

Mum, although she usually used WhatsApp; the communication blackout was proving alarming. Perhaps it was Dylan, the rat – fat chance if he thinks she would be replying to him. Perhaps it was just a mate asking her to join in with some fun expedition. That would be cool and a welcome distraction.

Emily finished her sandwich and rose from her chair. "Thanks Granny, thanks Aunt Cyn that was delish. Please may I get down?"

Granny asked, "Don't you want a brew, Emily?" as Aunt Cynthia simultaneously chirped, "How about a cuppa?"

"No thanks. I've got my water." She raised her refillable bottle in salute and dashed into the lounge, her hand already diving into her pocket.

David Merripen
Your Letter

Yay. He's replied.

A shiver of excitement ran through Emily as she selected his message.

It was one hell of a surprise getting your letter. You are correct in thinking that I am Julia's husband. It is such a shame that her mum started looking for her so late in the day. I am sure she would have loved to have heard from her during her life. She was so upset to have been given away and never knowing the reasons why, although she could guess what with it being during the war. She always hoped that one day her mum might turn up but didn't want to look for her in case it was a secret and it upset the apple cart.

You ask if you can meet us all. I talked about it within our family and I have to say that although we have agreed to meet you, to be honest, your request has been met with varying levels of enthusiasm. Please can you reply and suggest some dates.

Emily punched the air. "Yes!"

She read it again.

Poor Aunt Julia. It is so sad that she felt unloved by her mum – I know all about that.

"Granny, Aunt Cyn," she shouted through, "that email that pinged. It's from David Merripen, Julia's husband, and he's agreed to meet. Isn't that exciting?" She got up to show the message to The Boomers and, as she strolled through, wondered why there would be 'varying levels of enthusiasm.'

After a long day of Granny and Aunt Cynthia finding Emily little jobs to do – including Aunt Cynthia trying to show Emily how to repair her own patchwork bag without much success – Emily went to bed excited to know that she would soon be meeting people that knew Julia.

A last glance at her phone confirmed that there was still nothing from her mum.

Next door's dog yapping heralded the arrival of the postie. Emily woke, suddenly alert. When she heard the letterbox twang, she dashed down the stairs as a blue envelope plopped onto the doormat.

She picked it up. "Yay, it's for me."

The handwriting was very loopy and old-fashioned. She studied the postmark, Tunbridge Wells, as she headed for the kitchen to show The Boomers, flapping it at them, "I've got another letter. It must be Sarah Pennington."

As she slid into her place, Granny said coolly, "Pyjamas again, Emily?" but handed Emily a knife. She slit the letter open and extracted a piece of paper that exactly matched the colour of the envelope. Emily found it so odd to be opening a real letter at all, so unusual in this day and age, except for bills and official statements – yet here was her second in a matter of days. It was written in real ink, black or very dark blue. The handwriting was elegant, almost italic, but with a slight wobble.

The Boomers were looking at her intently. She took a deep breath and started reading out loud.

Mrs Jolyon Pennington,
Beech Court,
Willicombe Park,
Royal Tunbridge Wells,
Kent,
01892 557625

Dear Emily,

Thank you for your brief letter. I do indeed remember Julia Pennington nee Levett and knew her well. Her daughter Genevieve married my son Nicholas as no doubt you have already surmised. I do not know what it is that you wish to discuss about Julia, but I see no harm in telling you all that I recall if this is helpful to your family, in particular Julia's half-sisters.

I see that you reside in Sheffield, but should you wish to visit me in Royal Tunbridge Wells I would honour you with my time.

Royal? Royal Tunbridge Wells? And honour me with her time? What a laugh.

Please write to me forthwith or telephone me on the number I have given above to make arrangements.

Yours sincerely,

A rather spidery scribble.

Mrs Sarah Pennington

Emily shrugged, "Well, what do we make of that? Hilarious. Short and to the point. Such fancy ways. She must be a right old snob."

Granny muttered, "Who the heck does she think she is? Honour you with my time? My arse."

Emily burst out laughing.

Can't wait to meet that one.

THE MIDDLE

FIFTEEN

Emily woke up wondering where on earth she was. As she flopped out an arm to cancel her phone alarm she shook her head to clear her sleepy brain and remembered, "Kent. I've made it. I'm going to meet Julia's brother today."

She was looking up at a very frilly, floral lampshade and wondered just how many roses a person could squeeze into one room's decor. It was a little bit overwhelming to have quite so many variations of the very same flower in one bedroom.

Pink rose curtains, rosy sheets and pillows, a rosy bedcover in a different pink fabric, a tissue box with more garish pink roses, little bowls with no real purpose, rose prints on the walls, and even on the wastepaper bin.

At least the walls and carpet are plain, although a rather snot coloured green.

Reaching for her phone, Emily tapped WhatsApp and checked her 'Parents' group again. She had sent them a message before setting off from Loxley saying that she was off to Kent searching for Julia, thinking that they might respond and show some interest, or at least mention Great

Granny's house. They'd both read it, two blue ticks, but only Dad had responded with a bland, 'Hope you're successful. Have fun.' Still nothing from Mum. How long would this cold war last? She petulantly threw her phone onto the bed.

She wandered into the en suite shower room with more roses all over the walls, and the soap dish and tooth mug decorated in roses, of course. Overwhelmed by so much floral decoration, she closed her eyes as she showered and afterwards rummaged in her suitcase for fresh clothes – nothing pink and definitely no roses on it.

Today was the day she was meeting the first of her newly discovered family, and she wondered what they would be like. What should she wear on such an auspicious occasion? Probably not the harem pants that Granny disapproved of. Uncle Charlie was old, in his seventies, like Granny and Aunt Cynthia so would probably expect Emily to be smartly dressed for such a visit. Or would he if he was a farmer?

As he's so old, should I take out the nose stud and an earring or two? This is all so much more complicated than I ever thought it would be.

She plumped for some coloured jeans with a plain shirt and controlled her voluminous curls with a fabric hair band bought from an upcycling stall at the market.

She went down for breakfast, following the distinctive smell of bacon down a narrow, steep staircase. At the bottom, she instinctively ducked under a low doorway and stepped into a low ceilinged, beamed dining room crammed with three polished wooden tables. There would probably be more room for the furniture if there wasn't such an enormous open fireplace with a brick surround taking up most of one wall, and along the other a buffet table stacked with Tupperware containers.

Emily wasn't sure where to sit so hovered in the doorway. One table was occupied but all she could see was the back of a shaved head of indeterminate age atop hunched shoulders. Should she say, 'Good morning'? Probably not.

So, this is what it is like travelling on your own and staying in a B&B with a bunch of total strangers. A bit lonely and anxious making.

A cheerful young waitress with ginger curls and freckled face, looking like an archetypal country lass who had just come in from milking cows, bounded in carrying a plate and said merrily, "Take a seat and I will be with you in a sec. Breakfast menu is on the table."

So much enthusiasm this early in the day – and a bucolic accent to go with her looks.

Emily wandered over to the nearest table and had barely sat down when the friendly girl pranced over to her and with an enormous grin said, "Hi, I'm Katie. What can I get you? Tea or coffee? Something hot from the menu?"

"Coffee please, decaffeinated. I am just trying to work through what all the menu items are." Emily realised that this was the first time she had spoken to anyone face to face since her arrival late yesterday evening and her voice came out a bit croaky.

She read a long list of bacon, sausages, black pudding, field mushrooms, baked beans, grilled tomatoes, hash browns, kedgeree, kippers, and eggs cooked every way that was possible.

Emily thought she might just throw up at the thought of all that meat and fat on top of the angst, but was able to pick out one thing that she felt that she could eat. "Scrambled eggs please."

"White or brown toast with that?"

"Um, brown please."

"No worries. Help yourself to what you want from the buffet." She whipped away the menu and trotted off, leaving Emily feeling a bit awkward with nothing to look at or do.

Should've brought my phone down with me.

She pondered on her exchange with Katie, mesmerised by the way the woman spoke.

What sort of accent does she have? A new one on me. It's odd how you can set off from Yorkshire with the familiar warm burr from deep in the throat and suddenly find yourself listening intently to something so round and popping out from right at the front of the mouth. And why is she so weirdly energetic? She's like Tigger. Obviously a local girl with no other prospects, making the best of a boring job.

To pass the time and relieve the discomfiture, she decided to have a good look at the bountiful buffet but when she got closer to it the Tupperware tubs of cereal looked as if they might have been there for a rather long time, and there was evidence of crumbs and butter in some bowls of jam. She poured a glass of juice into a thick, cloudy glass. She thought it was probably orange. Back at her table she sipped at the juice. It turned out not to be orange, although she couldn't tell precisely what it was. It was very sweet and a bit metallic, but it was drinkable – just. She looked around the room trying to look relaxed. Not easy on your own.

Definitely should have brought something down with me to study.

The lively waitress appeared, clutching a tin teapot which she put on the table. Presumably coffee despite the non-traditional presentation.

"I see you are staying for a few days. Do you have plans?"

Delighted to engage in conversation with someone after

so much solitude, Emily replied, "Oh yes, I've discovered that I have a whole branch of the family that we didn't know about and I'm here to meet them. It's very exciting."

"They live round here?"

"Yes, some of them. I have a great uncle, Aunt Julia's brother, who lives in Lamberhurst. I'm going to see him today, and then a friend of hers who's in Tunbridge Wells. I'm seeing her tomorrow. Then my cousin lives over in Wiltshire who I'm visiting the next day after that, so a packed few days. Sadly, Aunt Julia died some years ago now in a tragic fire. She was adopted as a small girl so I'm going to see where she was..."

The smile on the waitress was getting to look a bit wooden so Emily thought she should stop.

Too much information?

Katie cut in with, "I think your eggs might be ready," and escaped to the kitchen.

SIXTEEN

Emily's journey to Oak Tree Farm was fraught with disputes with the sat nav lady.

"Are you sure that I should turn right here? It says no through road." Emily drove past the turning.

"Make a U-turn when possible," the sat nav lady then proceeded to whine for the next five minutes in her perfect received pronunciation.

"You have no idea how difficult it is to find anywhere to turn in these crazy narrow lanes. Please just shut up."

After a ten-point turn involving a bit of plunging into the hedge, Emily finally succeeded. As it turned out, the sat nav lady was correct. Emily apologised sulkily.

She turned into the entrance through the open farm gate which had a rickety sign next to it declaring 'Beware of the Dogs'. She drove up the rutted track, taking her time, looking around avidly at the home where her Aunt Julia had lived, drinking it in and savouring it all.

She was here, actually here, for her childhood.

Either side were grassy paddocks with wire square fencing and burly sheep that ignored her completely.

These must be the offspring of Julia's father's prize-winning fat rams that I read about when doing my newspaper research. They do look a bit on the plump side.

She clambered out of the car and took loads of photographs with her phone. An impatient beeping made her jump. Her arrival had coincided with the postie. She popped back into the car, crashed the gears a bit and then drove down the drive. To her right there was the wall of a wood framed solid brick barn backing onto the right-hand paddock. A round tower at one end sported a very jaunty looking hat on its roof, a sort of white cone with a pointy arm. Very odd.

As she passed by, windows and a front door were suddenly revealed. The barn turned out to be a house in its own right. A quite brilliant conversion. It kept the *olde worlde* look of a clearly agricultural building with black painted beams and window frames, but a glass door with side lights gave it a more contemporary look. The postie's van was trying to goose her back bumper. Emily pressed violently on the accelerator and shot forward. The postie swung enthusiastically into a parking area in front of the barn.

Ahead was the farmhouse, more of a chocolate box cottage, with the most amazing half brick, half hanging tiles façade under a dark grey tiled roof. The windows with their diamond shaped panes were sparkling magically. There were even stereotypical roses around the door.

I am being stalked by roses.

She went through another open wooden gate and parked behind a large black SUV of some sort and a silver town runabout. Her tummy fluttered in excitement. She had arrived at last.

I wonder what Julia thought as she was driven up to this

house for the very first time as a five-year-old girl? It's just so exciting to be here.

As she got out of the car a large, sleek black dog – she wasn't very good at identifying dog breeds – bounced up, grinning and waggling its whole body. "Hello dog, how are you?" She wasn't certain about touching it just in case it was a feral outside dog which she should 'beware of' as per the sign. She tried to sound confident and commanding, despite being very nervous.

The dog hurried off, then stopped and looked over its shoulder as if to say this way, so she grabbed her bag from the front seat, lifting it on to her shoulder with a grunt. *This thing is getting so heavy*, and followed. The dog took her around the side of the house, rather than to the more obvious front door, along a brick-paved path with ebullient plants billowing over it. A cloud of flowery smells arose, and she could hear a squadron of insects buzzing. Just such a quintessentially perfect country home.

The dog was sitting staring at the back door which was a stable door, both top and bottom wide open. Emily took tiny nervous steps forward in case there was somebody right there, trying to see if there was a bell so that she could make her presence known. She peered through a tumble of honeysuckle and roses – more roses – and was flooded by the most glorious scents but couldn't see anything obvious.

She took a deep breath and rapped on the top half of the open door. "Hello?" It came out as a quaver. She hesitated, cleared her throat, knocked again and shouted "Hello? It's Emily." In contrast, her voice now sounded like a foghorn.

A woman with a long face, terrible buck teeth and a wave of short blonde hair with a severe fringe appeared. Emily couldn't help thinking that she looked like a horse, albeit a very friendly one. "Emily! It's great to meet you. I saw your car arrive and then you just disappeared." Emily was clasped in a hearty bear hug and nearly suffocated as her head was drawn into an apron-covered bosom that emanated a smell of baking bread; it reminded her of Aunt Cynthia.

Once she could escape enough to be able to speak, she tried to explain. "The dog showed me to this door and..."

"Oh, Rufus, you are such a twit." The woman frowned at the dog who was looking at her avidly, his tail wagging enthusiastically as if he had just been soundly praised. "He obviously realised you're family and honoured you with the back door. Come on in. I'm Cathy by the way, Charlie's daughter, Aunt Julia's niece. Did you find us okay? Dad is so excited about meeting you."

Emily stepped into a kitchen with a large fireplace, flanked by horse brasses on leather straps, with a black Aga nestled into it. A huge bowl covered in a tea towel was on the warming plate, emitting a yeasty smell that mingled with the waft of freshly baked bread she had smelt on Cathy's clothes. Her mouth watered.

The rest of the room was taken up with a sturdy dark wood table surrounded by wheel back chairs except for a large throne of a carver chair at its head. To the left was a cramped area with a sink looking out over the car park and pale blue cupboards that looked as if they had seen better days. Several of the doors listed to the side in an overly relaxed way. The floor seemed to be an extension of the brick path.

Wow, Aunt Julia lived right here and ate in this kitchen.

"Now Emily, can I get you anything before we go through and see Dad? This is all so exciting for him."

Emily frantically looked around, trying to take in everything as quickly as she could. This was where Aunt Julia had grown up, in this glorious setting. "No, thank you. I'm so excited to see all this and to meet him too."

Then Cathy said in a much quieter voice, "Before we go through, I need to brief you about Dad. He's doing really well but he does get very muddled. It's a sort of dementia so he isn't too good on the here and now but – and this is the best thing for you – he is just so happy to talk about the past. He remembers it as if it just happened. Are you okay with that?"

"Oh yes, absolutely fine."

"I will redirect him as much as I can if he's going a bit off track. What is so wonderful is that he is just so thrilled to be remembering every little detail about his boyhood. This is the best thing for him. Let's go and meet him. Follow me." She disappeared through the far door. Emily followed, drinking it all in. Suddenly Cathy stopped and said in a conspiratorial tone, "By the way, he often forgets that Aunt Julia is dead – most of the time in fact. I think it's a coping mechanism. Would you go with it?"

"Of course. Anything that makes him comfortable."

Cathy turned on her heel and Emily followed her through a short, dark, cool hallway with one wall bulging with earthy coloured coats smelling of the outdoors. They emerged into a wonderful room sparkling with light from the diamond panes, with dark beams stretched across a low ceiling. It smelt of wood smoke and beeswax polish.

Sitting across the room in a low armchair was a lanky old man. He didn't have much left in the way of hair; what remained was draped over the dome of his head, but he had the most contagious grin. It wasn't the Uncle Charlie that she had imagined while doing her research.

"Is that you Julia? Oh, it is so good to see you. I can't believe it." He raised his arms wide in welcome.

Emily hesitated but Cathy stepped aside to reveal her. "Dad, this is Emily, Julia's great niece. Isn't that marvellous?

I told you about her and that she is here to hear all about Aunt Julia. Aren't you, Emily?"

"Yes, I am. It is so fantastic to meet you Uncle Charlie." It seemed so natural and cosy to call him that. "You have absolutely no idea how much this means to me."

"Come and sit down, do." He leant forward and patted the armchair next to him. A puff of dust and dog hair burst into the sunbeams streaming in through the windows. He looked at her expectantly, so she thought she'd better start things off.

She sank into the plump cushions of the armchair and settled her bag at her feet like a well-behaved dog. "So, Uncle Charlie, what can you tell me about Julia?"

"Where would you like me to begin?"

"Let's start at the very beginning, a very good place to start. You know, like doh a deer?" Emily grinned to make sure he knew she was making a joke.

Uncle Charlie looked completely blank and tittered a nervous, "Ha ha."

Cathy interrupted the awkward exchange. "Cup of tea, Emily?"

"Oh, no thanks, I have my water bottle with me."

"You, Dad – a top up?" Uncle Charlie reached for a rosy patterned cup and saucer and lifted it towards Cathy. More roses. It rattled alarmingly. "There we go, dear. Now as I was saying... What was I saying?" He looked puzzled.

"You were going to start at the very beginning of when you first met Julia."

I won't mention deer this time.

"Oh, I am too. This is such fun. When is she getting here?"

"I'm sorry Uncle Charlie, you've just got me, Emily, your great niece. Do you mind if I take notes? And I would love to take a few photographs if that's OK?" Emily withdrew her phone and raised it in preparation. Uncle Charlie looked confused.

"Is it okay if I take your picture?" Emily said, smiling.

Uncle Charlie jutted out his chin. "Of course, but where is your camera?"

"Um, this is my phone and it has a built in camera."

"Well I never. It's amazing what people can do nowadays."

"Smile, Uncle Charlie" Emily tried to capture the lovely smile that she had been greeted with but he just looked like he was having a passport photo taken.

Maybe I'll try again later when he's a bit more relaxed.

Returning the phone to her pocket, she dug around in her bottomless bag to liberate her 1/- notebook and sat poised with pencil ready, as if about to take dictation.

Uncle Charlie looked at her, puzzled. Emily put on a fixed smile. "You were going to tell me all about Aunt Julia, right from the beginning." Emily was so excited. She was here with Aunt Julia's brother and hearing her story first hand.

He shrugged, sat back and stared into space, took a deep breath and smiled happily. "The first time I saw Julia." He spoke as if he was reading a chapter heading. "We picked her up from Saint Christopher's in Tunbridge Wells. We all went – me, Mum and Dad – in the Rover all washed and polished for the occasion, all of us in our Sunday best. It was a filthy day. It was tipping down with rain and Mum shouted at me to keep out of the puddles as we ran for the car. I didn't, of course, and ended up soaking my socks and shoes. The drive seemed to take forever and not one of us said a word. The heater was on and my socks were sort of steaming and smelt like wet sheep." He chuckled to himself and his stomach wobbled. "The windscreen wipers marched across the screen, backwards and forwards. I remember how they thrummed in the silence. As we turned off Pembury Road, through an imposing entrance with its very own lodge, Mum reached out to take Dad's hand. I noticed that because they showed their affection very rarely".

Emily glanced at the family tree in her 1/- notebook. *John Levett and Margaret Levett. His parents, now passed away.*

"Dad parked up as close as he could. It was still pouring and we dashed in through the enormous front door. The door was giant size – well, it was to a small boy anyway – and there were fancy columns either side of it. It was very posh, an enormous house the likes of which I hadn't seen before. There she was, Julia, waiting for us in the cavernous hallway just by the side of a pillar." Emily pitched forward eagerly. *This is amazing.* "Oh, I can picture it like it was this morning: this tiny thing dwarfed by a nurse in a blue blouse and a crisp white apron with a fancy little hat crimped like a pie crust, and both of them made to look so small under the height of the ceiling. It went up and up." He looked up as he relived the moment. "Little Julia was very scruffily dressed, her dress a bit too short for her. You could clearly see the tidemark where it had been let down – even I could see that as a seven-year-old boy – and clumpy shoes that were in need of a good polish. Mum and Dad always made sure that I kept my shoes polished. I am guessing now that the children's home had to make do and mend with so many little children to take care of and clothes rationing only just finished. Her solemn little face stared at us, her eyes like saucers. She was hanging on for dear life to a golliwog. Poor mite looked as if she was shell-shocked. Totally rigid."

Even as Emily winced at that abhorrent word, a thrill of excitement ran through her.

"Do you know, Uncle Charlie, I think that" she

hesitated, unable to say the racist name out loud, "little doll was a gift from her birth mother. I have a letter saying so."

"Well, I never." Uncle Charlie was looking at her in bafflement.

That was daft. I shouldn't have interrupted but how incredible is that?

"But Uncle Charlie, there you were meeting Aunt Julia for the very first time at Saint Christopher's..." Pencil poised to take more notes, Emily looked at him expectantly.

"Oh yes. Mum walked towards her slowly like she did with the nervous animals on the farm. Dad held me back. She hunkered down to look at Julia eye to eye. She didn't say anything for a while. I'm guessing that she just smiled. She reached out her hand and very gently ran a finger down Julia's cheek." Uncle Charlie reached out, imitating this warm gesture. "The silence was broken by the click clack of shoes stomping into the hall and this fat cow of a woman came bustling in yelling, 'Please don't hang around. It's best to get going straight away for all concerned.' I tell you, she looked like a cow and she bellowed like one and all." He chuckled. "Well, she rounded us up and herded us out into the car. Mum sat in the back with me with Julia between us, her long, skinny legs stuck straight out in front of her, so Dad was all alone in the front, like a chauffeur as if we were very important people. Mum started telling Julia where we were going and all about the farm. I don't remember Julia saying a word; she just sat staring ahead. Mum took Julia's tiny hand in hers. I tried to do the same but Julia nearly jumped through the roof at my clumsy touch, and Mum glared at me so I just sat and stared at her instead. Always have been a blundering old sod."

Cathy came in with the ubiquitous rosy teacup, a biscuit balanced on the saucer. "Here we are, Dad. How are you getting on with Emily?"

"We're talking about Julia. Do you know when she'll get here? I am so looking forward to seeing her."

"She isn't coming today, Dad. Emily is here to ask you all about her, to hear her story. Isn't that lovely? Now, where have you got to?"

"This is gold. Uncle Charlie and his parents have just picked Aunt Julia up from the children's home."

"Good grief, I think you might end up having to stay the night. This is going to take a long time at this rate. You'd better have a biscuit to keep you going."

A delicious looking sugar-crusted shortbread was offered to Emily. How could she resist? She nibbled at the edge and it tasted glorious. It smelt of the kitchen when Aunt Cynthia was on a baking spree. "Oh, Cathy, this is just as good as my Aunt Cyn's."

Cathy looked askance but said with a smile, "I shall take that as a compliment." Emily blushed and turned back to Uncle Charlie.

Around a mouthful of crumbs, Emily prompted him to continue his story. "So, Uncle Charlie, what did Julia think of the farm when she arrived? Did she say anything?" She was desperate to hear more.

"She didn't say anything at all! Heavens knows what must have been going on in that beautiful little head of hers. Mum took her through the lounge and straight upstairs to show her the bathroom and her bedroom. Mum and Dad pulled out all the stops for her bedroom. They'd made up the bed with a pink candlewick bedspread and placed a special baby dolly with dark curly hair on it with a whole layette that Mum and Nan had spent hours knitting in front of the fire every evening. Dad and I stayed downstairs, so I don't know how she reacted." He shook his head.

"Did she take long to settle in?" Emily tipped her head

to show interest and encouragement. She so wanted to hear more.

"That little poppet was a princess. Such an adorable child. Quiet and so well-mannered with her 'Ps and Qs'; they had taught her well at Saint Christopher's. Mum and Dad, and me especially, loved her from the moment she became part of our family. She clung to Mum as if she never wanted to let her go. Very shy at first, chewed her nails terribly. Always hid behind Mum's legs, peeping out. The funny thing was that Mum was quite determined that she would be called Molly – that was the name of my sister that passed away – but Julia wasn't having any of it." *Like the Curate said in his letter!* "She would frown every time any of us tried to call her Molly and she spat out 'Julia'. I can't even remember how many times we tried but she was a stubborn little girl, bless her. Can you believe it, she started calling her baby doll Molly instead, so she had Golly and Molly as her inseparable companions." Uncle Charlie laughed and shook his head while Emily tried to hide her cringe at that name again. "It took her a while before her personality emerged but it was such a treat when I got a smile out of her, and what a smile it was. It lit up her face and her eyes would go really wide and she would just beam. Her eyes were the greenest green I've ever seen. Really startling."

GG's green eyes! "That's incredible. Great Granny Irene had those eyes and they have been passed down through the generations." Uncle Charlie looked at her, his brow crinkled with puzzlement. "Except I didn't get them, but The Boomers and my sister Ashley have..." Uncle Charlie continued to look at her in bewilderment. Emily decided to cut her explanation short. Interrupting the poor old chap had confused him. "Anyway, Uncle Charlie, please carry on. Tell me all about Aunt Julia." She smiled encouragingly.

"She was just so gorgeous, it's hard to describe just how perfect she was. She grew so tall and elegant and she did stand out!" He cackled. "Oh my, did she stand out. Have you seen photos of her?"

"No, I haven't."

"Where are they, Cathy? We should get out the albums for..." He had clearly forgotten who she was.

Cathy stood up. "Here we are, Dad, all right here on your table ready for you to show Emily. I am sure that Emily, Julia's great niece, would love to see them all." It was touching the way Cathy kept putting her dad right without contradicting him.

His trembling hand stretched out to retrieve an oblong, black cardboard book with a tassel on it, just like the ones in Great Granny's attic. He shakily put it in his lap and opened the cover. "Come round here... er, um. Look over my shoulder."

Emily was beside herself with excitement. She was actually going to see Aunt Julia. She went around to the back of his armchair and leant over, taking in his old man scent of soil with a hint of Marmite. Looking at the open album with its black and white photographs neatly stuck in with corner tabs, each with a handwritten note underneath and a heading at the top of the page giving a place and date, she got rather a shock.

Nobody at any time had thought to mention that Julia was black. Emily stifled a gasp and tried to close her mouth before she was spotted.

So GG's lover was a black GI. No wonder she was made to give Julia up for adoption. What are Granny and Aunt Cyn going to say about this?

The thoughts raced through her mind while Uncle

Charlie pointed at each photo in turn and lovingly read out the captions. Julia was indeed beautiful. She had stunning big round eyes, just as Uncle Charlie had said.

They must be as green as GG's and The Boomers.

A mop of frizzy hair sprouted wildly in all directions, and she had the most perfect mouth that Emily had ever seen, as if it had been Photoshopped: heart shaped and plump.

"Uncle Charlie, she really is so pretty, isn't she?"

"I told you, didn't I? You wait until you see the pictures of when she is older. She has just got more and more lovely as she has grown up. Mum loved making clothes for her, always running up little dresses. No more let down hems for Julia." Emily could imagine that and how lovingly her mum would have sewn them for her. *Like Aunt Cyn always did for me.* She glanced across at her bag, a patchwork of all those memories.

"Mum eventually learned how to cope with Julia's hair. Eventually! There are a lot of pictures with her hair all over the place." He slowly turned the pages, stroking Julia's hair in each picture. It did look somewhat untamed. "Mum's hairdresser wouldn't touch it and was so rude that Mum said she 'wouldn't darken their doors ever again'". Emily grimaced at his turn of phrase "By a stroke of luck, Mrs Stagg and her husband – farmers over at Brenchley – had done a stint of tobacco farming in Rhodesia, came back after drought bankrupted them, and she'd got involved with the workers' children and learnt how they did their hair into intricate little plaits. Mrs Stagg would come round, plonk Julia –" Uncle Charlie enacted the movement, "clutching Molly in one arm and Golly in the other – onto a kitchen chair and then she and Mum would crochet Julia's hair. Well, not crochet exactly, but that's what it looked like to me, constructing fancy creations. Julia sat there stock still in total silence as they tugged and tucked. Not a peep out of her even though they were tugging it quite hard." He turned the pages of the album. "Look – you can see the improvement as Mum got better at it."

"Is it okay if I take some pics of these? I'd love to show them to The Boomers."

"Yes, yes. Of course, although I don't really know what you're on about. Now let's carry on." Uncle Charlie turned the pages slowly, carefully examining every photograph. Emily was loving it and knew that The Boomers would be thrilled to see them, so she snapped away. Aunt Julia with Uncle Charlie, where Emily could see a glimmer of the old man in the young boy; Aunt Julia with Great Aunt Margaret and Great Uncle John; Julia with a kitten called Smudge; Julia clutching a black-haired doll, presumably Molly, and the other black doll; and Julia and Great Aunt Margaret with a cow labelled 'Daisy!' Julia's hair did indeed look much smarter as the photos went on; her face was permanently lit up with a delighted grin. More photos, Julia with a pony labelled Copper; Julia with Charlie and a blond-headed boy on a tractor; Julia with Charlie and the same boy around a birthday cake in the kitchen of this very house. In fact, the boy seemed to be in most of the pictures after that.

"Who is that?"

"Oh, that's Jolyon. You must have heard about Jolyon Pennington?"

"Yes, I have, but I'm not entirely sure where he fits in."

"Jolyon was my best friend from when we were knee high to grasshoppers. We both went to Lamberhurst School. We stayed best friends even when he went away to boarding school. The brother I never had. His family have a massive farm over at Lamberhurst, a thousand acres – not like our meagre two hundred. Very wealthy family, but he seemed to spend most of his time over here. I think his mother was a bit uptight. A great fellow. Julia took such a shine to him and they got on like a house on fire." Emily winced at the ill-advised phrase. "I think we all assumed that one day they would get married. Julia was so very disappointed when he married someone else. We had a big falling out over something. What happened, Cathy, that made it all go so wrong?" He looked distressed and Cathy stepped in.

"You had so much fun together as children, didn't you, Dad? You, Jolyon and Julia."

"We three got up to all sorts of mischief. Not always good, but always the three of us."

"Tell Emily some of the things you got up to, Dad."

He looked up at the ceiling, recovered his smile. "Well, we were quite naughty really. When it was hop picking, we were all expected to help as Mum and Dad worked as a pair going round tallying. They hired a bloke to work the oast just for the season."

Oast. She remembered the name from her research. *I must find out what an oast is.*

"We kids used to go round all the pickers and Julia would sing for them for a sixpence. She had ever such a good voice, an absolute natural." Emily nodded and smiled, remembering the cutting about the singing prize. "We used the sixpences to buy ice creams from the Italian chap who came round with his van. They were delicious, soft and creamy ice cream, nothing like those blocks we had at home, and they had a chocolate flake stuck in the top. The ice cream was twizzled into a cone." He twiddled his finger to create an imaginary ice cream. "That cone was essential because our hands were covered in hop pollen from picking, and it was so bitter to taste. We had it down to a tee. We slurped the top off with our tongues, crunched the stick of chocolate, licked the ice cream out of the cone, bit off the bottom and sucked out the rest. The dog always made an appearance, and he ate the tainted cones. Didn't seem to mind the bitter tang of it. Oh my, it was such a treat." Uncle Charlie smacked his lips.

"Why was that naughty though?" Emily was getting confused by this whole story.

"Ah, Dad thought we shouldn't take money off the hop pickers. When he caught us, he made us give it all back. But it wasn't half as bad as when we set the wood on fire. Have I told you about that?"

Emily couldn't help but feel alarmed, "No, you haven't."

He took a slurp of his tea and embarked on his next story. "Oh, Dad was furious. We were fiddling with a bonfire that Dad had damped down. We stirred it up by poking it with sticks and off it went. Whoosh." His arms shot in the air, his tea nearly went flying and a speck of spit landed on the photo album. "Totally out of control, started burning the trees and everything. Jolyon tried to put it out by filling his gum boots with water from the stream, but it was more than a little hopeless. I ran home, owned up to what had happened, and Dad called the fire brigade. We found it all ever so exciting when they came with their bells ringing and the firemen in all their waterproof gear, reeling out their hoses and squirting great jets of water into the wood." He chuckled and then his face suddenly became very solemn. "Poor Julia was clinging to Jolyon, completely terrified. She couldn't speak. Stayed silent for hours. She hated fire forever after that; petrified of it – wouldn't even sit near the fireplace. You could say it was almost a premonition, which makes the fire at Wayside Cottage even worse for her. And then something bad happened, a shocking fire, I forget now. Cathy, what was it about Julia and the fire?"

Emily was finding this all a bit bewildering as Uncle Charlie suddenly leapt forward into a whole new era, missing out decades. At least she knew about the two fires that he was referring to. She had the clipping of the one at Wayside Cottage and the one when Aunt Julia died.

Cathy caught Emily's eye, winked, and said, "Now, Dad, you were just getting going with your stories about when you were children. Do you remember that time when you rode out to Sparrows Green and you and Jolyon both fell off? Julia's pony, Copper, bolted and ran home with her clinging on for dear life. It must have been a long, long walk back for you boys. You're always telling us about that one." Uncle Charlie was suitably distracted.

"That was nothing. There was the time we found a pigeon that seemed very poorly. Julia felt so sorry for it that she decided to nurse it back to health. She kept it in her bedroom, fed it on cornflakes and gave it water in her dolly's tea service. It shat everywhere, pardon my French, and died under Julia's bed. Julia was bereft and Mum was so cross." Uncle Charlie snorted with laughter. Emily didn't find it quite so amusing.

Poor pigeon.

"It all sounds such fun. Where did Julia go to school?" Emily asked, trying to move the story onto more appealing aspects.

"She came to Lamberhurst with me and Jolyon. Mum used to pick up Jolyon and his brother Benedict on the way, shove all us boys on the back seat with Julia in the front out of harm's way. We always used to fight; it was what boys did in those days, all just a bit of fun. No seatbelts then either. However did we survive?" He grinned. "On Fridays, Mum would bring us all back to ours for tea and I remember the two boys, Jolyon and his little brother, Benedict, used to stay over quite often, top-to-tail in mine and Julia's beds with Mum shouting up the stairs for us to stop mucking about and go to sleep." He turned the pages until he reached one of Julia in her school uniform.

"She looked an absolute picture didn't she, her blouse so sparkly white? Mum always made sure we were turned out well. She was always having to patch up my shorts, darn my socks and once even," he burst out with a laugh, "oh dear, it does make me laugh, somehow Jolyon's tie ended up in with the calves who had a good chew on it, so she swapped the name tape from my tie to his so his mother would never find out." He reached for his tea, shaking his head; once he'd managed to get the cup balanced, he took a great swig.

"It wasn't all plain sailing though. In fact, there was a bit of a setback when she first started." He hesitated and stared into the distance, "She had settled in so well at home, but school was a different kettle of fish. Children can be very unkind and they hadn't seen a dark brown child before except in books. No-one had in Kent. It was very unusual. I most certainly hadn't. I don't think Mum and Dad had either before we adopted Julia. Everyone stared at her right from the start, and not in a nice way if you know what I mean." He shook his head. "They called her 'blackie' and kept asking to see her tail. It was in the war that the rumours started about black people having tails. What a lot of old codswallop that was. Mum said it was spread by the white GIs because they were so jealous of the attention that the black blokes got." Emily was horrified by such blatant discrimination and what people had said. "Mum said that the black GIs were utterly charming, really well-mannered and friendly whereas the white ones were brash and boastful, flashing their money around and treating the black ones like they were still their slaves. Disgusting."

So, GG had been enchanted by one of those 'charming, well-mannered and friendly boys' and she'd fallen in love despite the racial discrimination of others. True love. How romantic.

"Mum was so ingenious." He chuckled. "She did a very clever thing with the hens' eggs one teatime. We were having boiled eggs and soldiers, a favourite. Julia and I used to love collecting up those eggs. She was so gentle, lifting up the hens' light feathery bodies and drawing out their eggs. She was always so calm and quiet with all the animals." He looked lost in thought, shook his head, and sighed. "Julia."

Emily moved and falsely coughed to get him out of his reverie. "Anyway, Mum boiled up the eggs and when she put them on the table we were amazed. By some supernatural magic the eggs were all different colours. There was a white one, a red one, another one blue and the fourth was dark chocolate brown. 'Now Charlie, Jolyon and Benedict, you choose first. Which one would you like?'" Uncle Charlie seemed to be talking to someone imaginary. "I replied 'I don't know Mum. What's in them?' She chuckled, 'Eggs you nitwit.' I didn't get what she was going on about and chose the blue one just because it was different. Jolyon picked the dark brown one – I think he thought it might be chocolate. Mum turned to Benedict, 'Now, which one would you like, the red or the white?' Of course, he went for the red one because it was so outlandish. Julia got the plain white one. She was a bit miffed. 'Now you lot, on the count of three I want you to dig into your eggs.' Jolyon, Benedict and me always cut the top off with a knife but Julia liked to bash hers with a spoon and pick the shell off. I don't know what we were expecting but when me and Jolyon opened our eggs, we were a bit disappointed cos those magic, coloured eggs were all the same on the inside. Just eggs. We looked at Mum and I can remember her as if she were standing here, right now. 'Now you see – it doesn't matter what colour they are on the outside, they are all the same on the inside, just... like... us.' She grinned. Whenever anyone made stupid remarks to Julia like 'where are you from then, darkie?' we would just look at each other and say 'eggs.'" Uncle Charlie laughed uproariously, slapping his thigh. "We'd say eggs!" He carried on laughing for ages, shaking his head and muttering "Eggs!" He wiped his eyes. Emily waited for him to recover, thinking it was not so much funny as poignant and feeling very sad for poor little Julia.

"Even so, poor Julia did get so upset about being darker than everyone else. She kept washing her little hands over and over again to try and wash the colour off. She scrubbed them raw with the nail brush. And the teacher at school caught her chewing chalk during one lesson. Can you imagine that? She thought it might make her a bit whiter."

Emily gasped with horror. *How horrendous. Poor Aunt Julia.*

"Jolyon and I weren't having any of it, and every morning break and lunch hour we instantly swept her up. Jolyon was very popular at school – a good looking boy, known to be wealthy and a bit of a charmer even then, so it kept the nastiness away. It took some time before she had friends of her own in her class. Sad, really. What is it with people?" He sighed and looked forlorn. Emily assumed that it was a rhetorical question but nodded her head solemnly in agreement before wondering whether she should be shaking it instead.

"It's funny. No-one turns a hair nowadays if they see a black person in Tunbridge Wells, but it was very different then. It didn't really change until the Windrush when all the coloured people came here from all corners of the empire. It was in all the news, and then all the black groups became famous with their jazzy music and all of a sudden, we saw loads of Indians and Chinese and all sorts around the place." He went through the routine of precariously retrieving his cup and taking a big gulp of tea.

It was hard for Emily to imagine how it was before a multicultural Britain was the norm.

"Now, that reminds me. I remember when the Chinese opened a restaurant in Tunbridge Wells, must have been in the early sixties? Mum took us there with Nan. Dad didn't fancy 'foreign muck'." He chuckled. "Oh, but those deep-fried crispy noodles were like nothing we'd ever had before. And the waiters, they were all real, genuine Chinese people, all nattering away to each other in their sing-song way. They were teaching us to use chopsticks and the food was going everywhere. Oh, how we all giggled, sweet and sour pork balls shooting everywhere and staining the white tablecloth bright orange. It looked like a bloodbath." His whole body was wobbling and making the photo album bounce up and down as he laughed; he threw his head back showing the gaps where his teeth were missing. His teacup looked very precarious. "Oh my, those were the days."

Cathy clambered to her feet. "Talking of food, Dad, I think that's a good place to stop for lunch. Ham salad, I'm afraid, rather than anything exotic like chop suey." Emily was a bit embarrassed to reveal that she was a vegetarian, particularly as she was there on a farm surrounded by beef, pork and mutton on the hoof.

As Cathy helped Uncle Charlie out of the chair and to stagger into the kitchen, he looked back at Emily and said, "I hope there are coloured eggs to go with that ham." He laughed uproariously.

Emily picked up her 1/- notebook, grabbed her precious bag, followed them into the kitchen and took a seat at the table. An enormous mound of food was set before her. She tackled the pile of crisp lettuce and crimson red tomatoes, tucked into the slabs of delicious home baked bread – as delicious as Aunt Cynthia's. Slathering her slice with butter, she hoped she was doing her bit for the dairy trade and farmers everywhere to make up for not eating their meat.

SEVENTEEN

After lunch, Uncle Charlie declared that he was going for forty winks. Emily was a bit worried that she had worn him out, he seemed so fragile. He lumbered up from his chair and Cathy leapt up to put the kettle on the Aga for a cup of tea. Emily took it as an opportunity to shovel her unwanted ham, hidden under a lettuce leaf, into the bin. She hoped Cathy hadn't noticed.

With her back to Emily, Cathy asked "What sort of tea would you like? There's lemon verbena or mint growing just outside the back door, much favoured by vegetarians I believe, or you can have some good old PG Tips." Cathy turned round, a huge grin on her face, then laughed uproariously. "Oh, Emily, your face is a picture! Have the courage of your convictions. Stand up for yourself. Think of the prejudice that your Aunt Julia had to put up with. And her son, daughter and grandchild."

Emily blushed. "You're right, so much bigotry. And yes, I would prefer some mint from the garden."

Cathy went out of the back door and returned with a bunch of mint which she wafted under Emily's nose.

"It reminds me of GG's – that is, Aunt Julia's birth mum's – garden. And she grew lettuce and tomatoes too."

As Cathy turned to plonk the pickings into a mug Emily blurted out, "I didn't know she was black." She gasped. "Sorry, Cathy, that just popped out."

"I gathered that by the look on your face when you saw that first photograph. Why would you know? What difference does it make? And mixed race in any case."

Emily didn't know what to say.

"It's all very well you and I sitting here with our whiter than white privilege but imagine what it was like for them. Not only them either. Gran said that people used to spit at her when she was walking down the street and called her an 'n-word lover'."

Emily gasped. "Oh my God, people actually said that?"

"Nowadays, we have no idea how shocking it was for a white girl to have had sex with a black man. Just think of the stigma that your great grandmother must have experienced. Imagine the embarrassment of her parents. The shame."

Emily pondered and remembered the bit in Great Granny's letter where she had said about being kept hidden away. No wonder.

"My gran was instantly labelled as a slut for having a black child, even though she was clearly adopted. I grew up just seeing her as Aunt Julia, Dad's sister. I'm not sure when it was that I even realised that Aunt Julia was anything but Gran's daughter, I just thought that people were born in a variety of skin tones just as people had different coloured eyes. And Aunt Julia's were very green. It was only from other people's reactions to them that it ever dawned on me that Aunt Julia, Evie and Matthew might be different in any way."

Emily was confused, "Evie. Who is Evie?"

"Genevieve, Aunt Julia's daughter. A lovely name but it

was always shortened to Evie." Emily nodded, taking it in, and Cathy continued, "Even then it was Matthew's disfigurement that attracted most attention."

"Disfigurement?"

"Yes, Matthew was badly burnt in the fire at Wayside Cottage."

Emily reached into her bag for the cutting that she had on the fire and found her notebook instead, "Is it okay if I keep taking notes?"

Cathy nodded and continued, "He went through masses of plastic surgery but always looked different, poor chap. I was the same age as him so again I could see clearly that he looked odd, but he was just cousin Matthew. We played together right from when we were tiny tots. We were the best of friends and were in the same class at school. I think we did far more as families in those days and made our own fun in our homes. Anyhow, more of all that later, I'm jumping ahead of myself. Do you have any other biracial family members?"

"No, none at all. I come from a very proud, born and bred Yorkshire family. White, working class, but upwardly mobile. I've been reminded of the superiority of Yorkshire folk since the day I was born. God's own country and all that." Cathy chuckled. "This is going to be a huge learning curve for me. You?"

"Only Aunt Julia, her children Evie and Matthew, and Evie's son Daniel. Evie is relatively light skinned and has her mother's green eyes, and Daniel – well he's just Daniel. I guess you know about his problems?"

"Problems?"

"He was born with a cleft palate and a club foot, poor little lamb. All sorts of less visible birth defects too. It took ages before they could bring him home from hospital after he was born and he had to keep going back in for operation after operation to sort it all out."

More tragedy in Aunt Julia's life. Emily was sad to hear that and murmured, "Poor lad."

"He did get a much blonder version of the Afro hair, and it tended to do its own thing. One of his issues was hating people touching his hair, so it was difficult to tame it. People have this strange habit of wanting to touch Afro hair and they just go ahead and do it without asking, a bit like people wanting to pat a pregnant lady's belly. It made him very anxious."

Emily was worried. "You talk about him in the past tense. He hasn't, you know, passed away too?"

"Ah, I haven't seen Evie, Daniel or David for years. Or Matthew. Straight after Julia died, David bundled Evie and Daniel up and took them to a new job that he and Matthew got on a farm in Wiltshire. They basically ran away and have never been seen again. We did, of course, invite them to family events, always sent them an invitation in the post as it was the only way we knew how to contact them. We sent Christmas cards every year. I still do, I always will. Their number is ex-directory and they don't seem to use social media at all. I'm guessing that they're still at the same address that I gave you originally." Cathy shrugged and nonchalantly took a swig of tea.

Emily reached for her notebook and rifled through until she found the address that she had found on the electoral register. "There are so few Merripens in the country that it proved easy to find. Here we go." She turned the notebook round to show Cathy, who glanced at it.

"So, they are still there. They seem to have cut us dead. I'm not sure what it is that we're meant to have done. It's such a shame to have no contact at all with Julia's progeny."

Emily pondered whether she should admit that she had

already arranged to visit them. It seemed to be a sore subject. Perhaps David had some good reason for cutting ties. Maybe best not to say. She hesitated and the moment to say anything passed.

Emily stirred her tea pensively. "Great Granny's letter says that she wanted to marry her lover. They were secretly engaged but the army posted him elsewhere and he was never heard of again. Unbelievably cruel. I was a bit surprised. I thought it was because they weren't married but I am wondering now whether it was because he was black. Poor GG. How devastated she must have been."

Cathy nodded. "I read in Lucy Bland's *Britain's Brown Babies* that the GIs had to get permission from their commanding officer – always white – if they wanted to get married. In the States mixed marriages were illegal. Imagine that! And even though it was perfectly allowed in the UK, they would forbid it. Horrendous. You need to read up about it."

"I'd like that."

"I have some excellent books I can lend you, not just about the GI brides but the brown babies as well. That's what the media called them. And one that I particularly enjoyed was June Sarpong's *The Power of Privilege*. There are some great books out there."

Emily scribbled their names down in her notebook "It's funny how just in an hour or two your whole perception of race and colour can be turned upside down. I have a lot of thinking – and reading – to do."

Both sat in silence for a moment, sipping their tea.

"Anyway, I'll get down from my high horse now. Thank you so much for coming, Emily. This is just such a tonic for Dad, you have no idea. I haven't seen him as animated as this for years but... and it is a big but... I need to fill you in on some of the less frivolous and fun history before he comes back down."

"I want to know everything, I really do. I have a whole bagful of press cuttings about the fire at their cottage, about Julia's..." Emily hesitated, "inquest."

"I can cover a lot of that, but it is still a bit of a mystery. What do you know?"

Emily pulled out a fistful of papers from her bag, shuffled them like cards before spreading them out on the table in sequential order as if about to play patience.

"I have details of all the birth, marriage and death certificates and have drawn up a family tree and put them all in this spreadsheet." Cathy took the sheet of neatly laid out columns. "I suppose that they do tell a story in themselves, but it doesn't put faces to names and there is no sense of character. That's what is so frustrating about the whole genealogy science. It's so empty of a person's personality, disposition and essence. That's why it is so amazing to be here and meet you. Then I have the original note from GG." She put it in front of Cathy and smoothed it lovingly. "That's where all this started. This is the one I sent you a copy of." She paused and rummaged in her bag again. "And then there are the press cuttings from the *Kent and Sussex Courier*. Suddenly all their lives have come into being a bit more as I've dug into it. They've become people rather than just names. And I can't believe that I've now met Julia's brother in the flesh and seen all those pictures of her growing up."

She laid the printouts, that she had spent so long searching for, on the table in chronological order. Firstly, the story of the tragic fire at Wayside Cottage that had maimed Aunt Julia's son, Matthew. Aunt Julia was definitely right to have had her premonition about fire, it seemed, when those boys set fire to the wood.

The second was the piece headlined 'Babes in the Wood', the story about the frantic search and fortunate discovery of a ten-year-old Evie and a twelve-year-old Nicholas, son of Jolyon and Sarah Pennington. Emily could hardly imagine how frantic Aunt Julia must have been to have found her child missing.

The third and last was the tragedy of Aunt Julia's death. Emily shuddered to see the accompanying black and white picture of the burnt-out shell of a barn surrounded by fire fighters and their hoses. Emily suddenly twigged.

Jesus, it is the barn on the way in, the one that has been completely done up and turned into a house. I had no idea.

A shiver went down her spine. She had been admiring it without any sense of the disaster that had taken place: Aunt Julia's horrible death. She looked at Cathy, her face white.

"It's the barn, isn't it? The barn here on the way down the drive."

"Yes, it is. It's actually an oast house but barn suits just as well," Cathy replied softly. Emily tried to let it sink in. The place where Aunt Julia had perished. She felt tearful. By being here, seeing the barn, looking at photographs of Julia, suddenly her research had become real. Aunt Julia was a person with a personality and a face and a family who clearly loved her.

Emily changed the subject. "So, you call the barn an oast house. I have no idea what you mean."

"It's funny, isn't it? You grow up in a particular area of the country and take it all for granted. Kent is known as the garden of England and for centuries has grown all sorts of food stuffs including hops for flavouring beer. The hops are grown on tall frameworks made from tall poles and networks of wire which we called hop gardens. There are very few of them now, but you might get to see some on your travels. The permanent structure had strings looped through it for the hop vines to grow up. Every year the farm workers would 'twiddle' the hops to get them started growing up the strings." Cathy showed Emily the twiddling method with her hands.

"Oh, that's what the bit in the paper was going on about." Emily dug into her commodious bag to find the piece that she had uncovered in her newspaper archive search. "I'm beginning to get it now. But the oast house?"

Cathy continued, "I'll come to that. When it came to harvesting the crop, each string was cut and yanked down to lie across a canvas bin. The hop pickers would then pick all the hops into the bin. They were incredibly nimble and worked quickly, despite the amount of gossiping that went on. On a rotational basis the tally man would come along with a bushel basket and count each basket load into a big sack. Each picker would have the number of bushels that they had picked recorded in a book because they were paid on piece work. The canny old biddies – all very streetwise as they came from the East End of London – used to kick the canvas bin to fluff up the hops so that they maximised their volume."

Emily laughed.

"All the hops that had been picked were taken back to the oast house. They were all spread on the first floor of the roundel."

"The what?"

"The round tower. It's a drying oven with a slatted floor and a heater underneath blasting through hot air. The white cone on the top, the cowl, is the chimney to draw the air up through the hops to optimise their drying. After they were dried, they were packed into long tall sacks called pockets and taken away by the Hop Marketing Board."

"Well I never. Where I was brought up it's all been

about animal farming in the Peak District and stainless steel cutlery in the city."

"Dad stopped growing hops years ago. People like the Penningtons could afford to invest in the automated hop picking machinery but it wasn't worth it on such a small scale here. The oast was used variously as stables and storage. It became the thing to convert the redundant oasts into houses and that's what Dad did after the fire."

"So, the barn – the oast – who lives there now?"

"My brother, William, his wife Lizzy and their kids. Such an awful catastrophe has had some up sides. Not many, I must admit, but at least they have a wonderful home. It works well. Wills has a super comfortable house with all the mod cons and every conceivable environmentally self-conscious gadget that is going, and I live with Dad in the old cottage. I look after Dad and Dad looks after me, so we're set up for life."

"Haven't you ever left?" It came out rather rudely, Emily realised and blushed. "I mean, sorry... have you never married and had kids yourself?"

Cathy laughed. "Mum died when I was only fifteen, so I did rather feel an obligation to look after Dad, but when Wills married Lizzy and she moved in as 'lady of the house', I used it as an excuse to move out. I did have a long-term relationship, all very hush-hush. Like so many other couples in those bigoted days we pretended to be flatmates. It seems ridiculous now and I think if we had got married, we might have worked through things and still be together, but it wasn't to be. 2013 and the Same Sex Marriage Act were way too late for old 'dykes' like me."

Emily tried to hide her surprise. Cathy laughed. "Oh Emily, my dear, you have the most appallingly expressive face. You must learn to control it. But yes, yet another prejudice that I've had to fight against over the years. I think that's why I feel so strongly about what Aunt Julia had to go through. It's been tough but not as bad as she had it. But enough about me. Let's get back to our Aunt Julia." Cathy reached out and took the cutting of Aunt Julia's reported death. "Now, let's get down to it. What do you know?"

"Perhaps I'm reading too much into the newspaper reports but it looks, I don't know – unexplained, dodgy? I don't get the ligature reference and then what Sarah Pennington said..."

"Let me tell you what I know. I'll try and be as factual as I can so that you can understand what happened, but it's hard to stop my emotional connection from colouring the details. I can only give you an account from my own point of view."

"I quite understand." Emily looked eagerly at Cathy, pencil poised.

Cathy took a deep breath. "The facts are that Julia died in the oast, as you have now guessed, which was used as stables at the time. It had dry wooden beams and years of hay and straw debris scattered around. There weren't any horses or ponies by then; they were very much a thing of childhood. It burnt very quickly. By the time the fire brigade arrived, it was past saving. The fire is purported to have started from a Tilley lamp containing paraffin. There was no electricity in the barn. All the wires had perished years before, nibbled by rodents, which is why a paraffin lamp was always on the shelf just by the door to use for emergency lighting. Most of us, if we had any reason to go in there after dark, simply took a torch.

"Aunt Julia's post-mortem revealed, and I can quote verbatim, it's burnt into my brain, 'an upper airway free of soot, and carbon monoxide detected in the autopsy blood at 38%. Thoughts of rapid death in a fire were negated by the autopsy findings of trauma of the neck and tongue suggestive of ligature strangulation.'" Emily couldn't suppress a gasp, tried to cover her mouth with her hands. "You'd better write that down in full." Cathy waited for Emily to write down the exact words, prompting her to get them down correctly. "So, Julia was still alive, or maybe unconscious when the fire started. Her death was due to smoke inhalation and thermal burns with strangulation playing a secondary role. She was lying on her back when she died and had the characteristic pugilistic stance of a burn victim."

"Pugilistic?"

"Yes, like a boxer. The fire burns the flesh and then the muscles, which contract making it look as if the victim is in a boxing pose."

"Oh. How awful." It was suddenly becoming so horribly real for Emily. She couldn't take her focus away from Cathy's hideously descriptive portrayal of Aunt Julia's demise. Reading about it in the paper had been one thing but now that Julia had been brought to life through stories, photos and meeting her brother, she suddenly had a connection that made it feel personal.

"The ligature around her neck – a rope – was one of those blue plastic ones that get used on all farms for towing and tying on loads. It's made from polypropylene which is highly flammable. Burning polypropylene melts, producing drops of the melted flaming material, and that spread the fire. Drips would have fallen on to her clothes and flesh and she would have suffered horrific burns." Emily flinched. Cathy's eyes filled with tears. "We all pray that she was unconscious when her flesh was being burnt, but all of us are haunted by it and can't help but imagine how awful it must have been. Obviously, the parallels with Matthew were horrific. We hope that it wasn't a totally agonising way to die."

Cathy looked down at the table, closed her eyes and rubbed her forehead before continuing, "The obvious questions arose: was she trying to commit suicide by hanging herself, or did someone else put the rope around her neck, perhaps even to tie her in place? If the intention was for her to hang why did the ligature not do its job? The knot wasn't the correct one." A shiver went through Emily's body from her feet to her head leaving her scalp tingling. "Who started the fire? Was it a freak accident with the Tilley lamp being knocked over or deliberate? Who would have wished her dead? Could it have been murder?" Cathy put her head on one side and looked directly at Emily.

Emily held her look and tried to speak in a normal voice despite her feeling distraught, "Okay, so hence the inconclusive findings at the inquest. Suicide or murder?"

"One thing that I always wonder about is the rope. Each and every one of us present that night were involved in agriculture, so we were all experts in knot making, and would know how to make an effective noose that would have killed her straight away, except perhaps for Sarah." Cathy stared into space.

Did Cathy have suspicions about Sarah Pennington? Emily wanted to know so much more, so she prompted, "But the inquest must have gone into all that?"

"As you can imagine there were a lot of interviews, a lot of witnesses, a lot of explaining to do. But first of all, I have to tell you what I witnessed and who was there that night. I don't want to labour the point, but it just feels important to me that you know what it was like from someone who loved Aunt Julia. I couldn't help but wonder whether a fresh mind would see something that I didn't all those years ago. You can see why I don't discuss this in front of Dad."

Emily nodded in sympathy. "Absolutely."

"Julia turned up three days beforehand in one hell of a

state: wild eyed, hysterical. She just burst in through the back door. She was sobbing and pulling at her hair like a character in a silent movie. Very out of character. I was horrified."

"'What's wrong Aunt Julia, what on earth is wrong?' I asked her.

"'It's all my fault,' she said. 'I had no idea, but it is my wickedness that has brought shame and hell and everything that is awful to our family. Me. My fault.' She was literally beating her chest. I'd never seen anyone do that before.

"'Aunt Julia, please explain what on earth is happening. Can I help you?'

"'Baby Daniel,' she replied. 'Everything that is wrong with him, it's because of me. I can't bear to talk about it. I just had to leave. David is furious, rightly so, and Evie won't want to speak to me. I didn't know what to do so I left them and came home. Where's Charlie?'

"'He's just finishing up feeding the cattle. He won't be long.'

"'He's going to hate me too. Oh God, I can't stay here.'

"'Dad could never hate you, Aunt Julia.'

"'I don't know where else to go. It would be better for everyone if I was dead and had never been born.'

"I inadvertently shouted, 'No Aunt Julia, don't be stupid.' And then more softly, 'Sit down, calm yourself.' It felt odd talking to my aunt like that when I was such a naïve young thing, but it seemed to get through. She plonked herself in the left-hand chair, the chair you're in now, the place that she'd always sat since she was a child, her elbows on the table and her head in her hands." Emily couldn't help but adjust herself in the chair, the very chair where Aunt Julia had sat. "I placed a hand on her shoulder. She flinched. 'Now this is going to sound very trite but what I need to do is make you a cup of tea,' I told her. I busied myself putting the kettle on the Aga, getting out mugs and the teapot, ladled in a generous amount of tea – Julia needed something strong – and let the everyday clattering and clinking sounds soothe her. She started breathing deeply rather than sobbing. Then Dad came in and all hell broke loose again. Julia let out a shriek, jumped up, her chair toppling over with a crash, and threw herself at him.

"'Charlie, I can't bear it! I've done something so dreadful that I can never ever be forgiven.' She was almost howling like a dog. Dad wrapped his arms around her, squeezed her. 'Nothing can be as bad as all that now, can it?' Over her shoulder, he looked quizzically at me. I shrugged my shoulders. I didn't get what was going on. He stroked her hair and murmured 'Come on now, darling.' Kissed her gently, rocked her like a child and signalled to me with a flap of his hand to push off. Being an obedient daughter, I left them to it. I hovered in the lounge until I really had to start cooking tea and then I braved returning to the kitchen. Nothing more was said, and I was meant to ignore what had happened. That was that.

"Julia moved back into her old room which happened to be Wills'. Wills took it as the excuse he needed to move in with his girlfriend, Lizzy, now his wife. I had no idea what the plans were and whether this was going to be a permanent arrangement." Cathy shook her head and waved her hands as if to shut herself up. "Anyway, every night the phone would ring and ring. Dad answered it some of the time, I did when I couldn't bear to hear it ringing continuously. It was always David, Nicholas or Jolyon – never Evie – wanting to speak to Julia. But Julia didn't want to talk to them. It was very unsettling. Then, that horrifying night..."

Cathy paused and looked at Emily for the first time since she had begun. She was back in the present.

"I seem to live my life through the eyes of other people. I am the onlooker seeing but not really part of the action, never told what is happening and what people are thinking. That dreadful night..." Cathy shook her head slowly. "Anyway, the night of Julia's death. We'd just had tea. Ridiculous to remember so clearly but it was pork chops, mash and peas with onion gravy. Dad's favourite. Aunt Julia just toyed with hers. She was so distressed that she had lost her usual hearty appetite. I was scraping hers into the dog's bowl when the back door flew open and in came David. 'They're coming over.'

"'Good evening, David. So nice to see you after all this time. We didn't hear your car,' Dad said, rather sarcastically.

"'I parked by the oast.' He looked a bit taken aback by Dad's casual manner.

"Dad continued in the same calm way. 'Who? Who's coming over?' Julia was cowering in her seat. Silent.

"'Jolyon and Sarah. Probably Evie and Nicholas too once they get back from hospital visiting baby Daniel. They want a family pow-wow and since Mohammed won't come to the mountain...' he glared at Julia, '...the whole bloody mountain is coming to you.'

"'I'll just go, and you know... upstairs... for a moment...' Julia got to her feet, pointing at the ceiling and sidled towards the door. We all naturally assumed that she was going to the toilet until we heard the front door closing. She had legged it. David rushed across the kitchen to go after her but Dad stopped him in his tracks, grabbed his arm and pulled him back. I thought that David was going to hit him with the other, it was flailing so wildly. He was livid, I had never seen him so ugly. It was terrifying.

"'For fuck's sake, David. Let's just sort things out. We're too old to scrap like we did at the Elizabethan Barn all those years ago.' I had never in my whole life heard Dad swear, let alone use the f-word. I was shocked. He was glaring at David but said to me, 'I think it best if you go to your room Cathy. This could get tricky.'

"'Shall I go after Aunt Julia? See if she's okay?'

"'No, leave her be. She'll come back in when she's ready. She's probably gone to the oast. That's her secure hiding place.'

"The sound of a loudly revving car drawing up outside sent me scampering up the stairs to the sanctuary of my room. I peeped through the window without turning on the light and could see Sarah sinuously getting out of the car. She is like that, very serpent-like in all her movements, even in a time of crisis. Very snake-like overall actually. She had a cigarette on the go; she always has. I've never known anyone smoke as heavily as her. It's how she's stayed so thin.

"Jolyon clumsily got out of the driver's side, slammed the door and headed straight for the back door like a charging bull. Sarah dropped her cigarette and twizzled it under her shoe before sauntering after Jolyon. I stayed in my bedroom at the top of the stairs to listen. It was right above the kitchen, and I heard the back door open; it rattles in a particular way.

"'Right Charlie, where is she?' Jolyon was roaring.

"David responded just as loudly, 'She's bloody well not here, she buggered off as soon as I got here.'

"'Where's she gone?'

"'God knows.'

"Dad managed to get a word in. 'Good evening, Jolyon and Sarah. How lovely to see you so unexpectedly in my home.'

"'Sorry, Charlie. It's bloody rude of us to just charge in like this but we need to get a few things straight with Julia for the sake of all of us. If it is what we think, then for the sake of Evie and Nicholas we've got to get to the bottom of it, establish the truth. Jesus, what a mess. Obviously, we can't change what's happened to poor baby Daniel, but we've got to decide what on earth we do now.'

Emily didn't like to interrupt Cathy's story, but she was still confused as to what had happened to baby Daniel. Flicking back to her notes, she saw that she'd written about his cleft palate, club foot and other disabilities. *Need to check that out a bit more.*

Cathy continued, "Sarah jumped in with, 'You're just as much to blame, Jolyon.'

"'She's a witch. I didn't stand a chance.'

"Dad tried to stop things getting even more heated, 'Now for god's sake, just calm down all of you. What do you mean?'

"'She hasn't told you?'

"'I haven't a clue what you're talking about, but please just calm down. Come through to the lounge. Can I get you all something to drink?'

"Their voices petered out as they went through. I couldn't hear them in the lounge. I tried, even using the glass against the floor trick but it doesn't work with carpeting. So frustrating.

"Several things happened, and I can't exactly remember the order. The evening became a bit of a blur and afterwards everyone said that things occurred in a different order. Nobody could agree.

"I know for sure that Sarah went outside for a fag. Dad doesn't let anyone smoke in the house, particularly since Mum's lung cancer. I thought she went out several times; she says only once or twice. I could hear her walk through the kitchen each time: her high heels clacking on the brick, the distinctive sound of the kitchen door opening. On one occasion I swear I saw her walking down the drive towards the oast and walking around it as if to go in through the door, but she flatly denied it. Why did she do that if she had nothing to hide?

"At some stage in the evening I saw, and heard, a car draw up beside the barn alongside David's car. It stopped. The engine was turned off but the headlights stayed on. When the doors opened, the inside lights came on and I definitely saw Evie and Nicholas." She paused, looking stern. "I'm totally sure of that." She sighed. "Of course, the others and the police asked how I could possibly see who it was with the headlights dazzling my sight. I'm certain it was them. You can always recognise your own close family and friends from their shape and how they move, even at a distance. They disappeared into the dark, possibly into the oast house. Eventually, and I don't know how long they were lurking, they got back into the car and drove away. I thought it very strange that they didn't come to the house. Why wouldn't they? Why didn't they? Again, when questioned by the police, they denied having been there at all. Why? Did they go into the oast and talk to Julia? Another question mark.

"Dad, Jolyon and David all went out too, separately. I heard them each calling 'Julia?' from various distances. Dad and Jolyon, and possibly David too, would definitely have checked out the oast house because they knew it was Aunt Julia's favourite place to go and think. She always curled up and nestled in the hay and straw so it is possible that, as they all said, she was hidden in the dark and they didn't see her.

"We now get to the really horrendous bit. It was getting late. I had gone to bed and had eventually managed to get off to sleep despite all the drama. There was a sort of cracking sound like something really big breaking and the distinctive ping of shattering glass. In my dozy state, I couldn't think what it was and lay in bed listening with my eyes closed. When I opened my eyes light was seeping through my curtains, a very orange light like a sunset. I got up, curious but not particularly worried, opened the curtains and looked out. The oast house was ablaze. I instantly became wide awake with the surge of adrenaline that shot through me as I remembered Aunt Julia. Grabbing my dressing gown from the back of the door, and shoving on my slippers, I hurtled down the stairs and ended up in the lounge.

"They were sitting in the chairs and their faces all turned to look at me. Dad surprised, David and Jolyon looking angry, Sarah looking disdainful. 'The oast. It's on fire. Quick, call the fire brigade,' I told them. I was frantic.

"They all looked at me as if I was making it up. I dashed to the phone in the hallway linking the lounge to the kitchen and dialled 999, clumsily turning the dial on the ancient telephone because my fingers were shaking. Dad pushed past me and then the others, although I think Sarah stayed where she was. Or did she?" Cathy looked puzzled. "I gave the emergency services all the details. They asked seemingly stupid questions, needing to know who I was and my telephone number and just didn't seem to understand the urgency. I kept telling them to hurry up. They must have thought I was bonkers.

"Of course, we all must have been remembering the Wayside Cottage fire when poor little Matthew was so dreadfully burnt, and we all knew that the oast was Julia's favourite hiding place. The feeling of dread made me feel sick.

"As soon as they had finally taken down all the details, I ran, as fast as I could, out to the barn. Oh God, it was horrendous. The smell of burning, an acrid sickly stench, the thick pungent smoke. And it was so terrifyingly loud. Dad was dangerously close to the flames with a hose pipe in his hand. It was pathetic and made no difference at all. He was shielding his face from the heat. We saw later that his eyebrows had singed off. The rams that always live in that paddock were crowded against the far fence jostling to get away. David had moved his car to the end of the drive and was stationed there to guide the fire engines in." Cathy paused, staring into the distance, her eyes wide open. Emily could feel her heart racing in horror at Cathy's vivid description.

"In that situation, you are totally helpless and hopelessly useless." She shook her head, clasped her hands as if in prayer and lowered her head on to them. Emily, her heart pounding from the stark details of Cathy's ghastly account, thought it best to stay silent and waited for Cathy to speak again.

"The fire engines came eventually, making a racket from far, far away, but it was too late to do anything. The whole place had gone up like a tinderbox because it was basically an open space with centuries-old dried out wooden beams and floorboards and combustible hay and straw. I think Dad kept several of his farm potions in there too, including fuel for the mower and stuff like that. I suspect that some of the bigger bangs and crashes were those going up." Cathy raised her hands in a fountain and made a *pow* noise.

"The first thing the fireman asked was if everyone was present and correct. All the adults looked at each other, turning their heads time and time again to look at each other like a strange ritual. They didn't look at me. I think everyone knew then. One fireman said at the inquest that as soon as he arrived, he could smell that someone had died. Apparently burning human flesh has a unique odour." Emily winced in revulsion.

"It was Dad who finally voiced what everyone was thinking. 'Julia. We think Julia may have been in there.'

"'Are you sure?'

"'No. Yes. We'll go and search for her, but it is very likely.'

"Dad was weeping silently; his face was contorted, and I could see the tears shining on his cheeks." Cathy stroked her cheeks with her fingers. "They were lit by the fire. He organised us into two groups to look for her and suggested a planned route. Sarah immediately said she couldn't possibly go tramping around the fields in her high heels. She had a point but being in my slippers didn't stop me teaming up with Dad.

"We set off around the farm. I clung to Dad's hand. It was suddenly chilly and dark after the full-on heat and rage of the inferno. It was also very quiet. Every now and then Dad would call plaintively 'Julia?' He sounded like a cow when you take away her calf. It was horrible and haunting. I remained silent, fighting my own tears and trying not to let the sobs escape by swallowing them." Emily felt the quiet and the chill of the air and could feel her own tears welling at Cathy's eloquent description. She breathed quietly so she didn't interrupt.

"We could hear Jolyon and David doing the same in the far distance. Their voices held the same lack of conviction. Dad and I covered every inch of the farm's two hundred acres, at least twice. Like the forlorn cow, Dad's voice was breaking. My slippers and the bottom of my dressing gown were sodden.

"I'm sure that we knew she had gone, but there was the tiny hope that maybe when she'd left, she had gone further than the farm. Perhaps she would be hiding out in the woods where Evie and Nicholas had camped. Perhaps she had made her way back home. But I think Dad had recognised that particular odour too.

"By the time we got back to the barn, the firefighters

were damping down the last of the fire. Pungent smoke was still rising from the remains. It was difficult to see what had been there. Two of the brick walls still stood, a third jagged and leaning. The fourth, with the enormous double wooden door and a human sized mini door, had gone.

"The thought that Julia was in there was sickening. Unbearable. They couldn't do any further investigation while the place was still red hot. Maybe, just perhaps, she had escaped and run away. There was no sign of Jolyon or Sarah. The firemen told us that they'd driven off. There was nothing else to do but go back into the house. David was standing at the back door, his head in his hands. He was sobbing and keening. It was unspeakable, unbearable. His beloved wife." Emily felt cold. In just a few hours, Emily had got to know Julia as a real person. She knew now what she looked like, her face and personality. Hearing the graphic story from Cathy was so much harder than reading the bald statements in the papers when Julia had been a faceless stranger to her. Cathy continued, lost in the past.

"At that stage, I still hadn't got to the bottom of what the hell was going on. It didn't come out at the inquest. There was a conspiracy of silence. Each and every person could offer no reason that anyone might wish Julia any harm. All the questions revolved around who was where when, the comings and goings, and it was a nightmare with everyone saying different things. Families have secrets."

A cheery voice brought them back into the here and now and made Emily jump. She had been there, in the past with Cathy, feeling that catastrophe so intensely.

"Hello, love. Is Julia here yet? That was a nice little forty winks. I could murder a cup of tea." Uncle Charlie's choice of words made Emily cringe. She had been left hanging on a cliff edge with Cathy's story and felt exhausted.

Noticing her, Charlie said brightly, "Hello there. Nice to meet you. And you are...?"

"Hello, I'm Emily, Julia's niece. I'm here for you to tell me all about her."

Jesus, Uncle Charlie. What a time to wake up. What really happened? Had there been skulduggery?

EIGHTEEN

Uncle Charlie relaxed back into his armchair, teacup at his elbow, and beamed at Emily.

"Now, dear, what can I tell you?" Emily found it difficult to put Cathy's story behind her and start thinking cosy thoughts again.

"Well, Uncle Charlie, I have a very good picture of your childhood with Aunt Julia. It sounds idyllic. I would love to know how she met David, how he proposed, when they got married. Was it all very romantic?"

Uncle Charlie frowned. Emily was surprised as this was not the reaction she was expecting. "Well, you see, it isn't as simple as that. It never is. Julia is so beautiful inside and out that everyone who has ever met her falls under her spell. I did. I wanted to marry her." Emily jolted in surprise. Uncle Charlie noticed and looked rather put out.

I really must learn to control my face.

"Now, now, none of that, young lady. It's perfectly legal and there is nothing wrong in that. We're not biologically related. I love her, always have. Unfortunately, she sees me as a brother not a lover so that's an end to it." He harrumphed. "I won't be saying anything more about that." He turned away from Emily and took a long drink of his tea.

Emily tried to break through his sulk. "So, what about Jolyon? You said that you always thought that they would get married?"

Uncle Charlie took his time sipping his tea before turning back to Emily. "Yes, I did think that. He and Julia always talked about it growing up. I found it annoying because I loved her myself and saw him as a rival for her affections. When he went off to Agricultural College, he said that he would stay faithful to her, which he did. It wasn't while he was away that he let her down, it was here, right here, in Lamberhurst." He stabbed his finger on his thigh.

"Jolyon's parents put on an ever so fancy do for his twenty-first. Tent in the garden, disco, all the bells and whistles. I expected to be invited as an old friend, and an invite duly arrived, very posh card with 'At Home' written in fancy, raised type across the middle of it – but it was sent to just me, no Julia. I immediately questioned it with Jolyon. 'What's going on here?' Apparently, his parents vetoed Julia. They couldn't stand her being mixed race. They didn't want the embarrassment of having black people at their precious high society do; it would shock the neighbours and reflect badly on them. The bloody bigots had told Jolyon that if she was invited then they would call the whole thing off. They would have done, too. If Julia wasn't invited then I sure as hell wasn't going to go without her, so I declined, and not very politely either. It was never the same with Jolyon from that day on." Charlie harrumphed; Emily had noted he liked doing that but agreed with his sentiments.

"So, the story goes – according to who you hear it from – Jolyon was lavishing attention on Sarah Digby-Watson. A very suitable girl in Jolyon's parents' eyes: wealthy family, father something in the city, commuted every day from Wadhurst station into Waterloo. Others say it was the other way round or that because he couldn't have Julia he went on an absolute bender and got drunk as a skunk. It's always so difficult to find the actual facts in hindsight. Everyone swears their version is the truth." Emily could understand that, having heard about the apparent debacle the night Aunt Julia died. "What we can all agree on is that it was a shotgun wedding. Neither me nor Julia were invited to that either. I'd always thought I would be his best man and he mine. Sad really, a whole childhood friendship gone up in smoke." He sighed and shook his head.

Emily cringed at his use of the word smoke. Cathy's story was still pressing heavily down on her.

"To be honest, in my heart of hearts, I was delighted. With Jolyon out of the way, I thought that Julia would recognise her love for me. I felt a real idiot when I broached the subject, right here in this lounge, a cup of tea on the go, just like now. It was a bit sad because after that she kept her distance from me, avoided being in the same room alone, that sort of thing. I hated it. We've never really made our peace." It was clear to Emily that he had been besotted with Julia and that she was obviously very popular. It was nice to hear that she had been adored but sad that it had become awkward.

Uncle Charlie sighed and looked wistful, then reached for his cup and stared at the armchair opposite as if Julia might magically appear. He took a mouthful of tea, swallowing with a glug. "When is Julia coming, Cathy?"

"Not this week, Dad."

Emily had worked out that if she asked a question, it could help get Uncle Charlie out of his stuck record position. "So, how did she hook up with David?"

"Pardon, what do you mean?"

Emily realised he might not understand her modern parlance. "Sorry, I mean when did they get together?" She racked her brains for the old-fashioned term. "Step out together?"

Uncle Charlie nodded in understanding. "Well, he's quite a bit older than her, but as a farmhand he used to come along to all the young farmers dos. Nice enough bloke. Honest. Good cricketer. Very good looking in his gypsy way. Rumour has it that he was courting Sarah Digby-Watson at some stage but I think it highly unlikely. I can't see her going out with a farm worker, can you, Cathy?" He laughed. Emily couldn't quite see why it was so funny but went along with it and smiled encouragingly.

Cathy shook her head and smiled broadly. "No Dad, I can't."

"I also have a feeling that Julia thought giving her affection to David would smooth things over between us, make it less awkward. They looked good together as a couple. He's taller than her and she's very tall, those long, long legs up to her armpits. She's head and shoulders above me and Jolyon. Well, not shoulders, just head really. A handsome couple, as my mum would say." He looked into the distance with a happy smile, obviously recollecting Julia.

"When did they get married?" Emily asked. She knew the answer, but it was a good way to move the story on.

"Oh now, that was in 1967, wasn't it Cathy?" He roared with laughter and slapped his hands on his thighs. "You wouldn't know would you, love? You were still a twinkle in my eye. I'd have to check that with Julia but thereabouts. I bet it says in the photo album. Where is it, Cathy?"

"I'll go and get it, Dad."

"It was a fine old do, I must say. Mum and Dad pulled out all the stops. Fancy invitations, a tent in the ram's paddock behind the oast. David asked me to be his best man which was kind but also very hard. You have no idea what it's like watching the woman you love marry someone else. I stood there in Lamberhurst church at the chancel steps barely able to hold back the tears. Pathetic really. When they asked if anyone had any just cause or impediment, I had to clench my fists to stop myself saying anything. But what could I say? I had to stand there like a buffoon and pretend to everyone how pleased I was for the happy couple. What a prize idiot.

"Ah, here you are Cathy. Have you brought me a cuppa?"

"I've got the wedding albums, Dad."

"That's wonderful. I'm sure... er, um, would love to see them."

Emily took them from Cathy and opened the first page, carefully peeling back the tissue paper that seemed to be there to protect the photographs. She gasped. The tiny, black and white photograph she had found in the newspaper had been nothing like this. "Wow. Aunt Julia looks sensational. A bit like Beyonce. She is gorgeous, her figure, in that dress..."

Uncle Charlie looked at her quizzically. Was he wondering who she was or who Beyonce was?

"See, I told you Julia is beautiful. Mum made that dress, you know. She slaved over it night after night, sewing on lace and stitching all those tiny little pleats. She made the veil too, but they bought the tiara from Weekes, the department store in Tunbridge Wells."

"And is that your Dad with her? It must be, you look very like him."

"Oh yes. That's Dad. A fine figure of a man. He even

hired a morning suit for the occasion from Moss Bros. We all did."

Emily turned the pages and studied the pictures as they told their story. David, who was indeed very swarthy and handsome, a definite look of Poldark, was standing with a very youthful version of Uncle Charlie who had a mass of outlandish bushy hair, outside the church. There were images of the bride in the church porch with her dad; the bride walking down the aisle with a seraphic smile on her face, her arm tucked into her father's; the bride and groom saying their vows, looking lovingly into each other's eyes; the bride and groom kneeling in front of the altar; then together outside the church, first grouped with their parents then grouped with various unknown people. Then suddenly the pictures were of Uncle Charlie and David making speeches in a marquee with a stripy lining, and then the bride and groom cutting a cake. Emily took a picture of every single photograph.

"Mum made that cake too. Three layers of fruitcake. She's had plenty of practice over the years with the Christmas cake, so she did an excellent job. She was always very generous with the marzipan and the icing – the best bits in my opinion."

The last picture had the bride in a very short dress and big floppy hat accompanied by her new husband in very fancy chequered sports jacket and far too wide trousers, getting into an old sports car with confetti swirling around them. She recognised the drive and the house in the distance.

"I love that picture," Uncle Charlie said. "I think she looks like Marsha Hunt, don't you? It would look even better without David though." He cackled. Emily hadn't got a clue who Marsha Hunt might be. Suddenly his face fell and he looked mournful. "But where is Julia? She's meant to be coming." He looked at Cathy, getting agitated. "When is Julia going to be here?" Emily could see tears welling up.

Cathy suddenly piped up, "Right, Emily, it has been lovely to see you, but I think that is enough reminiscing for the day." She mouthed 'emotional' at Emily and inclined her head towards her dad.

Emily took the hint. "Absolutely. I must be getting off now. Thank you so much. I can't tell you how exciting it has been for me to meet you both." She rose to her feet, went and gave Uncle Charlie a hug. It was a bit awkward as he was sitting down but she hoped that he would realise, and remember, just how thrilled she was to have met him. "Bye then. See you later."

Oh God, how can I leave him looking so sad?

She gathered up her 1/- notebook and her miscellaneous papers, shoved them into her bulging bag and followed Cathy through to the kitchen.

"Thank you so much, Cathy. I can't tell you what this has meant to me. I've still so much to ask you both. Can I come back?"

"Of course. Now you've found us, I would hate for you to abandon us. How long are you here for?"

"Only a couple of days..." She was hesitant. Having not so far admitted that she was going to see David and Genevieve it seemed a bit too late to say anything now. "I'm off to see Sarah tomorrow. She's keen to talk to me about her friend Julia."

Cathy snorted loudly. "You're kidding me. I'd love to hear about that."

Emily wasn't sure what to make of that so just said, "Can I give you a ring so we can arrange something?"

"Of course. Now, off you go. Here are the books I was talking about, and I'll get back to Dad." Cathy gave Emily an enormous bear hug. Smothered once again in Cathy's ample bosom, Emily reciprocated warmly. She didn't really want to leave. Such lovely people. Her family.

"Thank you, Cathy. Thank you so much."

Rufus was lurking by the back door and joined her for escort duty again. She followed him back along the path to her car.

She climbed in and sat there for a moment, just trying to take it all in.

Why was Julia so upset? Why were Evie and Nicholas not telling the truth about being there the night of the fire? What had it all got to do with Daniel? And that Sarah sounded very suspicious lurking around the barn. What was she up to? So many questions. I need to find out the truth.

NINETEEN

Emily had learnt her lesson at breakfast, so she took her laptop with her when she headed out for tea.

She had booked a table at the Old Vine pub just across the road from her B&B. The waiter who showed her to her seat was a lanky, blond boy in super skinny jeans, a hideous plug in his ear, a long, hooked nose and pink uniform shirt; he looked like a flamingo.

As she took her seat, she obsessively looked at her phone for the umpteenth time that day to see if her mum had contacted her. At the very least a message of some sort, any sort, even if angry, would acknowledge that she knew about Great Granny's house.

She tapped in a brief message, "Met Aunt Julia's brother and niece today. Lovely people. Saw loads of pics of Aunt Julia. Amazing, Aunt Julia has GG's eyes!" Should she mention that she was mixed race? Probably better explained face to face.

The Boomers had told her not to phone as they wanted to hear the whole story all at once. It was probably a good thing because Emily hadn't got it straight in her mind at all. She used the time waiting for her Caesar salad – vegetarian version – to turn her notes into something more coherent. Swiping through her camera photos – she had taken lots of snaps of the family albums – she smiled to think that Granny and Aunt Cynthia would be thrilled to see pictures of their sister, even if her mum and dad weren't showing much interest.

The whole mixed race thing would be a bit of a surprise to The Boomers, that was for sure. She was feeling ashamed that she had reacted so extremely and had embarrassed herself in front of Cathy. What difference did it make to her perception of Aunt Julia? It definitely had, but Emily couldn't quite work out how. Cathy had been undeniably fair in pointing out that she had demonstrated a typical white privilege reaction. So confusing.

It had caught her on the hop, but it was amazing just how quickly she had absorbed the fact as she had got to know more about Aunt Julia. After everything that Uncle Charlie had told her about Aunt Julia as a small girl and all the prejudice that she suffered, Emily was firmly on the side of 'how dare they treat her like that'.

It was clear that Aunt Julia had had a wonderful upbringing. It was so reassuring that she had been adopted by Mr and Mrs Levett and taken into the bosom of their family.

Good phrase that... bosom of the family, very descriptive.

Emily couldn't help but think of Cathy's enveloping embrace.

In the photos of her joyful marriage to David, Aunt Julia looked very blissful as well as incredibly beautiful. It seemed that her marriage to David had probably been a happy one, but that whole section of her life had yet to be explored. Hopefully she would find out more when she visited David and Genevieve.

Julia had probably been a wonderful mum, but she

realised that neither Cathy nor Uncle Charlie had said anything much about that, nor about the fire at Wayside Cottage that had damaged Matthew. Emily realised she had learnt so much but suddenly found out just how much of the full story she still needed to uncover.

She certainly needed to find out more about Aunt Julia's actual death and realised now that Cathy had only told half a story. There was so much more to find out. Having spent so much time hunched over her laptop, Emily stretched her arms out to release her stiff shoulders.

Unfortunately, this coincided with the flamingo bringing her food, so her extended arms knocked the plate out of his hands. It crashed to the floor followed by the sudden silence that happens in these situations. Everyone turned to look. Emily blushed. "I'm so sorry. Really, I am. Sorry."

The flamingo flicked his floppy hair behind his ears and said through gritted teeth, "No worries, I suppose I'd better get you a fresh one and something to clear that up," Emily saw him raise his eyebrows up and down as he flounced off dramatically.

How rude. And he tells me to have no worries? I have even more worries now, what with my mum not speaking to me, my dad maybe not being my dad, being dumped by Dylan, and now the whole mysterious Julia situation. There is more to all this than meets the eye.

Emily was eager to meet Sarah Pennington the next day, to find out what had really happened.

TWENTY

Emily went down to breakfast the next morning armed with one of Cathy's books. The room was empty so she decided to tuck herself into the farthest corner. Unfortunately, she tripped over a chair as she squeezed past the tightly packed tables and staggered into the buffet. At that very moment the cheerful waitress, Katie, bounded in, looked at Emily spread-eagled against the pastry section and bit her lip, clearly trying not to laugh.

Emily struggled upright and managed to seat herself in the nearest chair. She took the menu and pretended to study it. Katie eventually asked, "What would you like today?" It came out a bit strangled.

"The same again please: decaffeinated coffee, scrambled egg and brown toast."

"No worries."

I wish everyone wouldn't keep saying that.

Katie returned moments later with the ubiquitous tin teapot. Emily noted that the waitress hadn't asked any questions this morning, so she decided to ask a few herself to prove she wasn't completely self-obsessed. "So have you worked here long?"

"No. It's a holiday job. I'm off to uni in September."

Emily was surprised how much this information changed her view of Katie, having taken her for a very middle-of-the-road country bumpkin with her freckles and rural accent. "That's great. What subject?"

"PPE, politics, philosophy and economics."

Emily tried to hide her surprise. "Sounds interesting. I read chemistry at Edinburgh." Emily was proud of that, and realised it showed in the way she said it. "So, where are you going?"

"Cambridge."

Unexpected. Emily's eyebrows shot up. So not just any university. "Wow. That's amazing. Um. Well done." It came out as a bit patronising, and she blushed.

Well that certainly took the wind out of my sails. I must learn not to make snap judgements about people. I wonder if the flamingo is going to Oxford.

Katie seemed to hear a call from the kitchen and hurried away, saying, "Excuse me." Emily pondered for a moment and then got stuck into *Britain's Brown Babies.*

Breakfast out of the way, Emily was so keen to pick up where she left off with Cathy that she phoned before leaving for her visit to Sarah Pennington.

She smiled as she imagined Cathy in the kitchen dashing to answer the phone in the hall. It rang for a long time and went to the answerphone. Emily wasn't prepared for this eventuality so garbled a message.

"Hi, it's Emily. Thank you ever so much for yesterday and I was just phoning to see when I can come again. I'll try again later. It's Emily by the way. Did I say that? Don't know. But it is. Thanks."

Having checked WhatsApp, and with still no message from her mum, Emily pulled on her cagoule, hitched her bag over her shoulder and dashed through the rain to Granny's car. She keyed into the sat nav the name of her destination: Willicombe Park, Pembury Road, Tunbridge Wells.

The sat nav directed her down a rabbit burrow of a lane but she was on her way. Emily was grateful for the sat nav lady's clear and concise directions because the rain made it hard for her to see where she was meant to be going. It was unseasonably dark, partly because of the rain clouds but also the huge number of trees overhanging the lane blocking out the light. Kent seemed to have so many more broad-leafed woodlands compared to Yorkshire. Same country but such unfamiliar scenery, houses, farm buildings and accents.

Emily diligently followed the sat nav's directions through a maze of unnamed lanes, past buildings with the same pointy hats as at Oak Tree Farm, clapper boarded farmhouses, and caught glimpses of little fields through gaps in the hedges. Suddenly, Emily came to a crossroads where the country turned abruptly from trees and fields into a townscape of modern houses along a straight road with unnatural planting and concrete parking spaces.

"This must be Tunbridge Wells."

She crept through urban streets and then more genteel roads with tall Edwardian townhouses either side, all very grand and identical. Turning randomly right and left as directed, the sat nav suddenly announced that she had arrived at her destination. A sign at the end of a short drive stated 'Audley Willicombe Park retirement village'.

Turning into the entrance revealed an enormous old white mansion nestled amongst a myriad of modern buildings.

Parking next to the palatial front door, Emily got out of the car and tried to work out where in the maze of modern additions Beech Court might be located. It was raining quite heavily so Emily sheltered under her black cagoule as she looked at a useful set of signposts pointing out the names of the various units.

I hope no-one is watching, I must look like a bat out of hell.

As directed, she followed a tarmac road around the corner of the mansion, past an enormous greenhouse that seemed to be tacked on to the side of the building, and scurried along the length of the house, dodging puddles. The house was huge. At the other end of it she found another useful sign pointing to a square block of flats, also rather out of keeping with the glamorous house, with a big brass sign saying 'Beech Court'.

Sarah Pennington gave her address as Beech Court, but she can't be occupying this whole block just by herself, surely?

Emily pushed open the commonplace front door and discovered a list of residents and their flat numbers. She trailed a wet finger down the list to establish which flat Sarah Pennington was in.

I wonder why she left that important fact out? To make her address sound posher?

Emily removed her cagoule, flapping it to get rid of the water, and followed a pine disinfectant smelling corridor until she found the right number. There didn't appear to be a doorbell, so she rapped on the door of the flat. It swung open creepily. She craned her neck around the half open door to peep into a very small hall.

The smell that had followed her along the corridor was instantly overpowered by something very citrus and lavender. It rang a bell in the deathly silence.

GG's Blue Grass? A good omen. Perhaps that's what all nice old ladies use.

"Hello?" Emily called tentatively. Silence. She tried again as loud as she could. "Hello?"

An ethereal distant voice, a bit gravelly, called out, "Come in and close the door behind you." She did so and followed the direction of the voice into a living room.

The room was a strange combination of dull magnolia walls, a dubious looking beige carpet, every version of floral fabric jumbled together on cushions, stools, and curtains, and antique wooden tables smothered by silver photo frames jostling with pottery knick-knacks.

A froth of white hair rose above the back of a rose patterned armchair facing the window.

These bloody roses are following me everywhere.

"Hello, Mrs Pennington. I'm Emily."

Nothing. She took several tentative paces forward and cleared her throat noisily. She didn't want to terrify the poor old dear to death.

"Hello, Mrs Pennington?"

The fuzz of hair jiggled alarmingly. Emily cringed.

Bother. Just what I had tried to avoid. Poor old lady will be alarmed.

She padded purposefully across the boring carpet with an eager, friendly smile on her face, nearly tripped headlong over a very low footstool but brilliantly recovered her balance before planting herself in front of the chair.

Her smile disintegrated when she caught sight of Mrs Pennington. She was stick thin and her face was like a cartoon parody of an old lady, with deep wrinkles and heavy lines drawn on for eyebrows. She wore an immaculately tailored suit with a navy velvet collar. It contrasted horribly with yellowed skin drooping from her face which was wobbling as she chewed vigorously. The layered bags under her eyes sagged, revealing a rather revolting crescent of red flesh. Her brown eyes, almost black, were super magnified by prescription lenses. She stared, bolt upright, glaring up at Emily, her lips chomping, twitching and dancing, and her wattle waggling. Emily felt queasy.

What is she doing? How weird.

Emily recovered her smile. "How lovely to meet you." She stooped to offer a wet hand to the seated hag and received a waft of Blue Grass.

This old woman is such a complete contrast to my lovely memories of a rosy cheeked GG.

The papery dry handshake was disconcertingly strong and withdrawn rapidly.

The wizened mouth stopped chewing for a moment. The woman stretched her alarmingly thin lips into a leer, then continued to chomp in a rather perturbing way while staring fixedly somewhere between Emily's eyes. Emily couldn't think what to say next so just smiled again. The silence, broken by the slushy mastication noises, was uncomfortable.

A croak arose from the old crone. "Well, my dear, here you are, what do you want to know?"

Emily jumped and tried to sound like a nice friendly young girl who was not horrified by the sight of this old woman and her extraordinary chewing.

Don't judge by appearances, Emily. You've been doing enough of that already today with Katie. She's probably just a lovely old dear.

"May I sit down?"

"Yes, yes." Chomp, chomp. One hand waved imperiously at a chair some distance away as she covered her thin lips with the other to smother a rasping cough.

Do I move it closer or sit far away? Where do I put my soggy cagoule?

Emily compromised by pulling the delicate embroidered chair forward a metre or so then perched on it, hoping it would take her weight. She leant towards Mrs Pennington, preparing to be charming but not knowing how to pitch her voice.

"As you know from my letter, I am a girl on a mission," Emily began. Mrs Pennington's head stretched towards her like a tortoise. "You can imagine my surprise when I learnt about Great Granny's... um... indiscretion." Mrs Pennington sniffed, flicked her chin in the air and her drawn on eyebrows wiggled. "I understand that my Aunt Julia was a contemporary of yours, a friend?" Mrs Pennington's head nodded jerkily. "So, I've come to see what I could find about my aunt to make her more real, so we can get to know her and to meet my blood relatives. I would love to know what you remember of her. You know, any stories, what she was like..."

"I see." Silence. Uncomfortable.

"So, I thought I could ask you some questions about Aunt Julia. May I take a photograph of you and take some notes?"

Emily bundled up her damp cagoule, inside out, and put it on the floor under the chair next to the heap that was her precious bag. Then she retrieved her phone and gestured with it at Mrs Pennington. The old woman shimmied in her chair, took off her spectacles, pushed an imaginary piece of hair from her face and looked at the phone, a small friendly smile playing on her thin lips. Her eyes lit up. She looked quite human. Emily took the photo, murmured her thanks and rummaged for the 1/- notebook and pencil in her voluminous bag, then flipped through the pages to the first blank one.

"You've been busy. Who else have you interviewed?" Mrs Pennington craned her wrinkled neck and replaced her glasses as if to read Emily's notes, even though she must be too far away to see anything much.

"My notes are mainly my research before I came to Kent. I've created a timeline from the newspaper cuttings and births, deaths and marriages, and I've noted down everyone's addresses, that sort of thing. But I have been to see my aunt's brother, Uncle Charlie, and had a long chat with Cathy, his daughter."

"Not a real brother, dear."

"Yes I know, but to all intents and purposes..." Mrs Pennington shrugged dismissively. "He was lovely and told me all about their childhood. It sounded so happy – playing on the farm, riding ponies and getting up to mischief." Mrs Pennington nodded but made no comment, so Emily continued. "Uncle Charlie told me all about him and Aunt Julia being brought up with Jolyon as if he were another big brother, how close they were. Apparently, he always assumed that Julia would end up with Jolyon but, as you know, she married David instead." Emily paused as Mrs Pennington's eyebrows shot in the air.

Oops. Must have said the wrong thing. Drat! Silly me, Jolyon married this woman, Mrs Pennington. Tactless. Well done, Emily.

Emily backpedalled quickly. "But of course, Jolyon married you, and you had your son. And then..." Emily glanced through her notes, "Nicholas! Well, he married Aunt Julia's daughter, Genevieve, my first cousin..."

Mrs Pennington was working her jaw and twitched her lips, pursing them like a dog's bottom.

"She was a black witch." Mrs Pennington spluttered, and out flew spittle and a lump of chewing gum.

Emily was so shocked that she gasped loudly.

What the...?

So much for the Blue Grass being a good omen. "Okay." Emily took a deep breath. How the hell was she meant to respond to that, and what should she do about the blob of gum that was glistening on the carpet at her feet?

I think I'd better ignore that.

"So, you didn't get along very well with Julia then?"

Mrs Pennington growled, "You could say that."

"Um, so why don't you tell me your side of the story. I would welcome hearing it."

I think?

Emily pinned her smile back on and poised her hand to show that she was ready to write something.

Mrs Pennington stared into the distance in a trance. Emily wasn't sure quite what to do, so she cleared her throat to remind the old woman that she was there. Had she noticed that the gum had flown out?

"Chewing gum is so very common," said Mrs Pennington, glancing at the floor. "My mother would have been horrified to see me chewing it, but they won't let me smoke even though I am purportedly in my own home. I have smoked all my life and chewing the gum is the only thing I can do to keep up my nicotine levels. Even so I just feel so out of sorts... so bad-tempered all the time."

The Boomers would agree about chewing gum being common. Perhaps the nicotine dependency was the cause of that vile outburst?

"So much for 'make yourself at home'. I paid a fortune to buy this flat and live in this terribly smart retirement village. It really is a magnificent set-up here, very genteel. It even has a spa and an on-site restaurant. Yet I must go right to the bottom of the garden and hide in the bushes like a naughty schoolgirl to smoke, and even then, the staff tick me off when they find me. But the gum costs more than the cigarettes and it really doesn't hit the mark. Put it in the bin, dear."

Emily eyed up the blob of gum and wondered how to pick it up without touching it. The thought was revolting, but she was worried that Mrs Pennington might be offended if she were to openly show her horror.

Oh bugger, I can't do this discretely. I'll just have to go for it.

She rummaged in her bag, feeling her way around until she found her pack of tissues. She took one out with a flourish like a conjuror, bent over and snatched up the globule, scuffed up the tissue and without thinking, popped it back into her bag.

I'll deal with that later.

Mrs Pennington looked shocked.

Oh my God, what did I just do? I shouldn't have done that. I should have asked where the bin is but it's too late now. This is so awkward and the old bat is making me feel so uncomfortable. That black witch remark...

She would have liked to leave then and there but if she was going to find out more about Aunt Julia she was going to have to ignore the weirdness of this clearly peculiar old lady. She decided it would be best to be kind, ignore the whole witch outburst, and maybe get some real nicotine into her to make her a bit more amenable. "We could always go for a walk in the grounds so that you can smoke if you were to wrap up well. It was raining when I arrived."

"Wrap up well? I am not a child!"

Emily cringed. *Oh, bugger. Wrong again.*

"I'm so sorry. I didn't mean it to come out like that."

Mrs. Pennington just looked at her with a disturbingly neutral look on her face; her jaw was sagging, and her unblinking eyes looked particularly terrifying magnified through her glasses. Still staring at Emily, her twig-like hand slithered to the side table in search of more gum. Emily noted that her nails were well manicured into coral red almonds. Unfortunately, the colour clashed with the yellow smoker's fingers.

"Would you like tea, coffee, or something peculiar in the lesbian tea line like all you young seem to want these days?"

Does she think I'm a lesbian? Why? Because I've been talking to Cathy? Does she even know about Cathy?

"No, I'm fine, thank you. I have my water." She smiled and patted the bag at her feet as if it was a cherished pet.

Emily turned back to her 1/- notebook, the pages covered with her untidy writing.

"Look, I am sorry. I haven't made a very good start, have I?" Mrs. Pennington slowly shook her head, her saggy wattle following just a beat later. "I really am desperate to find out everything I can. Why don't you start at the beginning when you first met Aunt Julia and just tell me all about it and why she... upset you so much?"

Mrs Pennington sat back and took a deep breath that rattled alarmingly in her chest, coughed heartily, and began.

"We all fancied Jolyon. A blond god. So charming. Handsome and fit. He always seemed to be taller than he was. I'm not sure that he even hit the six foot mark."

This is about Jolyon not Julia, but whatever, Emily thought, and dutifully noted it down anyway.

"I first met him at school in Lamberhurst when he was a very small boy and I was just a little girl. We were in the same class, and I noticed him straight away. Even as a five-year-old he had this air of supreme confidence and charisma which attracted everyone – boys, girls, and teachers – towards him." She stopped for a chew on her gum.

"That's where he first became best friends with Charlie. They were inseparable. I suppose that both being farmers' sons they had a lot in common. The fact that Jolyon's father had an acreage ten times that of Charlie's never really came into it. Not even when they were old enough to see the chasm between their situations and social standing. They were definitely the top dogs in the class, and as they went up the years they were looked upon as the 'in crowd'. If they deigned to speak to me, I was giddy with delight at being favoured. I yearned to get on their table at lunch to be close to them; they always seemed to be having the best time. Instead, I ended up next to a short fat girl, Penny Parsons, who smelt of stale digestive biscuits. She was always in perpetual motion, swinging her legs – they were too short to meet the floor." She paused, looked pointedly at Emily's legs, reached for her teacup, lifted it shakily to her thin lips and took a sip. Grimaced. Coughed. Spat out her mouthful of tea, including the gum, into the cup.

Emily shivered.

Oh, so gross. Yuck.

"It is odd that we were all there at the same school, all the main cast members of Julia's story. It was Julia's story, you know. She was the star, we were merely the supporting players to her drama with the big finish. Even David was there, although two years ahead of us and an unknown 'big boy' who wouldn't deign to speak to us little pipsqueaks."

Mrs Pennington put her head back, closed her eyes.

Oh God, she isn't going to go to sleep is she? At least she was getting on to Aunt Julia.

She started speaking again, her eyes still closed. "When Mr and Mrs Levett adopted Julia, Jolyon, Charlie and I were all in our third year of school. She, Julia, came from here. Did you know that?"

Emily was confused. "Um, here? What do you mean here? Tunbridge Wells?"

Mrs Pennington's eyes flashed open and gave Emily a withering look. "Here. This very place. It used to be a children's home called Saint Christopher's, a Doctor Barnardo's home."

So, this is the place that I found on the internet and Uncle Charlie was telling me about. Really? Incredible! I must look at the house again on my way out and take photos.

"That's amazing..."

Mrs Pennington continued as if Emily hadn't said anything. "They took in a lot of bastard babies during the war, as well as many evacuees. I don't know how many negro babies like Julia they ended up with." *Oh, I don't think you are meant to use the word negro these days, it's racist.* Emily thought of interrupting but thought that it was just an old lady's oversight. "Of course, it didn't have all the bungalows and houses around it. It was mainly just the house and extensive lawns. I find it a bit ironic, me ending up at the place where Julia started out."

It was hard for Emily to imagine. The place had been transformed and looked like a housing estate more than anything else, except for the crazily enormous house. She was trying to reconcile it with the description of the place that Uncle Charlie had talked about when they collected Julia.

"Anyway, that doesn't have anything to do with my recollections of Julia. Where was I?"

"You were saying that you were all at the same school."

"Yes indeed. Benedict, Jolyon's little brother, had just started in kindergarten. Julia came to the school sometime after she was taken in by the Levetts, but by then it was the middle of a school year, which can be an awkward time to start. All the friendship groups have been firmly cemented by then; all the little girls going round together holding hands, the boys fighting and jostling. Benedict was teamed up with a gang of naughty little boys who spent their time teasing the girls and playing kiss chase. He didn't want anything to do with Julia at first. She was just another girl and a very strange looking one as well.

"I remember her arriving on the first day of term led by Mrs Levett, her dark brown hand so incongruous wrapped in Mrs Levett's pale fingers. We were all fascinated by this little savage, for that is what we had been brought up to believe that all black people were in every story that we had ever read. *Little Black Sambo, Ten Little Nigger Boys...*"

Whoa! "You *cannot* say that!" Emily said. She felt a hot flush of indignation.

"I just did." Mrs Pennington's eyes opened and gave such a venomous, arrogant look that Emily was stunned into silence. "Anyway, we were apprehensive of that squiggly hair, her dark skin – she was very dark for a half-caste. She was just so different, otherworldly, and not like the rest of us. It didn't help that she had snot trickling from her nose." She snorted and pulled at her own nose and puckered her lips. "To be completely honest, I think I found her rather repulsive. At break times, I would see her sitting all hunched up, gnawing at her nails and looking rather feral."

Emily's mouth hung open at the bile that was dripping out of Mrs Pennington. It was vile and hateful. She had never met such an outright, bigoted racist in her whole life. It trapped her in the most awful dilemma.

This is appalling. Should I leave right now? But I want to know more, and she can tell me so much about Aunt Julia. But really, can I put up with this?

Emily's whole body was rigid.

"In retrospect, the poor child was probably traumatised, but we were all brought up in those days, as children of the empire, to consider negroes as a bit simple. I certainly presumed that she was retarded." Emily winced. "I don't think the other children in her class were very kind to her. They used to complain that she smelt sickly sweet and rather unpleasant. She suffered the usual things of unfriendliness: other people not wanting to be her partner, not wanting to hold her dirty black hand. They would ask silly questions like 'do you eat bananas' and 'where do you come from' and laugh uproariously when she said 'Lamberhurst'. She wasn't bullied as such, just stared at, and kept at a distance."

Emily was tingling with anger, her fists clenched. All the language of hate.

This is disgusting. Can I really take any more of this abhorrent vitriol?

A pathetic little squeak of "Please, I don't think..." was all Emily could manage. Mrs Pennington stared at her, a triumphant look on her evil face.

She's bloody well loving this. Well, I'm not writing any of this awful stuff down in my notebook.

"It didn't take long before Charlie and Jolyon realised what was going on and took on the role of bodyguards. The boys kept her between them and let her join in with their games as if she was a boy. Being surrounded and honoured by the 'in crowd' gave her a cachet that she wouldn't have ever earned just being herself. It was annoying for us aspiring acolytes because it made them harder to befriend without having to suck up to the little black picaninny too."

Emily thought she was going to lose her rag. Nobody used such hateful words today, surely. How could this hag come out with such detestable sentiments and expressions? Emily spluttered but no words came out. Mrs Pennington stared out of the window, away from Emily.

Emily's head suddenly exploded, she stood up and snarled, "That is enough." Mrs Pennington lazily turned to look at her, cocked her head on one side and brushed an imaginary piece of dust off her skirt. "Seriously, I am leaving. You can't talk about anyone like that. It is..." *Racist, inhuman, deplorable.* "...unacceptable."

Mrs Pennington shrugged. "Well, that is entirely up to you, dear. You wanted to come. You asked me to talk about Julia, and it now seems that you don't want to hear about her at all." Mrs Pennington smiled, like a crocodile, with no warmth; her eyes were steely. "If you leave now you won't find out things that only I can tell you. I've only just begun. There's so much more."

Emily was completely unsettled. *I do need to know about Aunt Julia. This is my only chance, but can I put up with that... with that...* She looked at Mrs Pennington who was sitting calmly, her hands folded neatly in her lap, her photograph pose, looking innocuous.

"So, are you going or not?" Mrs Pennington asked smugly.

Emily sighed. *I cannot walk away now.* Her mind made up, she sat down. "No." It came out as rather sheepish.

Mrs Pennington looked at her with a sneer. "So may I continue?" Emily nodded and tried to smile.

I am so feeble. I should have just left but after all Cathy's disclosures, and what she didn't say, this revolting woman must know what really happened.

"When Jolyon left to go to prep school, Benedict took over and became Julia's protector alongside Charlie, but by then everyone was getting used to her. I think she even had some friends in her class other than just having to be with Benedict. The initial shock and novelty of having a black girl at school had worn off, and our attention was moved on to the next freak to come along. An albino girl with thin white hair, transparent-looking skin and pink-rimmed eyes hidden by dark glasses. Children are rather horrid. Actually, I don't think they get much better when they grow up." She coughed again, a nasty rasping sound.

Emily shuddered. *Actually, it is you who is absolutely foul. What a bigoted bitch. I hope to God that she's going to tell me something that's of any use at all.*

Mrs Pennington continued staring over the garden as she waffled on, her hands fiddling and picking at her cuticles. Such a relief for Emily not to have to catch her eye. If she could see the thunderous expressions clouding her face, she would soon understand what Emily was thinking.

"After prep school, Jolyon went on to a boarding school in Canterbury, King's – frightfully fancy and a hilarious uniform with wing collars. He was so proud of it, silly chump. He was only at home for the holidays when he seemed to spend his time out on the farm with his father, the firstborn son ready to take over. As a teenager, he occasionally ventured out for young farmers events where he was feted and adored from an early age. We all went to the young farmers dos. There wasn't much else going on in such a rural area. I used to watch him from afar, really fancied him. He was a clean living boy, drank very little; he got into real ale and didn't smoke, unlike the rest of us. That's when I started smoking. Smoked ever since. Such a fuss they make about it nowadays; it hasn't done me any harm."

Emily frowned, wondering how she couldn't see what smoking had done to her: the deep chasms around her lips, the papery yellowed skin, the unhealthy boniness, the horrible cough. Emily tried to get the story back on track. "What was Jolyon like?"

"A gentleman. Beautifully mannered. I don't think I ever saw him drunk and out of control like the rest of us were after a lot of booze and partying." She coughed for a few minutes until she had found her voice again. "He wasn't that bright, didn't do too brilliantly at school. Scraped a few A Levels, enough to go on to Cirencester

Agricultural College like his father and grandfather before him. Farmers through and through." She jerked her chin in the air; her wattle wobbled.

"Charlie went to Wye College while Jolyon was at Cirencester. They were sowing their wild oats there, we presumed. Jolyon never showed any interest in girls at home. If he wasn't working with his father and the farmhands, he was just hanging around with Julia and Charlie. She was like a sister to him, I thought – wrongly as it turned out." Emily leant forward, rifled through her bag for her reusable bottle, took a swig of water. Mrs Pennington stopped talking, raised an eyebrow as if she didn't welcome the interruption, and waited for her to finish.

"With all the boys off at college there were suddenly so few eligible bachelors that I was left with little choice. I sort of went out with David, although we didn't go out much." She smiled impishly, it looked bizarre, and gave Emily a knowing look. Emily blanched at the implication. "The yin to Jolyon's yang. Tall, dark and handsome. A lovely twinkle in his eye but a rather childish sense of humour. My lover but totally unsuitable as a husband. A farm worker no less. He worked for Jolyon's parents." She gave one of her crackling laughs. "My parents hated hearing that I had been seen with him, a full-blooded gypsy no less, so appalling. I never took him home. It made them so cross, and I enjoyed the rebellion, but I couldn't possibly have married him. He was my bit of rough. He was very good in bed, so your Aunt Julia must have been very happy in the bedroom department even if she didn't win the golden prize – Jolyon." Mrs Pennington cackled, sputtering. Emily winced.

Too much information.

"So how did you end up with Jolyon?" Mrs Pennington looked at her fiercely as if she had forgotten she was there.

She paused and smirked. Emily thought she looked even uglier as her face collapsed in on itself. "It was his twenty-first. I was, of course, invited as one of the more suitable girls around the area. That's the way it worked then. All the mothers would scout around for the 'right sort of people'. Only those of a certain class qualified: daughters of doctors and lawyers, those that were privately educated." She paused and looked challengingly at Emily. "And snow-white English roses." She sniggered at her little joke which turned into a long choking fit.

Here she goes again. The racist digs. I hate this woman. This is all about her, not Julia at all. I've made my decision to stay but this is so painfully horrible that if she doesn't tell me something of use soon, I'm going to walk out of here.

Mrs Pennington, recovered, put her head on one side and then slowly on the other. She centred her head and stared unblinking into Emily's eyes. Emily didn't dare blink herself but pulled her mouth into what she hoped looked like a smile. Why did good manners kick in at the most inappropriate times? After what felt like minutes, Mrs Pennington inhaled deeply and wheezed, suppressing a rumbling cough. She chomped down on her gum only to find she hadn't got any; she reached for another piece.

Mrs Pennington's voice had become even more croaky. "I'm enjoying this. Talking about the good old days." She smiled at Emily condescendingly.

I really do hate you. I wonder if Julia did too. I'm learning nothing about her except how badly she was treated.

Turning again to look out of the window, Mrs Pennington rasped, "I charmed Jolyon. I looked wonderful. Dainty and raven haired with a fabulous figure dressed in a diaphanous gown that managed to look chaste and sensual all at the same time. David, as the farm hand, hadn't been invited of course. David was on car parking duty which was a little awkward." She smiled, looking rather pleased with herself. "Charlie hadn't made the cut either, despite them being the best of friends, which was bit odd. I presume it was because he was at a state school so not up to the Pennington's standards. No Julia either. I can't think that Jolyon's parents would have ever thought of inviting her in any case. It would have lowered the tone." She waggled her crayon eyebrows at Emily and gave another of those 'you know what I mean' nods while pointedly tapping at her papery pale skin. Emily flinched.

That isn't quite the way it happened. Thank goodness I spoke to Uncle Charlie first to hear the true version of this tale.

Emily was curious to see what she said next. "Jolyon had drunk quite a few glasses of champagne cocktail. It was hilarious; he wasn't used to it and got very tipsy, making a real spectacle of himself. He couldn't keep his hands off me for the slow dances. Really rather embarrassing." Mrs Pennington leant forward, paused for effect and pronounced in a simpering whisper, "And that was the night that Jolyon and I 'got together'. He did the honourable thing, bless him." Mrs Pennington looked as if she was winking but her wrinkled eyelids were so droopy it was hard to tell.

The whole thought is revolting.

Mrs Pennington turned to her side table and picked up a silver frame of a bride and groom and handed it to Emily. "There you are you see – Mr and Mrs Jolyon Pennington."

Emily found it hard to equate the beautiful young girl in the photograph looking so gloriously happy in her frothy white dress, enormous bouquet of lilies and cascading veil with the withered harridan with thin, snow-white hair in front of her. She squinted and peered closely at it and up at Mrs Pennington in the flesh, but it didn't really help. Sarah

Pennington was a truly exquisite creature at twenty-one. What happened to turn her into such a fright? Was it the smoking or the hate?

Jolyon was indeed very handsome, striking in a dark morning suit and knotted cravat with a single carnation in his buttonhole. His hair was fashionably long, a mop of hair with a fringe; she guessed it must have been the 1960s. Emily thought he didn't look quite as ecstatic as his bride; perhaps they had caught him at a bad moment, or perhaps she was just being mean minded because she couldn't stand this hideous woman.

"You look so happy." Emily managed to get out through gritted teeth. It seemed the right thing to say.

"Yes indeed." She smirked with triumph. "Jolyon and I lived happily ever after, had a honeymoon baby, Nicholas, and I kept fending off the siren Julia from getting her claws into my husband at every opportunity. Believe me she tried. Sadly, there was never another child for Jolyon and me. I regret that." Her voice accelerated and was steadily decreasing in pitch, almost conspiratorial. Emily found herself leaning forward to hear more clearly.

"I think we were all surprised when David proposed to Julia. I rather thought he would never get over me." She paused. "But Julia, as second best, did agree to marry him and it was all set, the white wedding at Lamberhurst church with the reception in a marquee at the Levett's farm afterwards. Nothing like ours, of course. All the guests in ordinary suits and the women in ghastly Crimplene dresses, horrible garish flowers. I suppose heritage will out. All very tribal and colourful." She smirked.

Stop with the racist jibes, or I might just leap up and slap you in the face.

"I caught them out though. Jolyon and Julia. He came home very late from David's stag do and I could smell *her* on him. Black people smell completely different to us, did you know that?"

I'm not answering that. I'll listen to her, but I'll not join in her lies. Emily merely stared at Mrs Pennington, letting her expression answer for her. The polite smile had disappeared.

"I did challenge him, but he came up with a cock and bull story about how the hens and stags had met up in the Elizabethan Barn, there had been a bit of a to-do with some fisticuffs, something do with the boys fighting over Julia, Charlie very drunk, the boys in blue called, and David and Charlie were dragged off by the police."

"I have that cutting," Emily chimed in, but Mrs Pennington continued without taking any notice.

"Typical for that class of people but not so good to inveigle Jolyon into their appalling behaviour. I was very surprised that Jolyon had gone at all. One doesn't normally party with the help. Anyway Jolyon, not involved of course, very nobly offered to get Julia home safely and they shared a taxi. Safely home, shared a taxi, my arse! He dropped her off at the Levett's farm and apparently decided to walk home. It isn't that far, I suppose, so that bit could have been true, but you can smell sex. I could smell her and sex on him. Bastard. He denied it over and over again at the time, but I knew it would come out in the end. Only one week before her marriage to David. Unbelievable."

"But..." Emily interrupted, very flustered by this revelation, but Mrs Pennington wafted a hand at her.

"After that, I had to think of ways to keep her where I could see her. Fortunately, she was kept busy producing her milk chocolate brats, first Genevieve and then Matthew. Matthew was much darker than Genevieve. He definitely looked very negro as a new born – bulbous lips, fat flat nose. Genevieve might have got away with being Spanish or something like that, a relatively light skin and curly rather than frizzy hair. Very much like yours in fact." Emily sighed loudly but was ignored.

"Anyway, in the end I persuaded Jolyon to move her and Genevieve into the farm cottage at the bottom of the hill when their hovel on Furnace Lane sadly burnt down. Poor baby Matthew. Burnt to a crisp although it was difficult to tell. A bit more blackened from the smoke and he ended up with a nose like Michael Jackson's" She guffawed. Emily cringed and clenched her fists, furious that the harridan was banging on again with racist slurs, quite deliberately she felt. "You have no doubt heard about all that?"

Through gritted teeth, Emily responded, "Yes, I have the paper cutting about it..."

"Julia tried to say it was my fault, the bitch, but she couldn't prove it." She leered in a malevolent way. Emily was tingling with waves of adrenaline.

What is that supposed to imply? Bloody hell, was it deliberate? The woman is completely insane. Would she be mad enough to set light to someone's home or harm Julia? Perhaps I am sitting opposite my aunt's murderer.

"Jolyon built a new architect designed house on the same footprint and moved his parents into it. He knew he'd make a fortune when it was time to sell it. It's a prime location, so handy for Tunbridge Wells."

Emily wasn't interested in that and wondered how to bring her back to Julia.

"So, the cottage that they moved to..."

"Right at the bottom of the hill, by the farmyard. I could keep an eye on her comings and goings. I engineered it so that she did the school run every day. After all, she was passing the end of our drive on the way to Lamberhurst and then – can you believe it? – she looked after Nicholas for me after school... for nothing!" She grinned. Emily thought she looked like a gargoyle. "I employed her cleaning the house. I did pay her for that, but it put her in her place." She wheezed and laughed wildly, stopped abruptly and stared at Emily. Emily leaned away from the malevolence in her eyes. "I made a mistake though. I did my best for years, managing to keep Julia away from Jolyon. I was always there, never giving them a moment on their own, but I couldn't prevent the black witch's spawn from seducing Nicholas and entrancing him into marriage. I blame myself, letting them spend so much of their early childhood together. He didn't seem to notice her colour. He treated her as if she was perfectly normal."

Emily closed her eyes in despair and rubbed the bridge of her nose. All this bile was bringing on a headache. How much more could she take? She wasn't sure it was worth it, but Emily needed to know more about how Julia died. She had chosen to stay but now deeply regretted that decision. Mrs Pennington continued, "We all tried to stop it for different reasons. We should have done – look how it ended. Have you heard about the poor cursed child?" Emily nodded. She had indeed heard about the child's disabilities from Cathy, so sad, but hoped she wasn't agreeing to the cursed comment. "Jolyon had a lucky escape from those contaminated, dirty black genes." She paused, nodding at the photo in Emily's hand. Her wizened hand shot out and snatched the silver frame from Emily as if she too was contaminated by association. "At least Nicholas escaped from the woman's clutches and her ghastly curses. We made sure of that. You can't get much further away than New Zealand." Her thumbs rubbed the silver of the frame as she coughed and spluttered again.

"When Nicholas fled and the she-devil... died," Emily noted the hesitation, "Jolyon fell apart. He slowly drank himself to death. He blamed himself, you see, for all that furore – and he blamed her as well of course." She shrugged her shoulders, reached out for another piece of gum then realised she was still chewing a piece. She chomped and chewed, her mouth distorting into hideous shapes.

Emily said, "But why did he blame Aunt Julia?" Mrs Pennington gave an unhelpful shrug of her shoulders. "I understand that you were there the night that Julia died. What happened? Why were you all there?"

Mrs Pennington put her head on one side. "Charlie told you that, did he? You could be right, although Charlie might have misremembered. I heard that he's gone a bit gaga."

"But it was Cathy who said–"

"A dreadful night. Best forgotten. I most certainly don't want to go over it again. Anyway, where was I? Jolyon was impossible, I just couldn't stay with him. He was vile and out of control. I was frightened that he might harm me during one of his drunken rages."

Emily was frustrated. This was why she had stayed rather than walking out on the vile bitch. She didn't want to hear about afterwards, she wanted to piece together what had happened to Aunt Julia on that terrible night. How did she die? "But do you think it was an accident, did Aunt Julia take her own life or, worse than that...?"

Mrs Pennington stared at her. Took a deep breath and rolled her lips together. "Do you want to hear what I have to say?" Emily nodded but was getting increasingly frustrated. Mrs Pennington continued wandering away from the whys and wherefores of Julia's death. "The farm sold overnight after just one advert in Country Life, to a Dutchman who wanted to turn it into an intensive veal farm. There was bit of a hoo-ha because Benedict wanted to take on the farm but couldn't afford to buy out Jolyon." She looked confused, her head still, tipped on one side like a bird, until the chewing started up again.

"There was plenty of money to go round. Jolyon gave the bulk of his to Nicholas to buy a dairy farm outside Christchurch. It took a while for Nicholas to accept such a huge sum but he did in the end. Appeasement."

"Appeasement for what? For having a disabled child? Surely Evie wouldn't have wanted that?"

"Genevieve wasn't there. Genevieve buggered off, taking the poor child with her. Tail between her legs." Mrs Pennington chuckled at her little joke, but it turned into a cough.

"Why didn't they stay together?"

Mrs Pennington stopped to glare at Emily and then continued. "Nicholas started again, found a nice New Zealand lass – the white sort with blonde hair, blue eyes, not an Aborigine. They had two little girls, one after the other, Amber and Kimberley. They were completely normal, no defects, so we know it wasn't Nicholas who had the problem."

Why can't she just stop with the racial slurs? She is so ignorant and it isn't even Aborigines in New Zealand it's Maoris.

"I bought myself a nice little townhouse on the Pantiles in Tunbridge Wells, had lunches with friends in Weekes, played a lot of bridge, popped up to town, a good life. Perhaps I should have gone to New Zealand but it wasn't really my scene and all my friends and family are here." She waved an arm. "Jolyon rented a flat in Sevenoaks. I don't know why there."

Emily's head was reeling from this sudden outpouring. She was confused how Mrs Pennington had suddenly fast forwarded the whole of her life story after so much early detail. It was all a bit muddled. Was it deliberate that she had skated over the most important parts? She shook her head in frustration.

"Please can you roll back a moment? I have so many questions to ask. How come Julia married David? Were they happy? What were their children, my second cousins like? How did your son get on with them? What caused the problems with Evie and Nicholas' child? Why did they part ways?" As she unleashed question after question, Emily rummaged frantically in her bag for a press cutting. She found the one she was looking for and shoved it at Mrs Pennington. "What do *you* think happened to Julia? The coroner gave an open verdict. Could it have been murder? Who could have done that?"

Mrs Pennington looked at her coolly, clearly understanding Emily's implication.

I bet she would've done, given half a chance.

"Well, it couldn't have been me, could it? Look at the size of me. Have you seen the size of Julia?" She cackled. It was horrible. "I suppose it could have been Jolyon, or indeed David or Charlie, that little trio of acolytes. All following Julia around with their tongues hanging out like dogs following a bitch on heat. Anyway, I've had enough now." She sat erect in her chair. "Go away. Too many questions. You're being very demanding and extremely irritating. I'm not being questioned under caution. You will have to come back tomorrow."

"I'm off to Wiltshire tomorrow to go and see David and Evie."

Mrs Pennington shrugged and stuck out her bottom lip; she turned away before swivelling back with a gleam in her eye. "Well, that is going to be very interesting. I wonder what they will say. Send them my... regards." She flung back her head and laughed manically before choking on her gum and struggling for breath. She coughed disgustingly; Emily could hear the phlegm bubbling deep in her chest.

Should I pat her back? Or perhaps I could just watch her choke to death...

She chose just to stare at the hag until it was over.

Once the frenzied performance had finished, Emily tried to end the meeting with dignity and pretend that the last couple of hours hadn't been a torrent of horrors. She stood up, shovelling her press cuttings and notebook back into her bag. "Well thank you so much, Mrs Pennington. It has been so kind of you to see me."

Why am I being so polite to this racist bitch? Too many years of training in etiquette from The Boomers.

Mrs Pennington didn't move, just looked at her, in a trance. Emily hesitated. "Well goodbye then." Emily looked directly at Mrs Pennington, her eyes blazing.

As she marched to the door, Mrs Pennington suddenly barked "You *definitely* need to come back. You most certainly do... I have so much more to tell you."

Now what?

Emily didn't know what to think. "Um, yes? Why?"

"No, you really must. I might tell you the answer to the biggest question of them all about Julia."

Emily stopped. What the hell is the old crone implying? Is there really a big reveal? Perhaps she can shed light on how Julia had really died? What on earth should she say?

"Bye then."

That was pathetic.

Emily escaped into the corridor in a rage, a rumble of laughter following her. It was a relief to be out.

So much for the Blue Grass being a good omen. Can I face going back to that hellish... that... troll bitch from hell?

Emily couldn't think of a better phrase to describe the awful old woman, and it was only by great strength of will that she resisted slamming the door behind her. As she strode, shaking with rage, to the front door Emily realised that she had left her cagoule behind.

I need to get out of here, right now. It will have to wait.

Back in the fresh air Emily took deep breaths to calm down. It had stopped raining and she sucked in the smell of wet earth to clear the all-pervading stench of racist hate.

Trembling with anger she stomped along beside the house towards the car. Suddenly she remembered what the evil crow had said about the grand mansion being Saint Christopher's. She pushed the clouds of rage away to remember what Uncle Charlie had said about picking Aunt Julia up from here. It was a relief to remember his delighted account of seeing Aunt Julia for the first time. It made her calmer.

There was a door at the side of the building that she eyed up, but her instinct said that the family had used the main entrance. The front door certainly looked very grand indeed with huge columns either side, an imposing tall black door, and an enormous lantern above it. It was just how Uncle Charlie had described it.

Well, I'm here now so might as well see if I can go in.

She crept up the ramp and pulled the weighty silver door handle. The door obligingly opened, although it was very heavy. It closed behind her very pointedly, all on its own, as if to hurry her in, and she was faced with a vast hallway. The interior was incredible, with more columns down either side, like a church, a tall ceiling painted white, and walls glowing in a gold shade of yellow. An enormous modern glass table was loaded with the largest lamps that Emily had ever seen and a bowl of pot pourri which perfumed the air. She nearly jumped a mile when she caught sight of a dog behind a pillar until she realised it was a statue.

Well, it can't get much posher than this.

Emily couldn't help but think that it hadn't looked at all like this all those years ago. Squinting her eyes, she tried to conjure up a nurse with a small black girl by her side, but it was too hard to imagine amongst all the glitz and glamour. She took a photo just the same.

At least I've seen it and can show The Boomers.

She stood for a moment thinking about Aunt Julia, Uncle Charlie, and Cathy and their connection to this place, but refused to think about the ghastly Sarah bloody Pennington.

Perhaps she would find out this so called 'answer to the biggest question of them all' from David or Cathy, then she wouldn't have to come back ever again.

TWENTY-ONE

The next morning, Emily was still reeling from her visit with the dreaded Sarah and awoke with a nasty taste in her mouth. When she'd returned from the odious Mrs Pennington's, her head was full of questions, the ones that Mrs Pennington had curtly refused to answer before dismissing her so abruptly.

Emily had worked out that she needed to make a very early start. Her sat nav lady had kindly informed her that it would take about two and a half hours to get to David's home. When she had made the appointment, she hadn't realised just how far it was, and had agreed to meet at nine thirty. To allow a bit of time for a break, to stretch her legs and have a pee, she needed to leave at six thirty.

She went down for breakfast at six and there wasn't a soul in sight, not even the genius Katie. The buffet was arranged with its array of dubious looking goods, the same ones for days, with questionably clean tea towels over each section. Lifting the edge, she didn't like the look of what was lurking underneath.

Bugger it. I will stop for breakfast on the way.

She made her way along the M25, dreadfully slow and

packed with vehicles for such an early time of the day, then down the M3, the road works limiting her speed to fifty and not a workman in sight. After that the sat nav directed her through a warren of roundabouts through a busy Bracknell. Arguments with the sat nav lady over which exit of the innumerable roundabouts resulted in her going round several of them twice. Finally, there were stops and starts and queues for no apparent reason approaching Reading.

So tedious. No wonder there's so much pollution from cars. So many of them, and all crawling along puffing out fumes. Where are they all going?

But at least the slow journey gave her plenty of time to think over everything that she had heard from Uncle Charlie, Cathy and then Sarah Pennington. The same story, but so different in many respects from the three of them. And still so many questions unanswered by Sarah Pennington. What was she not telling Emily? There was definitely far more to be revealed. But could she face going back? Emily was still seething from the racist language that had poured like vomit from the dreadful woman's mouth over and over again, let alone the foul chewing. It caused her to shudder, even now.

"Oh my God, I've still got that gob of gum in my bag. That is disgusting."

She stopped at the next services, rooted very gingerly around in her bag, found the repugnant piece of gum and threw it away, then calmed herself with a welcome mug of coffee and a not so special egg sandwich. Uncle Charlie's tale, more of a parable really, about the eggs came to mind. A good story.

All in all, it took her far longer than she was expecting to get to Wiltshire, certainly far more than the sat nav lady had decreed, so by the time she got through Hungerford she was running late. She hated being late and decided to stop in a layby off the A4 to call and explain herself. Surprisingly, she failed to get any signal on her phone at all. She'd never had this problem before.

Damn. I'd better keep going.

As she got closer to the address that she had been given, she drove through the most amazing scenery. Undulating golden downland fields stretched for miles, littered with mysterious lumps and bumps, and a most extraordinary hill, obviously man made because it was so symmetrical. It felt as if she was in a completely different country after the short rolling wooded hills and miles of hedgerows of Kent, the gaunt and glowering granite houses of Edinburgh, her busy home city of Sheffield with its industrious trams, and the small stone bordered fields of the Peak District.

What a diverse country we live in. Our different scenery, ways of speaking. Well, diverse in some ways but certainly not in others.

As she bowled along, she passed a spiky church spire, flashing supernaturally as it caught the sun; it stood like a sword amongst all the greenery in the valley below.

What a wonderful sight. What a mysterious county.

Directed off the main road, Emily swooped down a hill, passing charming black and white thatched cottages. She turned down a track and that was it, she was there. Her tummy flipped at the thought that she was about to meet Aunt Julia's husband and children. She found herself a place to park alongside a pair of rather prim Victorian semi-detached brick cottages.

Late. Not a good start.

She reached for her bag, stretched to loosen up after the drive and wandered towards the door of the formal cottage on the left. Dogs barked and the door was opened by a tall man with a full head of curly hair that was very dark and streaked with white. He looked bronzed and fit, in much better physical condition than Uncle Charlie.

He looks good for his age, just a more crinkled, grey streaked version of the David I saw in those photographs.

In a very deep, gruff voice he rumbled, "You're late." He didn't sound very happy.

Emily was embarrassed, "Yes, I'm so sorry. The traffic has been appalling and I tried to ring but there was no signal."

"That'll be the ley lines. They interfere with the signal between Hungerford and through Marlborough."

I have no idea what you're talking about.

Emily put on her best smile and held out her hand. "You must be David. I'm Emily, the one that wrote to you about Aunt Julia."

He hesitated for a moment, looking at her outstretched hand before enveloping it in a gnarly grip. He pumped her hand up and down several times while staring intently into her face. Discomfited, Emily blushed.

He growled, "You'd better come in."

She followed him into an immaculate lounge where he waved his arm at a sofa with three matching cushions standing to attention, opposite a spotless fireplace with an electric fire. As she sat down, she caught a whiff of chemical cleaning products.

"Tea? We don't drink coffee."

Emily found herself saying automatically, "Yes please, that would be lovely."

But I don't like tea. Why did I say yes? Why am I so nervous?

"The others will be back later so it's just us. I thought it best. Hope that's okay."

"That's fine. I'm looking forward to meeting my cousins."

"Are you?" Emily jumped. "I have to say that Evie has taken a lot of persuasion to meet you at all. You don't know much about them, then."

"Um, no."

That's why I'm here, surely.

"That's what I thought. Best to fill you in before you meet them, so you aren't too... you know."

Emily didn't know what to say. *What on earth does he mean? Too excited, too horrified, too disappointed or what?*

She managed, "Okay." It seemed the best answer to cover all eventualities.

"I'll get the tea." He disappeared out of the room and Emily had a chance to relax momentarily and have a good look around. There were only three photos on display that she could see from her place on the sofa; not as many as she had expected. They were reflected in the polished surfaces which were all exceptionally shiny and clean. Would there be a photo of Julia? She couldn't see her in any of them. She craned her neck round to search out other pictures but there was very little in the way of ornaments; everything was very minimalist.

She turned back to the three on the mantelpiece. There was a black and white photo of David and a woman in what could easily have been perceived as fancy dress by the fanciful nature of her hugely voluminous skirt. Emily looked again at the man with his slicked down black hair and the setting and realised it must be David's parents on their wedding day. The family likeness was striking. His father and he were interchangeable. Characteristics passed on, just like she shared Aunt Julia's genes through Great Granny.

Today I am going to meet my biological cousins. Amazing. I hope they aren't all as formidable as David.

One snap was of a family group wrapped up in scarves

and woolly hats, their arms outstretched on what seemed to be the top of a very windy hill. She could make out David, a woman who she assumed must be Evie, holding a small child bundled up in an all-in-one suit and a boy with glasses and a broad grin. A tail, presumably belonging to a dog, was captured disappearing off to the right. The second was obviously the same family, this time up against an enormous stone that towered over all of them, even David. She could see more of them because they were in t-shirts and jeans. Definitely Evie and her offspring. She must have married again or something. No doubt Emily would find out in a moment and the idea excited her.

David returned and looming over her he placed a mug on a coaster in front of Emily on the polished coffee table. She tensed up immediately. *Why do I find him so intimidating?* Politely, she said, "Thank you so much."

He took a seat in the armchair, leant back, placed his gnarly hands on the armrests and said bluntly, "So, what have they been telling you then?"

Blimey, he is forthright.

Summoning a smile, Emily said, "I've been hearing from Uncle Charlie all about Aunt Julia's childhood. It seemed idyllic being brought up on the farm and a bit about when you got married. Uncle Charlie said he was best man." David nodded briskly. "And then Sarah had quite a bit to say about you." Emily meant this to sound complimentary, but it came out as a bit sinister because she was thinking about some of the more intimate remarks, and it made her feel a bit queasy. "So, in terms of the story so far I've got up to when you and Aunt Julia got married..."

He interrupted, "Well, let me just tell you my side of all that. I want you to hear it from me as it all really happened, before the others get back. They don't need to be reminded of it all. I bet you've been told a whole lot of hogwash."

"Oh, okay. Well, that's great, thank you. I'd like to hear the truth." Emily tried to look eager and not embarrassed at how she might have come across. "Can I take notes?"

David nodded. Emily recovered her 1/- notebook from her bag that flopped at her side, looking very worn and untidy in this immaculate space.

"Right. Let's go back to the beginning. First of all, that Sarah. She was a real floozy to be honest with you. Most of the girls were happy to snog and suchlike but Sarah was quite happy to go all the way, and I don't think that it was just with me. She was a good looking girl, amazing dark brown eyes, and thick dark hair – almost black – and she was very small and delicate boned but trust me, very athletic. I wouldn't normally be quite so direct about people in my past, but she turned out to be a right pain. I wouldn't trust her as far as I could throw her."

Emily nodded, a bit embarrassed to be hearing so much about the sex lives of these old people. It was hard to equate this lascivious Sarah with the wizened creature that she had met. The only connection was that wedding photo where Sarah was indeed very pretty, in a twee sort of way.

"She dropped me like a hot cake when she trapped Jolyon. Poor foolish boy." He pursed his lips and shook his head. "It was at Jolyon's fancy party. His twenty-first. You have no idea just how snobby people could be then. Still are. They liked to rub the rest of our noses in it. As the Pennington's farmhand I did all the work getting the party set up. Not exactly in my job description but you can't say no to your boss, can you?" Emily shook her head in agreement.

"They had a huge fancy marquee on the grass – told you they were swanky people – and we had to use all the farm electrical leads for the band and the lights. I carried cases and cases of booze to behind the bar and put loads of champagne bottles into a big old tin bath, behind the tent. Filled it with water and then chucked in bags of ice they'd got from the fishmongers. It did smell a bit fishy." He snorted with laughter. Emily was relieved. When he laughed, he wasn't quite so scary.

"Anyway, I was only there to direct the cars and open doors as they dropped off their posh passengers in all their finery. I can remember Sarah arriving. She looked gorgeous in one of those dresses that shows nothing but promises everything, you know what I mean?"

I do, but I don't want to think about the old hag that way.

"She wouldn't even look me in the eye and just said 'thank you very much' as if she had never seen me before in her life. I was livid. Kind of knew then that I wouldn't be seeing her again. To be honest, no bad thing as it turned out."

"So, then you dated Julia?"

"Dated Julia?" It took him a moment to realise what she meant. "Oh my god, Julia. She was so beautiful. I never thought she'd even look at me. She always had eyes only for Jolyon from when she was tiny. I think everyone assumed that they would get married eventually, but they hadn't accounted for Sarah Digby-Watson, had they? I knew I was never more than a good lay to Sarah, and I can't imagine that it would ever have gone further than that, but she knew for sure that Jolyon was equally as besotted with Julia. Who wasn't?" He took a slurp from his mug of tea.

"Julia. Oh Julia. Always causing trouble without meaning to. The most wonderful girl in the world, just perfect. What made it harder for the other girls was that she had no idea just how flawless she was. She not only looked stunning, but she was just such a nice girl. Modest, wonderful sense of fun, an infectious giggle and an incredible singing voice." Emily was delighted to hear more about Aunt Julia's character. "Her being half black just didn't matter. It certainly didn't make any difference to the way I felt about her, although my parents were a bit iffy about it." He snorted again.

"Funny really after all the prejudice they had suffered from being pure blood Romanies and the racist insults that they'd had to put up with all their lives. To be honest, I never thought as her as being black, brown or anything else, just Julia. I don't think photos do her justice because they don't show the life force that shone like a... I don't know... I must sound like an idiot. You get the idea anyway." His voice had softened and Emily felt slightly less terrified by this romantic side of David.

"I got up the courage after a few beers and tentatively asked her to dance at a young farmers dance. She was standing by the entrance with Charlie, looking lost and uncomfortable – I guess because she didn't have Jolyon by her side. Charlie had his arm around her possessively, a bit too familiar for my liking to be honest. It made me a bit uncomfortable what with them being brother and sister. Although they weren't of course related in any way. I know that it is perfectly okay now, but I also know what people think and say in those situations. So much has changed." David seemed to realise he was gabbling because he stopped and looked out of the window at a pristine garden, raised beds filled with vegetables in serried ranks. He stared for so long that Emily wondered where he had gone inside his head.

"I didn't think she'd say yes when I asked her. To dance, I mean at that stage. But she did and I just fell for her hook, line and sinker. I'd never known anything like it, and me being an ordinary sort of bloke it took me by surprise. I would do anything for her, anything at all. What an idiot as it turns out." He sighed heavily. Emily was puzzled but didn't like to interrupt.

"We courted for over a year before I had the courage to ask her to marry me. When she looked at me, her face full of love, and said yes, I felt as if I would never breathe again." He shuddered, although whether in passion or disgust it was impossible for Emily to work out. "I know it was very old-fashioned, but we decided to wait until our wedding night. She was a virgin and to me she was such a goddess that I wanted it to be perfect." He shook his head.

Emily felt uncomfortable. *Why do these old people have to be so upfront about their sexual habits?*

Desperate to change the subject, Emily asked, "What happened at the Elizabethan Barn though?"

David started and looked at Emily questioningly. After a pause he spoke, "Oh, Charlie told you about that did he? It was stupid." Emily didn't like to say that it had been Sarah confirming the press cutting, and she just let him keep talking. "Charlie had way too much booze. I knew that he loved Julia. I suppose because we all did; not surprising really. He had fended off some yobs who were making racist remarks and then when I came over to claim her, he got all possessive. It was very, very stupid and to be honest he wasn't going to stand a chance against me in a fist fight, was he?" David laughed and shook his head, presumably at Charlie's ridiculous impudence. An image of the frail old man popped into Emily's head. "He'd just had one too many and was being all jealous. We'd been mates too long for that to get in the way. Anyway, when the organ started up with 'Here Comes the Bride' I couldn't have been happier. Julia looked so incredible, like an angel drifting down the aisle towards me. To be honest a few tears slipped out. Placing the ring on her long, elegant finger was overwhelming." David looked wistful.

Emily nodded with excitement, "I've seen the pictures. Aunt Julia looked stunning."

David turned to look at her as if he'd forgotten she was there. "She did, she did. Anyway, Mr and Mrs Levett put on an amazing spread in a big marquee in the paddock by the oast house. Charlie made a funny speech. I made a terrible one. I felt like a right idiot. I hate speaking in front of people, not my cup of tea at all. I only had eyes for Julia and just couldn't wait until we were on our own. In those days, at all weddings, the bride and groom went and got changed in separate rooms and then left in a car. I hated the outfit that I went away in, a ridiculous get up." Emily could see why, his outfit had been rather outrageous. "I would have been happier in my work overalls to be honest."

Emily was getting irritated. If he said 'to be honest' once more she might scream. She clenched her teeth instead.

"We got to the Star and Eagle in Goudhurst and there we had our wedding night." David's eyes unfocussed for a moment, but then he shook himself and sighed. Emily hoped that there would be no more information on this matter.

"We couldn't have been happier if we tried. Best friends, soulmates even. She was so funny getting the hang of being a housewife – useless at cooking, always burning things or serving them raw but oh, how we laughed about it. She blamed it on the cooker because they always had an Aga at the farmhouse. Just so much joy." He stopped, took a swig of tea. Shook his head at some private thought and continued, "When she told me she was pregnant I was even more thrilled. You just can't believe how it is when you're told that you have a child on the way. She was sick as a pig, not just in the morning but all odd times of day. She made me change out of my work clothes in the hallway because the smell of farmyard manure made her retch." He laughed suddenly. "I used to strip naked and dance through the kitchen waggling... oops, sorry. Excuse me." He must have seen Emily's horrified expression because he paused to wipe away tears of laughter and blow his nose.

While she waited for him to finish, Emily was suddenly desperate for a pee, but didn't dare say anything, waiting for the right point to interrupt. He was in full flood. She hadn't managed to say a word for ages. She hastily scribbled notes as it all poured out.

"When that little girl was born, I was over the moon. I loved her with all my heart and all my soul. We called her Genevieve after the actress who played Anne Boleyn in *Anne of a Thousand Days*. We saw it at the Essoldo in Tunbridge Wells. I forget her surname. Julia came up with it and I agreed, even though I'd have preferred something a bit more straightforward and English or from my Romany roots. Despite the fancy name, I don't think anyone ever called her anything but Evie – even Julia.

Except Sarah, of course.

"She was a good little girl, pretty like her mother with a shock of curly hair. Funnily enough it was curly like yours," he gestured at Emily's hair, "rather than frizzy like most people with black heritage. And the same beautiful eyes as Julia." He suddenly looked at Emily's eyes and evidently noted that hers were not up to Great Granny's standards because he shook his head slightly before continuing, "She didn't fuss all that much. I thought all babies were like that and couldn't understand everyone else complaining all the time. Then we had Matthew, and I got it. But I'm getting ahead of myself. I didn't mind about the lack of sleep. I would do the early evening feeds so that Julia could get some kip and she would take over in the night. We were such a team. So happy. We used to talk a great deal about how it felt for her having her own baby after having been adopted herself. She couldn't understand how anyone could ever let their baby go. I think it made her feel ashamed. She used to say how much her mother must have hated her to want to give her away. On a bad day she would have a good cry about it."

"But she didn't hate her at all," Emily interrupted. "I have a letter for her, but I don't know what to do with it now. I thought I'd give it to Evie."

He looked sad and grumbled, "I only wish now that her mum had contacted her when she was alive, so she knew why she had to be adopted. I mean, of course she did know in a way. It was clear that a young girl in those days couldn't give birth to a black baby without there being a whole lot of bother. I think it would have changed a lot of things for Julia if she'd heard from her real mum. Perhaps it might have changed everything." David shrugged. Since he seemed to have reached an intermission, Emily reasoned that perhaps this would be a good time to ask to use the toilet. With all the talk of his beloved Julia, he had settled into a far more approachable demeanour.

She leant forward. "Um, would this be a good moment to have a break?" David looked at her as if he didn't understand what she was saying. "Please could I use your bathroom?"

"Oh yes, by all means. You'd better use the toilet upstairs. Top of the stairs turn right. You have to give the handle a really good push, it's a bit dodgy."

"Thank you." Emily dashed up the stairs and used her time sitting on the loo to let everything she had heard sink in.

It's amazing how these old people like to talk about their past. No holding back.

She tried to forget the image of a naked David dancing

through a kitchen as she yanked the flush as hard as she could.

Emily returned to the lounge and as she sat back down, David said, "I seem to be going on a bit. Is this okay for you?"

He seemed far less fierce, so she was able to say with enthusiasm, "It's fantastic, thank you. I feel that I'm really getting to know Aunt Julia..." She couldn't think what to call him face to face – Uncle David? Somehow it just didn't suit. With Uncle Charlie it had felt just right, cosy.

"Shall I go on?"

"Oh yes, please do." Emily wriggled to get comfortable and eagerly took up her notebook.

"I'll fast forward the next few years of married bliss. Like any young couple we got into a rhythm and very happy we were too. Along came Matthew. Now, to be honest, he was a whole different kettle of fish. Such a whingy baby, never stopped crying and moaning. We were run ragged. I think Julia could see how you might like to give away a baby after all."

I'm sure he didn't really mean that. Well, I hope not.

"Evie was still an absolute delight. Thank God for Evie. I used to take her out a lot just to give her a break from her annoying little brother. She loved coming out on the farm with me, sitting on my lap as I drove the tractor – ploughing and sowing and rolling. Jolyon's parents, and Jolyon himself, didn't mind as long as I got on with the work, but Sarah would get a bit sniffy about it. 'Can't Julia look after her own brats?' That's what she called them. Brats. Very rude but I couldn't say anything to the boss's wife, could I? Even though I had shagged her in the past." Emily shook her head, cringed.

"And then there was the fire."

Emily sat up. *That was an abrupt change of subject.*

"Do you know about that?" he asked.

I hope he means the first fire. Surely, he couldn't have taken such a huge leap forward. "I have a press cutting about it." Emily rustled through the papers in her trusty bag, looking for it.

"It was horrendous. To be honest, I've never been so terrified in all my life, except perhaps for the other one. Julia was always very wary about fire, something about Charlie and Jolyon setting the wood on fire or something, so it couldn't have been worse for her. It all got very complicated. Let me see how to explain it." He paused, sat back in his chair and stretched. Emily placed the cutting on the coffee table.

"Wayside Cottage was small but perfectly fine for us. It came with the job. It had three tiny bedrooms upstairs, a kitchen and lounge downstairs with a bathroom added on the back as an afterthought. Not a pretty place at all, had rather a surprised look to it. Big garden though, which was great for Evie and Matthew, and I grew lots of vegetables. We were inundated with bloody vegetables." David chuckled.

Definitely less scary.

"There was a small open fire in the lounge. It was the only thing with a real flame as such in the house, and Julia was very careful with it because of her phobia about fire. She insisted on an electric cooker rather than gas. It was a winter's evening, the fire was lit, fireguard firmly in place, and I went out for a cricket club dinner with my mates at the Elephant's Head at Bells Yew Green just down the road. People don't do that anymore but that's how we did most of our socialising in those days. A pint or two of Shepherd Neame all standing around the bar, getting stuck into some steak and kidney pie, then the lads having a pipe or a ciggie, the occasional snob with a cigar, and a good old chinwag."

I bet that snob was Jolyon, even though he wasn't very good at cricket like David.

"Everyone seemed to smoke in those days, so we were in a lovely warm fug. It was like that in all the pubs."

Yuck. The last time I smelt smoke was on Uncle James and it was vile. Can't imagine how awful it must have been.

"Don't smoke now, filthy habit. Charlie Levett was there, of course, and Jolyon Pennington lording it over us all despite being so rubbish at cricket." He snorted.

That confirms exactly what I was thinking. We are definitely getting on the same wavelength.

"While I was out, Sarah came round to Wayside Cottage for some reason – very late for a social call if you ask me. She said it was something to do with the electrics which kept tripping out. We all know that was an excuse because surely she would have sent Jolyon for such a thing, or he would have spoken to me about it during the day. Julia, being polite, asked her in and offered her a drink. We normally had a bottle of sherry and a few cans of beer for such eventualities, but Sarah declined because she drank wine, and we didn't have that. Typical of bloody Sarah. I bet she knew that we wouldn't have anything so fancy. Anything to make Julia feel awkward, she did it all the time."

David leant forward and rumbled in a confidential tone, "Now this is where their stories differed. Sarah claims that Julia offered her a cigarette from a packet of mine that I'd left on the side and that she took one. But Julia said that Sarah had insisted that she try one of Sarah's. In any case they both ended up having a puff even though Julia had never smoked before. She says it was because she was so on edge; she couldn't work out why Sarah was there, she didn't want to be impolite, and it gave her something to do with her hands. Julia remembered getting one of my ashtrays and putting it on the coffee table in front of Sarah." David hesitated and his brow furrowed.

Where is this story going?

David went on, "Anyway, Sarah seemed to natter on to Julia, asking her loads of questions about the kids and all that. She never seemed too interested in them, so this was surprising in itself. Julia dutifully asked about Nicholas and how he was getting on. She'd often wondered why Sarah hadn't gone on to have another one but was far too courteous to mention it. Anyway, Julia said that Sarah never seemed to get to the point of explaining why she was there. Apparently, so Julia told me, Sarah suddenly said 'must dash' so Julia leapt up. She can't recall how it went from there, but she saw Sarah out through the front door which we only ever used for special visitors. She was baffled as to why she had come at all."

I'm baffled about where this story is going.

"Sorry, I know it must seem that I'm going on rather, but it's important you know this because of what the firemen found afterwards."

"What did they find?" Emily asked, pencil poised.

"I'll come on to that. I'm getting ahead of myself. Sorry. Anyway, Sarah left. Julia couldn't remember what time. She pottered around, damping down the fire and putting up the guard. Then she went into the kitchen to tidy up, went through to the bathroom to clean her teeth. Nothing unusual. She was certain about that – she did the same as she did every day.

"She went upstairs, poking her head into the lounge on the way to double check that the fire was out. She said that she remembered a smell of burning but assumed that it was the fire. She said she even poked at it again and spread the logs to be sure it was damped down before putting the fireguard back up. She went up the stairs and checked in on Matthew who made a fuss – he always did at the slightest disturbance, so he took a while to settle. Then Julia went through to Evie, gave her a kiss and a cuddle. She then went and got into bed. As usual.

"Chucking out time from the pub was ten, so I drove back home, reversed back into the drive and as I got out the car, I smelt smoke. It didn't smell like a regular bonfire, difficult to say how it was different. Then I heard it – a weird noise, rumbly and crackly. I went round the back of the house and then I could see it. The back of the house was completely ablaze. I know I screamed for help, yelled for Julia but then I had to decide. Did I tackle the blaze somehow, go into the house and get my family out, or get hold of the fire brigade? How the hell do you decide what to do first when that happens?"

Emily put her hands to her face in horror.

"I thought fire brigade first, they would be the most help. So I went to the neighbours, Mr and Mrs Beech, and hammered on their door – no mobile phones in those days, of course. They appeared, looking a bit surprised, Mrs Beech all in her curlers, but I yelled at them to get the fire brigade and then dashed back to the house. Then I charged inside and saw that the fire hadn't reached the kitchen yet. I went through to the back in pitch darkness and found the lounge door closed. I could feel the heat radiating from it, and I knew instinctively not to open it. Instead, I raced up the stairs into our bedroom and shook Julia. How the hell she had slept through it so far I don't know, but to be fair she was above the kitchen and she was very tired from so many sleepless nights with Matthew. She might even have popped a few pills. They gave out Valium like smarties in those days, so I don't rightly know.

"'Get up, get up!' I yelled. 'Fire! Fire!'

"'What...?'

"'For the love of God, get up.' She was suddenly wide awake and I could see in the gloom the tension seeping into her limbs. She scrambled out of bed, sniffed the air like a dog, her eyes wide open. 'Jesus Christ, I smell burning. What's on fire?'

"'Just get out of the house, Julia.'

"'Oh my God, where are the children?'

"'In bed. I came to get you first.'

"'I'll go and get Evie, you get Matthew.' She dashed out and that's the last I saw of her until we were all outside.

"I went to Matthew's door and it was firmly closed. We always kept it shut because otherwise we would be awake all night with his whimpering and wailing. Sounds a bit cruel now but you have no idea how bad he was. I yanked it open and was met by hell. Smoke and flames. It burned my eyes just to look. There was no way I could get through it to Matthew's cot even though it was only a few steps, so I went and yanked the heavy wool blanket off our bed, put it over my head like a cloak and went back in. I went straight to his cot, threw the blanket over it which killed the flames. With the blanket covering us both like a tent, I scooped him up and belted for the door. I raced down the stairs and out through the kitchen."

Emily found that her heart was racing. Reading an article in the paper was nothing like hearing it from David. It was suddenly so real.

"Julia was in the garden, in her nighty, clutching Evie and both of them were screaming their heads off. They were terrified as well as cold in the night air. Matthew was scarily quiet. I was terrified and thought he was dead. I didn't know what to do. Julia was useless, just screeching and out of control. I thought that if Matthew was burnt, and still alive, that I had to get him into cold water but I couldn't make out his injuries in the dark. To be honest, in my panic I eyed up the pond but luckily came to my senses. I dashed to the Beech's 'cos I knew that they were already up. Everyone was out of their houses by then, all watching but not doing anything very helpful if I may say so.

"I yelled at Mrs Beech, 'Water, water'. I don't think she understood so I rather rudely barged into their kitchen, put Matthew in the sink and turned on the tap. She followed and switched on the light. That's when I first saw clearly what had happened to him. I could at least see that he was breathing – rasping more like. His skin, oh God it was horrific. It was like melted cheese and tomato on a pizza that had been burnt, that's the only way I can think of describing it." Emily felt quite nauseous at that and instinctively clutched her patchwork bag to her for comfort. Thank God she already knew that he had survived, otherwise heaven knows how she would be feeling. "He was alive though and he was breathing in this weird way, really grating. I screamed at Mrs Beech to call an ambulance. To be honest I think I might have said 'fucking ambulance', pardon my French, I was so distraught. Mrs Beech would have been ever so shocked.

"I could hear the clang of the fire engines arriving then and hadn't realised at first that they'd had the sense to send an ambulance as well. I was just focused on scooping the water over my little boy's burning flesh. It smelled disgusting. His pyjama top had melted into his flesh. I wanted to vomit. I was scared that I was doing more harm than good and might kill him." He shivered and grimaced, a look of remembered horror crossing his face. Emily suspected that her face must look much the same. She felt sick.

"Thankfully the paramedics from the ambulance were

sent in our direction and took over. I can't tell you what a relief that was. They scooped him up, and I followed like a distraught mother hen. They took him into the back of the ambulance and fiddled about doing all the right things.

"It's hard to remember what happened next. I know that Julia came to the ambulance at some point with Evie and they all ended up going to the hospital together. For some daft reason – perhaps because there wasn't enough room – I said I would drive after them. When I got into the car, I realised that my hands were burnt. I don't remember when or how it happened, but as the adrenaline wore off the pain was excruciating. Nothing would have stopped me from chasing after the ambulance with my whole family in it, though." As David spoke he was rubbing the back of his left hand; for the first time, Emily noticed the ridges of scarred skin that disappeared up his sleeve and winced.

"Matthew survived – how, no-one knows, but his face and chest were badly burnt. His eyes were unscathed, thank God, but the rest of him was a mess. His nose and lips had just melted." David frowned and bowed his head. Emily pursed her lips so that he couldn't see her grimace.

"I can't tell you how awful he looked. It was so difficult to register that this was our bright, noisy little fellow. They wrapped him up in white bandages, layers and layers of them, until he looked like the Michelin Man. He was heavily sedated so hopefully he wasn't aware of the agony that his burns must have been causing him. Dear God, I knew how my silly little burns seared and stung. He was in hospital for months –five months and four days to be exact, and that was only the start of it.

"After that he had to have operation after operation. By a stroke of luck we had the famous East Grinstead Hospital on our doorstep that had dealt with the burn victims in the war, all those pilots that crashed down in flames. Matthew couldn't have had more expertise than that, but it took years. Years of grafts, years of building him a nose, building him lips. After all of that he still doesn't look right, but..." He tailed off. "What a childhood though. He was so bloody brave. It was ironic really that everywhere we went after that people stared at Matthew rather than Julia – not because he was dark skinned but because of his scars."

David suddenly sat forward, lowered his voice and said conspiratorially, "The firemen said that the fire started from a fag end smouldering under the settee. *Under* the bloody settee. Not behind the settee, not down the side of the settee, actually under the settee. There is no way that Julia would have casually allowed a burning cigarette to fester under the bloody settee. It was that sodding Sarah – I am quite certain of it. It had to be her. She was the one sitting on it. I went round to theirs the day after finding out and challenged her but, of course, she denied it vehemently. Of course she would. Jolyon wasn't too pleased and told me to leave in no uncertain terms. I had to of course, Jolyon's my boss. God, I hate that woman."

Emily blurted out, "I wouldn't put it past her." David looked at with surprise and gave a wry grin. He looked much less fierce when he smiled. "Anyway, I'm so sorry your family had to go through such a terrible time."

He nodded, "Thanks."

David suddenly slapped his hands on his not inconsiderable thighs. "Well, at least we've got that out of the way so when they all get back you won't be too horrified. Matthew is used to people staring but I think it kinder to be prepared. You see, we are a really strange bunch, and I haven't even got onto young Daniel yet. I need a break. I need to stretch my legs." He leapt to his feet surprisingly athletically for his age, went over to a table, opened the drawer, and removed a large red book.

"Here we go. Photos so you can get used to the idea." David handed Emily the book and strode out of the room. Emily breathed deeply and turned the first page. Colourful photos were neatly stuck in tidy rows on to a corrugated background. They were held in place by what appeared to be a sheet of plastic laid over them.

Thank God David has had the foresight to show me these. This way, I won't be shocked and won't offend anyone.

She rummaged for her phone and tried taking photos but the reflections from the shiny plastic made it difficult. Still, Emily was glad of a break to gather her thoughts after all she'd learned. Everything he'd told her explained why he was so cold and brusque when she arrived; he had been through a lot and, after all, he wasn't related to her in any way. He seemed to have warmed to her a bit but nothing like the warmth of the welcome she had received from Uncle Charlie and Cathy. Not as bad as Sarah Pennington though.

Why did he even agree to see me? He seems so effusive about Julia when they first got married but he doesn't seem to be quite so enthusiastic now. Perhaps I'm just overthinking this.

She took a swig from her water bottle and took the opportunity to remove her mug of untouched tea through to the kitchen. Rinsing it under the tap she annoyingly chipped the rim.

Should I own up?

She heard him clatter back through the hall so plonked the chipped mug on to the draining board and scooted back into the lounge; she didn't want him to think that she was nosing around. She picked up the photo album and was looking at it when David entered the room.

"I'm so sorry about Matthew," she said.

David flapped a hand at her. "Well now, let's be getting

on with things." Pause, "Julia. That's who you're here about, and the kids. Your kin."

Has he been reading my thoughts?

David reclaimed his seat. "We lost everything in the fire at Wayside Cottage. Everything. Photos, important paperwork, birth and adoption certificates, pictures, clothes, furniture, the lot. We were left with the clothes we were standing up in and the family car. Some of the clothes had survived because they were in wardrobes, but have you ever smelt fabric that's been too close to a fire?" Emily shook her head. "Gobbing. However many times they laundered the stuff it stank. We ended up throwing everything away."

"There we were at the hospital – Matthew very poorly, Julia in hysterics and Evie distressed, and everyone in their nightclothes. That's all we had left in the world. It makes you realise how you don't need so many things in your home."

Emily couldn't help but look around the room. *That accounts for the minimalism I suppose.*

"Everyone did rally round, especially Charlie and Lorna. They were incredible. They immediately made Cathy's bedroom into a dormitory for all of us, shunted Cathy in with Wills, and dug out every bit of suitable clothing they had. To be honest, the clothes didn't fit too well, what with Charlie and Lorna being so much shorter than either of us, but they made the effort and welcomed us royally. They were amazing." He stopped suddenly, looked at Emily and asked anxiously, "How was Charlie when you saw him, you didn't say?"

Emily was pleased to be able to contribute something useful to the conversation. "He was lovely, incredibly welcoming, very hearty and seemed really pleased to be talking about Julia. They were obviously devoted to each other."

"Indeed, they were." He nodded. "Indeed, they were."

"To be honest," *Jesus holy wept is it catching?* "He did get a bit muddled, but I suppose he is getting on a bit."

David snorted. "As am I." He shook his head. Emily wasn't quite sure whether to comment that he was in very good shape for his age while Sarah had become a raddled old harridan, but the moment passed. "I do miss the old bugger," he said wistfully. "Anyways, he and Lorna were just brilliant. Jolyon and Sarah were at least practical. They sorted out accommodation for us and we came out of it rather well. The house they put us in down the road from their mansion was bigger than Wayside Cottage – same number of bedrooms but just much larger, much nicer, and right by the farm buildings so extra handy for work. It was furnished as well, ready to walk into, which made life a lot easier.

"That Sarah doesn't miss a trick though. We had only just moved in and were scrubbing it clean when she descended in all her glory to 'make us feel welcome'. She dropped into the conversation that Julia might like to 'do something to keep her mind off things rather than being in the house alone all day between hospital visits' and 'earn some extra cash to replace all the things that we lost in the fire'. She, of course, made out that the fire was Julia's fault, no argument. Her mantra was, 'We were both smoking, weren't we? And of course, you weren't experienced at it. Easy to be careless.' I don't know how she did it but everything with Sarah was always presented as a *fait accompli*. It was impossible to say no or that she was wrong."

I can quite see that. She's a vile old bat.

"It drove me up the wall, but she always got away with it. How did she do it? Miserable cow. Anyways, it ended up with Julia agreeing to clean for her. She found it awkward I know. There was Jolyon welcoming her like a long-lost mate, hugging her and chatting away like a friend does and Sarah treating her like the daily help. I know that she actually was the help but even so, it was done in a very patronising and snobbish way. And the other thing she did was keep reminding Julia that Jolyon was her husband and not to get any ideas. Seriously? I didn't like it but there was nothing either of us could do and the extra money was a bonus. That woman was a nightmare."

"Still is," Emily chipped in and earned a smile from David.

I am at least making progress with this relationship. But hang on, what did I miss there? Would he realise that Sarah has told me about Jolyon cheating with Julia? Did David know about it at all?

"And do you know what, she also got Julia to pick up Nicholas and take him to school. Can you believe it? 'You're passing the door anyway so you might as well.' Then it would turn into babysitting for Nicholas too. She would dump him with us at the drop of a hat. No wonder he and Evie became so close – that led to all that crazy nonsense when they frightened us to death disappearing together."

"Oh, the 'Babes in the Wood' thing?"

"You know about that then?"

Emily eagerly reached for her press cutting and replaced the haunting picture of the burning cottage with it. "Yes, I did a sweep through the newspaper archives, and it came up. Just a small paragraph in the Kent and Sussex Courier but it was great to bring the whole family story to life. What happened?" She sat forward.

David chuckled, a deep rumble, "Little buggers. They were always playing together all around the farm. At the weekends they often took their dinner or their tea with them made by Julia, never Sarah." David shook his head.

"No, never bloody Sarah, always Julia." He made a sound halfway between a laugh and a cough, "Anyways, Julia made a picnic for Evie and Nicholas. I don't have a clue who came up with the idea. Sarah blamed Julia of course for putting nonsense ideas into their heads because she often talked happily about when she, Jolyon and Charlie used to camp out overnight when she was growing up. To be honest, it could just as easily have been Jolyon telling Nicholas about it. The first thing we knew was that by seven o'clock there was no sight nor sign of them. Sarah rang demanding to know when Nicholas was going to come home. We said we hadn't seen them. Matthew didn't know where they were, or he wasn't telling. Jolyon wandered down, sent by Sarah obviously, and we decided to drive around the farm to see where they might be. We weren't bothered at first but the more we hunted high and low and couldn't find them, the more worried we got.

"By nine o'clock Julia and I were both really concerned and we decided to ring the police. Anyways, the old bill came out at half past and asked loads of questions and at this stage Matthew finally owned up to knowing about their plan. Little bugger could have saved us so much worry. I was tempted to give him a right hiding." Emily winced, shocked at what parents thought was acceptable in those days. Luckily, David didn't notice. "He wasn't sure where they were camping but knew their general whereabouts, so we set out in the farm vehicles to hunt them down. Fortunately, the smoke from their fire was a bit of a giveaway and there they were, snuggled up in a den they'd made. As the papers picked up, they were a right pair of 'Babes in the Wood'.

"They'd been building that den for ages. It was a very good one to be fair, in the hazel woods up Sweetings Lane where they used to do the charcoal burning, in a great little sheltered clearing with an old fire pit and everything. Good choice. I was quite proud of the way they went about it. I thought camping must be in Evie's blood from her Romany roots." He harrumphed and shook his head but Emily was puzzled and couldn't see why. She took a breath to ask but David continued, "I wasn't so happy that they didn't tell us what they were planning to do, without question we would have let them, so I was angry when we found them. We gave them a right good talking to but they were safe and sound and had done everything carefully so weren't in any danger. Julia was livid – mainly I think because they had a fire going. Sarah was just as furious, but Jolyon was quite laid back about it. He reminded Julia about all the times they used to camp out with Charlie. I think that was what made Sarah particularly furious. She was always the green-eyed monster when it came to Julia and the stories of her, Jolyon and Charlie.

"Those two – Evie and Nicholas – were virtually brother and sister growing up. Ironic really, but of course we didn't know anything then. I bet that Charlie told you all about that – Sarah too; she would have revelled in it."

Emily was a bit confused. "Um, no. Told me about what?"

"You don't know? Oh. Well, I'm getting a bit ahead of myself. Let me press on to catch up. You do know that Evie and Nicholas got married, don't you?"

"Yes, I know that." Emily turned back in her notes.

"As you can imagine, Sarah was totally against it. She got quite heated. We all assumed it was because she didn't want her precious only son marrying the daughter of their farm worker and daily help – daughter of the hated Julia, and a mixed-race girl at that. 'I don't want grandchildren with a touch of the tar brush and hoops in their ears' she kept saying. It really annoyed me the way she made remarks like that. She made such a fuss you wouldn't believe – went on and on about it. 'Over my dead body' and all that. I think that made Nicholas even more determined, and certainly Julia was all for it. Can you imagine, her little bit of revenge on Sarah for stealing Jolyon from her all those years ago? If only we had known." David shook his head. Emily was intrigued. *Where is this going?*

"The wedding went off well. We thought we'd have it up at Sarah and Jolyon's. It made sense as Nicholas was their only child, but Sarah point blank refused. She was going to have nothing to do with it. She was against the whole thing. Over her dead body and all that. We should have taken notice in retrospect, but we didn't have an inkling."

"An inkling about what?" What wasn't he telling her? This was getting frustrating. So many hints.

David ignored Emily's interruption. "As a compromise, good old Charlie and Lorna came up trumps and we had it at their place, in the ram's paddock exactly where Julia and me had our reception, which was really nice. With the marriage itself in Lamberhurst Church, we had a bit of a re-run of the whole thing. It brought back some happy memories. I remember holding hands with Julia and saying the vows to her under my breath as Nicholas said his, and she did the same to me when Evie was saying hers. We were so happy, so delighted that our beloved Evie was marrying the man of her dreams – such a great lad. Nicholas, bless him, asked Matthew to be his best man. Sarah was fuming about that too, said it would spoil the photographs. I'd show you the pictures, but Evie burnt the lot. Ironic really, what with my own wedding photos going up in flames at Wayside Cottage and then Evie doing that deliberately."

Emily was missing something very important. "But why would she do that?"

"I'm coming on to that. Don't be impatient." David flapped a great big paw of a hand at her.

"Evie and Nicholas wasted no time having a baby. We were thrilled when she told us that she was pregnant. Sarah wasn't." David chuckled. "I think she was concerned that her grandchild would come out as black as the ace of spades, but that turned out to be the least of our worries."

"The disabilities, you mean. Now, I have heard about that." Was she going to find out what he was hinting at?

"Yes, the disabilities. Poor mite was born with a cleft palate and club foot. He was hideous to look at. Nicholas saw him as he was born and was horrified. They took him away and fiddled around with him for ages apparently, before bringing him back to Evie. They tried to explain, she told me, but even so poor Evie had a fit when she saw him, the gaping void in his face, the weird mounds of flesh on display, the twisted limbs." David shuddered. "You just can't imagine the horror of it all. Have you ever seen what those babies look like?" Emily didn't but knew that for research purposes she should look it up. "Evie had imagined that her beautiful baby would be born and that she would suckle him but there was just this space where his mouth and lips should be. He went straight into the special care baby unit." David shook his head as Emily winced at the graphic description.

"I'm so sorry." Emily was close to tears. *Poor little baby. Poor Evie. How shocking.*

"Obviously the first thing was for all us grandparents to take turns to visit. Me and Julia went first and just tried to act normally. I looked at him in his plastic bowl thing, and the first thing I thought was that he had been born a carbon copy of Matthew after he had been burned, the red gaping space in his little face. The same feeling of shock and – despite all your best attempts not to think that way –

revulsion. I made sure that Evie didn't notice my reaction and we discussed his weight, his blond curly hair and his skin colour being very much like Evie's when she was born, and how she had got quite a bit darker as she grew up. She asked me if I wanted to hold him. I was a bit squeamish at first but when you hold that little fragile body in your arms, it's amazing how you just love them. Someone of your own flesh and blood, feeling their warmth and life and the smell of them..." David seemed to be weighing a baby in his arms. "When it was Julia's turn, she helped to feed him. They had a super-sized teat on a bottle just like the one we used with the calves who wouldn't drink from their buckets." David was still staring into space, looking solemn. "It took both of us a bit of time to get used to what he looked like but after having the whole Matthew debacle, let alone the whole mixed-race thing, we were kind of used to it as a family. Not Sarah though, oh no." David shook his head and raised his eyes to heaven. "Apparently Sarah literally wailed when she saw him and called him cursed, the devil's spawn and all sorts of hideous things. Evie was so upset she asked her to leave, saying 'How dare you talk to me like that?' To be honest, how did she dare act like that and say such dreadful things?"

"What a bitch." Emily couldn't help herself.

"Indeed." David looked at her, eyebrows raised, surprised, and gave her a quick smile, "Things settled down when they came out of hospital. Sarah never took to the baby and wouldn't have anything to do with him until he was seven months old and had had the surgery to get him looking something like normal. To be honest, they did a very good job. They had to do an operation on his club foot as well. Nicholas and Evie wanted him christened but Sarah kept putting them off and said that the family christening robe wouldn't suit a black baby, except she used the N-word, then she couldn't find where she had stored it. It was ridiculous. She is ridiculous. Can't stand the woman. I hate her."

"I can see why. Was he christened?"

"Of course he was. Without a stupid christening dress. He wore a nice little romper suit that Evie and Julia had picked out for him at a swanky baby clothes shop in Tunbridge Wells and he was christened at Lamberhurst Church where we'd all got married."

Emily nodded in endorsement. "Good on them." She was most definitely supporting team Evie and Nicholas.

"I've never said what he was called, have I? Daniel. Daniel Charles Pennington. A good strong name. Charlie was over the moon that they'd gone for Charles. Matthew was made godfather. A genius idea, both of them sharing racial characteristics and all patched up. They were set to be soulmates from the outset."

"That's nice." *Poor sod, everything he's been through.*

"But then the questions started. Why had poor old Daniel been born with so many defects? The doctors were asking all sorts of strange questions. They had begun when he was born but I think they were being very careful and were more concerned about putting him right before worrying how he got that way. They started asking about how closely related Evie and Nicholas were. We kept saying that they weren't related at all but there were alarm bells going off. Can you imagine what that's like? What were they saying? What were they implying? Was it just a coincidence or was something odd happening? You can guess who put the cat amongst the pigeons."

Emily looked questioningly at David. "Sarah?"

"Yes, that witch, Sarah. She was the first one to say the unthinkable. It started as hints. She's the most devious woman I've ever met in my whole life. She kept goading

Julia, not Evie. 'Is there any reason that you can think of that there might be a problem? I can understand that you have no idea of your family history... That is the problem with being a child that has been given away, perhaps there was a reason...' She had a look on her face that said she knew something. Cunning bitch. Julia became increasingly uncomfortable. She looked worried. I kept asking her what was going on, but she just kept saying that Sarah was crazy. You know how it is when there's something going on and there's nothing you can do? I caught Julia looking at Jolyon. Jolyon looking at Julia, shaking his head. Sarah looking like the cat that had got the cream. Devious cow.

"The time came. It all came to a head. Sarah came round to ours with Jolyon in tow. Planted herself in the middle of the lounge, arms akimbo.

"'Now Julia, are you going to tell David about you and Jolyon, or am I?' Of course, I was mystified, completely baffled. Julia looked horrified, her mouth gaping open. Jolyon looked laughably witless. 'Well?' Sarah repeated. Julia looked at me and back at Sarah. Sarah looked smug.

"'Well did you or didn't you?' Julia looked like a bloody goldfish.

"'I...'

"'Did you or didn't you?'

"'It was only that one time and I wasn't married...'

"'But Jolyon was, wasn't he?'

"'Yes but that wasn't down to me.'

"'Black witch.'"

Emily sat up at those words. It is exactly what Sarah had said to her yesterday.

"I couldn't understand what she was trying to say," David continued. "It took a while before it dawned on me. 'Julia, are you saying that you and Jolyon...?' Julia burst into tears.

"'It was after our hen and stag night. When we met up in the Elizabethan Barn. You know what happened – the racist comments, the fight, you and Charlie getting taken in by the police.' She could barely speak from her sobbing, but I was getting the picture.

"'And...' I prompted.

"'Well Jolyon took me home didn't he? You asked him to. You told him to. We got a taxi.' She was looking at me, her eyes full of fear or something like that.

"'And then...' I prompted again. Julia squirmed.

"'You know how he's always felt about me and he wanted to talk about it and why he'd married Sarah and not me and how he'd regretted it every day.' Sarah was looking daggers.

"'And...' I was determined to get to the bottom of it. I was getting so angry. I could feel it boiling up in my head. I wanted to shout but I kept my cool.

"'We went into the oast house–'

"'Why the oast house?'

"'Because I didn't want to disturb Mum and Dad and, if they did wake up and come down, I didn't want to tell them that Charlie had been taken in by the police.' It was a reasonable answer but it sounded very dodgy to me. 'And I was pissed, had far too much to drink, I wasn't thinking straight. I had been cuddled up to Jolyon in the taxi, I was upset at how the evening had been spoiled, it felt good, the familiar smell of him, the warmth and I did feel very sad that he'd married Sarah and not me.'

"'What about me though, Julia? Weren't you thinking about me?'

"'Well, yes but no, not at the time. We weren't married yet. Look, I was so drunk that I could barely stand up...' She stopped, looked at Jolyon and pleaded, 'Jolyon, help me out here, please.' He shrugged, looked ashamed, and so he bloody well should have. 'You could say that Jolyon took advantage of me...' Jolyon gasped as Julia continued, 'You know I love you, David, I do. You know that I wanted to marry you.'

"'But you'd always wanted Jolyon, hadn't you? Sounds a bit like I was the second best doesn't it?' Julia just shook her head. I was boiling with anger. 'Anyways what did you think you could achieve by talking to Jolyon," David did the air quotes gesture around talking, "when he was already married with a child?'

"'I don't know. I wasn't thinking, I was just feeling. And it just happened.'

"'Did you actually, you know, do it?'

"'Yes.' Julia whispered. I was looking at her, so I don't know what Jolyon was doing, or Sarah even.

"'The week before we got married, is that right Julia?'

"'Yes.'"

Emily realised that she had heard about the infidelity between Jolyon and Aunt Julia from Sarah but hadn't understood the significance or realised that it was just before Aunt Julia's marriage to David. David continued, in full spate. "'So, what is it that Sarah,' and I glared at Sarah then, 'is suggesting?'

"Sarah stood to her full height, to be honest, not very tall but she did look imperialistic. 'Well, David, we know that the baby's birth defects are normally linked to the parents of the child being close relations. We've all read that, it's been hinted at by the doctors all along, so it got me thinking. I knew about your black whore wife and my husband. I'm no fool. I challenged him with it at the time and he tried to deny it.' Jolyon had turned away and was staring out the window, still as a statue. I hated him at that moment. 'I've had to do my level best to keep an eye on them ever since that evening. I have been thinking about nothing else ever since that misshapen, distorted child was born.' I winced, it was our beloved Daniel that she was talking about as if he were some object.

"'And what is your conclusion then Sarah?' I couldn't bring myself to say what I was thinking.

"'Has it not occurred to you, David, that perhaps Evie and Nicholas share a father?' I think I must have roared or yelled or something. Everyone, including me, jumped out of our skins."

A horrible frisson of cold travelled down Emily's spine. So, this is what Sarah had been getting at. She had told Emily about Jolyon and Julia but Emily just hadn't taken in the implications. Emily was horrified. She covered her mouth with her hands to try and suppress a gasp which came out as a squeak. Her skin crawled.

Dear God. That is appalling.

David was in full flood and continued without looking at Emily. "Julia started moaning, 'No, no,' over and over again; she crumpled and sobbed and hid in her hands. I went over to her to... I don't know what, certainly not to harm her in anyway. She leapt up, barged her way out of the room and fled. We were frozen. The next thing we heard was the car start up.

"'Let her go, the conniving black bitch.' That's what Sarah said.

"'In my wife's defence," I told that old harridan, 'I think you must be clear that she is not the adulterer here. Jolyon? What have you got to say for yourself? You are just as culpable.' Jolyon flapped a hand in my direction. He wouldn't look at me. 'Come on now, Jolyon.'

"Jolyon turned with disdain plain on his face. 'I don't give a flying fuck. All that is in the past and there is bugger all we can do to change it. All I can think of is Evie and Nicholas and their poor child. Someone has got to tell them.

In the circumstances, I think it ought to be me and Julia, but she's buggered off. So it had better be me. Agreed?' He looked at me, I hesitated then nodded, and then he looked at Sarah. She gave a curt nod. She looked so smug, it made my blood boil.

"'I just hope to God that that isn't where Julia has gone,' I said. 'Now please go, just please go.' They went and I stood there in the middle of my home and it felt as if my whole world and everything, just the whole bloody thing, had caved in.

"So, that's it you see. That's when everything came out."

Emily sat with her hands still covering her open mouth. She couldn't think of a thing to say. So that was why Sarah had been so keen to tell her all about Jolyon's 'indiscretion'.

Oh my God. Oh shit. Evie and Nicholas half-siblings. They'd got married and Sarah knew. And I know exactly where Julia fled to. Uncle Charlie's. But why didn't Cathy say anything about this?

She nearly jumped out of her skin when she heard the door open and a cheerful voice say, "Hello, we're back."

TWENTY-TWO

Emily couldn't help but stare at Evie as she came into the lounge. This was her blood related cousin, and it was an incredible thrill to be meeting her for the first time. The first thing that Emily noticed was Great Granny's green eyes, and the second that her long curly hair was just like her own. Evie stood there, statuesque and graceful.

Emily shook her head to clear the awfulness of David's story from her mind and hoped that for Evie it would all have happened a long time ago, in the past and that she had recovered from such a tragedy.

How the heck had she lived with it?

After the bombshell that she had received from David she was still trying to make sense of it. Having now heard what was meant to be the same story from all these different perspectives, Charlie then Sarah and now David, she was trying to fit it together like solving a puzzle, or a crime. She could hear other people scrummaging around in the hall – Matthew, Daniel? She suddenly remembered her manners, took a deep breath, found a smile, shoved her bag to one side and got to her feet.

"Hello, you must be Evie. I'm Emily, your cousin." In real life, the likeness to Aunt Julia, that Emily had seen in Uncle Charlie's photo albums, was incredible. The pictures that David had given her to look at just didn't do her justice. She was incredible, so charismatic.

"Pleased to meet you, Emily," Evie said in a voice that didn't sound particularly pleased.

"You have Great Granny's eyes," Emily offered with a stiff smile.

Evie stood behind David's chair and, instead of acknowledging what she had just said, leant forward and gave David a kiss on the cheek. David reached up to her, took her hand and kissed it, held on to it. It was nice to see them so close. "Hello love. Have you had a good time?"

"Actually, it was a nightmare." Evie looked at Emily and seemed to be addressing her rather than David. "Market day. The traffic is terrible, and we had to park up at the wharf because the Tesco car park was full. But we did get some goodies for lunch." After the bombshell Emily had just been told, this story of parking problems seemed to be totally inane.

I have to remember that while this is all new for me, they've lived with it for years.

"Did Matthew come back with you?" David asked.

Evie moved her gaze to David. Emily was relived as she had found her blank stare discomfiting. "No. He decided to go back to work but we managed a quick cup of coffee. He was on good form. Harvest is going well, and their yields are good, so he was happy about that. We had coffee and a cake at the new place in the market place. He's thrown himself heart and soul into fundraising for Rowdeford School – that's the children's special school," she added, swivelling her stare to Emily. "It's so great to have such a good school on our doorstep for all my special kids. But enough of our boring old life, what about you Emily? What has Dave been telling you?"

Dave, not Dad. Interesting.

Evie didn't look particularly enamoured to be meeting Emily, no welcoming hug and nothing about their relationship. Emily could feel odd vibes. It was completely different to the enthusiastic welcome she had received from Cathy and Uncle Charlie.

The 'kids' came in. Daniel was no surprise, thanks to the photo album. Looking through the pictures had given Emily a chance to look beyond the disabilities to find the person. He limped in, dragging his left leg, and his face was clearly patched up with a scar across his upper lip, uneven nostrils and his whole face seemed to be lifted on one side. The lenses on his glasses were thick. Despite all that, he had a cheeky grin and was obviously comfortable in his own skin. His blond hair framed his smiling face like a halo.

"Hey Dad, how are you doing?" he said to David, raising his hand to high five him. David obliged with a good thwack.

Dad? Not grandad? What on earth does the boy think his origins are?

Emily stood up, her hand extended, "Hello, Cousin Daniel. It's great to meet you."

He shook her vigorously by the hand. "Well, hello cousin that I didn't even know that I had."

Emily grinned back at him.

What a charming boy.

A skinny girl slithered in behind him. She had to be Evie's daughter, the child in the photographs. Squirming with shyness, she dodged past Emily and threw herself into David's lap. Snuggling into him, she twiddled dark curls and eyed up Emily with Great Granny's piercing green eyes.

David stepped into the melee of introductions. "Now, Harriet, this is your cousin Emily. Her great granny is the same as your great granny. Isn't that amazing?" His voice had become soft, soothing and gentle. The girl reached up and whispered in his ear in the same way that Ashley always did to Mum. Surely, she was too old to be acting in this babyish way. "She's come to meet us all." He chuckled. Having heard that Daniel was the result of an incestuous relationship had taken the wind out of Emily's sails, and now she was faced with this child. She wasn't sure how Harriet fitted into the proceedings at all, so what could she say?

Falling back onto what felt like safer ground, she asked, "So, Daniel, where do you go to school?"

Daniel roared with laughter and slapped his thighs, the image of David earlier that morning. Shared mannerisms but not genes. "How old do you think I am?"

"I'm sorry, Daniel, I'm not sure. I should have checked. I've written down everything I found out," Emily said as she reached for her bag of papers.

"Don't you worry, Cousin Emily, people often think I'm younger than I look. It is my handsome, youthful appearance." He did a dancing shimmy with a mischievous look, pursing his lips. "No, Cousin Emily, I left Rowdeford School years ago. I have been made to go out and work for my living. Mum and Dad cracked the whip, threw me out of the house and sent me to slave in Morrisons all day." He grinned.

Such confidence, so articulate and he calls them Mum and Dad. Convenience?

Evie put her hands together with a jolting slap and said, "I think it's time we had some lunch." Emily thought that the clapping must indeed be a genetic trait passed down from Great Granny.

They all trooped into the kitchen. David took his place at the top of the table and invited Emily to sit to his right. Harriet whispered in his ear. David said indulgently, "Harriet says, that's her place."

"Oh, I'm sorry, Harriet. I'll sit somewhere else," Emily said, keen to make a good impression but puzzled by Harriet's childlike behaviour. Harriet darted into the chair then reached over and took David's hand. Emily noted where Daniel and Evie sat then took the last vacant seat.

"Sorry about that, she's such a daddy's girl," David said.

"That's okay," Emily replied, her brain full of questions.

Daddy's girl? Did he just say daddy's girl? Perhaps they all call him Dad, except Evie who doesn't even though he was, but isn't. So complicated. Do I ask? Best not, see what happens.

"So how old is Harriet?" she went for instead.

"She's twelve, thirteen in December. Aren't you Harriet?" Harriet nodded. Emily was getting the distinct impression that Harriet wasn't entirely behaving her actual age, but perhaps she was just shy or playing up to being 'the baby' like Ashley did.

With that query out in the open, Emily was stuck again. She felt she should be asking questions but wasn't sure what to ask.

Evie placed a whole array of salads in plastic boxes on the table. Emily frowned, a reflex reaction when faced with synthetic waste. She quickly smoothed out her face, hoping her hosts wouldn't think she was disapproving of them in any way.

David clearly felt he'd spoken enough for the day and delved into the offered lunch with gusto. It was if he had forgotten about the bombshell he had lobbed in only minutes before everyone else's arrival. Evie was handing around the salads, ladling some on to Harriet's plate and passing it on. Emily helped herself.

Well, at least I can avoid the meat without making a fuss. One less thing to fret about.

"This is very kind of you Evie, thank you so much."

Evie responded, "No problem. Now, do tell me about what you have found out so far about Mum so that me and Dave can fill in your gaps. Who have you been to see?" It came out as a challenge rather than a request.

"Well, I did a lot of my research before I came – the joys of the internet – and have birth certificates, marriage certificates, that sort of thing, and several downloads from the Kent and Sussex Courier. Like The Babes in the Wood news story when you and Nicholas disappeared for the night." Evie raised her eyebrows and looked cold. Emily blanched. "Also, a tiny cutting about the police being called to your dad's stag night, it doesn't reveal much," Emily felt herself blushing knowing what happened after that, "the fire at Wayside Cottage and then, of course, about your mum when she died. I mapped it all out in a timeline and I've drawn up a family tree which I would love to pass across you to check that I've got it all correct."

Emily knew she was babbling to cover her nervousness. Leaning forward with the page open at the family tree, she knew that Evie wouldn't be able to see from such a distance but thought it might help to have it as a prop to avoid having to look at Evie's hostile eyes. "So here I start with John and Margaret Levett who had Charlie and Molly, who sadly died, and then of course Aunt Julia, your mum adopted as their daughter. I then have Aunt Julia marrying David, and then the births of you and Matthew." Emily was careful how she phrased that, being super careful not to mention anything about dads who might not be dads. She knew from her own experience that this was a difficult topic and Emily had no idea whether Evie would know that David had filled her in on the whole debacle. "I then have you marrying Nicholas Pennington and the birth of Daniel."

Emily paused before daring to ask, "I don't seem to have Harriet on it though, I need to add her." Emily looked at Evie with what she hoped was a questioning look.

Evie looked at Emily blankly, "Oh yes, you must add Harriet." *Well, that didn't help.* "So, who have you met so far?"

Having hit such a blank wall, Emily decided to answer Evie, "First of all I went to see Uncle Charlie who seemed more than delighted to reminisce. I heard all about Aunt Julia's childhood which was really nice. I'm sure that Great Granny would have been thrilled to know that she had been so happy. We looked at all the photo albums and, of course, I found out that you all seem to have inherited Great Granny's green eyes."

Don't think I will mention that I had no idea that Aunt Julia was black. That would be crass. It's odd how I've embraced the multi ethnicity of my newly found family. It seems now as if I've always known.

David suddenly said, muffled with his mouth full, "I thought all those photos were destroyed in the fire at Wayside Cottage."

Emily replied eagerly, "Aunt Julia's would have been, but Uncle Charlie had loads."

David nodded, "Of course, of course he did."

"You ought to ask him for some copies," Emily said enthusiastically, pleased to be on safer ground. "Aunt Julia looked so adorable when she was little. I can see the resemblance in Harriet, particularly Great Granny's green eyes."

When this mention didn't prompt Evie into enquiring further about her great grandmother, it seemed clear to

Emily that she didn't want to know about her own birth relatives. That was sad, as Emily had expected lots of questions about her as well as Granny and Aunt Cynthia.

Snappishly, Evie said, "We haven't been in touch with Uncle Charlie for years. Cathy keeps sending stuff but we think it best to keep ourselves to ourselves." She paused and more gently enquired, "How is Uncle Charlie? He's only a couple of years younger than Dave. Is he still farming, or has he retired too?"

Emily hadn't realised just how old Uncle Charlie looked in comparison to David. But on the other hand, it could just be that David looked exceptionally good for his years. His full head of hair made him look much younger.

"Uncle Charlie was a bit muddled. I think he has dementia. He kept asking when Julia was coming. A bit sad really. Cathy was very helpful and told me all about the night that," she hesitated, not wanting to talk about such gruesome things in front of the children, "Aunt Julia died." Emily smiled wanly, hoping for someone else to chip in. When they didn't, she tried, "I gather that you were all there that night at Uncle Charlie's?"

David looked at Evie intently; so did Emily. But then David was shaking his head and saying, "I don't think we have to go into that just now. Not in front of the children, eh?" Emily looked back at Evie and found her looking intently at David. David nodded his head.

What is going on?

When Evie caught Emily staring at them both, Emily hastily looked down at her plate and mumbled, "I'm hoping to go back there again before I go home." Silence. Emily had obviously touched a nerve.

Evie's eyes flashed and she broke the silence. "So, what did Uncle Charlie say about Mum and Jolyon Pennington?"

Does she know that I know? Emily wondered. *Did*

David warn her he was going to tell me all that stuff in advance?

"Not a lot really," she hazarded. "He seemed to talk most about when they were children. I think that that is the bit he remembers most clearly. He did confess to loving Aunt Julia and hoping that when she didn't marry Jolyon that she might marry him. So, that was a bit awkward." Evie looked at David and frowned; David shrugged. With so little encouragement, it was hard to keep talking but she soldiered on, "He told me all about the wedding at the farm and him being best man. And they've converted the barn that burnt – you know, the oast house – into a house for Wills, Uncle Charlie's son. Cathy is living in the farmhouse with Uncle Charlie."

Evie came to life, "So, he didn't say anything about what happened after Daniel was born?"

Daniel perked up, lifting his head from where he was shovelling in food and grinned happily. "Are you talking about me now?"

Evie said kindly, "No, lovey, Nanny Julia."

Daniel said sadly, "I don't remember her."

Evie patted his hand, "I know you don't."

Daniel turned to Emily, "She died in a fire you know. If she hadn't died she would have looked like Uncle Matty. His face is wonky, even wonkier than mine. Do you know, he was burnt in a fire too?"

Evie pursed her lips, "That's right, Daniel, your lovely Uncle Matty. Emily knows all about that, Dad told her all about it, didn't you?" David nodded, briefly raising his head from his plate.

Emily noted the reference to David as Dad again. "Yes, David told me about all the operations that Daniel had to go through, poor love." Emily added, smiling at Daniel who was eating with concentration again. Silence fell around the table except for knives and forks scraping on plates. Emily felt uncomfortable and piped up, "And then I went to see Mrs Pennington." In Emily's mind she was Mrs Pennington and not Sarah. Calling her Sarah would be far too familiar.

"So, how was Sarah Pennington?" Evie asked with an aggressive tone.

"She wasn't very nice. I got the definite impression that she didn't get on very well with your mother."

"You can say that again," laughed Evie. Not a happy laugh, more of a splutter. "Evil cow. She treated Mum like dirt. Nick told me once that she had called Mum her house slave. Appalling. She fought tooth and nail of course when Nick and I wanted to get married. She was despicable when Daniel was born, so it's hard to think of her doing anything nice for anyone else." Evie shuddered. "I don't want to see her again, ever. She can burn in hell." Emily was surprised at just how vehement she was in front of Daniel and Harriet, but they didn't seem to notice. In a caustic tone, Evie added, "So, enlighten us – what did that she-devil tell you?"

Emily was relieved that, on this occasion, she and Evie seemed to be in agreement and answered in a lighter tone, "Not a great deal when I look back on it. It was mostly vile remarks, very racist. She did say how she got to marry Jolyon which sounded a bit dodgy to me." *Dare I say anything about what she had said about David? It would be odd not to.* "She talked a bit about David."

David glanced at Emily. "All good I hope."

"Yes, of course." She wouldn't be repeating what Mrs Pennington said; it made Emily blush now that she was sitting there right in front of him. "On the whole."

David laughed. "Stuck up bitch."

Evie chipped in, "And what did she say about Mum?"

"Not a great deal really. It seemed to be mainly about

Jolyon and her, when they met, when they got married." Emily felt a bit awkward talking about Jolyon in front of Evie. "And then how they went their separate ways, but I didn't know why they had then." Emily stuttered to a halt.

Dear God, this is so hard.

What Mrs Pennington had said was now going through her mind on fast forward, tying in with the bolt from the blue from David. Should she call Jolyon 'your father' or would that be presumptuous? What could, and couldn't, be said in front of the children?

"But you do know now?" Evie paused, holding Emily's anxious gaze. Emily nodded. Evie continued coldly, her face expressionless, "And are you documenting it all, Emily, everything that everyone has been telling you?" Emily couldn't help thinking that Evie didn't sound very friendly.

"Yes. I've been writing up my interviews," that sounded too formal and uncaring, so she backtracked, trying to retrieve the warmer rapport that she had managed to get a glimpse of, "my, er, visits, I mean. I type it all up on my laptop in the evening back at my B&B. I'd love some snaps of you all to complete the picture."

Evie continued sounding ice cold, "And who are you going to share these thoughts with?"

Emily shivered, her attempt at lightness clearly hadn't worked, "I don't know really. Granny and Aunt Cynthia are desperate to find out all about Aunt Julia, their lost and found sister. And that whole branch of my family will be fascinated to hear about their cousins, just as I'm sure you are dying to hear about them." She knew she sounded overly jolly.

Evie wasn't to be swayed. "I think we'd like to check what you've written before you start broadcasting it, if you don't mind?" Evie smiled but it didn't reach her eyes. The silence was uncomfortable. Emily wasn't sure what to say to break it, but Evie took a deep breath and continued, "I'm not sure I really do need to know much about your branch of the family. It's all so remote from my life. Mum always felt abandoned and unwanted by your family, so there isn't really any feeling of connection. This is my family here." She gestured to those sitting around the table.

Emily couldn't understand Evie's assessment of the situation. "Have you read Great Granny's letter that I sent to David, where I explained how we found out about Aunt Julia? She didn't want to give Aunt Julia up. She loved Aunt Julia's father and would have married him and kept her baby if she'd been allowed. Cathy thinks it's because the Americans wouldn't let black people marry white ones; it was illegal. Look, I have brought photos of Great Granny, her mum and Granny and Aunt Cyn – your mum's half-sisters – to show you, to see if you can see family resemblances. They'd love to meet you." Emily rummaged in her bag to find the snaps, placed them on the table, and tried desperately to arouse Evie's interest, pointing at each person in turn. "And my mum and Aunt Jennifer and me and Ashley."

"I don't think I'm interested, but thank you," Evie said curtly. Silence descended. Emily looked at David but he was keeping his eyes on his food.

Where the hell do I go from here? We're still eating dinner. I can hardly take my leave without finishing it. But it's clear Evie doesn't want me here at all.

Emily tried a whole new tack in an effort to break the heavy silence, since it was clear neither Evie nor David were going to. *Jesus, this is hard work.* "So, do tell me about your life here in Wiltshire. It's a lovely part of the world."

Evie looked slightly taken aback. Emily felt foolish for asking such an inane question but at least Evie played the game and answered, "Dave has probably told you about working for Bob Frearson, hasn't he?" David shook his head. "Oh, well he's been a great boss and Dave's really enjoyed working for him after Jolyon and Sarah."

A definite dig about Jolyon and Sarah, and still referred to as Jolyon.

Evie continued with a sarcastic edge to her voice, "I don't think he realised how different it could be when you're given responsibility and allowed to get on with it. Bob's farm is very much the same size but nearly all arable. There are a few beef cattle which I like. I'm fond of animals and like to see them around, like in Kent, rather than just fields and fields of crops." Evie seemed to run out of things to say.

David chipped in, obviously keen to carry on the conversation while keeping it away from anything controversial. "But I've retired now, last year. Fortunately, this is a Crown Estate farm cottage that goes with the job, so even though I'm retired we have a protected tenancy for the rest of our lives. Matthew still works for Bob though. Nice to see him getting stuck in and he's stepped up into my shoes."

"Dave's my house husband now," added Evie with a smile. Emily was taken aback by her use of husband, seemed a bit odd. "He does the school run and looks after our Harriet when I go to work at the care home."

"And Dad looks after me," chirped Daniel.

Evie's smile when she looked at Daniel was stunning, like the sun suddenly coming out, a complete change from anything that Emily had seen up to this moment. She chuckled, an appealing low sound. "You don't need looking after any more do you, you nitwit." Emily was so pleased to see her looking so relaxed and could at last get a real sense of how Aunt Julia must have been.

Daniel laughed. "I'd starve if Dad wasn't here to feed us

all." Emily was still trying to take in the 'our Harriet' bit. Was she implying Harriet was both of theirs? Surely not. That couldn't be right.

With a laugh in her voice, Evie added, "I do work odd shifts, that's true. And your Dad is a much better cook than me."

They all seemed to be so happy. Gentle banter. Genuine affection. A tight family unit. Emily on the outside looking in.

David decided to join the conversation. "So, we moved here twenty years ago and haven't looked back. Daniel went through Rowdeford School which has given him a great start in life, as you can see from his precocious nature." David gave a mock glare at Daniel, who spread his hands and made a daft pose, his hands on his hips, with a huge grin on his face. "Harriet is now benefiting from the same. She tried very hard in mainstream school, but she needs to have a bit of a boost from the right sort of education to meet her special talents. Don't you, poppet?"

Ah, that explains her strangely childish behaviour.

Evie smiled at Harriet then turned to Emily, her warm disposition and genial smile changing in an instant; there was a challenge in her eyes. "As you can see, I do seem to produce very special children."

Poor Evie.

"They are our special children." David said gently. "Now, very special child Danny Boy, please could you clear the table and do the washing up with me and Harriet so that your mum can go through to the lounge with Emily? Harriet, my little darling, please can you help me and Daniel? Say yes, Daddy." Harriet didn't say anything but stayed where she was, looking at him.

Okay. Harriet is definitely his child as well as Evie's. I know that Evie isn't his daughter, so they're not blood relatives, but this still feels a bit creepy. I've only just got used to the idea of David not being Evie's dad. I'm not sure I've quite taken this new situation on board.

As she sat down in the lounge, Evie leant forward in her chair, an urgent look on her face. "Emily, Dave and I are not related. You do realise that?" Evie was almost whispering. Emily had obviously let her thoughts show on her face.

Cathy is right. Must take control of myself.

Emily nodded, but she didn't feel totally comfortable with the whole thing.

Evie glared, "I will say it again, we are not related. Are you related to Dave?" Emily shook her head. "Neither am I. It took me years to get over it, believe me. Dave has been my rock through all this horror story. He has loved me unconditionally all through my childhood and given me a sense of pride, a sense of belonging and sanctuary when others could be quite cruel. Our relationship was totally neutral for years, but I have always loved him and he has always loved me. It seemed perfectly natural for our bond, rapport, connection, whatever you want to call it, to develop into true love. True love in all senses."

Emily nodded but it came out as a bit extravagant, so she stopped abruptly, feeling awkward. "We live as man and wife, and as far as anyone around here is concerned that is what we are. Officially we have the same surname and Daniel always goes as Merripen rather than Pennington. We found out long ago that we could put the birth certificates right and everything, which would mean we could then marry formally. But we're beyond that. Why bother? We're content. We love each other. Happy ever after. Our funny, special family." Emily nodded again and tried a smile, even though in her heart she wasn't quite ready to sanction it entirely.

It's hard to switch just like that. Oh, but this research

into Aunt Julia's life is really challenging all my silly prejudices.

"Well, Cousin Emily, this is your newly discovered family." Evie sat back, spread her hands and smiled with a distinct sneer. "Now you're going to have quite a story to tell the rest of your family."

Emily responded, "Indeed. So, Aunt Julia, your mother? All the arguing the night she died – it seems like what you've told me explains all that, doesn't it?"

"I think it rather does," Evie replied.

"Well, that's the arguments explained, but the way Aunt Julia died –"

"Knowing how she died will not change anything," Evie interrupted. "We've all put that behind us."

"But were you there, with Nicholas? Cathy swears that she saw you," Emily persisted.

Evie looked angry. "The case rests as inconclusive, an open verdict, and it won't bring her back. Now, it has been lovely to meet you," her face said otherwise, "and I can't tell you what a joy it is to hear that my mother was loved by her birth mother. It gives us all some peace, but I want you to imagine, just for a moment, what my life has been like." She leant forward again, raised her hands and started counting on each long, slender finger. "The first thing, born to a mother who had been given away for being black but was actually neither black nor white. Me too. No-one can comprehend that unless it has happened to them. No-one at all. The small slights, the obvious restraint, always being treated differently." Emily wanted to express her sympathy and took in a breath ready to speak but Evie snapped, "Don't even say that you can imagine what it must be like. You can't." Emily jumped, feeling chastised. That was exactly what she had been about to say.

Evie pressed on her index finger. "The second thing: a

badly scarred brother who is stared at because however hard the doctors tried, they could never make him look anything resembling normal. I escaped untouched, not a blemish. Survivor guilt."

She moved to her middle finger, her eyes not leaving Emily's face. "Third: a badly disabled and disfigured son. Through no fault of his own. Nobody's fault apparently."

She stabbed at her ring finger, which Emily noted for the first time did carry a wedding ring. "Fourth: discovering that you had married your own brother." She made a face, mouthed 'oops' and shook her head then pushed her little finger back, too far Emily felt. "And fifthly, dear Harriet. My super special surprise child. Too old to be a mother. Definitely my fault this time." She held Emily's gaze. Emily was feeling a bit uncomfortable at the intensity of it.

"So, can you see, Cousin Emily, why I am done? My parents killed themselves, both of them, just in different ways. I've had enough. I just want a quiet life in my very own small world where I can love and be loved, surrounded by my flesh and blood, my real family. I want to be left alone. I don't want all this dredged up, and not by a person who claims to be family who I've never met and don't trust. Do you understand?"

Emily was frozen to the spot by the vehemence and venom in Evie's voice. "Yes, I do. Or rather, I am trying to."

David came in, looming over them where they sat. The atmosphere evaporated as if a bubble had been burst and the fresh air allowed back in. Evie stood up; her voice changed to bright and cheerful. "Hello love, Emily was just saying that she's got to be on her way." Evie smiled sweetly as she moved to take David's arm, but her eyes flashed at Emily.

"Yes, that's right," Emily said hastily, jumping up and fluttering about putting her belongings together, piling everything into her bag. She made doubly sure that she had everything, since it was very clear she wouldn't be invited back here again.

Uncertain what she could say in light of everything, she blurted out, "Thank you so much for your hospitality. Sorry to intrude. You have been very kind and it's been wonderful to meet all my cousins." Emily knew that she sounded pathetically and falsely jolly. "I'll let the rest of the family know all about you, or would you like me to check with you first...?"

"Whatever you want, Emily." Evie sighed, put her head on one side and leant into David. David kissed the top of her head. Emily didn't want to break their united front and so shuffled out of the lounge without shaking hands or offering hugs. She called out, "Bye Daniel, bye Harriet, nice to meet you," but got no response. She tried again with Evie and David, "Bye then, thank you so much." Evie and David followed in silence, herding her out. They watched her get into Granny's car and each raised a hand as she drove away.

Emily stopped just down the lane to catch her thoughts, and to have a pee in the bushes since she hadn't dared ask to use the bathroom again before she left. As she relieved herself behind an elder tree, a thought suddenly struck her.

Bugger, I forgot to give Evie GG's letter to Julia. And bugger again, I didn't get any photos.

~

Emily arrived at the B&B after a painfully slow drive back, during which her thoughts had jumbled and tumbled, falling over themselves in confusion. The long journey had given her time to muster her thoughts into some semblance of order and she was eager to get them written down, but where to begin?

It was hard to come to terms with the awful reality of what had happened to poor Evie and Nicholas. How shocking. How horrifying. It kept popping up in her head and made her shiver every time. Appalling.

It was nearly time for tea, which they all seemed to call dinner in this part of the world. Very confusing. She was still full of the 'lunch' – what Emily would have called dinner – that Evie and David had provided. It was sitting very heavily in her stomach. Needing to digest that as well as try and make sense of the revelations of the day, she threw herself onto her bed, exhausted.

It's all so complicated.

So many questions pinging around in her head made her feel queasy. Why hadn't Uncle Charlie told her what had happened, or had the horror of it all simply made him forget? Why didn't this all come out at the inquest into Aunt Julia's death? What excuse did they all give to the authorities for being at Uncle Charlie's that night if they hadn't come clean about the reason? She was very keen to follow up with Uncle Charlie and Cathy.

Emily was also seething that Mrs Pennington had been so perverse. Had she lied? The harridan. She must have done it deliberately if only by omission, she certainly wasn't the sort of person to hold back. Thinking about it, Emily couldn't be certain. She certainly hadn't told the whole truth, that was for sure. The whole meeting had been very abruptly brought to a close with that parting shot about 'more to tell'. She leapt off the bed, grabbed her 1/- notebook and scrabbled through the notes of only the day before. Unbelievable. Only one day before?

Yes, she definitely said that Jolyon had slept with Julia but not the consequences or when. Not even a hint. Obviously, Aunt Julia would have been horrified to find out what the outcome of her drunken coupling with Jolyon had resulted in. Emily shuddered. But could it be about how Aunt Julia actually died? Cathy could tell me about that.

So, I need to phone Cathy again and go and see her and Uncle Charlie. I'll do that first and then I won't have to go and see that hideous old witch.

Emily dialled Cathy's number, but it went to answerphone again. She was too uptight to leave a message.

She didn't dare talk to The Boomers until she had got her story straight. What on earth would she say?

And I still haven't heard a peep out of Mum. What is going on there? I'd better send her a message to show that at least I am not ignoring her – even if she is ghosting me. Perhaps she's sulking about GG's house and can't face talking to me at all.

She tapped in,

> Incredible. I met Julia's husband and daughter today.

What on earth can I say about all that?

Emily pondered and went for the easy option.

> Genevieve, Julia's daughter has GG's eyes. Incredible likeness. Will fill you in when I get back.

It all looked so straightforward when put in a short message like that.

TWENTY-THREE

By the time breakfast came around after a long, sleepless night, Emily was starving and completely knackered. Everything was still whirling round in her head.

How could it have happened? Poor Aunt Julia. Poor Cousin Evie. How awful to discover you had married your own brother. What a mess. So much tragedy in one family and two horrendous fires with dreadful consequences.

Somewhere around three in the morning, Emily had been convinced that Aunt Julia had been murdered by Sarah Pennington, simply because she was such an evil cow that she could have done it out of pure spite. Having not managed to kill her by putting a lit cigarette under her settee, perhaps Sarah had then had another bash at it in the oast. Emily had stared into the dark, her thoughts churning.

Or perhaps it was a distraught David losing the love of his life through her betrayal with Jolyon? But he wouldn't do that to Evie would he, murder her mother?

Or perhaps it was Evie and Nicholas, livid with what Aunt Julia had done, and the fact that they had been made to bear the consequences. Cathy said that she'd seen Evie and she had never owned up to being there when asked by Emily. She had seemed to brush off the question.

Perhaps Uncle Charlie himself, unrequited love and all that.

Or perhaps Cathy was lying about everything, and it was her all along. But why on earth would she do that?

Or maybe it was just that Aunt Julia couldn't face what had happened and had tried to kill herself.

She was going through it all again as she cleaned her teeth amongst the roses and then went down the steep stairs to breakfast.

The super intelligent Katie looked surprised at Emily's request for fried eggs, tomatoes, mushrooms, hash browns and caffeinated coffee. To be fair, she was starving having missed tea yesterday. All the scenarios were still churning around like a bad case of stomach ache, which she was likely to get after placing such a ridiculously massive order of food.

Damn it, I didn't really question Evie about that evening at all. Why were she and Nicholas there? Why did she deny it?

Mind you, even if I had asked her, would she have answered? She wasn't very forthcoming with anything else.

Emily was embarrassed to find that she had slammed her fist on her breakfast table. Her coffee cup rattled in the saucer and her fork pronged off towards a nearby table. "I'm so sorry, I really am," Emily offered, to appease a very surprised looking man in a suit who ended up being the recipient of a flying fork.

She kept herself to herself as she waded through the enormous plate of food that Katie delivered in her usual exuberant manner.

With her stomach groaning after way too much food, Emily staggered up the steep stairs to her bedroom, lay back on the rose spattered counterpane, and tried Cathy's number again. It was picked up on the fourth ring.

"Hello?"

"Cathy, is that you? It's Emily. I need to see you, urgently."

"Emily." Cathy sighed. "This is not a good time."

"I'm sorry." She hesitated. "Has something happened? Can I help?"

"Dad's had a stroke."

Emily was horrified, "When, how?"

"Day before yesterday." *While I was with the hideous Sarah Pennington.* "I went to bring him his morning tea and he was on the floor, poor love. God knows how long he'd been there. Fortunately, his duvet had fallen off the bed with him so at least he wasn't cold but even so..."

A dark thought crept into her mind. *What if all my questions caused it?* "That's awful. Poor Uncle Charlie. Where is he now? How is he?"

"Kent and Sussex hospital, and he's quite frankly not in good shape at all. He's paralysed all down his left side and he can barely speak." Cathy's voice cracked. "He keeps asking for Julia."

Emily winced. "I'm so sorry. Is there anything I can do?"

"No, nothing. It is what it is."

"Would it help if I were to visit him?"

Cathy sounded snappy, "I think that is probably the very last thing he needs at the moment. I can't help feeling that going over it all set him off."

"I am so sorry."

"For heaven's sake, Emily, please stop saying you're sorry, it's not your fault, I'm not saying that. I thought it would do him good. If he does die, he will die happy and full of lovely memories, as long as he doesn't remember about the bloody fire."

Cathy gave a deep sigh then said wearily, "Sorry, I am very tired and totally fraught, it's making me very emotional. Now what is so urgent that you need to see me?"

"I went to see David and Evie." She heard an intake of breath from Cathy.

Cathy slowly replied, "Okay." A pause and then bitingly, "I don't remember you saying that you were going to do that."

"I know. It was a bit awkward and you said that you hadn't been in touch with them so I didn't know whether to say anything to you."

Cathy gave a heavy sigh. "Oh Emily. I want to say 'grow up' but that might sound a bit rude." It did sound rude, and also exasperated, but Emily could understand where she was coming from. Cathy added more kindly, "Look, I'm sorry. Come over."

"When?"

"Now. I need to leave to go and see Dad at two o'clock. Come for lunch, I might even have some ham left over." Hearing the smile in Cathy's voice, Emily gave a small laugh, relieved.

Emily drove up the track which suddenly seemed to be so familiar to her. Rufus met her in his usual place and escorted her round to the back door. She knocked then called out, "Hello Cathy, I'm here."

Cathy appeared and Emily gave her an enormous hug. It felt especially good after the lack of warmth shown by Evie and David.

"I am so sorry, Cathy. How is Uncle Charlie?"

"Hey, don't you get over emotional again. Now come on in and tell me what's on your mind. You're wound up like a coiled spring. I wonder if you will ever learn how to control your emotions and reactions."

Emily felt deflated.

Oh dear. I'm hopeless.

"For heaven's sake, Emily. Chin up, man up, tits out! Come on..." Cathy draped an arm around her and drew her into the kitchen. "Cake. When I'm uptight, I bake. I do a lot of baking. What do you do?"

Emily had to think about it. "Aunt Cyn does all the baking and sewing, Granny grumbles and attacks the vegetable garden, but I think I google and do research."

"Ah, that explains your obsession with all of this. Just remember that this is about other people, not you. It isn't your story. Only weeks ago, you had no idea about any of us." Cathy snorted and added, "I can't even believe that you didn't know that Aunt Julia was half Black." Emily blushed.

"Now, sit down, eat cake, have a cup of tea, relax and then we can talk."

Taking her seat at the table, Emily realised that she was in Aunt Julia's place again. Cathy was clattering around with the kettle, teapot and mugs before nipping out of the back door to go and get mint leaves for Emily's tea. It reminded Emily of what Cathy had said about Julia arriving that night in such a state. It provided a moment for Emily to marshal her thoughts. She was desperate to get her questions answered but also aware that Uncle Charlie was fighting for his life in hospital. She kept quiet and waited for Cathy to be ready.

Cathy placed a mug of mint tea and a slab of lemon drizzle cake on a plate in front of Emily, then took the seat opposite. Cradling her mug between her hands, looking Emily in the eye, Cathy said firmly. "Now... go."

"I don't know where to start."

"What's freaking you out? Begin there."

"David says that Evie was Jolyon's daughter, not his." Emily waited for a reaction to this bombshell but Cathy remained remarkably unimpressed.

"Yes, that's right."

Emily was exasperated. "Why didn't you tell me that? Surely, I should know. It explains so much."

Cathy shrugged. "It wasn't really for me to tell."

Emily was thinking hard, crumpling somewhat inside at the thought that she was in a similar position – wondering whether her own dad was actually her dad. Surely a DNA test would help? But that was thinking about herself. She pushed such worries aside and came back to Aunt Julia. "But Sarah said that she needed to tell me the truth, the real truth. I thought she was suggesting that she knew something about how Aunt Julia died but now I'm not so sure. I think that it was about Jolyon fathering Evie."

Cathy put her head on one side, "Well, they all swept it under the carpet and got on with their lives."

This was proving so hard that Emily could feel tears gathering on her eyelashes. She scrubbed them away, but not before Cathy noticed and said, "I would've thought that's a good thing, don't you, Emily? Why the waterworks?"

She couldn't help but mumble. "David and Evie are living as man and wife."

Cathy leant forward and asked urgently, "What did you say?"

"They've got a daughter. David and Evie have a daughter."

Cathy shook her head in puzzlement, sat back, stared at the ceiling. After a deep breath, she said, "Well, that has to be a good thing doesn't it?"

Emily wasn't convinced, so offered a hesitant, "Yes."

"Are they happy?"

She was finding the whole thing just too much to take on board. It was all too confusing. "Yes, they are, very much so."

"So, Emily? It's all very well you coming along, digging around and making revelations but what about the rest of us? Sitting here, now, it doesn't affect me and it doesn't affect you. A week ago you didn't know any of us, for heaven's sake... and you didn't even realise that your blood relatives were black. It's all new to you and I'm sure that you are finding it very exciting..."

"That's a bit unfair." Emily sniffed.

That was a bit cruel but probably true.

Today's Cathy didn't seem quite so cosy, but she could understand that she must be under considerable strain with Uncle Charlie so unwell.

Cathy put her chin in her hand and continued. "Look, no-one knows how Aunt Julia died – whether it was by her own hand or any of the players that were here that night. Yes, I have speculated about it again and again and I admit that when you turned up, I did go over it yet again. It churned things up – the sense of injustice, families not being entirely truthful about where they were and when. They all seemed to have had motives for wishing her dead. Everyone seemed to be hiding something. I did set you off thinking and speculating, and I'm sorry because I shouldn't have done. That was very wrong of me. Perhaps if I'd known that you were going to see David and Evie, I would have said far less."

"But you knew I was going to see Sarah..." Cathy looked at her with her eyebrows raised. "I'm sorry, that sounded rather petulant."

Cathy nodded but with a half-smile on her face and

handed Emily a tissue. "Yes, I did. I didn't think she would reveal the big family secret after all this time."

"She didn't."

"There you are then. I've known this family a lot longer than you have, Emily." Cathy laughed and Emily nodded.

She's right.

Cathy was looking carefully at Emily. "We all have our suspicions and, in all truth, if it was murder, then the perpetrator should be brought to justice. But really, what difference does it make now? Aunt Julia died. All of those who are left are old fogies not far from their own demise. If they murdered Aunt Julia they will surely burn in hell, if you choose to believe in that hocus-pocus."

Emily knew that Cathy had a point, but it was difficult to step back having met all these people, her family. Cathy read her mind. "I know that you think of them as your newly discovered kith and kin, but really? Your branch of the tree has managed to live their lives oblivious to the existence of Aunt Julia and what was happening in her life. While you didn't know anything, there was no sense of hurt and pain, was there?"

She's right. I'm taking this so hard because of my nagging doubts about my own parents.

Even though she didn't feel much connection with the rest of her family, Emily did feel that she'd grown close to Cathy, and she felt a need to explain why she was so invested in all this.

After all, she shared her family secrets with me – it's only fair that I share some in return.

"I need to tell you why I think I am reacting so emotionally to this. At GG's funeral, we were all given her letter telling us all about Aunt Julia, and I was so thrilled to find out about it and keen to find her as GG had asked. I was so touched by her wish that Aunt Julia knew that she had been loved. Mum wasn't interested at all and then, totally pissed, she came out with the revelation that she had thought of putting me up for adoption. To top that she hinted that my dad might not be my dad. She just came out with it, with a sort of tra-la-la laugh as if it was hilarious. It wasn't in the remotest bit funny, and I was horrified."

"What did your dad say?"

"He said, 'Of course I'm your dad.' But beyond that he won't say anything to confirm it. Now there's a conspiracy of silence. Since they're not giving me any answers, I would really like to do a DNA test to find out one way or the other."

"Will he do that?"

"I haven't specifically asked him, but I doubt it. Perhaps I can steal his toothbrush."

"I don't think that will work. He would most definitely need to give his permission for you to do that." Cathy chuckled.

"Anyway, this isn't about me, it's about Aunt Julia, but I hope you can see why I have become so involved. It has been so cathartic to do all the research and try to get to the truth." Emily sighed, took a bite of the cake. It was delicious. Cathy took a long swig from her tea. "I now realise that David had to tell me the big family secret because otherwise I would have been shocked by his and Evie's daughter if I'd thought they were related."

"Exactly."

Emily was befuddled by all the conflicting information that she was trying to resolve. "Do you think I should see Sarah again? I mean, we both think she was planning to tell me that Jolyon is Evie's father, and I know that already. I don't want to have to go back if I don't have to but she did say that she had other things to tell me. Her exact words were "the biggest secret of them all". Perhaps she knows more about how Aunt Julia died."

"That's up to you, but personally, I wouldn't want to hear her gloat just for the sake of more secrets."

Do I want to know? It would be nice to be able to tell her that I know all about it and take the wind out of her sails, put an end to it. And maybe she can tell me how Aunt Julia died, even who was responsible. That is the key information that I'm missing.

Having put everything out in the open Emily thought she should confess, "I forgot to give Great Granny Irene's letter for Julia to Evie."

"Did she ask for it?"

"No. To be honest I don't think she was too pleased to meet me at all."

Bugger. Now I've caught the 'to be honest'.

"Each to their own. What are you going to do with it?"

"It feels wrong to open it and read it. One thing I thought of was to put it on Julia's grave. Does she have one?"

"Of course she does. Her remains were cremated," Emily winced, "and are interred at Lamberhurst Church. There wasn't room to put her next to her mum and dad, but she is close by."

Emily sighed. "Well, I really don't know what to do and where to go next."

"Go home, Emily. Go home to your family."

"What do I tell them?"

"Show them the pictures and tell them that Aunt Julia had a wonderful childhood, married a fine, handsome man to whom she was very happily married, had two children but sadly died in a fire. The inquest was an open verdict, delivered shortly after her first grandchild was born. Most importantly she was loved. She knew that she was truly loved. Let's face it, the whole lot of them – Jolyon, David and Dad – were all falling over themselves to love her." Cathy smiled.

Emily couldn't stop the tears. "I will. Thank you Cathy, thank you for everything."

Emily got up, leaving the remains of her tea on the table. Cathy rose too.

"Give my best to Uncle Charlie, won't you?" Cathy nodded, although Emily could see in her eyes that she wouldn't because he wouldn't know who she was. They embraced and Emily left through the back door. Neither Rufus nor Cathy escorted her out to her car. She knew in her heart that it was the last time she would visit.

As Emily clambered behind the wheel she felt very sad.

TWENTY-FOUR

Emily drove straight to Lamberhurst Church. The car park was empty. She rummaged in her bag to find the letter and climbed out of the car. Where should she start to look for Aunt Julia's grave? She hadn't the faintest idea.

I should have asked Cathy for more detailed instructions. Shall I ring? I don't think so.

She walked around the church and was hit by just how impressive it was, like two large buildings merged together alongside a tall tower. The tower was topped with a cone, just like the oast at Oak Tree Farm. A big church for such a small village, twice the size of the one in Loxley where they had said their goodbyes to Great Granny.

It was good to see the place where so many weddings had taken place: David and Julia's, Nicholas and Evie's. Daniel's christening too. She was trying to work out how many funerals it must have witnessed. She took pictures.

It struck Emily that churches weren't just religious buildings, they were a whole community's repository of life events. The whole story of Aunt Julia's branch of the family was registered here. She would find graves for John and

Margaret Levett, and probably little Molly's as well, if she were to look.

She tried the door but although the colossal handle turned and gave an enormous clunk it was obviously locked. She turned and wandered around in the shadow of the soaring solid walls and turning the corner, was surprised by a wonderful view of rolling hills, stands of trees and hedgerows that seemed to define the essence of the countryside in Kent. At that moment the sun came out from behind a cloud and beamed at her. It was a very spiritual feeling.

She strolled on, following the ancient path and wondering how many people had walked that way before her. Old tombstones, regimented in lines, marched across the graveyard. It amused Emily that every now and again a stone was leaning over as if trying to peer to the front of the queue. This was clearly an area for the oldest graves, so Aunt Julia was unlikely to be here. She wandered on, glancing at the names and the clues to a whole life lived.

> Isaac BALLARD 59 years tenant of Down Farm in this parish, who after 5 years of mental suffering died 22nd January 1884 in his 84th year. Also Catherine his first wife, 9th January 1831 aged 28.

> Mary Anne BALLARD widow of Isaac BALLARD late of the Down Farm Lamberhurst, 9th February 1896 aged 76. "A souccourer of many".

A life story all in a few words, recorded forever. Several surnames recurred again and again: Watkins, Boorman, Noakes. She hadn't seen a Levett yet. Emily found it mesmerising. So many people, so many lives, so many stories. Completely different surnames from those she was familiar with that Great Granny had recited so poetically: Marshall, Wright and Hepworth. With the variety of surnames, distinct accent and completely different scenery, Emily pondered that her family's distant home in Sheffield seemed to be an entirely separate country, even a different planet.

She took a path off to the left and could see that she was in a more up to date area with much smaller headstones, all packed much closer together than the old ones, with engravings that were short and to the point. They followed in date order so she was able to speed up to the year she was looking for.

Emily stopped in her tracks. There it was. A pale grey stone, only fifty centimetres high, standing in a garland of dandelions. She parted the weeds to read the words engraved on it more clearly.

Julia Levett
Born 23rd March 1945
Died 24th April 1992
Dearly loved.

That's it?

Emily was disappointed but she didn't know why. Why not Julia Merripen? Had David rewritten history? Who had put up the stone? Who had paid for it?

Bloody hell, this family. Every single time, more questions than answers.

"Oh, Aunt Julia." Emily sighed, staring at those few words. "I am so sad that I never got to meet you. It would have been so wonderful for you to be reunited with your sisters. I'm so sorry, but you were dearly loved – you really were – by your real mum, your adopted mum and dad, your brother, Jolyon, David, your children."

I'm not quite so sure about Evie.

"I hope that you're all up there having a fantastic reunion." Emily looked up to the sky. "GG won't know you're there so do go and seek her out. You will have to wait some time to meet your sisters; they are far too healthy and spritely to be coming your way anytime soon." *Except perhaps for Granny if she doesn't get her heart seen to.* The thought of The Boomers made Emily smile and feel an inner glow. She was loved too – not necessarily by her parents and definitely not by her sister, but she had been adored by Great Granny and The Boomers, that was for sure.

She took a few photos on her phone.

"I'm sure that you had such a happy life Aunt Julia, until your tragic end. I wish you could tell us what really happened that day." Emily sighed. "Look, I've got the letter here from your birth mother, GG. She was a lovely person and she didn't want to give you away at all. I promise. She asked us to give it to you, but we can't, and now I don't know what to do."

Now that Emily was here, she wasn't awfully sure what to do with the letter. She crouched down and sat cross legged next to Aunt Julia's grave and pondered. Should she open it and read it to her? That seemed like a betrayal somehow, it was too private and not meant for her eyes.

With a deep sigh, Emily asked, "Oh, GG, what the hell shall I do?"

A soft voice replied, "You could ask God."

Emily jumped out of her skin and twisted awkwardly to find out where the advice had come from. Her heart was pounding as she looked up at a figure silhouetted by the sun. Was it an apparition or a real person?

"I'm so sorry to startle you. I heard you chatting and wondered who you were talking to. I'm so sorry to interrupt."

Emily held her hand up to shield her eyes, hoping to be able to focus on the phantom. Emily was relieved to see that it was just a vicar, a short stout man with a polished head and one of those voices that aren't instantly recognisable as male or female. Emily sighed with relief. An actual person. "That's okay. I'm just trying to make peace with Aunt Julia."

That sounds bonkers.

"That sounds beneficial." The vicar moved out of the sunlight. "Would you like to talk about it? That's why I'm here, for just this eventuality."

Emily thought '*the answer to my prayers.*' That made her want to giggle, which didn't feel appropriate.

She tried to explain. "I'm Emily Walker. I'm a relative of Julia Levett, her great niece." She pointed at the headstone. "I have a letter for her from her birth mother but she has passed away so I can't give it to her."

"That sounds like a long story."

Emily scrambled to her feet clumsily and found herself inches from the vicar's face. She got a waft of extra strong mints before stepping back to a more dignified distance.

The vicar looked at her suspiciously. "Let's try again. How can I help?"

Emily didn't know where to start. "Well, GG, that's my great grandmother, gave birth to an illegitimate child during the war." *Don't think I'll mention that she was mixed race, it opens up a whole new conversation.* "She was adopted by the Levetts who farmed, still do, at Oak Tree Farm." Emily pointed in the direction that she thought it must be. "So anyway, when GG died, she asked us to find Julia, let her know that she was loved, and give her a letter. I had hoped to give it to Julia personally but I found out once I started researching that she passed away in 1992 so I was going to give it to her daughter Evie. But then Evie wasn't really too happy to meet me so I forgot and I didn't even meet Matthew so I couldn't give it to him either."

A look of bewilderment sat on the vicar's face. He was trying to disguise it with a benevolent smile. "Yes? But why don't you just read it?"

"Oh, I couldn't do that. It isn't for me to know what she said, that's between the two of them."

The vicar was not convinced. "But they have both passed on, have they not?"

Emily realised that the vicar didn't understand. "Yes, but... I don't know. It doesn't feel right. Please could you do it once I've gone?"

"Very well, but what do I do with the letter once I have done that?"

"For God's sake don't burn it whatever you do. Aunt Julia and fire are not a good combination." The vicar looked baffled. "Come to think of it I don't think that matters now. Perhaps you could set fire to it and put the remains on her grave, ashes to ashes and all that." The vicar nodded, looking a bit poker faced and didn't appear to want to say anything more. "Are you happy to do that? I would be ever so grateful..."

A thin smile, "Yes, yes, of course."

"Well, I can't thank you enough. I think I should go now." Emily turned to Aunt Julia's grave, kissed her fingers and bowed down to touch the stone. "Bye, Aunt Julia." She felt a bit weepy.

She turned away, "Thank you again..." It sounded a bit bald. *Like the vicar. What do you call a vicar?* "Thank you so much, sir."

She scurried away to a good distance before turning round and looking back.

Oh, bless his cotton socks, he is genuinely reading it. Thank you.

Emily felt a wave of peace.

~

On her return to the B&B, messaging Mum and Dad seemed the right thing to do even though Mum still hadn't responded. It enabled her to summarise the day. 'Went back to see Cathy today. Poor Uncle Charlie has had a stroke and is not at all well. Went to Aunt Julia's grave and left her letter there.' It was far too complicated to go into meeting vicars and such like.

Having found out so much and met Aunt Julia's family and offspring, her journey had come to an end. Surely she could return home now, knowing that she had done her very best.

She climbed into bed, switched the rosy lamp off and settled into her rosy pillow.

~

In the middle of the night, Emily woke up feeling uneasy. What was it that had made her so edgy? She tossed and turned in her bed of roses, unable to get back to sleep.

The realisation dawned that although her mission should be complete, she hadn't got any closer to discovering how Aunt Julia had actually died. It was the missing, final piece of the jigsaw and Emily was frustrated that she hadn't been able to fill that very last space.

Evie and David hadn't wanted to talk about it, neither had Cathy. Would Sarah be able to fill in the missing details? Was this what she had meant? Should she go back and see Sarah despite her being a racist pig?

Having now met the others in the saga she had become Sarah in Emily's mind rather than Mrs Pennington. She couldn't really remember why she had felt the need to be so deferential. It might be fun, in an odd sort of way, to call her Sarah just to see how she reacted, the stuck up bitch.

Emily smiled to herself and tried to switch off and go back to sleep. Plumping up the rosy pillow, she turned it over so that it felt cooler and turned on to one side and then the other.

Whatever she tried, the thoughts just kept going round and round in her head. Sarah did say that she had the answer to the greatest secret of them all, but did Emily even want to see the old bat again? She was the foulest, most racist creature that Emily had ever met. Emily sighed.

She nodded off with the tantalising thought that Sarah might be the key to resolving Julia's death.

TWENTY-FIVE

Emily dreamt that she had been running for her life down an endless corridor at Sarah's home. She was being chased by a sprinting Sarah in a wedding dress and veil, brandishing a bouquet of roses, enveloped in flames and screaming 'Julia, come back'. Dylan was skulking in front of her, barring her way. Emily was running as fast as she could but kept stumbling and her legs were rubbery.

When she finally wrenched herself out of the nightmare, she sat up in bed, genuinely out of breath and her heart was pounding. She could taste a distinct smokiness in her mouth.

Is this a sign? Hints of Great Expectations perhaps? But why Dylan? I haven't thought of Dylan for weeks. I am so over him.

Emily couldn't think what it might be a sign of. A warning to stay away and run for her life, or a definite omen to go back and seek the truth?

Exhausted, Emily dragged herself into the bathroom to scrub her teeth and get rid of the lingering bad taste. The buzz of her toothbrush was soothing and the everyday sound and gentle vibrations calmed her jangling nerves. Even the proliferation of roses looked benevolent today.

I wonder how Uncle Charlie is this morning.

Emily went down for breakfast and sauntered with confidence into the dining room. The suited man of the previous day had been replaced with a pinched faced woman in inappropriately high heels, heavy makeup and severely scraped back hair.

Katie came and took her order.

"Morning, what can I get you today?"

"Coffee, caffeinated, and a mushroom omelette please with toast."

I need fuel.

"Oh, that's different. Are you sure?"

Of course I'm bloody sure.

Emily smiled weakly and felt obliged to give an explanation. "Yes thank you. I need a bit of rocket fuel, I've been tossing and turning all night and I'm paggered."

"Okay." The waitress was staring at Emily oddly. *What did I say? Perhaps people down here don't say paggered, just like they call tea dinner and dinner lunch? I should have said something more universal like knackered except Granny always tells me that's rude.* "Coming right up." She pranced away and Emily found her thoughts swirling relentlessly.

The thought of returning home without resolving the final parts of the puzzle was overwhelmingly frustrating. Emily suddenly realised that the woman was glaring at her and barked, "Just what are you staring at?"

Emily blushed. "I'm so sorry, I was looking into space, not at you specifically. I really am sorry."

"Well don't. Look somewhere else."

"Of course, yes, I'm so sorry. At least I didn't throw a fork at you." *Why did I say that? She'll be even more confused.* "I am sorry, really."

Fortunately, Katie delivered her breakfast just then so Emily could stare steadily at the plate. She hoped the woman had stopped looking at her, especially when some omelette escaped and spattered down her front. She chomped her way through the toast deep in thought. By the time her plate was empty, she had decided.

I've come all this way, literally and metaphorically, I can't leave without finding out what really happened to Aunt Julia. I must *go and see Sarah Pennington.*

~

Emily shoved everything into her rucksack and said farewell to the swarm of roses.

Poking her head into the dining room, there wasn't a soul to be seen so she just left. Leaving through the front door without a word to anyone felt odd. She'd hoped to say goodbye and thank you to Katie and wish her luck at Cambridge, but it wasn't going to happen. Emily would never see her again, and Katie was unlikely to even remember her except when she was telling funny anecdotes about her menial holiday job to her equally brilliant friends. At least there would be plenty of stories where Emily was concerned.

Her focus turned to Sarah Pennington.

The question was, should she ring Sarah Pennington or just turn up? She had the ready excuse that she needed to pick up her cagoule. If she was there then it was a sign that Emily should have a final skirmish and if not, then it was a portent that she should just carry on back to Sheffield, return Granny's car and report back to her and Aunt Cynthia.

She stowed her rucksack in the boot, bundled her bag onto the front seat and set off. She decided to go to Sarah's via Aunt Julia's old haunts that she hadn't seen, not only to see them for herself but to record them for Granny and Aunt Cynthia. It also might give her jangled nerves a chance to calm down. The thought of Sarah Pennington made her jittery.

She went to take a picture of Aunt Julia's school in Lamberhurst. With its many angled roofs and buildings, and non-traditional windows, it looked far too modern to be the one that she, Charlie, Jolyon, Sarah and David had attended all those years ago. She took a photo anyway because she didn't know what else to do.

After that, she cruised along Furnace Lane in search of where Wayside Cottage had once stood. She guessed that it was the one right at the far end because there was an odd-looking modern monstrosity of a house that Emily assumed must have been the height of fashion in the late 1960s, a bit like the wallpaper in Great Granny's spare room. It was hard to imagine a small house being on the site, let alone a cottage on fire. Emily held up the press cutting but it didn't seem to match.

Backtracking, she sought out Aunt Julia and David's second home. It was hidden down a narrow and twisted back lane with a sign saying Hoghole Lane, exactly like in the *'Babes in the Wood'* piece. The name still made her giggle.

She drove cautiously around a particularly sharp bend on a steep hill hoping like hell that nothing was coming in the other direction and levelled out to see a fine cottage in front of her. It was very like Oak Tree Farm, obviously the same era, with warm bricks, hanging tiles and the same diamond pane windows. Home from home for Aunt Julia. It seemed to have a very happy demeanour.

How nice for Aunt Julia and David after all that trauma.

She parked on a track and wandered around the

perimeter. She didn't like to venture right in, and instead took her photos from a distance. A shaggy pony whickered to her over a gate.

Cute.

On the far side Emily found an array of farm buildings, all very grey and utilitarian. This must be where David had worked, Jolyon's farm. She could smell wafts of animal muck. It wasn't particularly unpleasant, just earthy and warm.

Here in this quiet place, Emily felt a connection to Aunt Julia that she hadn't found anywhere else. She took her time and imagined Aunt Julia playing with Evie, tending Matthew and helping him to heal from his terrible injuries, and David growing vegetables in the fertile looking garden.

A happy place. Tears welled, happy tears. This is where she would set her story about Aunt Julia.

She wandered back to her car where an irate man, driving the most enormous piece of bright yellow machinery that Emily had ever seen, was parked right up to her back bumper. He was on his phone and looking very angry.

Oops. Not such a good place to park.

She ran half-heartedly towards her car, more for show than it achieving anything very much, mouthed, "I'm so sorry", jumped into the front seat and started up the engine. She forgot to take the hand brake off so didn't go anywhere, and crashed the gears a few times. Taking a deep breath while flapping a hand at the irate farmer behind her, she could feel his disdain. Finally getting her act together, she shot out of the track and onto the lane.

Pull yourself together, Emily. Now, decision made, Tunbridge Wells and Sarah here I come.

~

Emily drove into Willicombe Village with swagger and parked. It looked a much happier place in the sunshine. "You have arrived at your destination," intoned the sat nav lady with authority.

"I know, and I'm ready to face the witch in her lair." Her trembling voice said otherwise. She grabbed her faithful friend – her patchwork bag – and knowing where she was going, marched briskly along the road, trying to look courageous, until she came to Sarah's block of flats. It all looked very neat and tidy, groomed and soulless after the abundance and looseness of Oak Tree Farm and the cottage where Aunt Julia and David had lived. Her stomach churned. Her bravado was deserting her. She felt sick with dread.

Is this a good idea? Can I face that bitch again? But what is it that she wanted to tell me? I can't miss this opportunity of finding out what really happened to Aunt Julia.

She stepped down the antiseptic smelling corridor and hovered outside Sarah's door, her stomach churning in fear. One half of her brain was yelling 'run you stupid idiot, run while you can.' A flash of her dream came to mind. The other half was purring, 'you really want to know, don't you.' She clasped her hands as if in prayer, took a deep breath and rapped sharply on the door with white knuckles. It didn't open like before. After waiting a moment, she knocked again as loud as she could – any harder and it would hurt her knuckles.

I will count to ten and if I don't hear anything I will go. One, two, three, four, five, six, seven, eight, nine, ten... right, that's it, she isn't here, I'm off.

Just as she was turning on her heel, the door opened a tad and Emily jumped out of her skin. The shot of adrenaline on top of her already heightened emotions was like lightning.

The ravaged, chomping face with its fluff of white hair appeared like an apparition through the gap. "Oh, it's you."

Emily tried for a bold, brave voice. It didn't come out quite how she had hoped. "Yes, it's me, Emily, Julia's great niece." *Did she need reminding like Uncle Charlie did? Just in case.*

"What do you want?"

"You told me to come back. You said that you had more to tell me about our family."

"*Our* family," she repeated in a strange sort of parody. "I did, didn't I? You'd better come in." She opened the door wide, turned and started making her way towards her chair using a silver topped cane as a support. Emily scooted in, closed the door behind her and felt horribly claustrophobic. The smell of Blue Grass had been forever tainted by this evil woman, and that made Emily incredibly sad.

Why on earth did I come back? She's just a hideous as before. She'd better come up with something solid about Aunt Julia's death. If she starts on her racist rants, I'm out of here.

Following Sarah across the room, Emily could hear Sarah's feet and stick scuffing the carpet, making a rather nasty scraping noise. Sarah levered herself down into her chair with well-practiced skill. Looking around, Emily couldn't see her cagoule anywhere so she sat in the same tapestry chair that she had used only a few days ago.

Only a few days? It feels like a year.

"I won't offer you tea. You don't drink it."

Blimey, she is sharp.

"Thank you."

There was a pause. Sarah was staring at her, her jaw still. Emily gathered herself and rummaged in her bag for her 1/- notebook. She was in no rush, she was damned if she was going to talk first and lose the upper hand. Sarah broke the silence. "Well?"

"I went to see David and Evie."

"Yes, you said you were going to."

Why do you manage to make everything sound so patronising?

"They filled me in."

"They filled you in on what exactly?"

Better just come out with it.

"About Jolyon, your husband, and Julia my aunt."

"Oh, that." She picked some imaginary fluff off her sleeve. "I told you about it. So?"

What the hell can I say now?

"Well, the consequences. You didn't tell me that..."

Suddenly Sarah Pennington burst out, "Dirty, black witch. She enchanted them all you know. Not just Jolyon but David and Charlie too. Those boys all vying for her favour, for years, endlessly, always Julia. She ruined my life." She glared at Emily and dropped her voice to a normal level, "Anyway, I told you about that. I am quite certain. So, what else, Emily, did David and Genevieve have to say?"

Emily was feeling indignant but kept her cool. She deliberately ignored the reference to 'black witch' and carried on in an exaggerated extroverted tone, "They seemed very happy indeed. They live in a wonderful area in Wiltshire, fabulous scenery. Their cottage is right in the middle of nowhere and they have incredible views of the Marlborough Downs."

"Ah, a travelogue. The highlights of Wiltshire." Sarah Pennington laughed and it turned into a coughing bout.

You cow. I'd forgotten just how much I loathe you.

Emily waited for the hideous phlegmy noise to subside before she made her next point. "That's right. David and

Matthew have been working for the same local farmer, a nice man, great to work for they told me." Emily smiled sarcastically. *Take from that what you will.* No comment from Sarah Pennington. "David has retired recently but he is looking very well, very fit for his age especially compared to Uncle Charlie and..."

Oops, I was about to say and you. Back pedal, too rude, but it is funny.

Emily suppressed a smile that turned into a smirk. "And Daniel, well he's an absolute scream. What a character. He's working in the local supermarket and seems very content. And Harriet. She's obviously got some problems but seems very sweet, very pretty. Most importantly they are just so close knit and loving as a family. It was great to see." Emily paused for a breath.

"Harriet? Who is Harriet?"

Bugger, hadn't meant to mention her. Don't know why. It just doesn't seem right. That made Sarah sit up. Doesn't miss a thing.

"Evie's daughter." Emily knew she was blushing.

Sarah was staring at her intently, head on one side. "Genevieve's daughter? I didn't know that she had married again."

I'm not going to say a thing about David.

"Oh, I don't think she has. It seems to run in the family doesn't it, the conceiving babies out of wedlock thing?" *Ha-ha, put that in your pipe and smoke it... Or chew some more nicotine gum.* "But anyway, they are very happy, and it was lovely to meet them. And Evie and Harriet have Great Granny's piercing green eyes. Julia did too. Isn't that incredible?"

"Indeed." The old hag was smirking and working her mouth. "You don't."

"No, but my sister Ashley does. It missed me but

Granny, Aunt Cyn and Aunt Jennifer all do. Obviously a dominant gene."

I am wittering and I don't know how to stop. Sod this woman, how does she make me feel so inferior? But I'm buggered if I am going to call her Mrs Pennington.

Sarah had adopted an irritated look, was squelching her gum madly and flapping her hand at Emily. "I'm really not interested in your family, dear. Have you quite finished?"

Emily didn't know how to respond. Her bravado seemed to be deserting her. "Yes," *This isn't going at all well. How am I going to find out what it is that she's hiding?*

"So that's it? You came to tell me that you had found out about Jolyon's adultery with Julia, but I already told you that. Why did you come then?"

Emily couldn't keep to her deliberate considered mannered demeanour, her patience had run out, and she burst out in a commanding tone, "It was you who told me to come back, and I quote, because I wrote it down in here," she flourished her 1/- notebook, "The answer to the biggest question of them all." She found herself staring aggressively at Sarah. That made a change.

"Do you know what, dear? I don't like your tone. I don't have to tell you anything. Anything at all. I think you have found out everything that you need to know." She rummaged around in her mouth and extracted a lump of gum and placed it an ashtray on her table. At least she didn't spit it on the floor. "Why don't you just potter back up north where you came from and leave us all alone?"

For God's sake.

Emily was furious. She stood up.

"I would like to say that it has been nice to meet you. But it hasn't. You are the most bigoted, vile woman I have ever met. All that is left is for me to say goodbye, Sarah." There, she'd said it out loud.

Sarah looked at her, "It's Sarah now, is it?" She smirked, put her head back and laughed although it sounded more like a gargle. It turned into another coughing fit.

Emily fled. She was shaking with anger.

Bitch. Bitch. Bitch.

TWENTY-SIX

Emily thrust her bag into the car, vaulted in and whisked out of Willicombe Village with no clashing gears or handbrakes. She was just too angry to be her normal incompetent self.

Stupid bloody woman.

She had four hours of driving ahead of her, plenty of time to get her head together. It seemed a long time, but she was very aware that the moment she drew into The Boomer's drive, she had to have her whole story in order. She needed to practice it because she had already shown how easy it was to let slip details that then sent her into a whole new series of explanations.

As she drove up the A21 and joined the M25 she decided to go over each of her visits and come up with the soundbites that made sense, were coherent and told a happy story.

She went over her chat with Uncle Charlie. How best to say that Aunt Julia was mixed race? How would the Boomers feel about that? She could describe the collecting of Julia from Saint Christopher's, the detail of the racist black doll that the curate had mentioned in his letter, the happy tales of fun on the farm playing with Charlie and Jolyon – all nice cheerful stories. The bullying and systematic racism at school? Not necessarily a bad thing to share. The Boomers had an equal right to know what life was really like for Aunt Julia and hopefully it would demonstrate how far things had changed since those far off days.

She carried on around the M25 and on to the M1. She glanced at her sat nav.

A further nearly three bloody hours on this boring motorway all the way to Sheffield.

She started thinking through Cathy's story. Aunt Julia's premature death only made sense if you knew about the inadvertent incestuous relationship between Nicholas and Evie, which was a reason for Julia taking her own life or someone else wanting to murder her. Emily cringed. The Boomers would need to know about Jolyon and Aunt Julia and the consequences of their infidelity.

Emily passed a sign for Leicester East Services and decided to have a pit stop. It had started to rain.

Bugger, bugger, bugger. I didn't even retrieve my cagoule from Sarah.

She was relieved to find a Waitrose and chose a tasty looking vegetarian salad. She got a Starbucks coffee, caffeinated, to fend off the inevitable droopy eyelids caused by the monotony of the motorway and the mesmerising thwack, thwack of the windscreen wipers. At the thought of the windscreen wipers, a memory of Uncle Charlie's story about collecting Aunt Julia popped up. A nice thought.

By the time she was sitting at a plastic table with her hoard she realised that it was not for her to censor Aunt Julia's story. As her half-sisters, The Boomers deserved to know the truth, not a sanitised version. They needed to see the inquest verdict. Thinking about that, and how it might make them feel about Nicholas and Evie's inadvertent incest gave her goose bumps. She shivered and sighed.

She mooched to the car, filled up with fuel and cruised back on to the M1.

She then considered the question of her visit to David and Evie. She could easily relate all the happy bits about their blissful marriage and their delight in their two children. The fire was a tragedy for Matthew but at least he lived, and the rest of the family were relatively unharmed, physically if not mentally.

No point in mentioning that it could have been a deliberate attack by Sarah. Unless you'd met her you wouldn't even consider it a possibility. I bet she did put that fag end under the settee deliberately.

There was the light-hearted story of Nicholas and Evie as Babes in the Wood. A cheerful tale with a happy ending and then there was the pleasure of Evie's wedding and everyone's joy at their union.

Except for Sarah's. Bitch. And she knew the possible consequences. Why didn't she say anything then and there? Why didn't Jolyon say anything? He must have known that Sarah suspected. So many bloody questions still. That cow has so much to answer for.

Everyone was thrilled when Daniel was born despite his disabilities, and he had turned out to be a decidedly happy and cheerful chap.

Except Sarah, she wasn't happy, and she bloody well knew.

And then Aunt Julia died, in all probability by her own hand. It did make sense and Emily was sad all over again.

I think I have this sorted. Good thing, that's the exit to Chesterfield. Not far now to Granny's.

THE ENDING

TWENTY-SEVEN

Emily parked in Granny's drive. She was exhausted not just from the long, repetitive drive but also the swirl of thoughts and emotions that were now lodged like a cyclone in her head. Who knew that her simple quest to find her aunt would become so complicated?

She clambered out, reached for her faithful bag which enfolded the precious 1/- notebook, her press cuttings and a phone full of pictures. She gave her bag a comforting squeeze.

She went to the boot and heaved out her rucksack. Before she could close the lid an excited shout from the door heralded Granny, her arms wide open and welcoming. "Oh Emily, it's so good to see you. How are you? What have you got to tell us? I'm so excited. Cyn's popped to the post office. She won't be long. Let me put the kettle on."

Emily stepped into Granny's comforting arms and felt the storm abate. "Absolutely Granny, all of that. It's fantastic to see you but first of all I am busting for a pee!"

~

Emily and Granny settled together at the dining table with a brew. Although Emily had resisted making a start until both siblings were there, she decided to plug in her laptop and get her phone pictures displayed in full screen size. Granny of course couldn't resist a preview and badgered Emily with questions when the first pictures of Oak Tree Farm popped up.

"Granny, behave yourself, you'll just have to wait." She said with a grin. She was determined to hold off the big news until Aunt Cynthia was there. They didn't have long to wait.

The front door opened and Emily could hear Aunt Cynthia yelling, "I'm back!" as she hung up her coat.

Aunt Cynthia's head appeared round the door. "Emily, love, how good to see you. Have you had a useful trip? We're dying to hear all about it. What were they like?"

Granny patted the chair beside her, "Cyn, come and sit down. Emily is being a right pain and wouldn't let me see any more photos until you got here."

Emily started showing the sequence of pictures she had taken at Oak Tree Farm and tried to tell the story through her eyes. She omitted to say that the picture of the oast was the barn where Aunt Julia had died because she wanted The Boomers to share her journey at the same pace that she had made her discoveries. She flashed up pictures of Cathy, the photo of Uncle Charlie looking like a police mugshot and then she let the bombshell casually drop by moving on to the first pictures of Aunt Julia as a baby.

Granny gasped. "Oh, look at her. Our sister, such a sweetie." Aunt Cynthia did her seal clap. "What a poppet. She's gorgeous."

Emily was surprised that neither commented that she was black and continued to point out who was who and related the stories that Uncle Charlie had told her of their enchanted childhood. Emily wondered how to go about telling The Boomers about the prejudice and bullying that Aunt Julia encountered because of her skin colour, but it became a natural thing to talk about when the pictures of Aunt Julia came up.

The Boomers nodded and expressed their sympathy. Granny said softly, "Poor mite. How different it was for us growing up."

Aunt Cynthia added, "Prejudice was terrible in those days. I can remember when books about black people had them all as cannibals with bones in their hair or as half naked savages. Shocking to think nowadays."

They were taking the fact that Julia was black so calmly that Emily had to ask, "How did you know Aunt Julia's father was a Black American? I got a real surprise, and you haven't turned a hair."

Granny frowned at her. "First of all, what difference does it make either way, Emily? Secondly, we old boomers aren't as daft as you think. We can google things too. While you were off on your mission south, Cyn and I looked into the background of the battalion that Mum told us about in her letter, the 320th Barrage Balloon Battalion. You didn't follow up on that did you?" Granny looked smug. "It was an all-black battalion, with white officers I hasten to add, because being stupid Americans they didn't think that the black people like Julia's father were good enough to be officers. Who are the savages here?"

Emily was so relieved that The Boomers were not behaving like the hideous Sarah Pennington. Her faith in the older generation had been restored. It was simply that Sarah Pennington was an out and out racist bitch.

Granny opened her iPad, fired it up as she spoke and brought up a page all about the 320th. Emily pushed her laptop back out of the way and sent Aunt Cynthia's cup of tea flying. Emily leapt up, sending her chair crashing backwards.

"I'm so sorry. I'll get a dishcloth."

Aunt Cynthia giggled. Granny growled, "Emily, you are just so clumsy, you don't change a bit do you?" Aunt Cynthia added with a pat, "It's so good to have you back, dear."

Emily mopped up the mess which was fortunately confined to the table, and they settled back down to look at Granny's screen.

"This says that the unit helped create a curtain of barrage balloons to protect the troops on the beaches from enemy aircraft. When the troops moved on inland, their job was to offload the stream of ships arriving to keep the invasion force supplied. Look at the pictures. One of these blokes could be him." They searched the faces together but were none the wiser.

Aunt Cynthia had a pleased smile on her face and added, "We tried to find out more about him but a fire in 1973 destroyed the US Army's Personnel Records Centre in St Louis. It destroyed most of the World War Two records that were there, so it would be too difficult to find him without knowing where he was from, not even which state. Shame that Mum didn't say."

Emily turned back to her slide show. She had decided on the tedious motorway drive that she should tell The Boomers the whole story of the night that Aunt Julia died from Cathy's point of view. Emily tried to relate Cathy's story of Julia turning up in distress and the terrible realisation that she had died in the fire while withholding why Julia was so distraught. It brought a lump to her throat. There was no point in hiding the uncertainty, the open verdict and she told them what Cathy had quoted from the inquest report while swallowing the hideous findings along with her tears. The Boomers sat in silence.

Granny was the first to speak, "Read that again, Emily." Emily did. It made her feel sick all over again. "Dreadful, quite appalling." Aunt Cynthia sniffed. "So, she was alive when the fire started but had the noose around her neck?"

"Yes," Emily whispered.

"So what is that all about?"

"I don't know," Emily mumbled.

Aunt Cynthia looked puzzled, "But would there be a chance of Julia attempting to take her own life? Why? What were they all gathered to discuss? Did you find out?"

"I will get to that but I'm doing it in the order that I found things out otherwise it gets in a muddle." Emily continued with her visit to Sarah Pennington. Looking at the screen, Emily felt that the photo didn't do her justice. She looked far too normal and pleasant, and none of that hideous chomping.

Granny was clearly puzzled by Sarah Pennington. She frowned and shook her head, "Why did you visit her?" while Aunt Cynthia was peering at the picture, "She looks nice. What has she got to do with Julia?"

"I tracked her down because she was the spokesperson mentioned in the paper after the Babes in the Wood incident, and after the inquest. Cathy implied that she was a family member and would be able to tell me all about Julia, in her letter, don't you remember?" Granny and Aunt Cynthia shook their heads. "She was a hideous crone. I hated her."

The Boomers looked taken aback at Emily's vehemence.

"Honestly, she was foul. I have never met anyone so racist in my whole life. Her language, the words she used, quite deliberately to shock, the bitch."

Granny growled, "Language, Emily," echoed by "Goodness me, horrible word from such a clever girl."

"But honestly, she was a bitch, there is absolutely no doubt about it. And she stole Aunt Julia's first love, Jolyon. I thought she would tell me why there was the big meeting – I was in the same place you are, why did they all descend on Oak Tree Farm?"

Granny, looking exasperated, prompted Emily, "Just tell us more of the detail, as it really happened."

Emily grabbed her 1/- notebook and talked The Boomers through the notes she had scribbled. Her handwriting reflected the rage she had felt at the time.

"Oh, I nearly forgot. This is such an amazing coincidence. Where Sarah Pennington lives used to be St Christopher's, the Doctor Barnardo's home that Aunt Julia was adopted from. Look, here are some pictures I took after I had realised, or rather after the old... erm, witch, had told me."

Don't want to upset The Boomers again.

Granny chipped in, "I've been busy too, Emily." She tapped the side of her nose and reached out for her iPad, fiddled about and brought up sites that referenced Saint Christopher's that she had found on the internet. The first displayed a whole lot of black and white photographs of groups of children in woolly bonnets and thick coats with a cohort of nurses pushing enormous prams. Granny peered closely at the screen. "Now then, I wonder if we can spot Julia in the pictures of the children." Aunt Cynthia crowded in to look. "Oh yes, let's see if we can, now we know what she looks like."

Emily got up and leant over Granny's shoulder. "Clever you, Granny. What an amazing find." They searched all the faces with excitement but couldn't find Julia. Disappointing.

Granny put her iPad flat on its face. "Well, we can't see her there."

"That's okay, I've got plenty more. Now, on to the biggest visit of them all. It turned out to be extraordinary." Returning to her seat, Emily fiddled with her mouse. A few clicks and Emily turned the laptop towards The Boomers. "This is David, Aunt Julia's husband."

Granny gasped. "Gosh, handsome beast. He looks very like my Pete," and from Aunt Cynthia, "He looks like Heathcliff, like a gypsy."

Emily thought that David didn't look in the least bit like Grandpa Peter, apart perhaps from the dark curls. Grandpa had only been about five foot eight and had a big beer belly. Love really is blind.

Emily talked through Aunt Julia's marriage to David, the birth of the two children, the dreadful fire, how Sarah had taken on Aunt Julia as her skivvy, and about the Babes in the Wood incident.

"Now this is where the story gets complicated," Emily said, taking a deep breath.

She had decided to explain the whole thing about Sarah outing Jolyon and Julia's indiscretion, and how that had resulted in Jolyon fathering Evie, leading to the disastrous, inadvertent, incestuous marriage to Nicholas, but she wanted to do it as gently as possible. However, although she started out softly, she couldn't control the flood of emotion and the whole story ended up pouring out in a torrent. The total horror of the situation was revealed.

The Boomers both gasped.

"That's awful," and "What a dreadful thing to find out."

"I was gobsmacked, to be honest with you."

I'm doing it again. I just think about David and start doing his catchphrases.

Granny frowned. "What a shocking thing to happen."

Aunt Cynthia had a look of shock on her face, "No wonder Julia was so horrified that night. Poor love. I can't really take it all in."

Granny barked, "Why didn't that Sarah say anything before they got married? She should have. What a callous cow. Our poor big sister and our niece. What a tragedy."

Aunt Cynthia was still looking wide eyed. "Imagine that happening to poor Evie. She must have been appalled. I shudder to think about it."

Granny couldn't stop shaking her head either. "Shocking."

Aunt Cynthia, her face looking pale, said, "It must have been horrendous. Do you think that is why she... perhaps... took her own life?"

"That's what I think, Aunt Cyn," Emily whispered.

Aunt Cynthia put her head into her hands and stared down at the table. Granny looked around the room with a frown as if seeking inspiration. Emily could see that they needed to process the whole thing so she waited until Granny gave a big sigh and said, "Well, lass. What else can you tell us?"

Emily repeated as much as she could remember from David's stories. In retrospect she realised that she had got very little out of Evie that she didn't know already. Aloud, she said, "Despite knowing that Evie and David weren't related it still felt a bit creepy finding out that Harriet was Evie and David's daughter. I don't know, a bit like when Woody Allen married his adopted daughter. It didn't feel right at all."

Granny frowned. "Give the poor girl a break, Emily. Thank God she's found love after a marriage that was appallingly disastrous through no fault of hers at all, poor darling." Aunt Cynthia nodded in agreement. "So, what does our niece, Genevieve, look like then?"

"There are no proper pictures of them."

Granny looked indignant. "Why not?"

"I tried to take a few shots of David's photo album but it was an odd one with a shiny plastic cover. You can't really see anything, can you?"

Granny and Aunt Cynthia leant forward and peered at Emily's screen. "You're right, such a shame," and a petulant, "Oh dear," from Granny.

"And then I was going to ask them if I could take a few pictures, but they didn't seem to be keen." *Evie couldn't get me out of there faster if she tried.* "I think that's it."

Granny asked brusquely, "Well, at least tell us what they looked like," and Aunt Cynthia more gently, "Were the children like Julia?"

"Evie is stunning. She is tall and graceful with dark curly hair, very much like mine, and has Aunt Julia's ever so long legs and..." Emily was about to describe her skin colour, thought better of it, "she has GG's green eyes and is gorgeous. I can see that she is very like Aunt Julia."

Aunt Cynthia sighed, "Our niece." Granny grumbled, "If only we had a picture of her."

Emily was a bit put out by their whinges. *Honestly, I did my best.* "Well, then there was Daniel, a sweet looking boy, a bit scarred from where they mended his cleft palate and a bit of a wonky nose and a pronounced limp from his club foot repair. He has a shock of blond hair. Now, he does have a Facebook page. And he is such a chirpy, sociable chap." Emily brought it up and showed the photos that he had posted. They were all selfies of him making crazy poses as he had done during her visit. "You see? He's a hoot." Sadly, there weren't any of the rest of his family. Perhaps Evie wouldn't allow that.

Granny chuckled. "Just look at that hair. Needs a good

haircut." Aunt Cynthia, "What a cute little chap. Such a big smile."

"And what about the little girl?" demanded Granny, echoed by Aunt Cynthia asking, "And the others, Evie's daughter?"

"Harriet is a pretty thing. With GG's eyes and her shy mannerisms, she reminds me a lot of Ashley. But she's a bit, you know... she has special needs."

Aunt Cynthia looked sad, "Oh no, poor lamb. Not her too. Poor Evie, what a tragic life."

Granny folded her arms. "What a right pickle, the whole palaver."

"Evie wasn't too keen to meet me at all. She was a bit hostile." *A bit? Very!*

"Not surprising really, having a total stranger coming along and poking their nose in your business, particularly with that dreadful discovery. I'd probably be the same. Wouldn't you Cyn?" Aunt Cynthia responded with a very brisk, "Too right I would."

Emily was a bit put out. After all, she had only been 'poking her nose in' in order to find out all about Aunt Julia for The Boomers' benefit. "Anyway, it all got a bit tense. I think the whole visit was a bit intrusive for Evie, not surprisingly. And I then went and forgot to give her GG's letter."

"Oh, Emily, you twit," Granny looked heavenwards. Aunt Cynthia shook her head with a soft smile, "Typical scatter brain, you'll be forgetting your own name next."

"I didn't know what to do so I took it to Aunt Julia's grave at Lamberhurst Church. It's a lovely spot with a great view, although of course she can't see it, but even so... and I took some pictures of it, here." The church looked wonderful and imposing on the screen and Aunt Julia's grave looked very dignified. "And then the priest came along. Gave me a real shock at first. But he kindly agreed to read the letter to Aunt Julia once I had gone, and he did because I looked back and checked. What a nice man."

Granny interrupted Emily's thoughts, "And what's this next picture?"

"I tried to visit Aunt Julia's school but it looked far too modern, can you see what I mean?" Granny and Aunt Cynthia nodded solemnly. "I wasn't sure it was the right one, but I took a picture anyway". Granny looked at her with a frown and a look that said she'd been daft again. "And then I went to their home in Hoghole Lane, and it really is called that, a crazy name but in a good way."

"Such a pretty place, don't you think, Cyn?"

"Oh yes, Rose. It looks ever so peaceful."

Emily didn't think she should mention the irate farmer on his mega sized tractor. "So, there you are. The epic voyage of Jason and the Golden Fleece but in my case Emily, her capacious patchwork bag, and her one-slash-dash notebook. I don't think I will ever find out what really happened on the night that Aunt Julia died. It will always remain an unanswered mystery."

Granny sat back and looked thoughtful. "What a lot they've all come through. Well, I guess that now we know all about our sister we – and she – can rest in peace, don't you think, Cyn?" Aunt Cynthia nodded in agreement. They both sat looking into space. Emily left them to their thoughts.

Granny suddenly said briskly, "Well done, Emily. You are to be congratulated on doing an excellent job. What a thrill – our sister, eh? All that remains is for you to send me all those snaps of Julia for us to keep. I love those wedding photos in particular, she looks spectacular. I'll get one framed and put it on the mantelpiece with the rest of our family." She smiled and patted Emily's hand. "Thank you

Emily, love, thank you ever so much. I think Mum would have been delighted that she had such a wonderful childhood full of love."

Aunt Cynthia nodded, a dreamy look on her face and sighed, a happy sigh. "Julia is at peace now." A long pause.

Suddenly, Granny clapped her hands, making Emily jump. "Now Emily, you need to go and make your peace with your mother. Have you heard from her?"

Emily's heart sank and she groaned, "No."

TWENTY-EIGHT

Her quest completed, Emily got the train back to Newcastle to her mum and dad's. She felt completely flat now that her mission had been accomplished and she knew that she couldn't put off facing her mum about Great Granny's house. The thought of it still made the hairs on the back of her neck stand up.

That was one thing she had learnt from the whole enterprise, you had to face up to reality, whatever that entailed, and however much it might hurt.

After the freedom of having a car, it was strange to be using public transport, but at the same time so much better for carbon emissions and giving her time to think. It would have been impossible to get round Kent and Wiltshire without the car though, so she supposed that she had to be more mindful of people who lived in such rural areas in the middle of nowhere. Something else she had learnt.

She got a bus from the station to home. As she got to the end of their road and started counting down the house numbers, her courage started to fade, and her stomach sank with a thud. She wasn't looking forward to this at all. She hoiked her patchwork bag up on to her shoulder. As it slapped her side it seemed to be giving her a pat of encouragement.

She arrived at the door, took a deep breath, put her key in the lock and went inside. "Hi, I'm home." Silence. She stood for a moment wondering whether they were perhaps ignoring her. She tried again, louder. "Hello?" But there was no-one in. A strange homecoming after the days of high emotion and discovery.

She opened the door wide and then wasn't quite sure what to do with herself. She bundled herself into the lounge, dropped her rucksack and bag and twiddled her thumbs, looking around. Nothing had changed since she was last here. It seemed an awfully long time ago. She checked her phone. No messages. She delved into her bag for her laptop, opened it and looked through all her notes from her adventure, and scrolled through the photographs.

It was very quiet.

After what seemed like an hour, Emily heard the front door open and the bustle of her family coming in. She skipped to the door and found that she was pleased to see them. "Hi. How are you all?" They seemed surprised to see her and had arrived back with an armful of fish and chips. The wrapped bundles made it hard to give them any hugs of greeting.

"Hello lass," Dad said but held his fish and chips in the air and side-stepped Emily, to show that he was encumbered, and marched towards the kitchen. Ashley scuttled past without making eye contact, hanging on to her bundle as if Emily might try and steal it from her.

Mum planted a kiss on her cheek as she trooped through after the others. "Hello stranger. Got a lot to tell us about we hear." She didn't sound very happy, but it wasn't really surprising.

Emily's stomach lurched as she tagged along behind. "Oh yes, so much. You wouldn't believe what I've found out. It's been amazing. I met Aunt Julia's brother – your uncle – and her niece and a friend, Sarah Pennington, who wasn't a friend at all as it turns out, more of an enemy... And they had a real set to because Nicholas and Evie got married not realising that they were brother and sister..."

Mum headed for the kitchen table. "I'm not talking about that malarkey. Mum told me that you had something to tell us about GG's will."

Emily flushed even though she felt cold. She wasn't entirely sure whether it was because she had been endowed with such a windfall at the expense of everyone else or because her Mum seemed so disinterested in everything that had filled her heart and soul for the last few days.

They all took their regular places around the kitchen table, each in the place where they had always sat throughout Emily's life. Just like Julia had had her appointed place. Dad reached for the Heinz ketchup and Henderson's relish from the worktop and plonked them unceremoniously on the table. They started unwrapping their packages. Wafts of chip shop smells filled the kitchen. Emily's mouth watered and she felt left out.

Mum was direct. "So, Emily, what's all this about the will?"

"Oh. I'm not sure of all the details really," Emily mumbled with embarrassment.

"But you've got the house?" Mum was the appointed spokesperson. Dad was, as usual, keeping quiet.

"I think so, yes." She knew so but didn't want to sound smug.

"Well, well, well. Lucky you." Mum sounded icy. Emily felt cold.

She wasn't sure what to say, or whether Mum had meant that as a question or made a statement, so she kept quiet.

Mum seemed too tight lipped to say anything more. After a long pause where Emily felt increasingly isolated and excluded, Dad put in his penny's worth rather more bluntly. "Well, Emily, since you've copped the lot what are you going to do for your sister?" Emily flinched at his choice of phrase. "And your Mum?"

And you.

She knew she had to say something and try to explain. "Look, I had no idea that GG had done that. Absolutely no idea at all. I haven't had a chance to even think about it because I have been so wrapped up in finding Aunt Julia." She realised that they were each tucking into their fish and chips and no-one had offered her any. She wanted to cry. They all looked at her, expecting more. Their chewing reminded her of Sarah Pennington and their unfriendly stares were like Evie's.

Mum asked angrily, "When did you find out then?"

Emily mumbled, "I read the will when it was sent out by the solicitor." Strictly speaking, that was true but not being good at misrepresenting the truth, she couldn't help but blush.

Mum stared at her hard and grunted. "Yeah, right."

Emily came clean. "I did read the will that was sent from the solicitor but I also got an inkling from The Boomers..."

"That's what I thought. You were in cahoots with The Boomers and didn't even think to tell me and your dad..."

"If Dad even is my dad, that is."

"Not that old chestnut, Emily." Mum raised her eyes to heaven.

Emily protested, "You were hiding things from me and not telling me the truth. It was you who suddenly announced that you thought about giving me away and that Dad might not even be my dad, and then won't talk about it. You have no idea how that makes me feel and having found out what happened to Aunt Julia and the consequences of not knowing who had fathered whom and the tragic result of all that, I really do feel that I have a right to know." Emily found that she was shaking with anger and out of breath.

Mum put her forehead in her hands avoiding Emily's furious gaze. "Emily, stop gabbling, you're making no sense at all."

"All it would take is a simple DNA test. That's all," Emily persisted. Dad seemed to be about to speak and then changed his mind. That made Emily so furious that she leapt to her feet and shouted, "I'll bloody pay for it then, since you're so hung up on money. It won't cost you a penny and it will be priceless to me, so that's fair. After all, as you said so offensively, I've now copped the lot."

"Emily, calm down." Dad tried to intervene; he reached grubby fingers towards her. "You're always such a drama queen. I'm your dad and that's an end to it. If we did take these tests then what would you do if it turned out that I was your dad or if I wasn't? Eh? What would you do? What difference would it make? Now sit down and calm down."

Emily just couldn't help herself, all her hurt, a lifetime of feeling unwanted had come to the boil and, even now, them hiding things from her. "No, I can't calm down. Either you say right now that you will take a test, or I'm going to..." she wasn't sure what she was prepared to do. "I'll walk right out of here and never come back." She breathed heavily and inhaled wafts of fish and chips. She felt starved of food and of affection from her family, who sat looking at her as if she was some strange monster that had walked in and was threatening their wellbeing. She wondered whether this was what Julia had felt when she thought that her birth mother hadn't loved her and hadn't known who her father was; whether this was how Evie had felt when faced with a phantom from the past digging up all those painful memories. She wanted to cry but she wasn't going to, she was determined.

"Okay, Emily. That's enough. You're being very rude and totally unreasonable." Dad spat out a bit of fish or something as he spoke.

"Okay, yes you will take a test?" She was speaking through gritted teeth. Her jaw was starting to ache.

"I'm not even going to answer that question, Emily."

Emily placed her hands on the table and looked at each of them challengingly in turn. Ashley was staring at Emily, her green eyes wide open. She stuffed a chip into her mouth, a ring of ketchup around her lips. Mum shook her head and raised her hands. Entreating or dismissing Emily couldn't tell. Dad just stared at her.

She could feel her body trembling. She closed her eyes. Total silence. She could hear her own breathing and Ashley smacking her lips. A tear escaped.

Emily opened her eyes and looked at each of them again, hoping that someone would find the right thing to say to ease her misery.

"For Pete's sake, Emily love..." Her mum looked at her pleadingly, but without moving from her seat to offer any comfort or reassurance.

Emily turned and left the room, burst into hysterical tears, and retreated to her room. "What the hell do I do now?"

TWENTY-NINE

Things were just as fraught the next morning. Emily steeled herself to appear at the breakfast table after a restless night deciding what she should do.

She had made up her mind. Now she had a house of her own and was old enough to move out, why not? All she had to do was tell her parents, and then it was over and done with. No point in waiting, she would go today, straight after breakfast. The sting of hurt flared up and made her catch her breath.

She procrastinated by packing everything in her room, glad of the giant zip bags that she had bought to take her stuff to and from Uni. Once that job was done, she knew that she had to go down and face them. She'd be as steely and determined as she could be.

Mum was flapping around after Ashley who was banging on about PE kit and a packed lunch; both of them ignored her arrival in the kitchen. Dad was sitting at his regular place at the table with a mug of tea and a plate covered in crumbs. A hint of toast hung in the air.

"Morning, love," he said, without looking up.

At least Dad is managing to behave normally. Whatever that is now.

"I thought I should tell you my plans..." Emily threw it out in her mum's general direction.

"I can't be blathering on now, I've got to get Ashley to summer camp and then I've got a staff meeting at work so I'm in a rush. We'll talk later."

"But I won't be here, Mum."

"Oh, for heaven's sake, Emily – you're not still in a strop, are you?"

"A strop?" Emily didn't know quite how to take that. She hesitated with her mouth hanging open.

"Well, anyhow, I must get going. So, bye love and see you later." As she passed Emily, she dropped a kiss on her hair and shouted far too loudly right by her ear, "Ashley! Get a move on, we're leaving right now." It made Emily wince.

"Bye, Mum." It came out as a whisper.

"Get yourself a brew and come and sit down, love." Dad patted the table in encouragement.

Emily flicked the kettle on and reached up for her camomile tea bags. She put them on the counter, looked at them enquiringly and then rustled through the cupboard for her other flavours, her 'lesbian' tea. A sudden flash back to Sarah Pennington and the lovely Cathy made her realise how her world had become so complicated since Great Granny's funeral.

She looked in the mug cupboard and wondered whether she should take the ones that were obviously hers, ones from Christmases and birthdays. The mug with the Periodic Table on it had been given to her by Dylan so she laid claim to that, not because of any sentimental reasons but simply that it was very useful. She left any that she wasn't completely sure about as she would hate to be accused of stealing from her family, even though they seemed to think that was what she had done by inheriting Great Granny's house.

Briefly considering some toast, she realised she wasn't hungry. Her stomach was too much of a churning pit, so she sat down in her appointed place and cradled her tea. Her dad was looking at her. He didn't seem angry.

"Right, love. Let's be having it. Where are you at?" He said it softly and folded his arms.

Emily was confused by the contradictory body language. "I'm definitely leaving. I should have moved out years ago. It's ridiculous to be living at home at my age. By this time next year, I'll have finished uni and heavens knows where I will be working."

"So, where will you go in the meantime?" Emily noted that Dad had taken it as read, apart from a quick surprised raising of the eyebrows. There was to be no cajoling or debate. He was clearly happy for her to go. She realised that she had hoped for some form of protest to show that he did care about her and wanted her to stay.

Trying to sound hearty, but failing dismally, she said, "As you both pointed out last night, I have done very well for myself and have GG's house, so I might as well go there."

He supped his tea and continued softly, "That sounded a bit self-righteous. You have to realise that it was very hard for Mum to be overlooked like that. I know she's got a bit of cash but it ain't very much in the scheme of things now, is it?" He paused, "And you hid it from us. That's the worst bit of it." Emily blushed. *He does have a point.* "As well as disappointed, she was very hurt." Emily considered this and could see that they were right to be so upset. When she had been so angry with them it had seemed the right thing to do.

Emily pursed her lips, not sure what to say. "I am sorry

about that, it was stupid of me." It sounded weak. "I'm going back to Loxley though. I think it's best."

"When?" Her dad looked so calm that it made Emily angry all over again.

"Today. Once I've got all my stuff together."

"What about your mum?" Emily shrugged. *I did try and say goodbye, but she wasn't paying attention as usual.* He paused, looking at her carefully before carrying on, "So that's it. That's what you're going to do?"

"Yes." Emily tried not to sound sulky.

Dad's voice remained measured, "Okay, so on a practical note, how are you going to get there? You can't take all your crap on the train."

"I don't know, I could hire a van or something."

"Or you could ask your dad if he could drive you there."

Emily was taken aback. Was this a genuine offer? "Really, Dad? But shouldn't you be going to work?"

"Now, here's the thing. It seems that I've been made redundant again." He looked at her wistfully.

Emily was dismayed. "Oh, Dad. I am so sorry. I had no idea, why didn't you say so?"

"We haven't really been given the chance, have we love?" It came out as a whisper. "Now, let's go and get your stuff and we'd better get going. It's a long drive there and back. Let's just hope that the old wreck will hold out."

Emily sat in the front seat of her dad's car. It was a strange sensation to be confined in the small space, within touching distance, but still so far apart. Emily had carefully not mentioned at all the whole 'Dad, if he is my dad' thing. It wouldn't have seemed fair when he had been so thoughtful and helpful retrieving her stuff, loading it all into the car.

The silence was covered by Radio 2, making it unnecessary to talk. After her sleepless night Emily decided it might be the ideal opportunity to have a nap. She closed her eyes and put her head back.

"Right lass, now I've got you all to myself and you can't escape, I think it's time for some straight talking." The pronouncement, loud over the dulcet tones of some middle-of-the-road tune made Emily jump. She looked wide eyed across at Dad who was looking firmly ahead.

"Okay?" Emily said hesitatingly. His voice didn't match what he had said. It was his usual understated tone.

He continued at the same level, "You've been off visiting half the country to find out about your long-lost other family and it seems to me that you don't even know what your own story is." He paused.

"That's true," Emily hazarded, hoping it sounded encouraging.

"I've been getting a bit uptight about your carrying on, you know that. So, I think it's my chance to have my say."

"Okay." Emily wasn't sure whether she was meant to be responding to each of his statements or whether she should just keep quiet, but she felt an urgent need to fill the gaps.

He turned the radio off. "When I met your mum, she was a lively young thing, great fun, always having a laugh and up to mischief. She was pretty – not in the way of the other overly made-up girls with their too-short skirts; she had class." *Emily tried to imagine her mum young, fun and lively. Not words that she would ever choose to describe her.* "She had a good job at Bramall's and had just got a promotion, so she was on cloud nine. They were going to sponsor her to do night classes to get a personnel qualification which would set her up for a future as a manager." He took his time looking carefully in both wing mirrors. "She wasn't a saint – liked a drink too much for that. We'd been going out with each other for a few happy months and then she got up the courage to tell me that she thought she might be pregnant. She was horrified and beside herself. She wanted to get rid, but she'd left it too late."

Another family member gaily telling me that I could have been terminated and never existed at all. Great.

"She eventually told her mum who was livid, the usual 'after everything that I've done for you' lecture. As you know, your gran isn't exactly a paragon of virtue herself, but she came down like a ton of bricks on your mum. Your mum took it hard because she had been trying so hard all her life to live up to your gran, find some way of pleasing her and making her proud. She'd found it difficult because there was Jennifer – always the golden girl, the pretty one, the tall slim one who tripped through life like a goddess with blokes worshipping at her feet."

I certainly know how that feels.

"You know what it's like, the way you keep comparing yourself with Ashley, a silly competition that's quite unnecessary. It's only you that does it. It's all in your head. Just be yourself."

Did he read my mind?

Emily drew breath to speak, but Dad said, "No, I haven't finished yet. You're listening to me this time. Anyway, your mum had to have the baby. She had a rough old time of the birth, on her own. I wasn't allowed anywhere near, and you ripped her apart. The midwives were right sourpusses and weren't very kind, said that she had brought it on herself being unmarried and all that. Poor Mum. They didn't want to keep her in hospital, so sent her home in agony with a baggie of drugs and this new, scrawny little thing."

"Me," Emily said softly, distressed.

"Yes, you. You were a dear sweet little thing with your mop of curly dark hair and brown eyes, but I wasn't allowed anywhere near you. The matriarchy – that is your rather scary family – captured their little princess and confined her to their castle. Can you imagine me, the weedy guy, that they pity and disapprove of, going round and demanding to see my daughter and your mum? You know what they're like."

Emily had a vision of Granny's best pugnacious face. She nodded and let a small dry laugh escape. "Yeah, Dad, I can most definitely see your point."

"Mum was struggling with the breastfeeding apparently, something else that I couldn't help with. You just kept crying and turning away, which made her think that you didn't need her at all, and your mum found it ever so difficult. Cried a lot. Looking back, it was a clear case of post-natal depression, but your Gran and Great Gran weren't having any of that. They thought that your mum was just being difficult and that she didn't really want you, so they took you over completely, which made things even worse for your mum. I did visit when I was allowed, and your mum was a right mess. She decided that the best thing for you was to have you adopted. She wasn't thinking straight, she was overwhelmed by the whole thing and felt a complete failure in the mothering department. As you now know, your Gran and Great Gran weren't having that either and so they engineered to pack her off back to work and stole you away. It wasn't the greatest time for your mum, that's for sure."

Emily was trying to assimilate this torrent of new nuances. It was hard to see her efficient, strong mum shown to be so crushed. "Why didn't Mum–?"

"Still haven't finished. You'll get your turn afterwards. Anyway, she rather left them to it, she didn't have much of a choice. She wasn't happy. I tried to get her out of it, get her to go out the pub, go dancing and suchlike because we could with our full-time babysitters, but she didn't want to go out and have fun. A light had gone out, she wasn't the same person. I didn't understand depression. Couldn't really empathise with it. I was determined to do the decent thing and asked her to marry me. I wanted to give her back her sparkle. She wouldn't. 'I've made my own bed, I'll have to lie in it.' That's when she started this stupid mantra 'how do you even know it's yours?' I was horrified. I knew in my heart that your mum wouldn't have two-timed me. She's got her faults, but she's too decent to do that to someone. I knew she was just trying to push me away, to make me feel like I had no responsibility to her, or you, if I wanted to leave. Which, of course, I didn't. I loved you both." He paused, checked all the mirrors and concentrated on changing lanes. Emily felt like she should say something, but this was all so huge that she couldn't think what she might possibly say. She needed to assimilate this new disparate perspective. It was difficult to imagine her mum depressed and struggling. She was always so efficient, organised and on top of things.

He started up again. "The turning point was Jennifer meeting the showy James. He was a flash Harry even then, not hard to imagine." He chuckled. "He'd just got his job with Grace Kennedy and so whisked Jennifer down the aisle and off to Jamaica in a matter of months. I don't know why this changed your mum's mind, but I think she realised she might be left living at her mum's, alone, for the rest of her life if she kept turning me down. Either that or she got fed up with me asking all the time." He chuckled. "So, she said yes. A bit reluctantly. Your Gran and Great Gran weren't best pleased. They'd hoped for something better than me, someone with ambition. And I'm obviously a deadbeat next to James." He sighed.

Emily felt awful for him that he felt that way. He was kind and solid and lived a quiet life, but it didn't make him a wimp in any way. Before she could think of something to say to make him feel better, he continued, "After the hoo-hah of Jennifer's wedding there wasn't much left in the pot for our wedding, but we were happy to settle for a quick in and out of the registry office and a pint at the Admiral Rodney."

"The Admiral Rodney, I had no idea..." It was so much easier to find things to say when it was about mundane things like wedding venues.

"GG took charge of you throughout the whole thing and was so wrapped up in you that she barely looked our way or acknowledged the occasion. It was quite hurtful." He sighed again and Emily was truly shocked that Great Granny could have been so unkind.

It certainly didn't seem to be the way she had always been with me, so caring and nurturing.

"So, there we were, the newlyweds with an adorable little girl with cute curls and big, solemn brown eyes. Such a pretty little thing." He smiled and glanced at Emily. It was the first time that she had ever heard her dad compliment her. It felt good. "With both of us working, we got together a deposit and bought our first home together. Your mum was beginning to relax and there was a glimmer of her former self, but it took a long time for her to... I don't know... find any real warmth for anyone. And I mean anyone," he added, glancing meaningfully at her, "you or me. Certainly not your Gran and GG. But I stuck it out because I loved her. She's a good person and I hoped that love would come in time."

Ouch, that must have been so hurtful for Dad to be thinking that.

"It had become the habit for you to go to your Gran's

every day and so it continued. We pottered along, grateful for the free childcare and your mum's wage to pay for the flat. I didn't earn much even then. Our little family in our own home. Your mum made it lovely, and we kitted it out, all on the tick – everyone did in those days. Then I was made redundant. 1993. First time and it hurt like hell. Yes, there was a recession, but we all thought that British Steel was big enough to protect us from all that. It wasn't. I hung in there for the first and second rounds of job losses but the third was a knockout blow. Your mum's job wasn't enough to keep up the mortgage and the HP payments, and she couldn't get a better paid job because she'd never gone to night school because of having a small baby. So, because I was no longer providing, our home had to go." Emily had no idea that her parents had once owned their own home. "I felt like a fool, even more so when James and Jennifer reported back on their growing wealth and exciting times in the sun. I always felt that your Gran and Great Gran disapproved of me even more, if that's possible. If that had been you or Ashley in financial straits I would offer to tide you over if I could." He gave a bitter laugh through pursed lips. "But your mum and I kept our heads above water. We rented a flat in Rotherham. It was cosy but nice enough. We were happy, that was what was important, and we loved you, still do." Emily's eyebrows shot up just as he looked at her. "I know we rarely say that – it's a generation thing – but we do, you know. Very much."

Emily was taken aback by this declaration, a first, and squeezed her eyes together to stop a tear escaping. "You still went to your Gran's every day, free childcare and when it came to schools it made sense for you to go to Loxley so she could pick you up at the end of the day. I used to come and collect you from your Gran's every day. Do you remember that?"

Emily murmured, "I do, sort of."

"The moment I put you in the car you would fall asleep, exhausted from a day at school, full of carbohydrate laden old-fashioned food and then hours of fun with your ancient relatives vying for your favours. I thought that you felt loved by us all." He sighed.

"But I did..." protested Emily.

"Just not by us, your mum and dad."

"That's not true..." It was an empty exclamation because as soon as she said it, Emily realised that he was right.

"It seems to me that this is what this sudden 'leaving home and going back to Loxley' is all about." He looked at Emily and nodded with his eyebrows raised. Emily looked away, feeling contrite. "Anyway, life carried on. I got jobs here and there, nothing that could be described as permanent but then it just got worse and worse. Your mum was made redundant, and we had to stop and work out what the hell we were going to do next. Your mum is efficient and clever, and loyal and hardworking – that's where your brains and work ethic come from. That's why we ended up moving to Newcastle. She was accepted for a good role in what they now called human resources, and we tagged along with her."

He paused, carefully changed lanes, "It were hard at first without the free childcare but somehow it was much better for us to be away from them. When the chips were down your mum proved to be as strong as your Gran and Great Gran any day. Of course, it niggled that Jennifer was still living the life of Riley with James and their hot and cold running servants, when your mum is just as good and intelligent as him – better even.

"So, roll on her thirtieth. We had a great party back in Sheffield with old friends. The Admiral Rodney again, it seems to be the go-to place. Your mum was chirpy and so much more like her old self. It was lovely to see." He paused, smiling. "And so, Ashley came to be. Your mum was terrified, scared that she would be ripped apart again, petrified that she would descend into post-natal depression, frightened that she wasn't good enough to be a mum. She panicked about how we would pay the bills while she was on maternity leave and who would look after this baby when she went back to work. She got herself into a right state again, just like she was after having you."

Emily found it hard to imagine her mum so vulnerable.

"So, she had Ashley. She had a planned C-section because there was so much damage down below. We managed to keep the matriarchy at bay, and she came home and we worked it out together. She was so surprised how much she loved Ashley. It took her breath away. There was no pressure, just us muddling along, so she could take her time to get to know her baby without judgement. She discovered what it is like to be a mum."

Emily was taking it in and trying to see this whole new point of view. A thought occurred to her, and it made her feel abandoned all over again, "But you sent me away to Loxley when Ashley was born. It was if you didn't want me at all."

Her dad looked shocked, "Yes, we did send you off to your Gran's. We thought it was the best thing to do for you while your mum recovered, and it also kept GG and your Gran away from the new baby. Also, a C-section is a drastic operation and there was no way we could cope with you bouncing around the place. Besides, we didn't want you to feel like a servant waiting hand and foot on your mum, or Ashley."

Emily thought about this different point of view, one she'd never considered before. *He could be right*. Emily had thought the world had finished challenging her unfair assumptions, but maybe not.

"And so we set off, this new enlarged family. We hoped that you would love Ashley like we did but you always seemed to resent her. It often happens that way with a new sibling. Your mum understood more than most because she knew how she felt about Jennifer, the golden girl with the beautiful green eyes – and there was Ashley with her blond curls and the family features. She tried so hard to get you to realise that you were two different people, loved the same but nurtured differently, not in some competition. The more she tried the more you pulled away and retreated to Loxley and The Boomers. I don't think she ever succeeded in that, do you?"

Emily blenched.

How do you answer a loaded question like that? Was it just petty jealousy? Am I really that shallow?

"We really did do everything we could to make you feel loved and wanted." He sighed, took a moment, then changed the subject to something easier. "We were so proud when you got into Edinburgh, but a bit scared of showing just how proud we were. I felt that if I overdid the praise that you might think that I was... I don't know, being sarcastic or something. That sort of thing doesn't come easily to a northern lad. But we were very proud. Still are. I find it difficult to know how to talk to you about it. You have experience of something that might as well be on another planet. There are things you say that I don't understand at all, and I feel too stupid to ask." He chuckled wryly. "But you didn't make it easy for us either. I remember you were talking about some dissertation, and it was just gobbledygook to me. You smiled at me in a patronising way and said, 'Don't worry Dad, I don't expect you to understand.' That made me feel this big," he added, pinching his finger and thumb together. Emily felt a stab of guilt.

"And what's with your posh friends and their fancy parties? Ceilidhs? What the hell is that all about? You even went to some boy's castle for his twenty-first and came back full of it. Really? You can't imagine how that makes me and your mum feel."

Emily prickled with shame at the realisation of how it must seem to them.

"You're always going on about saving the planet and criticising your mum and me when we're just trying to find a way to get from one day to the next. We make the money last by buying the cheapest, whether it is good for the planet or not. I know I go on about money, a lot, but we've never had much. I hate to see things wasted. At least we have that in common, eh?" He looked at Emily with real affection, and Emily felt warmed, in a comforting way.

Emily had never heard her dad say so much in her whole life and was exhausted from just listening and trying to process it all.

Why had they never said any of this before?

She thought about it for a moment.

Have I ever given them the chance?

"So, there we are. We arrived at the Admiral Rodney in Loxley for your Great Gran's wake, the headquarters of the matriarchy. Jennifer was arrayed in her grandest clothes, looking wealthy. Your Gran looked pointedly at Jennifer and then eyed Lisa up and down. 'Talk about chalk and cheese!' Can you imagine how your mum felt? Then that cocky James was talking about the new villa that they've bought and asking, 'Why don't you come and use it?' Everything that your mum feels that she isn't and rubbing our noses in the fact that we can't afford to go on holiday, and that we don't own our own home. Then there was The

Boomers lording over us with their imperious pronouncement about Julia and trying to make it out to be such a fantastic thing, this lost family member, to be found, to be told that she was loved. I wanted to shout at her, 'Aren't we good enough for you, the ones you know about?' And then to top the lot, Jennifer hinting about how we were going to have you adopted. And all the time, there you are, feting and adoring The Boomers, the ones who love you and cherish you, not like your wicked mum and dad."

Emily could feel a lump in her throat and tears building up. She tried to blink them away without her dad noticing. Looking firmly at the road in front of him, he seemed oblivious.

"I think that's why your mum was so off her head and drank too much. She couldn't cope. She was out of order and very stupid, I have to agree, but... she means well, your mum. She's ashamed of herself – and of me too – and ashamed of how our lives have turned out because I'm not the great provider. I am sorry about that. I don't feel so great about it myself. Most of all, she feels sad that she lost you so early on and never really got you back. That's why the silly outburst. Trying to make it out to be a funny joke when it's screwing her up inside."

Emily felt tears escape and drip down her cheek. She tried not to sniff.

"The final nail in the coffin was the will. I know we shouldn't have expected anything from anyone. We all have to make our own way in our lives, but it was hard that suddenly there you were, resenting us, rushing off on this enormous adventure to find your long-lost aunt and forgetting that we even exist. Then you deliberately hid from us that you were getting GG's house. That hurt. We couldn't think why you wouldn't even tell us yourself. We kept waiting for you to say something." Emily let out a loud sob. "It would have made a big difference to our lives. Plenty to cover the rent, or even buy a place of our own, and then maybe even a holiday, somewhere abroad rather than going to Scarborough again."

Tears continued to course down Emily's face. She felt dreadful and ashamed that she had hidden such a life changing event from her parents.

Dad sighed. "Okay then. I've had my say. That's it. End of. Your turn."

His face transformed into his usual deadpan expression. Emily had no idea what to say. She stayed silent. She was biting her lip trying to stop her sobbing. The quiet was deafening. She could see his point of view, but it didn't erase the years of feeling so left out of their family. How could she explain this to them in a way he would understand? Rummaging in her bag to find her tissues, blowing her nose violently, she frantically tried to find the right question. She found it.

"Dad, do you remember the fish and chips?"

"What are you on about? The fish and chips?" He looked confused.

"Well, when you all came home you sat round the table last night, not one of you offered me so much as a chip."

"Well, we wouldn't, would we?" he said with a shrug.

"Why ever not?"

"Whenever we go to the chippy or anywhere you always bang on about whether they might have fried your chips in the same fat as some meat or fish. You make out as if it's a heinous crime."

"Do I?" Emily had never thought about that.

"Yes, you do, love. You go on about it all quite a lot. Even the butterfly farm suggestion." Emily was confused. "You immediately gave us one of your hifalutin sermons. It's like living with a Jehovah's Witness. You're so adamant about your own opinions, lecturing us on how we're destroying the planet while you're the great saviour."

Emily thought about it. It stung but she knew that he had a point. It made her cry even more. She wasn't sure whether it was the humiliation or the guilt, and fresh tears welled up. She sniffed loudly and wiped frantically at her nose. Dad glanced across at her, patted her knee briefly.

"Come on, lass, you know you do."

She attempted to say "Thanks, Dad. You're right. I'm sorry." It was difficult to speak through the tears. Dad placed his hand on her knee, gave a comforting squeeze. After a long moment of silence, he broke it with, "Right, love, do you want to speak now?"

Emily shook her head, "No thanks, Dad, I think I just need to digest everything that you've said." *I really do need to process this.* "It's a lot to take in."

"Okay, love, but I'm very happy to listen." He looked at her kindly and she responded with a weak smile. He patted her knee and returned his hand to the wheel. "Right then, love, let's have the radio on again then, shall we?"

She nodded and let the sounds of the super jolly presenter cover her confusion.

Emily had imagined that she would stay in Great Granny's house, her house, but she knew it was totally impractical now that all the furniture had been disposed of. She got Dad to drop off the bulk of her stuff there and they went on to Granny's.

Emily had to go and knock at the door to make her presence known to The Boomers for the first time that she could remember. She stood shoulder to shoulder with Dad as they opened the door. At the sight of her dad, they looked alarmed. Emily stepped forward at which point they embraced her as they always did. "Come in, love," from Granny and "Come in, welcome home," from Aunt Cynthia.

It was odd how her dad's words had slightly altered how she felt about them. Could he be right about their streak of possessiveness?

Over her shoulder, Granny added, "You too, Mike. Bit of a surprise..."

Her dad just followed them in. "Just dropping Emily off but I'm parched and would die for a brew, Rose. Need to get off straight away, it's a long way back." Emily had never before heard him speak so assertively to Granny. Perhaps through this whole journey, literally and metaphorically, they were all changing, each in their own way.

THIRTY

Emily was back in her appointed bedroom at Granny's. She heard next door's dog yapping as it always did when the postie arrived. It reminded her of when she had been so eager to get letters back from Uncle Charlie and then the hideous Sarah Pennington. Knowing that there wouldn't be any post of interest to her, she lay back and thought about her mum and what she should do about their broken relationship.

She hadn't spoken to her parents since their big row and Dad's great reveal three days ago. She didn't know where to start unpicking it all and wasn't sure whether she should try. Did Mum know what he had said on that enlightening journey? There had been plenty of time for Emily to think about what he had said and she was beginning to understand where he was coming from. Thinking of some of her past behaviours made her tummy lurch in embarrassment and regret.

Life is very different seen through someone else's eyes. That was a lesson that she had learnt from her journey of discovery to find Aunt Julia and her lost relatives. Nothing could have prepared her for what she found; it was shocking.

Emily wasn't sure whether she should be openly apologising or waiting for her mum to do the big reveal to her too. She thought she might write to her but then that seemed a bit weird and old-fashioned after the whole Sarah Pennington correspondence. The thought of Sarah Pennington made Emily's flesh crawl.

Emily couldn't remember a time when she had been quite so confused and uncertain of herself. She felt in limbo but knew that it was up to her to seize the moment and sort things out for herself. Her whole existence and beliefs had been turned upside down and she felt uncomfortable, unsettled. She started flicking through the photos from her great adventure to find Aunt Julia, and considered the way her visits had gone.

She had written to each of them. A real letter. She had met each of them and listened with an open mind to what they had to say, whether she liked what she heard or not. It had turned so many prejudices and assumptions on their heads. Perhaps she could do the same with Mum. Let her talk, like her dad had. Really listen. It made her tummy flip but she should do it.

Not write a letter – that would be weird and freak Mum out. But an email would be good. She could write it and rework it until it said all that she wanted to say, and not send it until she was sure it was right.

Then they'd have to meet. Not here, but not at home either. Definitely not at Great Granny's house. Meet each other halfway. Neutral ground. Maybe somewhere on the Yorkshire Moors; it was beautiful there.

Emily climbed out of bed. After three days she had already slipped back into a routine. She yawned, used the bathroom, got dressed and trailed downstairs.

"Morning."

A short "Morning," from Granny who had her head in the paper. "Morning, love. Shall I put the kettle on?" from Aunt Cynthia.

"Yes please." She got out her periodic table mug and reached for her camomile tea bags. At last, the message had got through about the tea. She popped a slice of Aunt Cynthia's home baked bread into the toaster which made her think of Cathy, then got a plate and a knife and sat at the table.

"We need to talk, lass." Granny sounded brusque.

"Sure, Granny. What about?"

"Well, you've got all this holiday left before you go back to Edinburgh, and it seems that you're wasting it."

Emily had to agree. "Yup. You're obviously plotting something."

"I am."

Emily grinned, "Okay, what jobs have you found for me to do?"

Granny sat up poker straight like a chairman at a board meeting. "Number one, GG's house. We need to do something with it. It can't just sit there empty. It'll never sell if it's left to fester."

"I've been thinking about that. It might sound daft, but I was thinking of renting it out. Then I get a nice steady income from the rent."

"Much better to sell it, it would be the easiest thing to do, and you can get your cash in hand. We'll have to smarten it up either way. No-one would want to buy it how it is. The gas and electrics are sound but the décor is like something out of the ark. We need to decorate it from top to bottom. I've picked up these paint cards. The magnolia is nice and neutral, and we can get it dirt cheap."

Emily smiled to herself as Granny tried to get Emily to

do what she thought she should do. It was funny how much she did that.

"I've got the time, Granny. That's the whole point. I could do all that. I'll paint it and tart it up and then I can let it, unfurnished."

Granny looked doubtful. "When have you ever done decorating, Emily?"

"I can do that. I can learn. I can look on YouTube."

Granny waited and, getting nothing more from Emily, continued, "And the second thing is, your mum. What are we going to do about that? What do you want us to do?" Emily sighed. That wasn't so easy. You couldn't just slop on a coat of paint and whitewash that whole situation.

Emily sat back and stared at the ceiling. "You're right, Granny, I do need to sort it out and I do have the beginnings of a plan." It was easier to say that to the ceiling than directly to Granny.

Aunt Cynthia took her seat. "And what might that be, dear?"

Emily knew that it was something that she had to work out for herself. It was between her and Mum. So all she said was, "I'm working on it."

Granny was looking miffed and Aunt Cynthia somewhat surprised at this new Emily who seemed to be making her own decisions. There was an uncomfortable silence. Emily was inspired, "But, hey, Boomers, I need you to help me decide how to decorate GG's house – my house. I've never used a paintbrush in my life, and I'm sure to get paint everywhere."

Granny rallied. "I've painted more walls than you've had hot dinners." And Aunt Cynthia enthusiastically added, "I could run up some curtains. Mum's are in tatters."

Emily clapped her hands. *Oh yes, I've definitely caught that habit.* "Yes, to all of that."

Harmony was restored. The balance of power had shifted subtly, and it was a good feeling.

~

It was easy to find a place to meet Mum halfway: Mount Grace Priory, a National Trust property on the edge of the Yorkshire Moors. Emily's plan was to have a picnic – no money changing hands for food and drink – and then have a chat, just the two of them, with no-one else to twist the narrative.

The logistics were a bit more complicated. She had to ensure that Granny would lend her the car and that Dad would do the same for Mum on the same day. Emily knew that Mum wasn't that keen on driving, she always left that to Dad, and would have to be persuaded to come alone. Google Maps said it was only an hour from Newcastle. It would be an hour and a half for Emily from Sheffield. Plenty of time to rehearse her questions and prompts to get Mum talking and hopefully bring everything out into the open and clear the air.

She had to make certain that Dad would look after Ashley. It was a non-starter if Ashley was hanging around.

The hardest bit was the missive to her mum. It took two days before Emily was happy with her draft – and she wasn't going to let The Boomers anywhere near it. It wasn't easy to write. In fact, it was more problematical than any dissertation Emily had ever attempted. She only had one shot at getting it right.

Mum, I feel that we really do need to talk...

With all her ducks in a row, the message read over and

over until she was happy with it, and her fingers crossed, Emily hit Send.

Emily was perturbed to see just how quickly her mum wrote back.

> Emily, Thank you for your email. You're right. We need to talk. Good idea to meet at a neutral place. Mount Grace does look nice. I do understand why it must be just you and me, and Dad has said that he will be with Ashley for the day. Also, Dad says I can use the car although I'm not that happy about driving on the A1. Sooner rather than later, I think.
> Love Mum

Emily found that she was shaking as she read the message and tried very hard not to read anything into her mum's words. She read it about ten times.

Emily took Mum at her word and two days later was bowling along the M1 and A1(M) motorways to Mount Grace. Emily rehearsed her words every few minutes of the journey, but she still wasn't happy about the tone and nuances that she wanted to express. Waves of nervousness kept rippling through her.

As she drove into the car park, she looked out for Dad's car but she couldn't see it. She exhaled with a loud "oof," having found that she had been holding her breath with anxiety.

She messaged, 'I'm here. Let me know when you arrive,'

and then sat tapping her fingers nervously on the steering wheel.

Emily saw Dad's car creeping in. Knowing that Mum always looked for the widest space possible to avoid any mishap – she wasn't adroit enough to reverse in – Emily waited.

She sat in silence, her nerves frayed, until she got a message, 'I'm here. Where are you?' Emily emerged from the car and pretended to look around as if she hadn't seen her mum drive in, did the 'there you are' look of surprise and wandered over.

They looked at each other for a moment without saying anything. Emily was the first to speak, "Mum." She stepped forward and gave her a hug. She made sure that it lasted a bit longer than her usual greeting to show the intensity of the feeling.

"Well, love. Here we are." Emily looked at her mum and caught a look of fear or panic on her face.

What is she thinking? I thought she would look, I don't know, belligerent. Do I look the same?

"What's the plan, then, love?", she said softly. Where was her normal self-assurance? An uneasy smile. *Why is Mum nervous?*

"I thought we could have a look at the church and the monk's cell, stroll around the gardens, and then have a bite to eat. There are picnic tables by the orchard. I've got dinner here." She patted her stalwart patchwork bag. It gave her comfort.

Mum lifted a plastic carrier bag; Emily tried not to grimace. "I didn't get much, a few sandwiches, cheese and pickle and egg and cress." Clearly, she had tried very hard and chosen vegetarian fillings. Emily appreciated it but was so on edge that she didn't know whether to comment on it or not. They set off.

"How's Dad?" Emily knew that her voice was a bit squeaky from the tension.

"He's fine. Hasn't found another job yet but it works out okay because he can look after Ashley 'til she goes back to school." Mum sounded equally strained.

Bugger. Even a simple question gets tainted with echoes of our disagreement.

"And how is Ashley?"

"She's fine. Enjoying spending time with your dad. Very easy to please." *No, Emily, don't take that the wrong way.* "And how's your Gran and Aunt Cyn?"

"They're good. Aunt Cyn is determined to run up new curtains for GG's house which keeps her busy. She's loving it. And Granny is helping me by instructing me on the decorating. She thinks she's rather good at it but in truth she's not such a good teacher. It turns out that I'd rather she didn't." Mum laughed.

At least it didn't trigger any comments about GG's house coming to me. This is exhausting.

Mum changed the subject to safer ground. "Heard from that bloke of yours?"

"Dylan? No, thank God. You know what, sitting back from it, it turns out that I was more upset about being unceremoniously dumped than I was about losing him as a boyfriend. When I think about it, I'm not sure that we had that much in common." Mum chuckled and Emily began to relax a little.

"It can go like that." Mum's voice sounded less tense. Long silence. "Look, there's the church. That should be interesting."

Phew.

They wandered through the church and marvelled at how small the monk's cell was. It reminded Emily of her rooms at home, both Newcastle and Sheffield. She always drew the short straw wherever she was.

They were fascinated by the monk's garden and carefully read all the labels on the herbs and flowers to see what health benefits each provided. Emily pinched the mint and sniffed it. "I think it's the same variety as in GG's garden."

An answering non-committal "Hmm," from Mum.

They then strolled to the orchard, found a picnic bench, and sat down. They mirrored each other, delving into bags and putting the picnic goodies on the table between them and spreading out serviettes as plates. Emily placed a samosa in front of her mum. "Lamb."

Mum glanced at her, appreciating the unspoken gesture. "I think we should make a start."

"Yes, tuck in," Emily said, grabbing a sandwich.

"Emily! What are you like?" Mum laughed naturally for the first time since she'd arrived. "You know what I mean. Who goes first?"

"Oh." Emily put the sandwich down. "Sorry. I really am hungry. Well, I'd really like it if you could just talk to me about when I was born, even perhaps before I was born, and my childhood. Dad said a lot, but I need to hear it from you, how you felt."

"Okay. I've thought about it and planned it all out in my head, gone over and over it, but it's hard to know where to start." Mum took an enormous breath and let it out in a long sigh.

Emily nodded in agreement, "I know, Mum. I know."

She paused and stared into space. "I was horrified when I found out I was pregnant. We'd been taking precautions of course, we weren't stupid, but the pill wasn't a hundred percent, clearly."

"We?"

"Your Dad and me." Emily raised her eyebrows. "I know, Emily. That was really stupid of me saying what I did. I was pissed, I was angry, I was upset. Whenever I'm with The Boomers, they seem to reduce me to some sort of silly child who can't do a thing right. That whole revelation released all sorts of memories, like when I told your gran and she hissed at me, 'Whose is it then? Or perhaps you don't even know, you hussy.'" Emily gasped, shocked. Granny was often brusque, but she had never heard her being cruel. "You know what she can be like, Emily, when you don't meet her standards." Emily immediately thought of curt comments about wearing pyjamas to breakfast. Mum stared into space for a moment and then sighed. "I was embarrassed having even said it afterwards. Daft, I know. That's why we kept fobbing you off. It was difficult to explain, to backtrack." She took a bite of the samosa. "That's good that is." She chewed on it and swallowed.

Emily waited, not entirely convinced, and wondered if she'd need to prod her mother, but Mum eventually continued, "Your gran was not at all helpful. Before that, we'd had a good relationship. Not close. Not cuddly and outwardly loving, never a word of praise, but respectful and encouraging. You know your gran. It was her that came up with the idea of night school to get a proper personnel qualification, made me ask my boss. I think she was crushingly disappointed when I let her down by getting up the duff." She sighed.

"Do you think she had an inkling about GG and her indiscretion?" Emily asked.

"No, love. That was obviously a complete surprise to her. If she had known, I don't think she'd have been quite so shocked or been so cruel. She was disappointed in me. I think she had high hopes of me becoming a personnel manager, really climbing the ladder and getting to the top."

"But you still could have."

"Your dad's a dear soul but he isn't the upwardly mobile type, a bit old-fashioned, can't see him as a house husband holding the fort while I forged a career. Gran could see that, she always looked down on him. And it wasn't going to happen."

"But you still could. Even now. You aren't that old." Mum laughed. "You've got years to go," Emily insisted, "you're not even forty yet."

Mum chuckled, "Sometimes, love, you sound very like your granny."

Do I? They were both quiet for a moment, a comfortable silence, and took bites from their snacks.

A thought struck Emily, "Why did you marry Dad then? You didn't have to."

"No-one wants used goods, love. Everyone knew about the pregnancy and even if I'd had you adopted everyone would've known."

To Emily it sounded like convenience and she asked rather crossly, "Didn't you love him?"

Mum stopped, obviously thinking about her reply. "I don't think I knew what love was then. I'm not sure that I could feel anything at all at that time." Another hesitation. "I liked him. He was kind and considerate, looked up to me, made me feel good about myself. He actually seemed to fancy me in preference to the long legged, blonde, Jennifer. That didn't happen very often." A wry smile. Emily was disappointed and took a breath to protest but Mum continued, "But I did grow to love him. He's always been so supportive, he's consistently taken my side when The Boomers are having a go at me. We suit each other. We'll never be a great big passionate, romantic story, but we do love each other. Very much actually. He's a good man."

Emily was relieved but still had another question, "Why didn't you have me adopted?"

"I couldn't, love. No way that I could have done." She paused. "I never could have done that." She shook her head. "Giving birth to you was a nightmare. I know that your dad told you about the four-degree tear, right from my vagina through to my back passage. Afterwards, I was a wreck. Today they would diagnose me as having PTSD, it was that traumatic. I kept getting flashbacks, still do sometimes, lying there my legs akimbo while they spent hours carefully stitching my undercarriage together into some semblance of order. Any bodily function after that was painful and precarious for months. It wasn't a good start to motherhood." She shook her head again, as if trying to make the memory go away. She shuddered. "But then it got worse."

Emily reached out a hand, her mum covered it with hers. "How could it get any worse than that? It sounds horrendous."

"The moment your GG set eyes on you it was weird." Mum paused. "She couldn't keep away from you. Mum and Aunt Cyn took it as wanting to help me out, I was in such a state, could barely walk to the toilet, had accidents, it was humiliating. She tried to get me to nurse you, but I couldn't get the hang of it." Mum laughed, more of a snuffle. "I thought you didn't like me – silly to think now, you were just a tiny innocent baby." She looked pensive. "So anyway, GG whipped you away and started feeding you herself with formula, making me instantly redundant. I was in too much pain and mental turmoil to care." Mum sipped at her orange juice. "I get it now, of course. I suspect that she saw your dark curls and had her own flashback." They sat, each quietly mulling over their own thoughts.

Emily tried to imagine how difficult that must have

been. It was all far easier to understand with hindsight and she could see exactly how it must have appeared to her poor mum. "And you'd never have understood that if it wasn't for her letter from the grave."

"Not knowing what was going on in GG's head at the time made it impossible to recognise why she did what she did. Mind you, your gran was nearly as bad. She was besotted with you. Her first grandchild, and she always said that you got your hair from my dad. He'd not that long passed away. They almost fought over you." Mum sniffed with a sort of humming sound, staring into the distance.

"Not easy for you, Mum," Emily said, gently squeezing her hand, amazed at her mum's revelations and trying to take them all in.

Still looking away, her mind in a different place, Mum said, "No, love. It wasn't. I thought that their obsession would die down after I married your dad and we moved into our own place, but it never really ended. Every excuse they had, they'd have you round there. Yes, it was wonderful that you received such loving care while I went to work, and it did give me the chance to work longer hours and make something of myself, even though I never did do that qualification. Gran didn't let up about that and I sort of resented it and dug my heels in in protest. Ridiculous really, cutting off my nose to spite my face, but you know what she can be like when she gets an idea in her head." Emily nodded, thinking of Granny and her insistence that she should sell Great Granny's house.

"But what they did was fanatical. They love bombed you so much that I didn't feel that there was any space left for me. You were just as infatuated with them. 'Granny doesn't cook the chicken like that,' you'd say as you picked at my offering. 'Aunt Cyn is making me a new dress. We went and chose the material and it's really cool.'" Mum glanced at Emily's bag. "I bet there's a remnant of that one amongst that little lot." Emily looked at her bag too. The love that Aunt Cynthia had put into making it was still there, but it had shifted in some way by her mum's disclosure. Emily was assimilating this new perspective and it was changing her frame of reference.

"Every weekend it was, 'I'm bored, are we going to Loxley?' And not just The Boomers. 'GG says that if I eat all my vegetables I will grow up into a strong and clever girl.' I'm quite certain that she gave herself all the credit for you going to university." Mum let out a harsh 'hoof' sound and shook her head. "It was hard." She stared across at the trees looking sad. "You were totally bereft when we moved to Newcastle. You were homesick for weeks, months even. You blamed it on me and your dad. You were a ball of rage. When we got to Newcastle, you insisted on having the smallest room and arranging the furniture in exactly the same way that it was at Granny's house." *Did I do that? I don't remember it at all.* "And so it went on. You even refused to come home after staying with the Boomers when Ashley was born. 'Do I have to, Mum? Can't I stay here?' It was..." Mum paused, her hand on her chin, "...heart-breaking."

It was a vague memory but she could now remember that she had felt that way and revelled in the way that she was feted and adored by The Boomers and Great Granny. Now, hearing about the effect that it had had, Emily was horrified that she had behaved that way. She could see how that must have hurt her mum.

"Even now, when we go and see The Boomers you greet them like the long-lost loves of your life. I can't think of a time that you have ever – and I do mean ever – been so happy to see me or your dad." Emily tingled with mortification, squeezed her eyes together and put her head in her free hand. "Sorry, love, that came out as a bit harsh."

But actually true.

Rubbing her eye, Mum continued, "When you came home after GG's funeral, I tried to get you to join in with me and Ashley but you wouldn't. I'd taken time off work, it was my annual leave, and I hoped that you'd enjoy spending time with us. It hurt that you didn't want to, and that finding this Julia was more important than your sister and me." She sighed heavily, "And I was upset when you suddenly announced that you were going back to Loxley. If only you'd said I could have made arrangements for Ashley and I had wrongly assumed..." She shook her head. "I got my knickers in a twist because the one big thing that any working mum dreads is not having childcare. It's just so worrying, you've no idea how taking any extra time off is held against you, and I panicked. I'm sorry about that, love. That wasn't right."

Mum turned and looked squarely at her, reached over, took Emily's hand away from her face and held it. "Right, lass. It's your turn."

Emily's head was spinning. "I need to think. Can I just go for a short walk?"

"Of course." Mum patted Emily's hand and relinquished it. Emily eased off the bench and strode off rapidly before her mum could see her tears.

Where to begin to unpack all of that? It was suddenly so obvious. How could Emily not have seen it before?

She'd had a wonderful time with The Boomers and Great Granny. She could recall so many happy times, so much laughter and fun and cuddles. And yes, Mum and Dad were boring in comparison and always seemed to be doing dull things like grocery shopping, cleaning the house instead of making it messy with paint, paper and glue, cooking mundane food rather than baking sugary goodies. Even changing the beds instead of getting outside in the sunshine had annoyed her, because she much preferred to go off exploring the common or paddling in the river.

She could clearly remember the sadness of being wrested away from Loxley. It had been traumatic, ripped from the bosom of her 'family'. She had felt betrayed.

Ashley. Now Ashley was a different situation. She hated that her little sister was beautiful and blond and had the green eyes. Always being snuggled by Mum. No room for her. 'Shush, don't wake Ashley.' 'Gently, you'll hurt her,' when she tried to hug her. She recalled watching Ashley on Mum's lap when Mum was coaching her to read. Ashley was very uncooperative, but Mum was kind and gently cajoling. Emily couldn't remember a time that Mum had ever done that with her. Mind you, she hadn't needed cajoling. She loved reading. Perhaps that was it. Emily did find Ashley very irritating but was that really Ashley's fault? Maybe it was Emily's own 'green eyed monster' that was generating these perceptions.

Then the really big one. Great Granny. Transferring her love for her lost child, Julia, to Emily. Thinking of it like that was a bit sad. It wasn't really Emily that Great Granny had adored so lavishly but a memory of her darling daughter, given away. It was hard to process and somewhat ironic that it was Emily who had made all the effort to search for Julia and bring her back to life.

As she wandered through the gardens, Emily wasn't looking at the fine planting and the well-tended borders. She was working on untangling her whole life to date and seeing it through her parents' eyes.

Thinking back, she could see the love and attention that she had received so unreservedly from The Boomers, and from Great Granny, but now she also appreciated it from her parents' point of view. It must have hurt them so much to have been pushed away. In all honesty, she hadn't really ever given them a chance. It made Emily quiver with mortification and embarrassment. She hoped that it wasn't too late to make amends and change that.

With that thought she hurried back to her mum and took her place at the table. "Okay, Mum, I think I understand. I'm so sorry." She put her hands out on the table. Her mum took them in hers. "When Dad spoke to me so openly it was a revelation. It made me look at my childhood with a very different perspective. I've never considered things from your point of view before and now that you've given me such a full and frank account, I feel terrible. I've taken you and Dad for granted and I can see the mistakes that I've made. I do love you both, I really do, and I am just so sorry." Tears sprang to her eyes. Looking at her mum she could see that she too had tears trickling down her cheek but was also smiling wanly. "I know that I can be very irritating banging on about the health of the planet, my health and eating habits. I do realise that..."

Her mum gave a small smile, "You can, love, you most certainly can." Her eyes were twinkling.

"And I say sorry all the time which must be annoying, and I talk out loud for no good reason and I know that you don't like the way I dress or the stud in my nose." Emily squeezed her hands.

Mum raised her head and opened her eyes wide in protest. "I've never said any of that."

"You don't have to. I can see it in your face. You show every emotion, just like me." Emily grinned to show she was laughing at herself. "And I do hate the way you lavish attention on Ashley, but I get that now..." Another squeeze and a grin.

Mum looked askance, "Do I? Do I lavish attention on her?"

Emily squeezed her hands, "You do. And I can see why. You're her mum, she deserves all the love in the world. It's all good." Mum smiled, one that reached her eyes. "So..."

"So?" Mum looked serious.

"Thank you Mum, for talking to me today. Openly, frankly and... with love." Her mum never used the 'L' word. A warm squeeze of her hands from Mum. She clearly understood. "I don't think I have anything left to say. I have listened which has been the right thing for me to do. I wish we'd had this conversation years ago, but we didn't."

"Are you sure, love?"

"Absolutely, Mum. Dad opened up a whole new way of looking at things. I've gone over and over it in my mind, but I needed to hear that from you."

"What about your point of view? Shouldn't I be listening to that?"

"No, Mum. Anything I could say would sound childish and stupid and selfish. So, I'm okay. More than okay. Now that I recognise that, I am truly sorry for my inappropriate behaviour and that I haven't understood you. We're a complicated family." She looked intently at her mum.

Mum's face took on a picture of anguish. "But can I ask one more thing? You've never invited us to Edinburgh. Are you ashamed of us?"

Emily squeaked in protest, and sat back, withdrawing her hands from under her mum's. She felt mortified, knowing that mum was right. Why had she always been reluctant for her parents to visit her? Was it because she was a different person in Edinburgh and that if they were there, she wouldn't be able to be two divergent people at once?

Emily blurted out, "It's difficult to put it into words, but

I'll try. I'm trying to think this through as I go along." Mum nodded briefly, but the sad look remained on her face.

Emily took a deep breath. "When I'm at uni, I'm Emily the studious undergraduate, wanting to save our planet from extinction. I'm respected and an equal with my peers, whatever their background and monetary worth. It's easy to relax and just be myself. I can be whatever I want to be, and not necessarily the same thing every day." Emily gave a wry laugh, "Funnily enough, when I'm with The Boomers I realise now that I revert to being a child, just like you said that you do. My clumsiness comes out, I'm very deferential, I don't question their opinions and I allow them to treat me like a silly kid. In short, I lap up their extravagant preferential treatment. It makes me feel special." Emily paused, surprised by her own insight.

Mum asked, "And at home, with us, your dad and me?"

Another big breath. "Whenever I'm at home, I feel that I'm judged as the Emily I used to be as a child. Exasperating Emily, the irritating big sister, the plain, even ugly, daughter," Mum choked and Emily looked at her and said sincerely, "Yes, Mum, I do feel I am the ugly one, who is wasting everyone's money with grandiose ideas above my station."

Mum let out a weak, "No, Emily, no..."

"Being clever isn't enough. Whenever I tell you about uni, both you and Dad get a glazed look as if you aren't interested."

Mum gasped. "No, Emily. It isn't like that at all. I just don't get half of what you're talking about and I don't want to look even more stupid to you by asking questions. And it's hard because Ashley, bless her, just hasn't got your brains at all. That's why I spend so much time with her, trying to help her keep up at school, which isn't easy. We try not to rub her nose in it by pointing out how amazingly clever you are. And she just doesn't have your brave personality. You always seem to be so on top of everything and so sure of yourself."

Emily put her head on one side and considered this point of view. "I'm beginning to understand how we've just been so blind to each other's perspective. We really should have had this conversation years ago." Emily reached out for her mum's hands again. She squeezed them and smiled softly. Emily was trying to make sense of it all.

After a long silence, Emily said, "I'm sorry. I really need to put this all together in my mind and get my head round it. I'm confused, Mum. My whole belief system, my whole life has just been turned upside down."

"I'm so sorry, love." Mum nodded.

Emily knew that this was the moment to be open about everything, "And about GG's house..."

Mum interrupted. "I think we both understand now what that was all about, don't we, love?"

Emily nodded. "It's amazing how many ripples have come from that one event. Major life-changing consequences, and not just for GG and Aunt Julia."

"Have you decided what you're going to do with it?"

"I had. I was going to keep it, although Granny keeps telling me that I should sell it." Emily chuckled and raised her eyebrows, "I was thinking of letting it out so that it provides me with an income and then, when I leave uni, I could think again depending on the housing market. But, Mum, I could also sell it right now and we could share the proceeds, particularly to tide you over until Dad gets another job. Honestly, I'm grateful for anything that I get from GG."

Mum smiled, "Listen to you, Emily. You, our little girl, sounding so grown up, but it's yours. You deserve it and it'll set you up for life and leave you without a university debt hanging around your neck. We've managed perfectly well up 'til now and we can carry on perfectly well. We want **you** in our lives, Emily, not your money." Another strong squeeze of her hands and a shake. "Don't give it another thought. Anyway, I should think that you've got a lot of work to do there to bring it into this century." It was said with no hint of envy.

"Thanks Mum. You're right, I have a lot to do. I don't think anyone else shares GG's taste in wallpaper." She hesitated, wondering whether or not to ask for help but decided it might be too soon. It would also get complicated with where they would stay and how much time they would spend with The Boomers.

"Now, Emily, I want to get back before the rush hour traffic gets going, but I think there's a couple of things to say before I go." She paused and then gently shook Emily's hands, "I do love you, Emily. Can you forgive me?" A first time she had ever heard that word from her mum, used in that way.

Tears sprang to Emily's eyes. "Yes, of course, Mum. Totally, but only if you can forgive me too."

Mum nodded, unable to speak because she too was weeping.

After a minute, they released their hands and both wiped their eyes. Mum busied herself packing up the inevitable detritus that accumulates after a picnic, and rammed it all into the carrier bag. It seemed very mundane to Emily after all the emotion.

They walked in comfortable silence back to the car park, finding a bin to consume the rubbish, and stopped by Granny's car.

"This is me, Mum." Emily put down her bag and opened her arms. Mum stepped in and they shared a warm embrace. It felt comfortable and comforting. A flash of a memory of Cathy, except Mum smelt of lamb samosas instead of bread. Emily smiled. "When do I get to see you again?"

"I tell you what love, I'm a dab hand with a paint brush, so I'll come and help you do up GG's house. Gives me a chance to see Mum and Aunt Cyn as well, show that I'm fine about the house and all."

Emily grinned, "I'd like that."

"So would I. Bye, Emily love."

And I'll leave it at that, not complicate it with logistics.

"Bye Mum, see you later. Love you." She felt at peace.

Emily drew up outside The Boomers' house. Her car journey back from Mount Grace had seemed much shorter than the drive there; it was funny how that happened, when you were dreading something. But the journey home had still given her time to digest everything her mum had said.

The meeting had been cathartic, but Emily was a little sad that she and her mum had managed to miscommunicate for so long. At least now they had a way forward.

Granny opened the front door with Aunt Cynthia peering over her shoulder. It made Emily shake her head at the recollection of Mum's awareness of just how they pampered and mollycoddled her. A perfect demonstration. Emily's interpretation of it had shifted in just one short meeting with her mum, followed by over an hour of dissecting and analysing every aspect of her family relationships.

Emily knew she was going to be dragged in and plonked at the table before the interrogation commenced. Holding her bag in front of her as a defence she clambered out of the car and called out with a grin, "You know what I'm going to say... I need a pee." The Boomers laughed and stepped aside so she could head straight up the stairs to the bathroom.

She came back down to find them both at the kitchen table. Granny patted the tabletop. "Come and sit down, lass. Tell us all about it."

Aunt Cynthia added eagerly, "Do take a pew, dear. The kettle has just boiled."

Emily knew this would happen so she was prepared. "Mount Grace was fascinating. A really great place to visit, you should go there, you'd love it. We liked the monk's cell, it made my room look enormous in comparison, and the gardens were glorious."

The Boomers chuckled but Granny had a look on her face that showed that this was not what she had meant at all. "So how was Mum? Did you have a good chinwag? Sort things out?"

"We did. We were so lucky with the weather that we were able to have our picnic outside, so it was great."

Still not what Granny wanted. She frowned. "So what did you talk about?"

"It was interesting. Mum talked to me for the first time about when she found herself expecting with me and how she felt afterwards, so damaged and so lost –"

Granny interrupted, "That isn't quite how I'd have put it..."

Emily chose to ignore that. "But tell me, what do you remember about how GG was with me? Mum had a fascinating take on that."

Granny looked confused. "She adored you, lass. Worshipped you. She stepped up to the plate and helped your mum when she was... struggling."

Aunt Cynthia added with a smile, "Couldn't keep her hands off you."

"Yes, that was what Mum said." The Boomers offered

up identical frowns. "What Mum reckons is that when I was born with my dark curly hair, she sort of fixated on me as if I were Julia."

Granny harrumphed. "That sounds a bit far-fetched to me. Your mum has some strange ideas."

"But could it have been true?" Emily persisted. "Knowing what you know now?"

Granny stayed silent and frowning, but Aunt Cynthia spoke up. "I suppose so. Mum could have seen a hint of Julia in you, but we didn't know about it so wouldn't have considered anything like that at the time."

Granny continued to stay very still until suddenly she slapped her hands on the table, making Emily jump. "So, your mum was okay about the house, then?"

"Actually, she was. She understands and it isn't an issue."

Granny looked surprised. "So, no bad words?"

"None. It was good. Really, really good."

Granny paused, looked at Emily as if trying to work out what was really going on. "Well then, time for us to get on with doing that house up so you can sell it."

"Yes Granny, it is very much the time for **me** to get it all together."

THIRTY-ONE

Two days later Emily was sitting at the table with The Boomers having tea, her faithful bag at her feet, when her phone pinged, muffled within the depths of all the other stuff that she kept in there. A WhatsApp. Emily automatically reached down to retrieve her phone to read it. *I bet that's from Mum.*

Granny growled, "Emily."

"Sorry, Granny," she sat up straight and continued tucking into her stuffed pepper. Emily pondered about Granny's reaction. That was a typical example of how Emily felt she reverted to being like a child with The Boomers. She wondered whether she should have just excused herself from the table and read the message like an adult or whether it was the right thing to do to comply. After all, it was The Boomers' home, their rules. It was just good manners.

It's complicated, but my attitude has most definitely shifted.

When tea was finished and The Boomers were on to their cups of tea, Emily did excuse herself from the table.

She stopped herself from saying 'please may I get down' as she had always done since time immemorial and avoided asking specifically for permission by saying, 'Thank you for my tea, it was lovely.'

Far more appropriate.

She grabbed her bag, slumped in an armchair and rummaged for her phone. The WhatsApp message was from Mum.

> **Mum**
> When can we come and help out with the decorating?

Emily smiled.

Mum and Dad arrived at Granny's front door with Ashley in tow. Mum was the first in. "Hi there, we're here." Emily greeted her and Mum gave her a warm hug; it felt good. Mum followed up with nothing too sentimental, just a good practical mum comment. "Your dad's brought his drill and toolbox, just in case."

Dad gave her a kiss on the head. "Hey up, lass."

Ashley just walked past as if she hadn't seen Emily at all. Emily couldn't resist. "Hi, Ashley. All right?" Ashley looked back at her with a frown on her face, shrugged and carried on into the lounge.

Some things will never change.

Granny eased herself out of her armchair. "Hello, Lisa, love. Good journey?" She came forward and gave Mum a smacking kiss in the ear. "Hello, Mike." Dad stayed out of kissing range.

Aunt Cynthia hovered, delivering little pats on any

arms that she could reach. "Hello, Lisa, hello, Mike. I'll just go and make us all a brew."

As Aunt Cynthia headed for the kitchen, Granny opened the conversation, "So you've come to help our Emily out with the house then? That's big of you."

Mum looked a bit worried, as if she wasn't sure what to say. Emily could see what her mum meant about her relationship with Granny. It was the first time that she had bothered to observe their interaction. Dad stepped in. "Well, Rose, sooner she gets it rented out then the sooner she stops sponging off all of us. That's got to be a good thing, eh?" He said it with an almost straight face, but Emily, with her new understanding of her dad, read it as an attempt at a joke.

Granny bristled and looked sharply at Emily. "I thought you were selling it, Emily?"

Emily tried not to mumble but it was hard to change her behaviours all in an instant, "Well, Granny, I've had a think about that..."

Granny ignored her, "And anyway, Mike, we don't mind looking after her, she's a good lass and does her bit around the place. She can stop here for as long as she likes."

Emily thought she should intervene. "It's really great of you to look after me, Granny, thank you. But Dad's right – if I can get the house in a good condition, everything will be so much better. Now, there's a lot to be done at GG's and we don't want to waste the day. So let's have a brew and then be on our way over."

Aunt Cynthia bustled in carrying a tray with the family brown teapot and other requisites for a Yorkshire cup of tea. "I've baked some parkin," was met with a resounding chorus of "Ooh, yum," followed by a round of harmonious chuckles as they all realised that they had sung out in unison.

As they settled with their teas, Mum asked Granny, "Now, Mum, we can't imagine that Ashley is going to be much help to us so I wonder if she could stay with you. Is that okay?" She looked a bit nervous about asking. Emily hadn't realised before how subjugated Mum was in the presence of her own mother. Old wounds clearly ran deep. Perhaps she'd never thought to observe their interaction in the past. It was as if Emily had suddenly become aware of everyone around her in a way that she never had before.

"Of course she can. You'll enjoy that won't you Ashley? Aunt Cyn has got all the makings of some buns so that'll keep you busy, won't it?" Ashley didn't bother to reply, just leant in toward her mum. "And we'll make everyone's dinner, too."

Mum was puzzled and looked at Emily. "I thought we said we'd all meet up at the Rodney for dinner?"

Granny replied instead, "It would be just as easy to come here and save you a few bob. Let's do that. After all, Mike's all about watching the money." She winked at Mike. "And I've got some macaroni cheese that needs eating up."

Seeing her mother's worried look, Emily decided to step in. "Actually, Granny, *I'm* paying for dinner. I would like to treat you all – Mum and Dad for kindly coming and helping out, and you and Aunt Cyn for everything that you've done for me."

Granny mumbled ungraciously, "That's big of you, Emily." Emily blanched; this wasn't the Granny who normally went along with Emily's ideas. It felt like a game was being played between Granny, Mum and herself and she was only just becoming aware of the rules.

Dad, rather to Emily's surprise, seemed to pick up on the atmosphere. "Well, Rose, how's that vegetable garden of yours? We've had awful problems with carrot fly this year, what about you?"

Granny was back on top. "Did you plant alliums between the rows like I said?"

"I like to use marigolds like my mum always used to."

"Well, that clearly isn't working. Alliums are the only answer..."

The argument continued as it did every year when the conversation came round to carrot fly. The non-combatants supped their tea, except for Emily who was washing down her delicious gooey parkin with water from her reusable bottle, until they were ready to head off to Great Granny's house.

The moment they stepped outside Granny's house, Mum ticked Dad off. "Why did you go and have to bring up the carrot fly? You know it always gets her going." Dad shrugged but Emily noticed a slight smile. She was noticing so many nuances.

At Great Granny's, they stood looking at each other, wondering who was going to take the lead. It was Emily's house so, by rights, she should be in charge, but all the same she turned to her mum and said, "Right Mum, you're the best organiser I know... organise us." Emily thought that Mum looked quite pleased.

Mum decided that the best approach was for Dad to do all the gloss paint, the skirting boards, the window frames, and the doors. "Mike, you're the most dextrous of us all, and I can't see Emily or me doing it as neatly. We'd get the paint everywhere, we're so clumsy." Emily had never before heard her mum refer to herself as clumsy. "Emily and I will do the emulsion together. It's more fun being able to chat and with two people working together it keeps up the pace."

"Good point, Mum. When I've been working on my own, I bore myself into a stupor."

Dad nodded. "Suits me. I could do without you two blathering while I'm working."

"Let's get to it." Mum clapped. Definitely a family thing.

Tins opened and paint stirred, rollers at the ready, Emily and her mum started from opposite corners. Mum piped up, "Last one to the other's corner makes the brew." They set off at a pace. After a few minutes of vigorous rolling, Emily was spattered head to toe in fine speckles of grey.

"Hey, Mum, we need music to paint to. What do you like?"

"None of your weird modern shouty stuff, that's for sure."

Emily laughed. "Something from the olden days then – Eighties or Nineties?"

"Yeah, why not. We had some good stuff back in the day. I remember me and Jennifer used to wind Mum up by singing 'Like a Virgin' and dancing around the lounge to it in a very flirty Madonna-ish sort of way. She was not impressed. That was the first time she called me a hussy. We were only about thirteen."

Emily was taken aback and decided to ignore the unkind comment. "I'll have to find that one then. I'd like to see a replay of the dance moves that so shocked Granny."

Emily fiddled with her phone, finding hits from the eighties and nineties and put it in its dock. The dulcet sounds of 'I Want to Break Free' boomed out.

Mum immediately started rolling in time to the music with a wiggle of her hips and a Freddy Mercury tilt of the head. Emily laughed and joined in. It was so fantastic to see this side of her mum – one that Dad had alluded to but Emily have never seen before. Mum sang along for a verse or two; she knew all the words, then in a normal voice she said, "I did too."

"What?"

"Wanted to break free. Me and Jennifer thought that your Granny was so strict compared to everyone else's mums. We couldn't believe it when she gaily divulged her hippy background and seemed happy to talk quite openly about smoking weed in the days of free love. Bit hypocritical really."

Emily thought about this. "Granny is a bit of a stickler I must say, always has been with me. But I've always known that under that scary exterior she's a right softie." Emily paused and smirked. "You're right though, I'm always on my best behaviour with The Boomers. You're not going to believe this, but I've only just stopped asking to get down from the table after a meal."

Mum burst out laughing. "Emily, I can't believe that. How old are you?"

Emily grinned. "I know." It felt so good to be laughing and joshing with her mum. It was as if a switch had been flicked on. "Thanks, Mum, for coming and lending a hand. It means the world to me."

"Enough of that soppy claptrap, Emily." Emily smiled to herself. Mum sounded more like Granny than she would ever know. "It's my pleasure and it's good to be spending time with you."

The next song on the playlist, 'Wake Me Up Before You Go Go', lifted them out of their moment of sentimentality and got their paint rollers going nineteen to the dozen.

~

Granny was determined to make a point at dinner so for her meal at the Admiral Rodney, she only ordered a starter, a duo of pate. "That's plenty enough for anybody." She leant back and patted her stomach. Emily wasn't going to be deterred and asked for a main course, vegetable curry.

Dad went for the steak. "Medium please, and none of that fancy foreign sounding sauce, thanks."

Mum ordered a burger and chips for Ashley and chose the gammon steak with triple cooked chips for herself. Aunt Cynthia raised a hand. "Same for me too." Emily saw as Granny scrutinised them in turn, looked down at their waistlines and gave a sniff. Mum and Aunt Cynthia both pointedly refused to look at her.

Orders given, Emily wanted to talk about her mission to find Julia. "So, Aunt Julia."

Granny started off. "You know what I think, love. We've found her. It's a sad story but at the end of the day we know that she was loved."

Aunt Cynthia added, "A terrible tale. Awful for you to find all that out, Emily."

Mum asked, "Have you been in touch with them at all since you got back?" Emily was pleased that she was showing such interest.

Emily shook her head. "No. I did write a thank you note to each of them, and I attached a photo from last Christmas when we were all together here so they could see their northern relations. I wanted them to see that all of you have GG's eyes like Aunt Julia, but I didn't hear anything back, not even from Cathy. I wasn't particularly surprised."

Mum nodded. "Shame really. So, what are you going to do next?"

Emily frowned. "You're right, Granny, there isn't anything more to be done is there? I guess I'll just go through my notes and pictures on occasion and just remember the whole thing as a great adventure." The thought that it was all over made her feel sad, but there was no denying she'd learnt a lot along the way.

Mum suddenly piped up, "Talking of Christmas..."

Granny frowned and cut in with, "No-one was talking about Christmas."

Mum smiled nervously. "Emily mentioned the photo that we had from last Christmas which made me think..." Mum looked anxiously at Dad, seemingly for support. "Well, it'll be the first Christmas without GG, so we can't all stay with her, can we? We can't even gather at her house if Emily's going to rent it out. I think the time has come for us to have Christmas at ours rather than yours, Mum."

Granny was silent for a moment, her mouth pursed. "So, what you're saying is that you don't want to have Christmas with us?"

"No, Mum. I'm not saying that at all. We want you to come to us for Christmas."

Granny sat up straight and spluttered, "But we've always had Christmas here, since you were a babe in arms."

"Yes Mum, and it's been wonderful, but we think that the time has come for me and Mike to take the strain. We'd love to start doing Christmas our way, the next generation." Dad nodded his support.

Granny looked horrified. "Where will we all stay?"

"I'll work something out. Emily won't mind sleeping on the settee, will you love? You've plenty of experience with strange sleeping places while you've been at uni."

"That's true enough. There was a time when six of us slept in one room at a Travelodge, it was a laugh..."

Mum interrupted with, "Anyway, Mum. I thought I'd give you some forewarning. Aunt Cyn, I hope you'll still be making the Christmas cake and the mince pies?"

"Of course, dear, and the Christmas pudding." Aunt Cynthia grinned. "And I'd better be baking some nut loaf monstrosity for Emily."

"And Mum, I hope you'll be providing the parsnips,

sprouts and carrots fresh from your garden." Granny harrumphed.

The awkward silence was broken by, "Now who's having the pate?" The food had arrived. Emily was relieved to be able to say, "The pate? That will be Granny."

It was a release and everyone visibly relaxed. Except Granny.

THIRTY-TWO

It had seemed to take Emily forever to sort out Great Granny's house, although in reality it had only taken five weeks in all, even with the help of Mum and Dad. Still, that was far more than the one month she had naively anticipated at the start.

Emily was standing in the hall of Great Granny's house – her house – waiting for the agent to come round to discuss letting it. She desperately hoped that they would approve of her decorating choices.

She had painted away a lifetime of memories, creating a blank canvas for a new era to begin, and was very proud of what she had achieved. In doing so, she had made some new remembrances, dancing with her mum, choosing colours, and teasing dad about his extreme attention to detail.

Emily hadn't realised that Great Granny's bequest included some of her surplus cash. She had felt very guilty all over again; it should have gone to Mum. But most of it was immediately consumed buying paint, flooring, carpets, and fixtures and fittings.

Emily decided on one last tour of her house while she had it all to herself.

The bathroom now had a shower, over a screened bath with a crisp white vanity unit and toilet. Great Granny had never taken to showering. The spare room had lost its sixties' aberration wallpaper to a soothing range of gentle tones of grey. Great Granny's bedroom looked vast without its furniture and all its frills. It smelt of fresh paint, Great Granny's Blue Grass had completely evaporated, but as a silly personal joke Emily had decorated it in a warm green blue. It had made her mum chuckle. Emily had chosen a muted yellow for the tiny back bedroom. She envisioned it as a nursery, a home for a new generation of babies.

"I'm really pleased. I think it looks very good. Hope you think so too, GG." Emily beamed with pride as she walked down the stairs, following the run of grey carpet that linked all the rooms together.

At the bottom, Emily poked her head into the kitchen. The units weren't very up to date, but after a very grown up evaluation of the pros and cons of fitting new ones, she had come down on the side of 'it will do'. The oak lookalike floor laminate that went through the ground floor gave it a far more contemporary feel than the blue lino and swirly patterned carpets that GG had favoured.

Emily strolled through to the lounge. Just like the kitchen units, she had prevaricated over replacing the fireplace but decided in the end to leave it and keep it as an original vintage feature.

She wandered to look out of the dining room window across the garden to the trees on the peaks far in the distance. Everything was getting to the end of its summer showiness and settling into more autumnal tones.

The doorbell rang. It would be the agent.

She said softly, "What a long way I have come."

THIRTY-THREE

Emily returned to Edinburgh at the start of the new term to find everyone else trickling back after the long university holiday. It was strange to be back in this alternative world of tall grey buildings, streets that behaved like Escher paintings and the surreal Arthur's Seat looming over the city.

Emily had secured a modern studio flat, not very beautiful inside or out, very plain and uninteresting, incredibly practical, but she had plans.

She had chosen it so that she could walk to lectures, a zero carbon footprint, but even more so because the sun streamed in through the window, and she could line up all her herb plants along the ledge. She was watering them with a wonderful old aluminium can that she had found in a junk shop. The Boomers would be proud of her green fingers.

Mum's right. It has always been The Boomers that come to mind before my own mum and dad. Thank God I have learned that I don't have to choose between them, I can enjoy them, and love them, all.

It was the first day of lectures and Emily set off jauntily

in anticipation of making a start on her final year. She was thinking about what colour she could use as an accent colour to make her flat more cheerful. Now she'd mastered that life skill on Great Granny's house, *my house*, she wanted to resurrect it. She was contemplating a sunshine yellow throw and some scatter cushions.

It was Sod's Law that one of the first people she bumped into as she walked towards the King's Building was Dylan going the same way. It was awkward because she couldn't ignore him – that would be very odd – but engaging with him meant walking the rest of the way to the chemistry block together.

He looked smaller somehow, skinnier, and weak. How on earth had she even dated him, let alone cried when he dumped her? She decided to play it cool, hitched up her patchwork bag and opened with, "Hi, Dylan. Good vacation?"

"Yeah, you?" He looked sheepish.

"Excellent as it turns out." She grinned to herself, feeling superior. "Did you get away? Go abroad? Have exciting adventures?" She realised that she sounded hearty and quite unlike her normal cool, laid-back self.

"Nah, it didn't work out. Because I had to do my retakes, I couldn't go away so I worked at the local pub. I did pass them though and at least I've got a bit of cash set aside."

"Congratulations."

"Thanks."

They walked along, automatically getting into step with each other and staying at least one metre apart. Emily tried to imagine holding his hand as she had before. It wasn't very appealing. She glanced across at his mouth and tried to remember kissing him. Yuck. How her perspective on life had changed in so many ways in such a short space of time.

He clearly wasn't going to ask Emily anything else, so

she decided to launch into a monologue to break the awkward silence. "Well, Dylan, let me tell you about my holiday. As you know, my great granny passed away and at her funeral it was revealed that there was a long-lost great aunt who had been adopted as a baby. I went on a mission to find her. My adventure took me to Kent and Wiltshire. It was incredible, an extremely complicated story including a possible murder. I inherited a house which was amazing, and then I spent hours and hours doing it up before letting it out to a lovely young couple..."

Dylan interrupted, "You inherited a house?"

"Yeah. I did. Oh look, we're here already." Emily bounded up the steps ahead of Dylan. "See ya." She looked back; he looked gormless, so she waved and dashed away.

A week in and Emily was feeling dissatisfied. She sat at the desk in her flat. She was meant to be reading an enormous tome on analytical chemistry but her mind kept wandering.

Her life seemed to have split into four distinct contradictory chunks: university, her fellow eco warriors and her dinky little flat. 'Home' in Newcastle where her parents were, 'home' in Loxley where The Boomers and her house were and she had always felt most at home. Fourth, the world of Aunt Julia that she had no reason to go back to even though it was so significant to her. Each of those other lives seemed to be miles away as she sat there procrastinating at her desk.

Her friends had been vaguely attentive when she regaled them with everything that she had been through over the summer: Dylan dumping her by text, inheriting Great Granny's house and the epic mission to discover all about Aunt Julia. They weren't that interested, however.

They couldn't appreciate the colossal changes that Emily had been through. It was too far away in a different universe, a place that didn't touch their existence in Edinburgh and their exclusive academic bubble. Castles in the air, like Edinburgh's, were other people in another world.

A bit like Aunt Julia's family living in a parallel universe until I went to see them. They're still there now, living their lives, but I can't touch them and I have no idea what they're doing. They don't care a damn what I'm doing, thinking, saying.

Emily sighed and leant back in her chair, nearly tipping it too far and flailing to regain her balance.

Uncle Charlie, is he recovering, will he pull through from his stroke? I hope so, and I hope he can find happiness when he looks back at his life, even though he never won Julia. Will Cathy find herself a nice girlfriend and live happily ever after? The Merripens living in their idyllic world full of domestic love, despite all their difficulties, they have a far simpler family life than mine. And Sarah Pennington? I hope that bitch chokes on her bloody gum.

She was restless and decided that a mint tea might be the answer. She got up and edged around her bed to tweak off a sprig of mint. As she sniffed it she was stirred with memories: Great Granny's garden and Cathy's magical home with the diamond windows where Aunt Julia had been so happy. She flicked on her kettle and while it boiled, resolved to pull herself together.

"Right Emily. Sort yourself out. You need a plan."

Tea made and back at her desk, she rummaged in her patchwork bag to retrieve the 1/- notebook, spread it out, and couldn't resist reading every entry she had made. When she eventually got to the end she turned over to a fresh page, a new chapter.

"Now, what am I going to do?" As she thought, she tapped a Biro against her nose, not realising that she was leaving numerous blobs of blue ink.

She wrote, 'The Plan'.

Firstly, she knew that she had to get her head down and study hard for her final year. She was determined to get a first just to show everyone her worth. And she would. She must. Then the world would be her oyster.

Why an oyster? What's that got to do with anything?

She wrote: 'Get a first. Attend all lectures and laboratory sessions. Study diligently.'

Don't get distracted by rereading the whole of my notebook and then writing big plans?

Emily knew she had to address everything she had discovered on her journey about a lifetime's worth of prejudices. Not just the white privilege – although that definitely needed to be addressed – but the other advantages such as happening to have been born with brains and being lucky enough to go to university. And inheriting a house from your great grandmother. She scribbled: 'Think about privilege.' It didn't quite hit the mark in capturing the issue but she knew what she meant by it.

And there's nothing you can do about the way you look, but you can change how you think.

Emily thought for a moment of Daniel, his cheery disposition and total acceptance of himself.

I can do that too.

And my family. The family that I always had, even before I knew of Aunt Julia's existence.

She needed to fully accept that everyone thinks about things from their own viewpoint and to each of them it can look very different. She thought of how both her mum and her dad had opened up to her and revealed a perspective that she hadn't understood. She wrote: 'Try and understand where they are all coming from. Build bridges between the generations.' This was much harder to distil into a simple strategy, but she realised that she had learnt a great deal from her quest to find Aunt Julia. She rifled back through the 1/- notebook again and looked at where her journey had begun.

She smiled and for the first time in days felt a frisson of optimism. "Right Emily, you need to get on with the plan, not just talk about it."

The most obvious and pressing thing to tackle first was definitely her mum and dad. Their honest, heartfelt conversations had unlocked a channel of communication that Emily needed to keep open. She needed to show them that they were loved just as much as The Boomers and that she did need them in her life. It was essential that they meet face to face as soon as they could, before they fell back into a lifetime of bad habits, unconscious patterns of behaviour, and slipped back into entrenched positions. She remembered what her mum had said, that she had never invited them to her university world before. It made her feel sick just thinking about that moment, but it was something she could remedy very easily.

"Strike while the iron is hot."

And what the hell does that mean? Ridiculous, all these crazy sayings.

Deciding that writing a plan was good but acting on it was better, Emily sent them an email.

Hi Mum and Dad,
Why not come up on the train to Edinburgh for the day? We can have a family outing. The journey along the coast is wonderful. I can feed you haggis, neeps and tatties!

Let it be my birthday present to you both. What do
you think? Love Emily x

It wasn't very eloquently written, a bit stilted and short but an olive branch all the same. Perhaps spending time together as a family outside home might give them all a chance to open up again and listen without prejudice to each other's point of view. It could become part of their family's way of communicating rather than them all hiding behind imaginary barriers.

It was nearly time for her organic chemistry lecture and it looked like it might rain, so she busied herself putting her books together and finding her jacket. She missed her black cagoule. Bringing Sarah Pennington to mind made Emily's blood boil.

That bloody woman.

Mum replied almost immediately to her email, just as she got to the King's Building. A good sign, Emily thought.

That would be great. It has to be a weekend because
of work. Name a date that you are free and we will
organise things this end. Mum x

Emily checked her phone diary and replied before she went into the lecture theatre.

How about 15th of October. Is that any good?
Emily x

Would they come? It was only a matter of weeks. Would they find an excuse to postpone it?

Emily, you're doing it again. Things have changed.

When Emily came out of a fascinating talk on isomerism, Mum had replied.

That's great. See you then, love. Mum x

Emily discovered that she was feeling happy. She was looking forward to seeing her parents and having a normal day out. All those silly concerns that she used to have when anticipating a family gathering – wondering if she would say or do the wrong thing, or that things would kick off – had dissipated.

I think I've found my place in the bosom of my family. A flash of Cathy's ample chest came into her head; it seemed a faraway memory, but it still made her smile.

And while she was thinking about her family, she dialled The Boomers for a chat. She still talked to them regularly, but she had also found a way forward with her nearest and dearest kin.

Granny answered. "Hello, Loxley 4196."

"Granny, hi. How are you? Have you been to the hospital yet?"

"Yes, Emily. I have. They're talking about putting in a stent, whatever that entails. The doctor did tell me about it but it all sounded a bit gruesome, poking things down my veins, so I stopped listening."

Emily chuckled, "Granny, you are so naughty. You should listen. And how is Aunt Cyn?"

"She's driving me mad, as usual. She misses you so she keeps baking. We're both going to explode from eating too much. At least she's found somewhere to dispose of some of it..." Emily was confused. "The family that have moved into GG's house love her parkin. We take it over to them, have a brew and tell them all about the old days in Loxley. They're looking after the place really well, it's all very neat and tidy."

So, the incorrigible Boomers had found someone else to

nurture in her absence. Emily wasn't entirely sure what to say so murmured a noncommittal, "Is that right?"

Granny carried on, "We even told them all about Julia, and we're taking all the photos around next time we visit." Emily was alarmed. She hoped that her tenants didn't mind being ambushed by The Boomers. Perhaps she should check it out with the managing agent. "And she's expecting, which is a thrill. Me and Cyn have offered to take the little boy out so that she can get some rest, and she'll be glad of some help when the new one arrives."

Sometimes there was no stopping The Boomers.

THIRTY-FOUR

Emily strolled back from her lecture on biomolecules, which had been fascinating. It was raining and she still hadn't replaced her cagoule. *Must do that. Wonder if the old bitch has found it? What if she actually wears it? Yuk!*

Her phone pinged. Mum had WhatsApped her. When this had happened in the past it had made Emily anxious but now, she looked forward to seeing what Mum had to say. It was often a snippet of news, like success at work or an achievement of Ashley's.

Mum
Got a letter for you here. It's very blue. Do you want me to hold on to it and bring it up with me when we come or shall I send it on?

Emily
Ta mum send it on please.

Mum
Will do. How are you?

Emily
Good thanks. Just been to excellent lecture. You?

Mum
I'm okay. Work is busy but fitting in study for CIPD course. Think Dad might have got a job. Interview yesterday. Went well he thought. Cross fingers. Will forward letter.

A few days later, the letter plopped onto the mat of Emily's flat with Mum's rounded handwriting, forwarding it on. Emily took one look at the blue coloured envelope, the handwriting in blue-black ink, caught a waft of a familiar scent and her stomach lurched.

Blue Grass. It's got to be from Sarah.

Holding it gingerly by one corner, she slumped into her one cosy chair, needing complete comfort in order to have the courage to read it. She pulled her patchwork bag onto her lap as protection and slit the envelope open with a finger. A thought popped into her head, *not nearly as efficient as with a knife*, happy thoughts of Granny. She extracted two pages of paper that, just as before, exactly matched the colour of the envelope. Taking a deep breath, inhaling more Blue Grass, she started reading.

Beech Court,
Willicombe Park,
Royal Tunbridge Wells, Kent
Dear Emily,
I assume that you remember me, Mrs. Pennington, following your visit in August.

Cheeky cow. Mrs Pennington! You're Sarah to me you stuck up, patronising, racist bitch.

> *I have been having great heart searchings since your visit and feel that I should not leave you without the truth. I am dying. We all are but, in my case, sooner rather than later. Lung cancer. I have asked that this letter be sent to you upon my death. Somewhat ironically, I feel with the parallels of your Great Grandmother's letter from beyond the grave.*
>
> *First of all, I am so sorry to be the one to tell you that Charlie Levett has died following a second stroke. He was a kind man and highly respected within the community.*

Emily sighed, "So sad, for him and for Cathy, but not really surprising." She read on.

> *When you visited, I told you to come back because I had more to tell you. I did, but when you returned you were so rude that I dismissed you without giving you the information that you desired. Knowing that I am going to die, I feel it cathartic to tell you the whole truth, a deathbed confession as it were.*
>
> *Why you? I don't know why, except that you seem to have a thirst for Julia's personal story, poking your nose in and digging up things that the rest of us have left buried. I will leave it up to you*

whether you reveal what I am going to tell you to "your family".

I must also make quite clear that I did not lie to you or to anyone else. I have never lied, but sometimes people took my truth the wrong way.

What on earth does she mean by that?

Julia hung herself.

Emily flinched at the inhuman bluntness.

I found her in the oast, I knew she would be there. I entered through the door and couldn't see anything in the dark. I lit the Tilley lamp and as I lifted it to look around, I saw a body dangling from a beam. It was motionless.

I thought that it had to be her after everything that had been going on. I approached gingerly, hoisted up the lamp, it was not a pretty sight, and ascertained that it was indeed Julia. One had to be completely certain. I was shocked but I wasn't at all surprised.

I stood for a long time trying to pull myself together and wondering what to do. I thought it best to go back to the house and tell the others. As I turned to leave, I raised the lamp for one last look and was horrified to see those piercing eyes of hers wide open, staring straight at me. I dropped the lamp, it broke and the debris on the floor immediately flared up. I fled. I hate to say this, but

I think in retrospect she may have still been alive at that point.

I panicked and fled. I smoked a cigarette and decided that it was best to pretend that I hadn't even been to the oast. It would have complicated things. I returned to the house and tried to forget what I had seen.

Emily leapt to her feet. She was shaking and horrified.

"What the hell! Why didn't you go and get help from the others? You could have saved her."

Murdering bitch. I knew it, she had to have had more to do with this. If you think you got away with this, you've another think coming.

She found herself pacing around the confines of her room.

Do I call the police? Cathy will want to know. Or will she? David and Evie definitely need to be told. At least Uncle Charlie didn't find out before he died.

She marched around, she couldn't stand still, trying to work out what to do, saw the time and realised that if she didn't leave soon, she was going to be late for her laboratory session. She couldn't miss it; such an absence might hinder her getting a first. Even so, she couldn't resist reading the rest of the letter quickly. She couldn't not after that bombshell; she'd not be able to pay attention, wondering what it said.

She was expecting an explanation of what happened next, but Sarah just changed the subject entirely. Why did she not go and tell everyone straight away? Any sane person would have done so. She could have told them about the fire but Cathy had said that she was the one that raised the alarm, so obviously not. Still so many questions.

Emily was baffled but read on.

I must also tell you about Jolyon. Part of the reason for Jolyon's early demise was his poor health. He was an alcoholic in his later years but also Jolyon had LADA which in full is Latent Autoimmune Diabetes of Adulthood. It is a form of Type 1 Diabetes. Doctors tend to rule out diabetes when presented with the classic symptoms by adults because most mature people who develop it are overweight and Jolyon was extremely lithe and athletic. It only really came to light when we were trying for a sibling for Nicholas. You may be interested in some of the more obscure side effects that his disease can cause. Knowing your predilection for snooping around, I am certain that you can find out all about it.

Yours sincerely,

A scrawly signature.

Mrs Sarah Pennington

The letter seemed to have stopped very abruptly.

What is she saying? What has this got to do with the murderous cow leaving poor Aunt Julia to die in the most painful way possible?

Emily shuddered, grabbed her laptop from her bedroom, googled 'LADA'. Frustratingly it came up with a list of links for cars.

What the...?

The clock was ticking.

Damn. I'll have to get back to it.

Emily packed Sarah's letter and her laptop into her bag, grabbed her house keys from the hall table and dashed out of the door towards the King's Building, her head reeling.

So it was that bloody Sarah. Murderer. I'm glad that you're dead, and I hope it was as horrible and slow and painful as it was for poor Aunt Julia.

THIRTY-FIVE

Emily was working diligently on her chemistry experiment, but her brain was like a tornado.

Even on her deathbed that disgusting woman was lying and prevaricating. The bitch must have realised that Aunt Julia was still alive. Perhaps if she'd got the others, they could have saved her.

Emily carefully measured chemicals to the nearest gram, checking three times; her hands were shaking but it was vital to get it right. Then poured them into a flask, added the requisite amount of acid and swirled the flask to mix. She then lit the Bunsen burner, being extra careful not to burn her fingers as she had done many times before.

What is this crap about diabetes? What is she saying? What else is there to say?

She knocked her flask against the Bunsen burner, it cracked and she lurched for the sink before the contents could go up in flames. A chorus of "Emily!" arose from around the benches accompanied by laughter. They were all used to her.

"Sorry."

Bugger. I nearly set the whole lab on fire.

Emily shivered.

~

Lab session finished, Emily scuttled to the Brucks Street Café for lunch and reread the letter from Sarah.

"That racist bitch from hell." A girl at the next table looked at her questioningly. "Sorry, I'm just talking out loud. I've got this letter..." The girl's expression turned to horrified and she quickly gathered up her laptop and mug without any further eye contact with Emily and moved to another table. "I'm so sorry. I didn't mean to offend you," Emily called after her.

She sighed and moved on to the strange, seemingly innocent second part of the letter, muttering out loud as she reread it. She looked up to make sure she wasn't terrifying anyone else before typing into Google, 'Latent Autoimmune Diabetes' and bingo. She read the description from the authoritative Diabetes Charity. 'As a form of type 1 diabetes, LADA is an autoimmune disease in which the body's immune system attacks and kills off insulin producing cells.'

So, what is Sarah going on about? What is she getting at?

She tried the next link about symptoms: 'The symptoms of LADA are the same as type 1 and type 2 diabetes: passing urine a lot, feeling very thirsty, getting tired, getting thinner. And whereas being overweight is a major risk factor for type 2 diabetes, people with LADA tend to have a healthy weight'

She said about that. It can't be something innocent. It must be significant. I can't believe that she abandoned Aunt Julia. It's monstrous.

Emily felt outraged all over again then pressed on, following more links but couldn't find anything significant.

It reminded Emily of going through all the microfilm when she was studying the Kent and Sussex Courier back copies at the British Library. That seemed to have happened a whole century ago.

She read the letter again. 'It came to light when we were trying for a sibling.' And they only had Nicholas.

Perhaps that is the clue. Did he become infertile after fathering Nicholas... and Evie?

She added 'infertility' to her Google search. The results came up and she clicked through to the Diabetes.co.uk site.

'A number of issues can cause infertility in men with LADA. These include:

Erectile dysfunction; Reduced sperm quality; Retrograde ejaculation; Hypogonadism (low testosterone).'

Sounds a bit gruesome. But it might be relevant.

'Reduced sperm quality: Diabetes can lead to reduced sperm quality through DNA damage to the sperm and lower sperm volume, but diabetes as such does not appear to affect motility of sperm (the ability of the sperm to move towards the egg).'

Okay? So Jolyon could still father children.

'Retrograde Ejaculation: Another problem that may result from autonomic neuropathy is retrograde ejaculation. This occurs if nerves are unable to control the muscles of the bladder from closing at the point of ejaculation, which results in semen entering the bladder rather than exiting via the penis.'

Yuck, but that does sound like you can't make a child at all.

Emily thought long and hard. Low or no sperm. Infertility?

Oh bugger. Is Sarah telling me that...

Emily frowned, read it again.

Please God, no. Was Jolyon incapable of fathering a

child? But when? They had conceived Nicholas okay. Hadn't they? But...

A cold feeling started somewhere around Emily's heart and spread through her body, up to her brain. Every hair on her body stood on end.

Oh my God. It was NOT Julia and Jolyon's infidelity that created Evie.

Emily felt nauseous. A trickle of ice down her spine.

Sarah and David. Sarah was sleeping with David. She said so. She dumped him at Jolyon's twenty-first and then claimed to be pregnant by Jolyon. That's why they got married. Nicholas must be David's child.

Emily's head was spinning; she could barely breathe.

That means that Evie is David's daughter. Sarah knew that. She bloody well knew that.

Emily thought she might faint.

No, no, no. Evie ***is*** *David's daughter. Sarah lied. That bitch, she blamed it on Julia. That's what she was on about, that stuff about "my truth".*

She couldn't help herself. She yelled, to everyone in the café's astonishment, "No, no, no... no. Fucking Sarah, she knew, she bloody well knew."

Not knowing what to do with herself, she leapt to her feet, her coffee washing across the table.

I can't tell the Merripens. I can't tell Cathy. Who can I tell?

Strangers stared at her as she stared wildly around.

This is too much. I can't endure this on my own.

She moaned, "What do I do now?"

She could only think of one person who she could share this with, someone who would hold her hands and help her carry this burden.

In one swift move, she threw her laptop into her patchwork bag, grabbed her coat and dashed out of the café.

~

Sitting on the train, Emily fumbled with her phone and made a call. No reply, it went straight to the messaging service. The journey seemed to be taking forever. For just under one and a half hours the thought kept returning. Every time she remembered the consequences of her discovery. It wasn't Aunt Julia... She didn't have to kill herself... Sarah could have saved her... she couldn't help but shake with anger and distress. "Fuck you, Sarah."

Waiting for a bus outside the station was agonising. Why did they never come when you're in a hurry? She leapt on the moment the doors opened and hovered by the door all the way to her stop. Getting off, she started running.

Fumbling her key in the lock, Emily was surprised when the door suddenly opened and she fell into the hall. "Emily! What are you doing here?"

Emily threw her arms around her mum, her bag falling to the ground, and sobbed into her shoulder. Mum patted her back and rocked her, waiting for her agitation to subside.

She kissed the top of Emily's head, "Come through to the kitchen, love. Let's have a brew and you can tell me what's going on." Mum picked up the abandoned bag and Emily felt herself steered towards the table, where she slumped heavily into a chair.

Mum fiddled around, clattering with mugs and kettles. Emily couldn't help but think of Cathy doing the same for her, and that she had done the same for Aunt Julia. Delving into her bag, she retrieved the letter from Sarah and placed it on the table.

A mug of herbal tea was put in front of Emily. "Thanks, Mum." Mum had remembered that Emily didn't drink tea, that was kind.

"Okay, Emily. Let's hear it love." Mum's hand reached out to cover one of Emily's.

Emily pushed the letter across the table. Mum read it. She had obviously reached the bit about Aunt Julia, "Whoa, this is appalling. No wonder you're upset. She's actually admitting being culpable for killing Aunt Julia. Good God." She carried on, reading the rest. "What is the rest of this that she's saying?"

"Jolyon suffered from Latent Autoimmune Diabetes. I looked it up and found out that it had made him infertile. That is what Sarah Pennington is getting at."

"So?"

Emily sighed heavily, "Sarah had an affair with David and then, when she became pregnant, coerced Jolyon into marrying her. She claimed that Jolyon was the father. Nicholas was actually David's child."

"And Genevieve?"

"David's daughter."

"That's awful. So Genevieve did inadvertently marry her own brother but not quite in the way that she had thought. That is so sad, for all of them. Poor loves."

Emily was indignant, "But Julia attempted to kill herself because she thought it was her fault. It wasn't. It was that bitch, Sarah bloody Pennington." Emily was getting worked up again. She could feel the horror of it rising through her chest. "The worst thing is that Evie and David are living as man and wife..." Tears cascaded down Emily's cheeks again. She sniffed and whimpered, "What should I do?"

Mum looked thoughtful, shook her head and seemed to stare around the kitchen for inspiration. Emily waited. Mum said softly, "Will it make any difference if the truth comes out? Will it make things any better for anyone – or worse?"

Emily had to think about that. Was it right that Sarah Pennington had got away with it?

Mum spoke again very gently, "Look Emily, searching for Julia has uncovered a whole lot of family mysteries. The people concerned, the Levetts, the Penningtons and the Merripens, they had to live with those secrets all their lives. We didn't." She paused. "That hideous woman, Sarah Pennington, is dead. She will surely be rotting in hell. Aunt Julia is sadly dead, and nothing can change that, as is Charles Levett. Those that are still living have found a peaceful life for themselves. Haven't they?" Emily nodded and tried to take it in. "And we have our family here." A squeeze of the hand. "By embarking on this whole journey, I think we've uncovered our own connections, brought it all out into the open, and we can look forward to a better life together. All of us. Your dad and me, Ashley and The Boomers." She paused, squeezed Emily's hand. "My take on this is that, by searching for your lost relative, you've actually found your own family." Emily nodded. Her mum was right.

Mum whispered, "I think you have to let it go. Can you let it go, love?"

Emily agreed. It would do far more harm than good to tell anyone. It wouldn't even make her feel any better. She sighed.

Mum patted her hand. "I have a suggestion." Emily looked at her. "Why don't we take that vile woman's letter and burn it?"

It would certainly be cathartic.

Emily agreed, "Yes, Mum, let's do that."

Mum found a box of matches. Emily took the letter, holding it like an offering, and they went out in a procession to the garden.

Shielding the letter from the breeze, Mum struck a

match and Emily held the blue envelope over it and twisted it so that it flared like a candle. It burnt very quickly, but Emily held it gingerly by a corner until it was well and truly alight, staring at it with great concentration. She watched as the letter turned to ashes, thinking of everything that had happened and letting each thought melt away with the flames. She watched as it drifted away, melting into nothing.

Turning and putting her arms around her mum, Emily said, "Thanks, Mum. Thank you for everything." She gave her mum a squeeze. "It's over."

Emily looked up to the sky and whispered. "Rest in peace, Aunt Julia."

THE END

SENSITIVITY REPORT

WRITTEN BY: CATHY OLAYINKA GOODMAN

The writer of this Sensitivity Report is a person of mixed racial heritage, and I did not find anything in the book that shocked me, as, sadly, this kind of prejudice, whether open or inadvertent, has been my experience throughout my life. My opinion is that it is preferable to treat the subject openly rather than take the attitude that literature is not the place for it. However, a reference in the jacket blurb and the online description to give readers a 'heads-up' as to the content of the book and allow anyone who would be offended or triggered to avoid it, is essential.

This familial search story examines prejudices that are both deliberate acts and unwitting patterns of thought and behaviour, with regard to disability, illegitimacy, and (in passing) homosexuality, but in particular to racial prejudice. It is a carefully thought out and realistic examination of white privilege and the attitudes endemic in our society from the older, "non-u" or "politically incorrect" generation right up to the present day – as embodied in the young, university level narrator. It reveals how easy it is to be racially prejudiced without even being aware of it or to use terms which may denigrate and cause pain without any conscious wish to do so. The older characters use slurs such as 'half-caste' and 'frizzy hair' and even 'golliwog', which are today acknowledged as being disparaging and demeaning.

At the same time the book includes characters who are blatantly and proudly racist, such as 'Mrs Pennington', whose racist agenda appears to be emboldened by feelings of jealousy, inferiority, and, ultimately, the desire to cause harm from beyond the grave and to have the destructive last word. Sarah Pennington is truly repulsive, and not just because of her racism: the physical description of her, raddled by age, infirmity (and the evil secrets she carries to her deathbed) is gruesome, and clearly signals to the reader that her words are the expressions of a noxious personality. It contrasts well with the startling, beautiful green eyes of the GG family.

There is a good deal of dialogue in the book, and some of the conversations are so realistic, with the use of extreme racist insults and slurs, as to seem to have been written verbatim. In order for readers to believe this story, and understand the motivations behind it, it may be useful to include some reference to the author's racial heritage, and a Foreword which recognises that, although fiction, the story is intended to be an examination of prejudice. Otherwise there may be a backlash because of the 'Mrs Pennington' character, and other racist events described in the story.

ACKNOWLEDGMENTS

Thank you so much for reading Searching for Julia. I love to hear what people think of my stories so if you have any thoughts on the book that you'd like to share you can find me on my Facebook page @LizzyMumfreyAuthor or on Goodreads.

Thank you to all the people who take my over enthusiastic writing and turn it into a honed novel. I have had the absolute honour of working with an editor, Charlotte Bond who has taught me so much about writing and helped me knock my narrative into shape, as only the best personal trainer can.

Robin Phillips of Author Help has been a steady and wise hand on the tiller steering me to produce Searching for Julia as a professionally published novel.

My especial thanks to Lucy Bland for her permission to use actual stories from her nonfiction book, Britain's Brown Babies and her encouragement when she read the first draft of the novel.

My incredible family are a constant support, encouraging me in my writing. My husband, Bob, has to put up with erratic meal times when I disappear into my fictional worlds. My darling daughters, Philippa and Francesca, are especially supportive and reassuring. My sister Diana and her daughter, Erica Manwaring, both authors, give me forthright and effective feedback on my drafts. I often need it.

ABOUT THE AUTHOR

It is easy to say that I am "just a housewife". I am but I have had a wonderfully capricious life being many other things as well - all of which I draw upon in my writing.

I have a large extended family, a wealth of colourful friends and colleagues and endless triumphs, misadventures and embarrassments which add colour to my writing.

I was brought up as a Kent farmer's daughter, one of four girls, went to a typical old fashioned all girls school, got thrown out of Bristol University and then spent the customary years in London having an outrageously fun time.

I got married unwisely young and then consequently "unmarried". I became a single parent working all hours that God gave (all in IT) to keep my two wonderful twin daughters in ponies.

I then met and married my beloved Bob and since then I have had a wonderful time as a farmer's wife (full circle?) putting on a any number of madcap events to raise money for charity, creating a life skills course for children with special needs, sailing the Atlantic and exploring the world, documenting my travels in what became an avidly read blog ...which started me writing...and I just can't stop.

ALSO BY LIZZY MUMFREY

Fall Out

Be Careful Who You Marry